What Readers Are Saying About *The Underwater Window*

The Underwater Window starts fast and moves along with a 6-beat kick. Dan Stephenson knows swimming, and he brings out the richness of the sport. But you don't need to be a swimmer to enjoy this great story of friendship and rivalry.
— Rowdy Gaines, 3-time Olympic swimming gold medalist,
Hall of Fame inductee, Olympic swimming analyst for NBC TV

There's romance in this story, just below the surface. What's most endearing about Doyle Wilson is not the all-consuming pursuit of his swimming goals, but his growing awareness that there's more to life, and that swimming is preparing him for it. I enjoyed this book immensely.
— Janet Evans Willson, 4-time Olympic swimming gold medalist,
Hall of Fame inductee, Author of *Janet Evans' Total Swimming*

Everyone wants to know what it feels like to win an Olympic medal. Dan Stephenson has captured that moment and many like it in his book, *The Underwater Window*. On many occasions, I caught myself saying, "Yeah, that's exactly what it was like." If you want to discover how to build a champion in life (not just in the pool), read this book!
— John Naber, 4-time Olympic gold medalist, Hall of Fame inductee,
Author of *Awaken the Olympian Within*

This engaging and easily readable novel, written by a world Masters swimming champion, plunges you deep into the fascinating fast-lane world of Olympic swimming competition. But *The Underwater Window* dives far deeper than most sports novels—hitting the very bottom of why we race, and what of life is left when we get too old to win our heats.
— Jonathan Rowe, Author of *The River of Strange People* and
A Question of Identity

Take the plunge into *The Underwater Window*, but be prepared to be pulled along until you reach the finish wall. *The Underwater Window* provides a very realistic view into the passion-filled world of elite athletes. Reading it is like a race, not a workout. I laughed, I cheered, I rode the waves of ad   ok to swimmers and non-swimmers alike.
—Brian Goodell, 2-time Olympi   uctee

D1468802

The Underwater Window

by Dan Stephenson

To Mary – I had a
great time – let's
do it again.

Dan Stephenson

For Tracey

CHAPTER 1

There are four strokes in swimming, and one is named "butterfly." It's the most photographed stroke because it looks so graceful. Both arms come out of the water at the same time, while a powerful dolphin kick surges the body forward. What spectators don't see is that butterfly is wicked hard. It requires the coordination of a Chinese gymnast and the strength of a Bulgarian weightlifter. It tires you out quickly, and by the end of a race, that beautiful stroke produces unbearable agony.

The stroke's namesake epitomizes the sport of swimming. When you look at a monarch butterfly, you see a colorful, elegant creature, his stained glass wings stroking the sky to make him look lighter than air. As you watch him flit from leaf to petal, you don't see what got him there—the time he spent as a caterpillar, straining his 4,000 muscles, chewing through plants, storing up energy for the great challenge ahead. You don't see the 5,000 miles he covered migrating to Mexico and back, 25 million wing strokes, one at a time.

I sat in the ready room in Brisbane trying not to think about butterflies. The flock in my stomach put me at the brink of nausea. The room was small with no windows, the air heavy. Marco, the guy at the end of the row, stood up suddenly and ran to the trash can by the door. He leaned way into it and spewed. I could hear him retch, even though I had earphones on. Marco stood back up, wiped his mouth with the sleeve of his sweat jacket, and returned to his chair.

I tried not to dwell on the fact that the race I was about to swim might be my last. A poor swim would end my career. A great swim would give me a reason to press on, take a shot at the Olympics.

I tried not to think about the tiny hole in my sharkskin swimsuit. I had punctured the fabric with my fingernail in the struggle to pull the thing on. I fretted that the hole would grow into a massive rip. It was just above my right knee, staring up at me every time I looked down.

I tried not to daydream. Dreams are for kids. When I was eight years old, I had dreams. I was a star then, and people told me I was going to go to the Olympics. I believed them. The next year I started watching the Olympics on television. I cheered for the best swimmer and imagined myself, like him, on the medal stand, my hand over my heart, singing the national anthem. I was going to be an Olympic champion, not just in one event but in several—the best swimmer that ever lived. That dream faded, then died, as my repertoire shrank and my competition grew. At age 24 I had goals, not dreams. Goals are hard, cold numbers: a time, a place.

I tried not to think about the kid in the next chair, the Australian teenager who kept looking at me. He wanted to psych me out with his goofy grin. The kid had too many teeth. He was a freak of nature. I tried to psych him out by ignoring him.

A ready room is no place special. It's a holding tank for swimmers before the finals at big meets. It's part of the choreography. The meet officials want everything to happen on schedule, including the march onto the pool deck right before the race. They don't want anyone getting lost, so they herd us together twenty minutes ahead of time. You can't leave. You can't do anything but sit there, thinking about your race. Or you can pull something on the guys you're trying to beat. It's a breeding ground for psych jobs.

Even if you can tune everyone else out, a ready room is hardly a place for quiet relaxation. The adrenaline pumping through your veins makes it difficult to sit still. Your brain is hard at work, reminding you of everything bad that can happen: a false start, a missed turn, a half-stroke finish. You have to push those thoughts out and concentrate on every aspect of the task ahead. You play the race over and over again in your mind and if you do it right, you see yourself touching first. It takes all the mental strength you can muster.

The ready room in Brisbane was makeshift, as they often are—a converted coach's office with a lone door leading out to the pool deck. It had four yellow cinder block walls and exactly eight folding chairs. You can't be comfortable in a pressure cooker anyway.

The clock on the wall of the ready room had a sweep second hand that swept glacially, in stark contrast to the scoreboard clock outside, which had numbers for tenths and hundredths of a second—numbers that spun so fast they blurred. Watching the ready room clock only made me impatient.

I put a towel over my head and turned up my music. I closed my eyes and tried not to think about Archie, my teammate two chairs over. I tried not to focus on his two inch height advantage, his huge feet and hands, his condorian wingspan. I tried to forget his world record time, 3:39.59, though it was tattooed on my brain.

The exit door of my mind was jammed with unwanted thoughts that refused to leave.

All of a sudden, two marshals in white uniforms entered the ready room, stood us up, got us in a line, and led us out onto the pool deck. As we marched, I could hear music blaring and fans cheering, overpowering the music in my earphones. The spectator stands were one level above the pool, so the cheers wafted down from a cloud of witnesses.

I quickly scanned the stands to spot my parents. I smiled when I saw them looking at me, waving. They had come all the way from Michigan to Australia to watch me swim one race in the World Championships. This was it.

We paraded like penguins until we were behind our lanes. I sat down in a chair behind lane 3, the lane assigned to the third-place qualifier. The other swimmers sat down in their chairs, all except Archie, who already had his sweats off. He was stretching and fixing his goggles. *Sports Illustrated* once described Archie's pre-race routine as "intimidating," but he's not trying to intimidate anybody. He doesn't do any shadow-boxing or spitting in people's lanes or anything like that. Archie's not thinking about you. He's focused on his own performance.

The thing is, though, you can't look at him or you'll be psyched out. Take my word for it. If you watch him, it'll be like watching your neighbor drive home in a new Jaguar. You will admire. You will envy. You'll see a machine built for speed.

The most impressive thing about Archie is his back. If you saw Marlon Brando shirtless in *A Streetcar Named Desire*, you know what I'm talking about. Archie has twice as many muscles as Brando. And it's not just the size of the muscles, it's the *definition*. His lats stand out the most—so far out, he looks like he has wings. His back is a gnarly trapezoid.

When Archie breathes deeply, which is part of his pre-race routine, his muscles inflate with his lungs. That will intimidate you if you watch. But he's not doing it for show, and his muscles aren't pumped up just to look pretty. Every single one of those muscles has a purpose. They're consummate swimming muscles.

Archie also drives a Jaguar—a gold one. My ride is an old Taurus, solid brown.

The overhead music stopped and an Aussie voice boomeranged off the walls of the natatorium.

"And now, ladies and gentlemen, the finals of the men's 400 meter freestyle. In Lane 1, from Brazil, Marco Carvalho."

Marco popped up from the chair behind his starting block and gave a little wave as a polite cheer descended from the stands above us. I glanced over at Marco and smiled. I had already sized him up. I'd touched him out at the Pan Am games the previous summer. Marco was a D-man, a long distance specialist, better at longer races than the 400. I wasn't worried about him.

"In Lane 2, from Australia, Graham Dowling!"

The announcer said that name with more verve, and the crowd erupted. Graham was a hometown boy from Mooloolaba, just up the coast from Brisbane. He was only 17 and clearly a rising star, one of the Australians' brightest hopes for a gold medal at the next Olympics. The cheering for Graham went a little long, I thought, and the announcer waited it out. As Graham turned to sit back down, I reached over and shook his hand. My dad taught me to do that when I was little. Respect your opponents. As my hand slipped out of his, I looked up to see a banner in Aussie green and yellow with Graham's picture. "He'll probably beat you," the banner said. It was pointed right at me. I glowered at the girls holding the banner, but they didn't see me. I had finished ahead of Graham in the prelims, though I knew he was sandbagging. He was likely to bust out in the finals.

"In Lane 3, from the United States, Doyle Wilson."

I get embarrassed when I hear my name over a loudspeaker. I stood up and attempted a wave, but I'd forgotten to unhook my earphones, and my thumb got caught in the cord on the way up. The right earpiece slid off my ear and onto my cheek. Smooth move for the folks back home. They show the intros on TV for a big meet like the World Championships, tape-delayed in the U.S.

My arms and legs were shaking. I was the oldest swimmer in the race, and I'd had a lot of experience in big meets. You'd think I'd be used to the pressure, immune to it, but the introductions always produce a Pavlovian response in me. I get jittery. I used to worry that the nervousness would sap my strength. Then I noticed that the more nervous I got, the better I swam. After running the data points through my brain, I decided that the jitters were my friends. I began to welcome them. I started thinking of adrenaline, not kryptonite, running through my veins.

"In Lane 4, from Japan, Takashi Osawa."

Takashi was the top qualifier from the prelims, but no one was calling him the favorite. I knew exactly how he was going to swim the race: take it out like Jack the Bear and try not to finish like Winnie the Pooh. I love swimming next to a guy like that. I can ride in his wake. And Takashi *always* came back like Winnie the Pooh. I fist-bumped him. He was a friendly guy, always smiling and nodding. He spoke zero English.

"In Lane 5, from the United States, Hunter Hayes."

I can't help but snicker when they announce that name because the guy who owns it has always hated it. He thinks it's too effete; what he wants to be is street. He used to be desperate for a nickname. I called him Archie one time as a joke, and he liked it. He didn't even know why I called him Archie, but he didn't care. So he took to calling himself Archie, a name his parents hated. Maybe that's why he liked it.

Archie is my arch nemesis. I started swimming against him in high school. He's two years younger than I am. Any record I ever set, he wiped off the board within two years. Archie's name is all over the walls of the high school pools in Michigan: Hunter Hayes. I did him a favor giving him a nickname.

I've had a lot of nemeses. However, a person can have only one *arch* nemesis—someone who is always there, opposing you, making you mad. Someone you hate to lose to. Someone who makes you work harder, who brings out the best in you. There can only be one Archie.

I ticked off the reasons I hated Archie: 1. He had beaten me almost every time we raced—27 times out of 29 races lifetime, not that I was counting. 2. He stood in the way of my one final goal: a gold medal in the 400 free at the Olympics in Paris. 3. He kept getting better and better at more and more races, while I struggled to hang onto just one race. 4. He was a golden boy, supremely gifted. 5. He was living *my* dream, and I had it first.

On the flip side, Archie and I were teammates who trained together, from the same country, the same state, the same city, the same club. He was my buddy, my friend. We hung out together.

Archie acknowledged the crowd, smoothly performing a 360-degree wave. I glanced past Takashi and mouthed "good luck" to Archie. Though I was working up the hate side of my feelings for Archie, I hoped he'd win if I didn't.

"In Lane 6...."

I stopped listening to the intros. It was time to do my final race prep. From that point on, I stared straight ahead, down Lane 3, between the green and yellow lane markers. Without moving my head, I secured my earphones, removed my sweats and fit my goggles over my eyes, making sure the suction was tight. I visualized the start and went over the strategy. I'd done this a million times, so there was no use trying something different. I was tuned to race frequency. I barely noticed when the crowd erupted again for the other Australian swimming in Lane 8.

The starter called us up with a long whistle. We mounted our starting blocks. "Take your marks…." It was dead quiet for three seconds while I did the little foot dance to position my toes, leaned down, and grabbed the front edge of my starting block. BEEP.

And so it began, like it always begins, with a bang. They used to start races with pistols, and now they use an electronic signal, but that's not the bang. The bang is the instantaneous reflexive action of every muscle in the body, from the toes to the face. Every muscle in all eight bodies, right down the line. The big muscles in the legs provide the push. The arms fling forward and lead the way, first out and then down. You streamline your body and squeeze your ears with your arms, preparing for the moment when you strike water. It's like being shot from a cannon.

The mind is also coiled, then released. You're full of thoughts and pressures until the beep, then everything is quiet. It's a relief to be in the water, finally, performing instead of thinking about it.

I hit the water and the counting began. First there were the underwater dolphin kicks: one, two, three. Then I surfaced and began counting my strokes: 28 strokes on the first length and 32 on every length after that. Next to be counted were the lengths of the pool—eight lengths of the 50-meter pool. There were numbers everywhere. Ten meters on the dive, 5 meters on every flip turn, 1.4 meters per stroke. Everything measured, everything timed.

My start, as usual, was only average. When I reached the surface at ten meters, Takashi was already at 11 meters. I'm always behind after the start but it's okay, the 400 is a long race. My strategy was to relax on the first 100 anyway, let Takashi get out ahead, and pass him on the third 100.

I immediately angled for the lane marker near Takashi. When you're dragging off somebody, you have to find the sweet spot. It's between 0.5 and 1.5 body lengths behind the other swimmer. The closer you get to his side of the lane the better, and when he gets close to your side, it's a bonus. Takashi was on my side of the lane, and the sweet spot was there for the taking. I rode along in his wake.

I like the 400 free because there's so much room for strategy. It's not a flat-out sprint, nor is it just an endurance test. You need both speed and endurance. And a good plan. It's one of the few races where the lead is likely to change hands more than once as the swimmers carry out their various strategies. One guy wants to grab the lead and try to hold it. Another guy saves everything for the end. Others make their moves earlier. If you make your move too early or too late, you can blow the opportunity to win.

My first 100 felt smooth, and I let Takashi inch further ahead. Graham was right with me as we turned at the 100, and we were both almost a body length behind Takashi. When Takashi got more than a body length ahead, I could see past him underwater. What I saw was that Archie was behind Takashi as well, but ahead of me. That meant I was a little off pace if I was going to win. Archie always saves up for the end. My strategy required me to get ahead of Archie and try to hold him off at the end.

As we came into the wall at the end of 200 meters, I had fallen further behind. Takashi was way out ahead. Graham and Archie were both ahead of me. For all I knew, I was in last place.

Time to get going, I said to myself. As I pushed off to start the fifth length, I came out with a burst. A big kick at the end of the breakout put me high in the water and it felt good. Halfway down the fifth length, I could already see Takashi getting closer. I caught Graham and started to pass him. The Aussie banner flashed in my mind. The probabilities were shifting in my favor.

I caught Takashi near the end of the third 100. I could no longer see past him underwater, so I still didn't know what was going on in Lanes 5–8. I was ahead of everyone in my half of the pool and Takashi was dying. I seemed to be in the lead.

I didn't hit my turn quite right at the 300. I took a little extra glide going into it. As I came out, I was anxious for air. That extra split second of glide meant an extra split second without air. I started to notice how heavy my arms felt.

I angled back toward the middle of the lane after passing Takashi and Graham. I didn't want them dragging off me. As I got further down the pool on the seventh length, I felt the need to know what was happening on the far side of the pool. I usually breathe on the right, but took a quick breath on the left so I could glance across on top of the water. Good. Still ahead of Archie. I thought I detected a splash way over there, though. One more look: definitely a splash. I wondered if the other Aussie, Ian Sinclair, was out there. He was so far over, in Lane 8, that I couldn't tell precisely where he was. Maybe a little ahead or a little behind. Either way, it was race time. As we headed into the final turn, I felt like I had a chance to win. As I broke to the surface after the turn, though, I felt absolutely dead. We have a term in swimming called "oxygen debt." The demand by the muscles for oxygen is greater than the supply. With 45 meters to go, I had oxygen creditors banging on the doors of all my muscles. I was approaching oxygen bankruptcy. My arms felt like rubber.

This happens every time. It's *supposed* to happen. The first time it happened, I backed off. I didn't want to injure myself. I had no idea how much I could handle. Over time I learned not to panic when the pain fills me. Like the stress before the race, I welcome it because I know it's happening to everyone else, too. You can hold your stroke together and you can take a lot of pain. Your opponents are as dead as you are, maybe deader. The last 50 is all about guts, training and mental toughness. Whoever has the most wins.

With 40 meters to go, my peripheral vision triggered a thought that was lodged in both my short-term and long-term memories: here comes Archie. He saved more for the last 100 than I did. So did Graham. They caught me. They passed me. But Archie just inched ahead of me. Usually when he passes me he whizzes past. Something wasn't right with him. Which meant: maybe I can get him this time.

I overheard my brain talking to my muscles. "Fight harder. Dig. Keep it together. Relief is coming soon." I kept my head down for the last six strokes and hit the wall hard.

Touching the wall at the end of a race, or a hard set in practice, brings a moment of physical pleasure that is hard to describe. The first breath is the most delicious bite of air you can imagine. The assault on your muscles has suddenly stopped and they're rejoicing. The arms that were dead can rise again for a fist pump if you've won.

Even before I turned to look at the scoreboard, I knew the news wasn't all good. Graham and Archie had beaten me, I was pretty sure, though it was close. The telltale sign was that the Aussie crowd was going berserk. That meant Archie hadn't won either. As I turned to look at the scoreboard, I noticed Graham in the fist-pump position, arm straight up. Without my glasses I had to squint to see the details on the scoreboard. The first thing I noticed was a "2" next to Graham's name. He got second. Why was he so happy then? The "1" belonged to Ian Sinclair, who won it in the outside lane. The Aussies swept us. Archie got third and I got fourth. No medal for me.

My time was 3:42.88, a second under my personal best. Graham and Archie were in the low '42s. Sinclair went 3:41. Takashi came in last after being under world record pace at the halfway point. I felt sorry for him.

I was also curious about Archie. His time was slow for him, three seconds off his record. He was having a stellar meet, too, with three wins already under his belt. I wondered what was up.

Mostly, I felt a sinking feeling in my stomach. My time was good, but not good enough. Still three seconds off the world record. And more important, there was a new dog in the fight—Sinclair. My odds of a gold in Paris were getting worse instead of better.

I'd never met Sinclair. He was 20 years old and considered only the Australians' second-best 400 man. No one expected this. He pulled the classic "outside smoke" routine, qualifying eighth and getting an outside lane. Having an outside lane provides a physical advantage, because only one person's turbulence washes into your lane instead of two. The outside smoker is off the radar of the top qualifiers, who focus on the competitors in the middle lanes. It's a risky strategy, though. Many a prime swimmer has tried it and failed to qualify for the finals—missed it by a whisker, trying to cut it close.

I don't know if Sinclair tried to qualify eighth, but once he did, he was an excellent outside smoker. He was pretty much out of my vision and thoughts. I wondered if Archie knew he was there.

Before I climbed out of the pool, I shook Graham's hand.

"Great race, Graham."

"Thanks, mate, you too."

I couldn't help but look up in the stands. Why were those Aussie girls still pointing that banner at me?

I treaded over to the lane marker that separated me from Takashi. He was draped across it as if to avoid drowning. I had never before seen him without a smile. There was nothing I could say to him, because I didn't know his dialect. I gave him a manly, one-arm hug, a pool hug.

I looked up into the stands one more time before leaving the pool. My mom had been watching me since the race ended, and when I glanced her way she smiled and clapped her hands so I could see she was proud of me. My dad had his plain face on. I knew he was proud of me even if you couldn't see it on his face. He was just wondering what I was doing with my life, that's all.

Out of the pool, I looked around for Ian Sinclair. He was talking to a TV reporter. I stood near them, off camera, waiting for the interview to finish. Ian was so excited he was talking too fast for American TV audiences. I used to love that Australian accent but I was starting to grow less fond of it.

"Ian. Doyle Wilson. Congratulations."

"G'day, Doyle. Nice to meet you. I guess I got lucky getting that outside lane."

"Well, keep up the good work."

"Oy'll have to, with this young pup pushing me here in the Down Unda." He pointed with his thumb toward Dowling, who was drying off with a towel nearby. "See you in Paris next year."

I knew what he meant about the "pup." Friendly rivals push you harder than hostile ones. Teammates push you every day, and the motivation is different. I knew this from years of swimming against Archie. What stuck with me, though, was the "Paris" comment. I knew *he'd* be there. It seemed unlikely that I would.

You have to start cooling down soon after a race or you'll tighten up big time. After speaking to Ian, I made a beeline for the warm-up pool. When I got there, I jumped right in—fell in is more like it. I almost landed on Archie.

"Did you see Sinclair over there, Arch?"

Archie un-suctioned his goggles and shoved them above his eyebrows. "Yeah, I saw him."

"Really. Why didn't you run him down?"

Archie moved in close, like he was going to speak directly into my ear. Just then, Coach Curtains appeared out of nowhere. Curtains was the Assistant Coach for the USA team and our club coach back home.

"Archie, what happened?" Curtains was yelling. He was mad.

"I don't know, Coach. I guess I just didn't have it in the tank."

"Looked like you did not put pedal to metal. I hope you were not saving up for the backstroke."

Archie was attempting a tough double—the 400 free and the 200 backstroke on the same night, barely half an hour apart.

"No way. I didn't see Sinclair until too late. I'll get him next time."

"Hell, you are the world record holder. You swim your own race and they look out for you. If you did not have it in the tank, then we are going to have to train harder. And if you bagged it…."

"I didn't bag it, Coach. What was I at the 200?"

"One-fifty-one. Couple of hundredths. If you had thrown in a :53 on the last 100, you would have run him down."

"I promise to train harder."

"All right. Now get moving. You have twenty minutes to work the lactic acid out of your muscles."

Archie pushed off the wall and started swimming slowly down the warm-up pool. I followed him. When we got to the other end, he stopped and so did I. We slid our goggles to our foreheads in tandem. We could see Curtains watching from the other end.

"Did you bag it?" I asked. I knew the answer.

"I bagged it." Of course he did. "Just at the end, to save up for the back."

If Curtains heard him say that, Archie'd be toast. Curtains is all about supreme effort. And if Coach Ableman, the U.S.A. head coach, heard it, he'd probably throw a chair.

"You just gave the Aussies a lot of testosterone," I told him.

"I know, but the only thing that matters is the Olympics. They won't touch me in Paris. I'm more worried about you."

"Me?" I didn't believe him. Archie doesn't worry about anything, least of all me. "Archie, you bagged it and still beat me. I guarantee you I left it all out there."

"You train harder than I do. And you got somethin' I don't."

"What do I have that you don't?" It sure wasn't speed. He had oodles of that.

"I don't know. All I know is, you got somethin' I don't."

He was positioning his goggles as he said that, and pushed off again as he finished speaking. I followed him again. This time he flipped at the wall. I stopped. I looked up at Curtains. He was kneeling down above the gutter and clapped me on the shoulder.

"Your third hundred was amazing, Doyle."

"What was it?"

"Fifty-four five."

"You mean amazing for me, right?" It wouldn't have been amazing for Archie.

"I am talking about how you took over the race, how you went from last to first. Swimming is not just about the clock. It is also about racing."

"Seems like a couple guys raced past me at the end."

"You were hanging in there. Real close to getting second. You might have picked it up a little too soon after the 200 turn. But you should be proud. Personal best, right?"

"Right."

There was a pause as Archie came back around and flipped. Curtains stood up to avoid getting splashed, then he knelt down again.

"By the way, we have to talk about the coming year. You have a decision to make."

"I know."

"When we get back to Michigan we will talk it through."

The decision had been on my mind since before the race and it was weighing heavier by the minute. The scoreboard had added some weight. The decision was staring at me, wearing the visage of my father.

Curtains wasn't saying what he wanted me to do. He wanted me to think it through, and if I was going to continue, I would need to re-dedicate myself to the task. I didn't want to think about it.

"Do me a favor, will you?" Curtains was looking at his finals sheet, so his mind was off me. "Keep your eye on Archie. Make sure he gets ready for the backstroke. And psych him up, will you? I do not want him bagging this."

"Will do, Coach."

I pushed off and did an easy 200. Then I was ready to get out, talk to Archie, join the rest of the team and lead some cheers.

It was a sign of respect that Curtains wanted me to talk to Archie. That felt good. Archie didn't need any psyching, but I relished the idea of telling him that Curtains had put me up to it. I liked the big brother role.

CHAPTER 2

For me, the hero of the 2008 Olympics was Jason Lezak. I know, most people say Michael Phelps was the hero, with his eight gold medals. Phelps was phenomenal, but he was expected to win. What Lezak did was not only surprising, it taught young swimmers an unforgettable lesson: never give up.

Jason Lezak anchored the 4 x 100 freestyle relay for the USA team. He started more than half a second behind Alain Bernard of France and passed him on the final stroke to win. To understand the significance of this, you have to go back eight years.

Lezak was a solid sprinter and relay swimmer even before 2008. He swam in the 2000 and 2004 Olympics and picked up a handful of relay medals in those Games. In 2000, he was on the favored USA team in the 400 freestyle relay. Gary Hall, Jr., the star on that relay, had promised that the Americans would "smash the Australians like guitars." The Australians won, and Lezak had to watch as the Australians mockingly strummed their air guitars.

In the 2004 Olympics, Michael Phelps was trying for seven gold medals and he ended up with six. One of his missed chances was in the 400 freestyle relay, an event the Americans had a chance to win, but lost handily to the South Africans and the Dutch. Lezak was on the American relay and watched the South Africans celebrate.

In 2008, Phelps was trying for eight gold medals in eight events in order to best the Mark Spitz standard of seven-for-seven. He was favored in every event except one: the 400 freestyle relay. The French team was dominant, and its star, Bernard, owned the 100-meter freestyle individual world record. On the eve of the Games, Bernard was asked about the relay and reportedly said, "The Americans? We're going to smash them. That's what we came here for."

Lezak had the pressure of past U.S. failures, Bernard's taunt, and Phelps's gold medal quest all on his shoulders. When he dove off, Lezak was .65 seconds behind Bernard. Bernard pulled further away on the first 50, touching with his feet at 21.20, the fastest 50 meters ever swum. Lezak came out of the turn almost a full second behind—an eternity in a sprint.

"I'm not going to lie," Lezak said later. "When I flipped at the 50, it really crossed my mind for a split second that there was no way." Then he told himself, "I don't care how bad it hurts or whatever," and he got down to business. With 25 meters to go, Bernard still had a commanding lead. With ten meters left, Bernard started tying up. Lezak stayed strong. Bernard lost his stroke and flailed weakly into the wall, turning to peek at Lezak just before the end. Lezak kept plugging, and touched .08 seconds ahead of Bernard. The Americans won, and Phelps was on his way to eight golds with an assist from Jason Lezak.

Lezak won only one individual Olympic medal, a bronze in the 100 freestyle in Beijing, an event won by Bernard three days after the relay duel. He was a good swimmer. But on August 11, 2008, for 46.06 seconds, Jason Lezak was beyond good—he was great. He rose above himself and went seven tenths faster than his next best swim. He swam out of his skin, out of his mind. On that day, at that time, in that place, he transcended his training and his past. He exceeded the sum of his parts.

I hauled myself out of the warm-up pool and took a long hot shower, not to get clean or wash the chlorine off, but just to feel the water running over me. That hot flow soothes the muscles and the mind. I finally got out because I had some work to do.

I put on my U.S.A. sweats and went back out on the pool deck, looking for Archie. I found him in a corner with his earphones on. He looked like he was sleeping. I sat down by him and tapped him on the leg. It took two taps for his eyes to open.

"Hey, Doylie, what's up, man?" He said that a little loudly, then pulled out his ear buds.

"Curtains told me to psych you up for the backstroke."

"Wow. I appreciate that. Take your best shot." I knew he didn't need it. He was just being polite.

"The thing is, you know you've got the talent to beat everyone here. You know how to race better than anyone. You've gotten good coaching."

"Yeah…," he said, but he was waiting for more. He was looking at my lips, like he expected something really profound to come across them.

"I guess what I'm saying is that you have this—I don't know—gift. I don't want you to waste it." As soon as I said it, I wanted to take it back.

"Yeah," he said. "I'm aware. It weighs on me, you know? Like a responsibility. Like it's a chore." This wasn't going in the right direction.

"Arch. Look. I think Curtains knows you bagged it at the end of that 400. You're gonna be dog meat if you don't show him something in the backstroke."

He smiled a big, genuine smile, and that made me smile. We were both relieved, I guess, that I was now playing the role of messenger instead of guru.

"Got it," he said. "I'm psyched." He stood up, gathered his stuff and started hopping up and down to show me how psyched he was. "Thanks," Archie said over his shoulder as he ambled off.

Archie has a unique walk. He extends with the toes of his back foot, giving the effect of a small bounce. He couldn't carry a jug of water on his head like the women in Kenya; he'd be drenched. Yet, like everything else about Archie, his walk looks effortless, like he could go on forever.

It was time for me to fill another role. The USA team had elected me captain. I don't know why—I wasn't the best swimmer on the team. I had no clue how to be a captain at that level. Every swimmer on the USA team knew how to get psyched. They didn't need any guidance. Maybe just some encouragement, some togetherness. I decided to go lead a few cheers.

As I approached the USA team bench, I got a few pats on the back for my 400 free. Coaches, swimmers, trainers, everyone seemed pleased with my performance, but they were reserved, like they weren't sure how I viewed it. I was the captain, so I figured it would encourage the team if I acted like I was happy with my swim.

"Personal best," I said. "But we've got to kick some kangaroo butt before this night is over!" This drew some hurrahs. I don't swear much. I just never got into the habit. My teammates undoubtedly seized on the word "butt" and thought it was pretty edgy coming from me. I heard the word echoed a few times after I said it.

Our team got rowdy when Archie was introduced for the 200 backstroke. We whooped and hollered and made the announcer wait before introducing the next guy. This was an unfamiliar event for Archie. He was seeded fourth, swimming in Lane 6. His ability to make a World Championship final in the 200 back was a testament to Archie's versatility.

It was dead quiet for the start, then the beep, which triggered both the whirring of the clocks and a big yell from the crowd. You feel sheepish yelling at the start of the backstroke. The swimmers arch through the air, enter the water and stay under for five seconds or more. They can't hear you.

Archie stayed down the longest and came up ahead. One of his gifts is the upside-down underwater dolphin kick. He does it better than anyone, which is why Curtains had him try the backstroke in the first place. He'd done some blazing times in practice, but he had trouble learning when to come up. You have to surface in less than 15 meters or you're disqualified. Archie kept going too far. He had never won a 200 back in a major competition, but he was getting closer.

This time, Archie surfaced at 14.5 meters. I gave a thumbs-up to Curtains, and he winked back at me. Archie was already half a body-length ahead of the pack. These were experienced backstrokers he was racing against, including the Aussie world record holder. On every turn, Archie stayed down a bit longer and went a bit farther than they did. Coming out of the last turn, he was a full body-length ahead. Let's see what's in his tank now, I thought.

Archie didn't die and he didn't bag it. He won that 200 back pulling away and set a new world record. His fist was in the air before the next guy finished. Kangaroo butt duly kicked. I detected a smile on Curtains' face.

After the last race that night, I hustled upstairs to catch my parents. They were leaving Australia the next day and hadn't seen a whole lot of me during the meet. I was hungry, so I suggested we grab something quick at a place in Brisbane I knew they would like: the Detroit Diner. It served American food, Detroit style.

On the drive over to the Detroit Diner, I sat in the back seat of the Holden Commodore my dad had rented, staring out the window. It was raining and there wasn't much to see. Everything is backwards in Australia. The seasons are switched. Water swirls down the toilet in the wrong direction. The steering wheel is on the wrong side of the car and they drive on the wrong side of the road. In the warm-up pool, you have to swim down the left side of the lane or you'll run into an Aussie—in America, we circle on the right.

My dad had driven in England, so he acted like he was a pro. My mom, on the other hand, was white-knuckling the armrest.

"Hey Dad," I said. "How do you like driving on the left?"

"It's not so bad." My mom turned around and looked at me. She didn't say anything, but the look of terror on her face suggested she disagreed.

So much for that conversation. My parents aren't big talkers. My mom grew up on a ranch in Wyoming, the third-oldest of seven kids. She loved mountains and animals. The nearest neighbors were more than a mile away and they didn't socialize much. She came to Michigan for college, met my dad and stayed in Michigan. She's an expert horsewoman—my athletic genes came from her. They sure didn't come from my dad.

My dad is a numbers guy, so he doesn't put much stock in the finer points of polite conversation. He grew up on a farm in northern Michigan, went to college at Southern Michigan University, and got a degree in accounting. He worked at a big accounting firm in Detroit for two years and hated it. He took a job with a small auto supplier. That company hit it big, and my dad became the CFO. When he came into a bit of money, we moved to a small farm outside Huron Springs. My mom works with the horses and runs the farm, which has become a big enough operation to employ three outside workmen. My parents love it there, and I do too, but I'm no farm boy. I grew up in pools.

"Did you guys go see the koalas?" I was trying to start another low-key conversation.

My mom answered. "Koalas, kangaroos, wallabies…we've had a marvelous time. We met that Ian Sinclair's parents. *Very* nice people."

Sinclair having nice parents was an unwelcome fact. The thought that he had parents at all was inconvenient. He was the enemy. In swimming, this is usually the case. Your enemies are nice people from good families. A swim competition is called a "meet;" you go there to swim "butterfly" and "free." It's hard to imagine friendlier words. Yet you're willing to almost kill yourself trying to beat your opponents. There is an eternal dichotomy in swimming between love and hate, between friendliness and combat.

"I can't believe you guys came all the way over to Brisbane to watch me swim."

My dad answered this time after a glance at me in the rearview mirror. I didn't want him doing that—he needed to watch the road.

"This is our payback for all of those weekends going to swim meets in Benton Harbor and Ferndale and Fort Wayne."

"Akron," my mom said. It was her personal unfavorite. They had driven me all over the Midwest during my age group career. They'd do all that driving, then be stuck all weekend in a stuffy pool with a chlorine gas cloud hanging over the stands. My mom, in particular, having grown up in the land of wide open spaces, seemed claustrophobic in natatoriums. They'd watch heat after heat of boring races. It had to be utter drudgery. Sort of like swim practice.

We arrived at the diner, parked and sat down. I looked around for other swimmers, but I didn't see any. You can always spot them. If they aren't wearing sweats, you can tell from the hair, or lack of it. We ordered and waited for our food.

The booths at the Detroit Diner were made out of old car seats. The menus unfolded like road maps, and the plates looked like hub caps. The owners of the diner had equated Detroit with car culture, a caricature we'd become used to.

I knew it was time to talk about my upcoming decision, but I didn't want my parents to know how much it was weighing on me. I kept trying to distract them with small talk.

"What did you think of Archie's backstroke, Mom? Pretty intense, huh?"

"He's very talented," my mom replied, and it was a clipped answer. She liked to talk about Archie, and would have said more, but she knew it was time to get serious. She and my dad had probably been talking about it before I joined them at the pool. I decided to let her off the hook and didn't try any more small talk.

I've had some major talks with my dad, most of the time sitting across from him at restaurants. The drug talk, the sex talk, that kind of stuff. In the sex talk, he was so nervous he could barely get the words out. I was a foolish kid at the time and thought it would be fun to mess with him. I already knew everything he was telling me, but I asked him a bunch of questions to prolong it. Like "why do men have nipples?" He sweated a lot. I'm kind of embarrassed I put him through that. The sweat at the Detroit Diner would be mine, not his.

My dad has this face that usually looks all serious, with the corners of his mouth headed downward slightly. When he smiles, though, you get teeth and dimples—the change from serious to happy comes out of nowhere.

When my sister and I were little, my dad would do this thing where he'd start growling like a bear in the next room. My sister would scream and we'd run through the house with him chasing us. Eventually he'd catch us, and rub his scratchy chin on our bellies. It kind of hurt, but we laughed ourselves to tears. My dad played both roles perfectly—scary guy and fun guy. The years had made the corners of his mouth go down a bit further, and the dimples came out less frequently. Working for decades in the auto industry had taken a toll on his face.

The food came, and I went to work on two burgers, fries and a milkshake. As soon as I took my first bite of burger, he started in.

"So, Doyle, that was a pretty good swim for you, don't you think?"

I nodded, then took a few seconds to chew. "I was hoping for better."

"It was your personal best. You made the World Championship team and represented your country well. Seems like a good way to go out. Why don't we celebrate the end of a great career?"

He had turned the smile on, and his dimples were out. I looked at my mom, and she was smiling too. It would have been easy, a happy moment. It would have pleased them. I smiled back.

"This might be the end, Dad, but I'm not ready to decide right here and now. I don't want to make any rash decisions. I want to talk to a few people, weigh the pros and cons. I'll probably decide next week."

The dimples receded until his face was in full glower. I'm told I have his face, but he gets a wicked five o'clock shadow starting at about noon. Mine had been shaved as smooth as a stingray right before my race. I risked being disrespectful if I didn't make my face look serious. It was hard to do. For several hours after a race you're still on an adrenaline high.

"You'll be 25 by the time of the Olympics."

"I know. But 25 is not that old, Dad. Lots of swimmers are peaking in their late twenties. The Olympic Committee pays living expenses and I've got a suit contract and math tutoring, so I can handle it financially. If I don't continue, I may always wonder whether I could have done it."

"Done what?"

It was the question of my life. I pondered it for a few seconds, devouring food as a cover for stalling.

What could I reasonably hope to accomplish? Make the Olympic team? Maybe get a medal? So what? That wasn't going to bring me any money or fame. My dad knew that I no longer had dreams, just goals. His point was a good one—the upside was too tenuous and not big enough.

"You know…done my best. Made the Olympic team, won the gold. I don't know if this was the best I can do."

He sighed, then launched into the prepared portion of his remarks.

"Doyle, you have gifts beyond swimming. Even time is a gift. You don't want to waste your gifts." Omigosh, he was using the same argument on me that I'd used on Archie.

"I know, Dad."

"You had a good academic career, not just a swimming career. You've gotten into two good medical schools, you've already deferred a year, and you're risking your spot if you delay any longer."

"But Dad…."

"Enroll."

The word reverberated through the restaurant. I looked around to see if the whole restaurant had heard it. Everyone stared back at me, the word "enroll" written on their faces.

"Everything you say is true, Dad. I'm weighing it. But I have this feeling inside." Wrong word, my dad would not be persuaded by feelings. I didn't know how to explain it. I'm not even sure I understood it myself. "I know I'll never get to the top, where Archie is. It's just—I really want to be great *once*. You know?"

But he didn't know. I could see it in his grizzly face. And how could I expect him to know? How could I expect anyone else in the world to know? Even my best friend didn't know; in fact, he was part of the problem. Who could I tell? Who would understand?

I looked at my mom and she didn't know either. My mom and I weren't always close. She favored my sister, which was no surprise since my sister could ride a horse before she could walk. When my twin nieces were born, I fell out of medal contention. Still, I had to give my mom credit for trudging along to all those swim meets. She must have heard the pain in my voice. She reached across the table, squeezed my hand, and the pain drained away. My mom loves me without having to understand. Did I mention that Doyle is her maiden name?

My dad loves me too. I know that. Shoot, these talks aren't easy for him. He does them for my good. I told him so, and thanked him. He had made darn good points, a compelling case. But it wasn't going to be decided in Brisbane at the Detroit Diner.

There was an awkward silence. I tried to break the tension.

"Do you guys have time to watch me eat a hot fudge sundae?" They both smiled. The dimples made an appearance. My dad drank coffee and my mom sipped tea while I dipped my fries in the whipped cream. We talked about the Tigers' chances for a pennant.

On the drive back to the team dorm, I stared out the back window of the Commodore. The rain was getting torrential. I wanted to stick my head out into it to soothe my aching brain. Why did I have to think about this now? Why couldn't I just enjoy the trip? My future was starting to close me in like lane markers.

What's the big deal about being an old swimmer? There have been lots of successful swimmers older than 25. Dara Torres set an American record at 41, after having a baby, for goodness' sake. I knew, though, that it was different for Dara Torres. She was a swimming goddess. She got money and fame from the sport. I was not at that pinnacle. I had to make a life beyond swimming, and the only question was when to start.

I wished I could talk to Molly. She always sees the big picture; she knows how to reassure me. I made a mental note to catch up with her as soon as I got back to Michigan.

I arrived back at the team dorm close to midnight. It wouldn't look good for the captain of the team to violate curfew, so I had to say hasty goodbyes to my parents. I dodged the raindrops, ran through the front door and jogged into an open elevator. I knew right where the "5" button was, so I pressed it and simultaneously took stock of the elevator. There was one other occupant, Camille Cognac, a 22-year-old sprint freestyler from Baltimore. I noticed she hadn't pressed a button.

"Camille—hi. Going to 5?"

"Yeah. Nice 400 tonight. I thought you were going to win it there for a minute." A pause. "I was cheering for you."

Something about that pause made me nervous. Or maybe I'm just always nervous around women. Anyway, I was nervous.

"Thanks. Nice swim in the 100 free yesterday." What a slow elevator.

Camille had already won two golds and a silver in Brisbane, and she had another chance for gold in the 800 free relay the next day. She won the 50 free at the last Olympics and achieved some notoriety when she posed for a men's magazine shortly after that. "Tasteful," was the word commonly used by other swimmers to describe the photos. Camille had dated several swimmers, including Archie, if you can call it dating when neither party is serious.

Finally the elevator reached floor 5. It took about five seconds for the doors to come open, but it seemed like an hour. I waited for Camille to get out, then I followed her. She turned around as soon as I got out, stopping me with my rear end barely clear of the elevator door. I glanced back instinctively to make sure the doors closed.

"Hey," she said, "can you come down to my room for a minute? I want to show you something."

What could she show me? I'd seen the magazine; there was nothing left to see.

There was only one light in the whole hallway, halfway down, flickering. It took me a couple seconds to figure out what she really wanted. I was tempted. But I was scared.

I looked at Camille in that dark hallway in Brisbane, and what I saw was one of the magazine photos. The photographer had tried to make Camille look like Marilyn Monroe. It wasn't hard to do, with her chlorine-blonde hair and her bountiful pectoral region. Her lips were parted slightly as if she were whispering something, her eyes half open, her hair tousled. She was holding up two of her Olympic gold medals, which covered…well, they didn't cover much. The thing that stood out most to me was the tattoo on her left hip. It was a shark. A twisting mako shark, ready to lunge.

I was NOT afraid of Camille. I was afraid of the shark.

"I really can't," I answered, trying to inch around her. She blocked me with her hip. *That* hip.

"What's wrong, got a girlfriend back home?" Her eyes were radar-locked on mine and she was touching my arm. She was in charge. I was sweating.

"No…yes…I don't know." All those answers were true. "Look, don't you have the relay tomorrow anyway?"

"Yeah, but only at night, so I can sleep in."

The elite swimmers don't have to swim the prelims of relays. There are alternates to take their places, and the U.S. is so stocked with talent, the alternates almost never fail to get the relays into the finals, which is all that matters.

She grabbed my hand and said "c'mon, my roommate's there. I won't hurt you." She reached past me and pushed the elevator button. The doors opened right away. She pushed the "4" button and down we went.

She pulled me toward her room without saying anything, and I had a chance to assess the situation. That's what I like to do—evaluate. I'm cool and rational, someone who doesn't fly on impulse. So I counted the facts. First, it would be a violation of team rules to enter her room. Second, I did have a girl back home—Molly—and although there was nothing official about our relationship, I had the nagging feeling that it would be cheating on Molly to hook up with Camille. Third, I really was scared—even after the initial adrenaline spike wore off. I had no experience with women like Camille. She wasn't the type that had ever been interested in me. I was used to shy, cerebral women. How was I supposed to act around someone like Camille? Fourth, my cowardice was a perfect complement to my confusion—why was Camille interested in *me*, of all people?

On the other hand, Ay Chihuahua! Camille has it all—a great face and a perfect swimmer body. No guy could fail to be attracted. No male could resist.

The fact that Camille's roommate would be there calmed me a little. I wasn't expecting an actual hook-up. I was flattered by Camille's interest in me. It felt good after a disappointing swim, a tough talk with my parents, and what looked like the imminent end of my career.

We got to her room. She opened the door, poked her head in and glanced from side to side. "Hmm," she said. "Looks like Josie's not here." She yanked me into the room. The door closed behind us, and I was officially in violation of team rules.

The room had suits and towels draped over chairs and lamp shades, leaving the light low and no place to sit except on one of the beds, which turned out to be Camille's bed. She let go of my hand, and I sat on the bed. I had no idea what was going to happen. Camille walked across the room, which wasn't far, opened a dresser drawer and pulled out a tank top. She turned her back to me and removed the sport bra she'd been wearing. I tried not to look, like I know you're not supposed to look directly at the sun when you're swimming backstroke outdoors. For a brief moment, out of the corner of my eye, I saw her bare back and legs, interrupted only by her tiny athletic shorts, which had been rolled over at the top to make them even shorter. I looked away, but the image stayed emblazoned on my mind. My throat felt parched, my palms drenched. She put on the tank top and turned toward me.

"Much more comfortable," she said. She walked past me toward the lone small desk in the room, pushed some things aside, and picked up a book. She brought it over to the bed and sat down beside me. "Here's what I wanted to show you."

What?! She really wanted to show me something? I was disappointed, yet relieved. Surprised, curious, bewildered. The signals were mixed. Ambiguity is one of my least favorite things.

I took the book in my hands. It was an old hardback *Ulysses* and weighed a ton. It was in good condition. I thumbed through it and found a torn piece of a heat sheet on page 35—evidently a bookmark.

"Camille, are you reading this?"

"Yeah, but there's so much I don't get. Like this Stephen Dedalus guy…. I just feel like if I could talk through the beginning stuff, I can get over the hump. You've read it, right?"

"Umm, yeah." I scratched my left temple. "But I'm no expert on it." I'd studied it in college. It was like swimming in molasses. I couldn't get past the fact that Camille, of all people, was taking on *Ulysses*. I thought she was a dumb blonde. Maybe it was a ruse, a snare tactic.

She took the book back from me, put it on her lap, and started leafing through it. She said some words, and I heard them, but they didn't register. She bowed her head toward the book, and I turned slightly, putting my nose in close proximity to her neck. The smell of female skin is ordinarily pleasing to the male olfactory senses, but when it's combined with chlorine, it intoxicates me. I moved my face closer and closer.

Camille was saying something, and I was in another zone altogether, when the door came open and Josie leaned inside. She looked right down at me, and

I glanced up at her across Camille's neck, while Camille completed a question about a fox burying his grandmother. She lifted her head, causing her neck to crash into my nose and knock my glasses catawampus.

"I can come back," Josie said, continuing to look only at me.

"No," I bleated sheepishly. "That's okay. I gotta get going, and Camille has the relay tomorrow." Josie looked at Camille, who nodded. I stood up, straightened my glasses and my clothes. Camille got to her feet as well.

It was now crowded in the little dorm room, and my head was swimming. I felt unsteady, like I needed to hold onto something, but I dared not touch any women. I slithered around them, made it to the door, muttered "goodnight, ladies," and got myself into the hallway. There was air out there, cool air, plenty of oxygen. It started to revive me. I took a few steps, then turned around to look at their door. Just then Camille poked her head out.

"Sleep tight, Doyle," she sang. "We definitely have to continue this sometime soon." I waved and tried to force a smile.

I shuffled down the hall, into the elevator, and finally got to my room. Once safely inside, I stood there in the dark, assessing what had just happened. My roommate, Brick Lehman, was swimming the relay the next day, and he was asleep. I didn't want to wake him up. It was so quiet I could hear blood pumping through my veins. I was still sweating. There was no chance of sleep for a while.

My mind raced. The thing that bothered me most was my loss of control under pressure. It messed with my self-image. I'm the guy who likes pressure, who wants to anchor the relay, the guy people look up to, the steady one. And I let her drag me down that hallway and call all the shots. She put me off my feed.

It all started with the shark. Blasted shark. Here I am, fresh from being conquered by Archie for the 28th time and getting a serious talk from my dad. I get into an elevator on my way to catch some Z's, and this starlet looks at me like I'm lunch. Who wouldn't be dithered by that?

And why was Camille interested in *me*? She's a star—no, a constellation—and I'm at most an asteroid. I'm not in her league. Or am I selling myself short? Can I really get a woman like that? If only I was more suave, more experienced....

I felt embarrassed about violating team rules—a minor infraction, perhaps, but it gnawed at me. Josie's stare said she was surprised that I, Doyle, the upstanding team captain, was behind a closed door after curfew with a female teammate. And what about Molly? We were both technically free to fish other streams, but it didn't feel right.

The most hilarious notion of all was Camille's interest in *Ulysses*. How ironic would it be if her intellectual curiosity were real—if she was the one who wanted to talk books, while I was only interested in smelling her neck? Maybe I completely misunderstood her. Maybe I miscalculated the situation. Maybe it would've been different if I'd been in charge. I made a mental note to re-connect with Camille down the road sometime with the control re-apportioned.

I stripped down to my boxers and climbed into bed. I could hear the rain overhead. I could hear Brick breathing. Good. I hadn't awakened him. But sleep was elusive. I thought about Camille. I thought about my future. Then I started thinking irrelevant things like why is there a Detroit Diner in Brisbane? That was the first stage of the mind-drift that ended in sleep.

The last day of the meet was weird for me because I wasn't swimming. There was no going through the usual meet-day routine: wake up early, drink some power juice, eat a banana, get in the pool for a warm-up, stretch, take a shower, re-shave my legs and arms, get some breakfast, rest a little, get back to the pool for prelims, warm up again, get stretched and rubbed down, swim my race, warm down, take another shower, eat lunch, take a nap, hang out, eat a snack, get to the pool for finals, warm up, stretch, psych up for finals, swim my race, warm down, take another shower, eat like a pig, go to bed. Now that I was done racing, I could do what I wanted. I didn't even need to take a shower—I was clean from all the swimming the day before. I did have to eat like a pig, that's one part of the routine you can't skip.

It was *really* strange watching the finals of the 4 x 200 free relay on the last night of the meet. I'd been on that relay many times. The 200 free was one of my best events when I was younger, and I had anchored the 800 relay in the national championships, the Pan Am games and the previous World Championships. I always did much better on relays than in individual events. Now the 200 was outside my shrinking repertoire and, hence, I was not eligible for the 4 x 200 relay. I was a watcher, a cheerleader.

The Australians thought they could beat us in the 800 relay. Because it was the last event of the meet, the crowd was raucous. I wanted to make sure our guys heard from us, so I led the team in a "U—S—A…U—S—A…U—S—A" cheer. That one is not real hard to lead. Then I led the Hawaiian "Icky La Boomba" cheer. That one requires the leader to yell himself hoarse.

My roommate Brick gave our team a slight lead on the first leg, but the Australians put Dowling and Sinclair on the second and third legs, and led by a body length after 600 meters. As Archie dove off to anchor our relay, I was afraid he jumped. It was a great start. I looked at the officials and the scorer's table, and was relieved to see no sign of a DQ (disqualification). Archie caught the Aussie anchor halfway down the third length, and passed him on the home stretch. Another gold for the Yanks. Archie finished with his bronze in the 400 free plus five golds—two in relays and one each in the 200 free, 200 back and 200 fly. Camille ended with three golds and a silver. Not a bad haul for the king and queen of American swimming. They would get a lot of press buildup in the coming year as the media tried to boost interest in the Olympics—the quadrennial creation of swimming darlings.

CHAPTER 3

I love water. I like to immerse myself in it. When I dive into the pool at the start of a workout, I stay under for a while, gliding under the surface. When I take a hot shower after practice, I stick my head in the water flow, letting it roll down my back and face. I prefer body surfing to board surfing because I want to feel the waves on my whole body, not just my feet. I prefer snorkeling to scuba diving because the absence of tanks frees me to move around in the water better. I go down deep, swim upside down and look back up toward the surface. Seeing the fish is fine, but what I really want to see is the water. Clear blue water. Twenty feet down, the water at the Great Barrier Reef is a blue I've never seen in a crayon box.

Why do I like water so much? I like things that are simple, clean and elegant. I like things that are predictable, measurable, quantifiable. I guess that says something about me. Water and I were made for each other.

Water has some fascinating qualities. Its density and viscosity are ideal for swimming. Those qualities also make possible the circulation of blood, which is mostly water. The human body is mostly water. Every living thing on earth is mostly water. The earth itself is mostly water. Water is the fluid of life. Scientists searching for life on other planets look for signs of water. I took a lot of science courses in college.

Water is beautiful. In my home state of Michigan, there are few things more resplendent than a sunset reflecting off Lake Michigan, a waterfall in the Upper Peninsula, or a gentle snowfall. Water is useful. You can cook with it, drink it, wash things in it, play in it and use it to create electricity. When iron and steel are heated and then quenched in a pool of cool water, the metal becomes hardened. It's like what water does to swimmers.

Molly says water is spiritual. Moses parted it. Jesus walked on it and turned it into wine. There's a verse in the Bible that says the earth was "formed out of water and by water." The Qur'an says "Allah has created from water every living creature." These sayings conjure up images of a Creator using water in the recipe for the dough of life, and using water like a chiseling tool. Water is part of the mixture of every living thing, and it has the power to dig out great rock canyons.

Water has a dark side. It can kill and torture. It makes things rust. Water seeks its level. It goes through tiny cracks and seeps in without being invited. Swimmers get it in their eyes, ears, noses and every other crevice. It gets into our brains. We can't escape it.

One of the great things about being on a U.S. national team is the trip home. Your performances are over and the pressure is off. You're at a physical and emotional peak. You're usually in a foreign country. And if you have special permission, you don't have to travel home with the team. Archie and I had special permission. We'd made plans to fly up to Cairns and take a boat out to the Great Barrier Reef.

The day after the meet ended, most of the team headed for the airport early in the morning. Archie and I slept in, then had lunch with a couple of our teammates and said goodbye to them. We packed up and hauled our stuff outside the dorm to wait for our ride to the airport. It was a brilliant day, and we had our sunglasses on, our faces pointed up. T-shirts, shorts, sandals, no cares: classic chilling.

Archie's phone rang. I know all of Archie's friends and I know the ringtones Archie has assigned them—all rap. This was not one of those. It was an old style phone chime, his tone for "unknown caller." He flipped his shades to the top of his head and scrunched his face to see the caller's number. He looked at me, then back at the phone, and answered it. He turned his back to me and walked a few steps into the shade of a rubber tree. I resumed the ray-catching position.

Though I couldn't make out any words, I could hear Archie's voice becoming more animated. The conversation went on longer than I expected. Archie likes short calls. I didn't care, because I had my face in the sunshine and I was on my way to the Great Barrier Reef.

He jogged up to me. "Guess who that was. Greg Norman." He was stoked.

"Who?" I heard the name, but it was from left field.

"Norman. The Shark! He's like the most famous bloke in Australia."

"The golfer?"

"Yeah, the golfer, but he's way more than that. Got his own wine, man, and a clothing line, runs a bunch of businesses. He's like a zillionaire and he's married to that crazy tennis chick." He was doing that thing with his eyebrows where they go up and down real fast. That crazy tennis chick, Chris Evert, was old enough to be Archie's mother, and she had split from Norman long ago.

"Okay, I know who Greg Norman is, but why did he call you?"

"Saw me on TV last night. He's here playing in some golf tournament. Wants us to have dinner with him."

Here was the good and the bad of being Archie's sidekick, in one package, like medicine in your ice cream. I knew that Greg Norman only wanted to meet Archie. He didn't invite "us" to dinner. But hey, I got to go along, because I'm Archie's buddy.

I remembered why we were standing out in the sun in the first place, and I guess I must have furrowed my brow. Archie looked at me like I was unfortunate in the head or something.

"Dude, why you grimmin' me?" he asked.

I wasn't grimming him. It's just that I had spent hours and hours making plans for our trip, researching the snorkel spots, the boats and the accommodations, studying the flight schedules and crossing all the t's. We had paid money. We had a plane to catch, and all subsequent activities depended on our catching that plane. While it sounded kind of neat to schmooze with Greg Norman, it was going to rain chaos on our plans.

"I mean, it sounds like fun, but what about our flight?"

"No worries, mate!" He had picked up some Aussie slang, and it fit him like a Speedo. "All I know is, this guy wants to meet us, and it's gonna be vast. The Reef'll wait for us."

I don't know how many times this has happened. I plan everything, and it's not like it's easy because Archie has likes and dislikes. I stick to the schedule. Archie messes it up. It doesn't worry him, because he doesn't worry about anything. I clean up the mess, I get us back on track. I sighed.

"Maybe Chrissie will be there," he said, doing the eyebrow thing again. I'm not sure I can precisely define the subset of women to whom Archie is attracted, but I learned long ago that age is not an issue.

"They're not together anymore, Arch. Your information is stale." As usual. I spotted our car approaching. "Do you know where to tell the driver to go, or do I have to figure that out?"

"He's got a boat. We're having dinner on the boat. He said we could head over there right now, even though he's not gonna get there for a while."

We schlepped our stuff over to the car and heaved it into the trunk. I told the driver there was a change of plans. "Take us to Greg Norman's boat, please." The driver nodded and we took off.

As we drove up to Greg Norman's boat, our jaws dropped. It was vast. The driver dropped us off with all our stuff, which we carried over to a gangplank that went up to the boat. A guy in a blue blazer with gold stripes on the cuffs met us at the top, and introduced himself as the captain.

"Oy'm Will," he said. We introduced ourselves, and he started showing us around the ship. We got to the bridge and Archie saw the throttle.

"How fast does this baby go?" Archie queried.

"She'll do about 20 knot," Will replied, but he winked and said "if we fang it." Will had a slight resemblance to the shark-hunting sea captain in *Jaws*. He had a gold tooth and gray stubble on his face, but it was neat and trimmed, and he wore pressed white slacks.

Will showed us all the toys next. There were three more boats on board for various activities. There were a couple sea-doos and a submarine—a submarine? I could see the gears turning inside Archie's head. He let Will get ahead of us, then he whispered to me.

"Can you imagine us in a submarine at the Reef?" No, I couldn't. "Let's get old Norman to spin us up to the Reef on this barge."

I whispered back, "she only does 20 knot. Knots. It's over a thousand miles up to the Reef, and that's more than two days up and two days back if we fang—if we floor it the whole time. Besides, maybe old Norman needs his barge in the meantime." This is why I plan things. Archie isn't the most realistic planner. He thinks he can have everything.

Will brought us back around to a nice room with comfy chairs and a flat screen TV, on which an Australian Rules football game was playing. A guy in a waiter getup came by with a tray which was sporting two flutes of champagne. Archie and I looked at each other, shrugged like "why not?" and took our flutes. "To old Norman," Archie said, clinking his flute on mine. We drank, and pretty soon we were munching on giant prawns and trying to understand Footy.

Finally old Norman sprinted up the gangplank. He didn't look that old. Blond, tan and tall with big shoulders—he could have been a swimmer. His formidable chin arrived first.

"Hunter?" he said, looking at Archie.

"Archie," said Archie as he grabbed Norman's outstretched hand and tried to arm-wrestle him. It was a stalemate.

"Greg Norman. Call me Greg."

He folded my hand in half as I muttered "Doyle, Doyle Wilson." I managed to look him in the eye as he measured me up. His eyes were shocking. The color, yes, he's famous for that, but the wattage was discomforting. I had to avert.

"Glad you guys could make it. Listen, we're gonna have a great meal here, then I'm afraid I've gotta run back to the course. I'm in the hunt, ya know? But

I watched the swimming on TV last night and I can't tell you how impressed I was. Archie, you made our Aussie kids look like shark bait."

"Well," Archie said, modestly as usual, "they did beat me in the 400."

"What do you swim, Doyle?" Norman asked me. I mean Greg.

"The 400." I could tell I didn't need to apprise him of the fact that his shark bait had beaten me.

"Whujja win, Archie, about five gold medals?"

"Yup," I said, answering for Archie because I know he doesn't like to talk about the medal count. He thinks it will jinx him.

"And what about Paris next year, what's the goal?" He was looking at Archie, not me.

I started to answer, but Archie opened his mouth so I stopped. He closed his mouth again, and I got ready to answer, but he beat me.

"Best ever."

I guess he figured Norman was a guy who would know what that meant. And he wasn't exactly giving a medal count, so maybe there'd be no jinx. He smiled at Greg. It wasn't really a smile, it was a grin. No, it was a statement, made with teeth and lips but no vocal cords.

The Shark smiled even bigger than he'd been smiling already, only his was more like a statement, too. Their eyes were also making statements. If you'd passed your hand between their faces, you'd have been electrocuted. It was sickening.

"I *thought* so," Norman growled. "*Tall order*, my friend. Tall order indeed. Good on ya."

The waiter guy came back and ushered us into this glamorous dining room with a big chandelier over the table. We sat down. It turned out that there were two uniformed waiters. They were both busy. They brought out turtle soup, a nice bowl of salad and finally, tah-dah, what we'd all been waiting for, the surf and turf. I don't know what they call that combo in Australia, but my plate had a thick cut of Greg Norman brand Wagyu beef and two "bugs"—what Australians call lobsters without the pinchers. We drank Greg Norman wine, of course.

During dinner, Greg regaled us with stories of his youth in Queensland. He loved the ocean, was always going fishing at the Reef, sometimes fishing for sharks. He caught a few, too. Those were the days, apparently, because now they're trying to ban shark fishing at the Reef.

I was getting full, and feeling a little sleepy, when Greg put his elbows on the table and leaned toward Archie.

"Tell me, Archie, what makes you do it? What *drives* you?"

Archie glanced at me to tell me he had it. "I like to go fast," he said. "I like the feel of it. It's fun."

Greg stared hard at Archie for several seconds. Eye to eye. Then he nodded. "Simple," he said. "Brilliant." He took a sip of wine and swished it around in his mouth. Then he leaned forward on his elbows again.

"What makes you go so *fast?*"

"I guess it's because I work hard. Guys like Doyle push me pretty hard in practice."

Hard eye contact for several more seconds, and then Greg said "*fascinating.*"

I could see Greg summoning up all of his eye strength for one final question. "What do you *think about* in a close race?"

"I think I'm going to win, that's all. I *know* I'm going to win." Greg looked extremely satisfied with this answer.

I was a spectator to all this, and I kept a straight face, but on the inside I was rolling my eyeballs and saying "oh brother." Greg should have asked *me* those questions about Archie. I know exactly what drives Archie and why he goes so fast. I could have lectured all night on those subjects, and my lecture would have been footnoted with references to equations, angles, muscle fibers and lactate levels. I have all the data catalogued and indexed in my mind. But he didn't ask me, so I didn't say a word.

In a way, I suppose, there was some kind of real communication going on that had nothing to do with words. Maybe Greg wanted to measure Archie's intensity: the handshake, the stare, the grin, the *emphasis* on the words and not so much the words themselves. Maybe that's how superstars communicate with each other, on a level higher than linguistics. Like the dolphins in *A Hitchhiker's Guide to the Galaxy*—a series of clicks indeed. Mere mortals like me could never hope to understand.

I was feeling like a potted plant when all of a sudden, a waiter came hustling in. On his hand was a tray. On the tray was a dish. On the dish was ice cream. On the ice cream was hot fudge, and on the hot fudge, a cherry nestled in a bed of whipped cream. There was only one sundae, and I got it. I knew why, too. Archie had tipped off the waiter. He knows what I like.

"Guys, really, this is too big for me," I said. "You have to take some." But Greg was content with coffee, and Archie had another glass of Greg Norman wine. The hot fudge sundae was my special treat. It occupied me while Greg and Archie bonded some more.

"So what's next for you blokes?" When he asked that, I realized that we hadn't fixed our messed-up plans. Greg was completely unaware that we even had a problem. But my mouth was stuffed, so Archie answered.

"We were supposed to fly up to Cairns today and take an early boat for the Reef in the morning."

"The Reef? You guys are headed up there?"

"Well, we were. But we missed our flight. It's okay, we can probably catch another flight tomorrow."

"Nah, you'll miss a day at the Reef that way." He thought about it for a second. Then he grabbed his cell phone. "Nigel. Greg. Got a couple guys here on the boat who need to get up to Cairns." Pause. "Tonight." Pause. "You got it." Click.

"Looks like you guys are in luck," Greg said. "I don't need the jet for two more days. Nigel's ready to fly you up to Cairns, but you gotta go quick. We'll have a car here in five minutes to take you out to the airport."

I rolled my eyeballs and said "oh brother" on the inside again. Outwardly, no one noticed a thing. Luck had shined on Archie and gotten him out of a mess that he'd never even worried about. I got some of the glow from that luckshine.

Archie took another slug of wine, Greg slurped some coffee, and I downed a big spoonful of ice cream. We got up and walked out of the dining room, onto the deck, and down the gangplank. Our bags were at the bottom.

"Sorry this was so short," Greg said as he massacred my hand again. "It was good to meet ya, Doyle." Then he turned those laser eyes on Archie. "Archie, keep it up, friend. Good luck to ya."

Nigel flew us straight and true. We landed in Cairns just past midnight, and made it to our bungalow around one o'clock. We got a couple hours of shuteye and then dragged ourselves down to catch the six o'clock bus to Port Douglas. We made it all right, got on our boat, and slept all the way out to the Reef.

Archie and I had done a bunch of snorkeling, and we were good at it. We didn't use masks, just clear swimming goggles, and we didn't need no stinking snorkels. Each of us could comfortably hold his breath for almost two minutes. We knew how to blow our ears out so we could go really deep. We wore fins for speed.

We were getting ready to dive off when the dive master came around.

"You blokes've done this before, havya?"

"Yeah," Archie said. "We're pretty much experts."

"Rippa." The guy looked us up and down. "Just gonna weah the budgie smugglers?" He was staring at our Speedo briefs. I glanced around and saw that everybody else was wearing wetsuits.

"Heck yeah, the water's warm and we like the freedom of going Speedo." Freedom is one of Archie's favorite things.

"Suit ya'selves," the dive master said. "You know about the Irukandji, right?" The three of us looked at each other for several seconds. "Jellyfish the size of a fingernail," he continued. "Can't hardly see 'em. The sting doesn't feel like much at first, but after half an hour, it's blue murder. Backache, headache, vomit. It can mess up the heart rhythm. Couple blokes have bellied up from it."

I talked Archie into wearing stinger suits.

This is the thing about Australia. It's an incredibly beautiful place, great weather, friendly people. But it has great white sharks cruising the coasts. Sea wasps. The ten deadliest snakes. Irukandji.

With beauty comes danger. Ah, Camille. Hadn't thought about her for a while.

We snorkeled ourselves to exhaustion and ate a giant meal on the boat. It was one of those clipper ships with tall masts and big sails. The sails were down as we lay anchored for the night. Archie and I decided to sleep on the top deck, using piles of towels for mattresses. It was warm, so we didn't need shirts. The stars looked like sea spray splashed across the southern sky. They made me wonder about the grand scheme of my life.

"Arch," I said, as we both faced skyward, "you dated Camille Cognac, right?"

"Yeah, not for long. Pretty hard when you live so far apart. But we had some fun."

"The thing I'm wondering is, is she…nice?" That sounded really dumb. "Nice" wasn't really what I was looking for, but it was the only word I could think of.

"Nice? Yeah, she's a real nice girl. I mean, she likes to have things her way. Kind of, I don't know…determined."

Archie doesn't talk about the gory details of his love life, even to me, for the same reason he goes silent on the medal count. He propped himself up on one elbow and looked down at me as a big grin grew on his face.

"Do you like her, Doyle? I can fix you up!"

Archie can get any woman he wants, and he knew I was nervous around them. He had taken it on as a mission to get me hooked up. I was pretty sure, though, that despite his good intentions Archie would not select the right woman for me. I'd have to do it myself.

"I'm curious about her, like what makes her tick. She initiated a discussion with me at the dorm down in Brisbane. Kind of an interesting discussion. She's started reading *Ulysses*."

"What's *Ulysses*?"

"It's a book by an Irish author named James Joyce. Kind of a famous book. Hard to read. Doesn't seem like something she'd be interested in, which is why I'm a little confused about the whole thing."

"Hmm. She's actually kind of smart, though you wouldn't know it, the way she acts sometimes. Likes to watch PBS." Really?

We both thought about it for a minute. Then Archie, still propped on his elbow, started working his eyebrows up and down again. "*She* initiated?"

"Yeah."

"Dude, you're in. Camille gets what she wants, and she wants you. Go for it, man."

"Thanks. I'll think about it."

He got off his elbow and we resumed our stargazing. He was quiet, probably to let me think about Camille. But I was already off Camille and onto bigger fish. The stars were bearing down.

"You know," I said, "I have to make a decision when I get back to Michigan. I've been out of school for two years already, not really doing anything but swimming. My dad thinks I should hang it up, get on with my life, and he has a good point. I might not make the team, or get a medal. It might be a big disappointment after investing a lot of time and effort."

He propped himself up again.

"Don't even talk like that, Doyle. You're there. You're gonna make the team, no sweat. And win a medal—at *least* silver." He winked. There was no way that Archie could even imagine himself winning less than gold. It wasn't in his DNA.

"The Aussies are getting tougher," I reminded him.

"You're gonna butter the Aussies." He thought about it for a minute. "Besides, it's *Paris*. You and me. Think of the babes."

It was a futile conversation. I don't know why I started it. Archie and I know each other like brothers, but we're from different planets. His world is about babes, the absence of sweat, and buttering people. It's a cool world and he loves it. But I'm not from there.

"So, basically, you think I should keep swimming."

"You got it. No-brainer. Black & white." He unpropped himself and we gazed up.

My world had a million shades of gray. I love black and white and hate ambiguity, so Archie's world had a lot of appeal to me. But what could I do when the gray enveloped me like a Michigan winter fog? My brain was starting to hurt again. It wouldn't be decided on a clipper ship in the middle of the Great Barrier Reef. I would need to collect the data, hear a lot of voices. Archie's view didn't carry much weight, frankly. But I appreciated it.

I propped myself up on my elbow and tried to give Archie one of those intense Norman stares. "You're a prince, Arch—a duke at the very least." I blinked. "Thanks for your confidence in me. And it's mutual, you know." It's easy to have confidence in Archie and he doesn't need it, because he has enough of his own.

The stars seemed to be growing, and it made me feel small. Swimming in the ocean the next day further punified me. We encountered a trio of reef sharks. I felt a chill when I first saw them. Archie was swimming underwater ahead of me, and he kept getting closer and closer to the sharks. He showed no signs of stopping and we were way past my comfort zone. I grabbed his leg. That may have been imprudent under the circumstances—it probably scared the crap out of him. But he stopped, and we surfaced for air before going back down to watch them from a good 20 feet away. As we watched, I grew more comfortable. The sharks did not try to eat us. I marveled at their sleek airplane bodies, built for swimming, their elegant, effortless movements. That was the day sharks became a little less scary to me.

CHAPTER 4

Swimming is counter-cultural. Swimmers are misfits in the world at large. Our culture says "if it feels good, do it." Swimming does not feel good. The very purpose of swim practice is to make it hurt. Races are largely about pain management.

Our culture says "gratify yourself now." Swimming involves delayed gratification. You peak for two meets a year. Every practice is geared toward the next big meet, which may be months away. Swimmers know they have to do the work today, day after day, in order to reap the reward tomorrow. For Olympic swimmers, the training strategy may have a two-to-three-year timeline.

Our culture says "make things easier on yourself"—buy fast food at drive-throughs; use the remote control so you don't have to get off the couch. Swimming is inconvenient. Swimmers take the hard road. We wear baggy suits and paddles to increase resistance. We do no-breathers. We swim butterfly.

Our culture says "entertain yourself constantly." Entertainment is a huge industry; being bored is a drag. Swimming is institutionalized boredom. It numbs the mind. You force yourself to do hard, boring things over and over. There is no scenery. There's no chance to socialize with your head underwater.

Our culture says "it doesn't matter who you are, it's how you look." Swimmers have hair that gets bleached and frizzed, then they shave it all off and look like cancer patients. Their teeth get discolored by the chemicals in the water. Swimmers develop monstrous shoulders, which is okay for guys, but female swimmers think the shoulders make them look unfeminine. Swimmers don't have time to make themselves look pretty.

Our culture says "celebrity is everything." We're fascinated by celebrities. We want to know what they do in private, what's in their trash cans. In swimming, there is maybe one celebrity per generation. It's not enough to win an Olympic gold medal. You have to win more than four gold medals to be remembered by anyone outside of swimming circles by the time of the next Olympics. Do any non-swimmers remember Matt Biondi? Five golds, a silver and a bronze at the 1988 Olympics. Or John Naber? Four golds and a silver in 1976. If you want to be famous, swimming is not the most rational route. And celebrities don't attend swim meets.

Our culture says "show me the money." There's hardly any money in swimming. The rare swimmer may make some money in endorsements, but there is no professional league and little prize money. Swimming takes up so much time, most swimmers can't hold regular jobs while they train. In almost every swimming family, it costs a lot of money to swim when you add up swim club dues and travel expenses, not to mention the extra food.

The countercultural aspect of swimming is one of the things I dig about it.

"DEEDLY DEE, MOLLY B." I texted a message to Molly to get her attention. I needed to talk to her about The Decision. It was 10 o'clock in the morning. Archie and I had arrived home from Australia the previous evening and I hadn't slept much.

"DDD." That meant: "deedly dee, Doyle, I'm on your wavelength." It also meant she was busy, or she'd have typed it out. She was at work.

Needless to say, I'd be mortified if any of my friends ever saw the texts I sent to Molly.

"READY 4 A BREAK?"

"S." She had reduced the word "yes" to a single letter.

"BHH IN 10?"

"K ***." The asterisks meant she was excited.

I got there first. BHH is Brewhaha, one of those non-chain coffee shops that hoped to become a chain when it grew up. There are lots of places like that in Huron Springs. Coffee and comedy is the game plan, and they have local comedians do stand-up on Friday nights. The concept didn't take off. The good thing about Brewhaha's failure to make the big time is that the coffee is cheap and the service is great. People know me there.

"Doyle!" I heard my name as soon as I opened the door.

"Nolan!" I shouted to the guy behind the counter. Like half the shop workers of Huron Springs, Nolan was a grad student, trying to stay above the poverty line while pursuing an advanced degree. He was wearing a t-shirt that said "Brewhaha Staff—The Perks Are Great!"

"Hey man, where you been?" he asked.

"Australia," I answered, walking up to the counter.

"Cool. Swimming, I suppose. Want the usual?"

"Not yet, I'm just posting until Molly gets here. What's on tap?"

"Today we have a dark roast from Tanzania. Scones are orange peel."

I turned around to analyze the table situation and just then Molly came into view outside. It seemed like slow motion as she walked, oblivious to my stare. It always makes me smile to see her. Molly changes her look all the time, but in some ways she's the same yesterday, today and tomorrow. She wears a faint permanent smile, like it's a natural feature of her face. If Camille is a shark, beautiful and dangerous, then Molly is a dolphin—playful and smiling. Molly has a strong protective instinct. In the 1963 movie *Flipper*, a dolphin drives away sharks when they threaten a boy. I don't know if that's true to life or not, but I do know this: Molly would totally do that for me.

Please tell me I'm not the only guy who compares women to aquatic creatures. It's probably a swimmer thing.

Molly walked into Brewhaha with a hairstyle I hadn't seen before, except maybe in a 1960s movie with Natalie Wood. Her hair fell straight down, then right before it reached her shoulders, it did a flip turn and pointed north. It was a perfect match for the corners of her mouth. Everything about Molly seemed to point upward.

She had on a relatively short skirt, revealing her knees—knees I like but rarely see. Above the skirt, a brown cardigan over an untucked shirt. I don't know what they call that style, but I see it on a lot of teenagers around town. There's more to her changing looks than just playfulness. It's also a by-product of social ineptitude, which I also like about Molly and matches my own. Or it could symbolize her well-known desire to revisit happier days. Anyway, I always smile when I see a new style; they all look good on her.

Molly was wearing her work smock. She was working part time for Dr. Sandoval, the optometrist, while pursuing a Masters in Clinical Psychology. Her schedule was brutal.

"Hey, Moll. Thanks for coming down on short notice. I got a crave."

"It's a slow day at the eyeball factory," she said with a wry smile. "My hankering hit at the same time as your crave. Coincidence? I don't think so." Molly doesn't believe in coincidences.

We hugged the way friends hug. Molly is five-foot-six on a tall day, and I'm six-three, so I have to lean down when I hug her.

I met Molly the summer after I graduated from college. I'd been noticing the math equations on the blackboard getting fuzzier. I was walking in downtown Huron Springs one day between summer swim practices and Dr. Sandoval's sign caught my eye. I walked in. There was this girl behind a counter who noticed me. I noticed her. She was wearing glasses.

"Can I help you?" she asked.

"Yes. Can you make me look like Brad Pitt?" She came closer, studying my face. "The young Brad," I said, "like in *A River Runs Through It.*"

That was the first time I saw the wry smile on Molly. "Umm. No. But I can make you look smarter."

Smarter?! Don't I look smart already? What I need is to look hunkier. The thing is, though, this girl looks pretty smart in *her* glasses, so she probably speaks the truth.

"So, then, you propose to make me look like Bill Gates?"

"I was thinking more along the lines of Cary Grant in *Monkey Business.*"

Wow. This girl can think on her feet *and* she likes old movies. Talk about the whole package.

I squeezed my chin to create a dimple, like Cary Grant's. It made her laugh. "I'm Doyle," I said, trying to imitate her wry smile, which didn't work because wry smiles are asymmetrical, and I'm a symmetrical kind of guy.

"I'm Molly," she said, pointing to the embroidered name on her smock, right above the caduceus. We shook hands. I got my eyes checked then and there by Dr. Sandoval and bought a pair of glasses. They make me look smarter.

I've got a bunch of pet names for Molly: Moll, Small, Holy Moly, Mb, 42, and several more. I thought maybe her parents were literary types who named her after Molly Bloom or Moll Flanders. Turns out her dad is an aerospace engineer who uses molybdenum alloys. So she was named after element 42 on the Periodic Table. Not a precious metal, or a noble metal, just your basic hard-working high-melting-point metal. Highly alloyable.

As I looked at Molly in the coffee shop, after the hug, I was glad I was wearing my glasses. I don't always. She was wearing hers.

Molly and I sidled up to the counter. She greeted Nolan: "Hello, she said, to No One in particular." Nolan got the nickname "No One" from his little brother, who couldn't pronounce "Nolan" when he was a toddler. Nolan smiled.

"Gimme the Tanzanian," I said. "Big. Two of those orange peel scones. And whatever she's having." I looked down at Molly. "Moll, I got it. Whatever you want." She ordered a cappuccino and a zucchini muffin. I paid and we sat down.

I looked up at Molly after stirring my coffee and she was grinning at me so hard it made me laugh. "What?" I said.

"Your hair! What'd you do, buzz it in Australia?"

"Not quite, but yeah, I wanted it short."

"Seems to be growing in kind of fluffy-like."

I reached up and felt it. "Don't you like it short?"

"I do, I love it short." She took a sip of her cappuccino. "Within reason."

"Oh hey, I brought you something." I pulled it out of my pocket—a platypus keychain. Not much of a gift, really, but I knew she liked monotremes.

"Awww. Thanks, Doyle. If I ever get a car I'll know right where to put the keys."

I love small talk with Molly, but I became keenly aware that she was on a break and our time was limited. "I did get a crave," I said, "but I actually need some advice from you." We both sipped our drinks. "I got fourth in the World Championships."

"Nice," she said. "I saw you on TV. I liked it when you knocked your headphones cockeyed." Shoot, I was hoping nobody'd noticed.

"Getting fourth was bad news, I'm afraid." Molly needs to have these things explained to her. When she plays video games, she doesn't care who wins. I suspect she loses on purpose sometimes so no one feels bad. That's one thing I *don't* like about her—I'm usually on her team.

"I'm 24 years old," I continued. "For a swimmer, that's getting pretty old if you're not at the top. At some point I've got to start living a real life, and it looks like now's the time."

She casually pushed her Natalie Wood hair behind her left ear. "Are you ready?" she asked.

"Yeah, I'll probably just choose one of the med schools."

"That's not what I meant." She meant mentally ready. She's into the mental side of things. And she knew I wasn't mentally ready. She has a way of subtly getting to my weak point.

"Swimming's been a pretty big part of my life. It's not easy to think about moving on. There's a big unknown out there."

She took a sip of cappuccino, and when she put the cup down, her face had lost its usual brightness. She extricated herself from her work smock and hung it over the back of her chair, then pushed up the sleeves of her cardigan.

It didn't seem all that hot in the coffee shop, so I wondered if something had come over her.

"Sorry. I was thinking about…" she sighed "…I know what you're talking about."

I hadn't intended it to be such a downer. The scrunching of her sleeves had revealed a band-aid on Molly's forearm. It was a Batman band-aid, black on yellow. She's always wearing band-aids to hide various things. It isn't just for fun, or to revisit her childhood, though that's part of it, I'm sure. She has a fear of minor health issues. I think, to borrow a phrase she has used on me, that the band-aids give her a veneer of protection.

I thought the band-aid might provide an opportunity for levity. I reached across the table and touched it. "Can I take a look?" She nodded. I gently peeled it back from the end closest to me. Underneath was a pink-red spot on her arm, with a little bump. I ran my finger over it. There was a little crust on it, like dried oozing. "Does it hurt?" She moved her eyeballs sideways and back: no.

I put the band-aid back on and applied a little pressure to make it stick. "That looks kinda bad, Moll. Maybe you should get it checked."

Her eyes welled up with water, and when I said "checked," she burst into tears. She bowed her head while the tears gushed out. I could see them dripping onto the metal table. I reached my hands across. I held one of her hands and put a pair of napkins in the other. She squeezed back on my hand and dabbed at her tears with the napkins. I'd seen this a bunch of times before. I'd sit there wanting to help, wanting to say something, wanting to put my arms around her. Wanting to solve the problem. Wanting to save her. But I knew from experience, the best thing to do is wait it out.

Molly's mother died of Lou Gehrig's disease. I knew about that disease, thanks to *Pride of the Yankees*, starring Gary Cooper. Gehrig was one of the greatest athletes of all time. The disease that bears his name struck him in the prime of his life. Amyotrophic Lateral Sclerosis—ALS—slowly takes away your muscles, your ability to move, and ultimately kills you. An athlete can hardly think of a more horrific way to go. The coordination goes early, then the ability to walk, then you can't speak, or even turn your head.

Molly had told me stories about how she and her mom learned Morse code so they could communicate. Near the end, her mom could move only her eyes. Eyes up was a dot, sideways a dash. She told me about reading books to her mom and how she would cry at the sad parts, but the only way Molly could tell was by the tears. The funny parts were the hardest—her body would struggle to let it out, but it's impossible to laugh without functioning muscles.

Few people have heard the stories. She doesn't want people to know how bad it was. She tells select people—people she can trust. You don't really know Molly if you haven't been told. Once you know, you can see the effects.

During her college years, Molly took care of her mom and also looked after her dad and younger brother. While other college students were drinking beer and going to clubs and hooking up, Molly was at home after class, emptying catheters and giving sponge baths. It stunted her social growth. In a way, I can relate—being a serious swimmer did that to me, too, in a comparatively miniscule way.

The ordeal left Molly pathologically close to her father. Maybe that's my spin on it, but if I ever wanted to take her on a "date," I would have to ask her father first. It's not his rule, it's hers. She'll spend time with me alone only if it's in a public place. If I want to hang out with her at her place or mine, I have to invite other people along, or she does. These rules are not specific to me; they apply to all male friends of Molly. I didn't get the rules at first—I thought "what is this, the '50s?" That was before I heard her talk about her mom. I get it now, and I like it. Molly has principles. She's different.

I hadn't gotten to the point of going to see Molly's father. When I first met her, she occasionally talked about a guy named Peter. They'd been high school friends and played in the church jazz band together. He was on a law school path, had a plan for their life together—he sounded like the kind of guy everyone would think was "right" for her. When the ALS came, Peter couldn't stick it out. He skated before the end. Her friends told me Molly was shaken—mad—not only at Peter but at God. After a while she talked like it wasn't meant to be. Then she stopped talking about Peter.

The Peter story and the dating rule told me that Molly wasn't interested in having a casual boyfriend. Her family was already running low on permanence, and she didn't want to take another hit. I, on the other hand, had never wanted a serious girlfriend. I'd been focused on swimming. I was never interested in romantic games. I was too serious, too driven, too…something.

The hair trigger crying is another mark left on Molly. The ALS started with something small. Her mom was healthy, happy, busy raising her kids and watching Molly reach high school milestones. At Molly's graduation, she was snapping a photograph and dropped the camera. No one thought anything. But she got it "checked," and after a zillion tests, the grim diagnosis came. So Molly is wary. Every bump is cancer, every ache a tumor. Potentially.

The sobbing slowed. It seemed safe to say something. "Probably just an alien seed, Mb. Planted under your skin. You're lucky to be chosen."

She smiled, and good news—it was wry. "You sure it's not arm cancer?"

"Could be the Ebola virus. Or flesh-eating bacteria."

"What kind of doctor should I see for that?"

"Dr. Seuss."

"I can see why you're headed for med school."

And that brought it back around to me. I like it when we talk about me. That was the whole idea when I texted her—to talk about me. It usually is. I always feel selfish and petty returning to my problems after one of her sobs. But this is another thing I've learned. Don't dwell on her problems. Talk about me. She likes that. It helps her.

I let go of her hand and she gave a squeeze before our hands came apart. She's a squeezer. My mom does that too.

"Yeah…" I said, "…med school. Even choosing a school is a big decision. Should I stay in Michigan and go to SM, near my parents, near…"—near her, but I couldn't say it—"…near home, or should I punch my ticket to Cali?" Few people in Michigan would pass up an opportunity to move to the Golden State.

"I don't want to talk about that. I want to talk about the ready thing. Tell me how you feel."

Ordinarily, an invitation to talk about my feelings would drive me up the wall. In this case, it saved me from having to talk about the med school choice. Med school in California would mean goodbye Molly. She had to know that. She was a factor.

"Oh, you mean ready to quit swimming? Everybody's got to retire sometime. It's no big deal."

She studied my eyes. It can be a little disconcerting, the eye thing, but I'm used to it. She's an expert at it, after having spent so much time looking into her mother's eyes. She knows the codes.

"Not a big deal? Are you lying to me?" Fortunately, she said it with a smile. I'd never lie to Molly, not intentionally. She'd detect it right away.

"I don't think of it as lying, really." Wishful thinking, deluding myself, stretching a bit, BS. "All right, it's a big deal."

"You're such a guy, Doyle. Of course it's a big deal. If the end of swimming makes you sad, it's okay. Be sad."

It was the budding psychologist talking. I guess it was sad. I tried to look sad for her. I squinted my eyes and pouted my lip. It brought back her wry smile.

"Okay, what you need is a child psychologist. I've got a classmate I can recommend." She started to pack up the trash on the table.

"No—I get it." I made the universal "slow down" sign—palms toward earth, downward motion, like the end of a butterfly pull. I took a deep breath.

"I guess I just saw it going differently. Especially the end. I visualized it a thousand times. I'm dressed in USA sweats, my hair is wet, I'm on the top step of the podium, holding flowers, waving. Smiling. I can see it right now, in my mind, as clear as any photograph."

"Hmm." She put her hand to her chin. "And it's hard to give that up?"

"It's hard to quit without accomplishing the goal. And what's the new photo going to look like? Will there even be one? I can't conjure one in my mind—believe me, I've tried. Doyle in a lab coat, looking through a microscope. Doyle in an operating room, cutting open a patient. Doyle in an office, putting x-rays against a light box. I can't even paint those pictures. It gets fuzzy when I try."

"I think I understand." But she didn't. She couldn't. Molly was never a swimmer.

"I've had one mission my whole life. I don't see anything on the horizon as a mission. And I can't imagine living a mission-less life." I'd gotten myself kind of worked up. When I was done, I leaned back and slumped down in my chair.

"I'm so glad you let that out." She did seem glad—energized even. Her eyes were lit up.

"Still think I need a child psychologist?"

"No, now I think you're normal. I can tell you something that might help you, though." I nodded. She sighed. "I—my life isn't exactly going the way I pictured it either."

I hadn't thought about that. Her picture was more messed up than mine. And maybe she *did* understand. Maybe she understood it better than I did. In these talks with Molly, I rarely come away with the problem solved. What I come away with is a reminder that the universe doesn't revolve around me, that other people have problems, that I'm not alone, that there are big principles at play. There was an awkward silence.

"So what do we do, Mb?"

"You make a new reality. You take a step of faith, move forward, adjust. The fact that your future is going to be different than you pictured it doesn't mean it won't be good." She said it mechanically, like she'd memorized it. "That's what I'm being told, anyway."

"Who's telling you that?"

"My pastor. My professor. My counselor."

"How do you know it's not a load of crap?"

"I don't."

We both stood up and silently gathered the garbage. She reinserted herself into the smock, and we left Brewhaha. Dr. Sandoval's office was about five blocks away. "Okay," I said as we walked, "here's what I really need to know. Is swimming like an addiction? If I quit, am I going to go through withdrawal? Will I need a replacement addiction or something?"

She laughed out loud when she saw I was serious. "I'll look it up in the DSM," she said. "Actually, what you have is an obsession—all you swimmers. It's a little different."

We rounded the corner and came to Dr. Sandoval's. Molly stopped, so I stopped, and we faced each other while she spoke. "The way you opened up to me back there..." she paused for two seconds, "just...thanks." I was still chewing on that when Molly said "Hey, I've got to go." She climbed the first two steps, then turned, reached down, and ran a couple fingers through my hair. "I'm really proud of you," she said. "Nice hair."

I wanted to kiss her, but I knew the rules. She bounced through the doorway.

I kept smiling after Molly disappeared. The look of her face stayed on my mind—slightly swollen from the crying, upturned mouth, flip turn hair. I remembered the feel of her arm, her hands. Molly and I hadn't touched much, so I was still getting used to her smallness, her softness, her lack of muscles. I liked it all.

As I walked home, it started to come together. Maybe I was ready after all. Go see Molly's father. Enroll at SM. Quit swimming. None of it would be easy. But it seemed right. My gut was saying do it. It sounded like a plan.

CHAPTER 5

The flip turn is unique to swimming. A wave of force and momentum moving in one direction instantly changes and goes the other way. Perhaps the fast break in basketball is similar, or the interception return in football, but those happen rarely and are unexpected. Flip turns are a regular part of swimming.

To execute a flip turn, the swimmer somersaults into the wall feet first, then pushes off and begins swimming the other way. But those are only the basics. Mastering the technique requires much more.

The flip is not a straight-over somersault. You have to dip your shoulder going in, so that your feet hit the wall pointing sideways. You twist at the waist so you can push off on your stomach instead of your back. Your head is upside down briefly, and you can get a snoot full of water unless you blow air out your nose—exactly the right amount of air at exactly the right time. You have to hit the wall just right—not too close and not too far. When you hit it right, you can explode off the wall with your leg muscles. You streamline after pushing off, then do dolphin kicks and finally a powerful arm stroke to break out at the surface. Too deep on the pushoff and you waste time; too shallow and you get hit by the wave that followed you into the wall. It takes precision, timing, strength, and focus.

Turns have to be attacked. You take a strong last pull and a big kick going in so you can hit the wall hard. There's no room for pussyfooting.

Initiating the turn at precisely the right moment is critical. The wall might come up on a half-stroke and you have to adjust by taking another quick stroke, or a longer glide in. You need to spot the wall three strokes out to be able to make the necessary adjustment.

When you see a really good swimmer do a flip turn, it looks fluid and effortless. Try it yourself and see how hard it is. How do you become a master of the flip turn? Like the golf swing or the jump shot, you have a thousand things to think about but can't think about any of them while you're executing the maneuver. You have to do it over and over again in practice, honing the technique to the point where it just comes naturally. Then, when you're in a race, all you have to do is spot the wall and habit takes over. Your eye has seen that distance before and tells the muscles what to do. An elite swimmer does about 150,000 flip turns a year. It can add up to a million in a career.

In swimming, as in life, the ability to change directions quickly is invaluable. Fine tune with practice. Spot the wall. Attack. Blow air out your nose. Explode off the wall.

It's hard to overestimate the impact coaches have on the lives of their swimmers. A swim coach is like a CEO, a military commander, and a parent rolled into one. There's a bond between swimmer and coach that often lasts a lifetime. I couldn't make The Decision without talking to my old college coach.

Robert Dewey, the men's coach at Three Rivers College, resurrected my swimming career. Early on in high school I'd become a fairly big star, and most people assumed I'd be going to Southern Michigan on a scholarship. However, I injured my shoulder at the start of my senior year and was told that I either had to get rotator cuff surgery or stay out of the water the rest of the season. My parents didn't want me to have the surgery, so I stayed dry for six months. The big schools backed off. I could have walked on at SM, but I was disappointed about the scholarship and not sure that I belonged there. I thought about packing it in.

I met Coach Dewey for the first time when he approached me at the state high school meet my senior year, which I attended in street clothes. Three Rivers had never been on my radar screen. It's a small liberal arts school outside Kalamazoo, Michigan, with an excellent academic reputation and a modest swim program. Coach Dewey was also a math professor at the school. I got offered a full academic scholarship to Three Rivers, which, being a Division III school, could not give athletic scholarships. My parents loved Coach Dewey. The academic scholarship sounded better to them than an athletic scholarship. I took it, thinking that I was probably signing away my chance at swimming glory.

The facilities and training at TR were far below the elite level at SM. Coach Dewey offered to support whatever kind of training I wanted to do. We started slowly, until I became more relaxed about swimming and started enjoying it again. If I wanted to stay late or do an extra practice, he was there—it was often just the two of us. He let me design workouts and we discussed everything about training and technique. I was a math major and had him as a professor in two of my classes. He became, like many coaches become with their swimmers, a second father to me.

I didn't have to call ahead with Coach Dewey. I knew I was welcome to drop in. He loved it, in fact. I always knew where he'd be—one of three places, depending on the time of day: at the pool, at his office in Jules Hall, or at home. I figured by the time I got there, he'd be home. I saddled up my Taurus and headed for the House of Dewey.

I love my old Taurus. It won the Ubiquitous Car of the Year award the year it was made, and that was 150,000 miles ago. It's been through a lot with me, including several near-misses on icy Michigan roads.

I stopped at an Arby's drive-thru and got four sandwiches and a big order of curly fries. I smothered everything with horsey sauce. I had a big travel mug of water with me to swill it down as I drove.

The drive between Huron Springs and Three Rivers reminded me of swim practice. Not much to look at. Lane markers, a stripe down the middle underneath. Done it a million times, back and forth.

Radar Love by Golden Earring came on the radio and I turned up the volume. This is a famous swimming song. A high school kid named Brian Goodell was in the Olympic finals of the 1500 free in 1976. He had worked with a sports psychologist who taught him that when it was time to "turn it on" in a race, he should bring a particular song to mind. Two-thirds of the way through the race, Brian was languishing in third place and hurting. He popped *Radar Love* into his mind's cassette player, or maybe it was 8-Track back then. The rest is history. Brian turned it on, ate up the deficit and won in world record time.

Brian Goodell would have been a huge star at the 1980 Olympics if the U.S. hadn't boycotted. The song reminded me of another reason to quit swimming—I could invest a ton of time in it, get my hopes up, then have everything disintegrate due to something beyond my control.

Coach Dewey and his wife, Laura, lived on a tree-lined street in Three Rivers just a few blocks from the campus. The houses were old but well-preserved, nicely landscaped. Many of the neighbors were professors. There were always people walking up and down the sidewalks, especially in spring.

Laura came out the front door to greet me. "Doyle! It's so good to see you. Do you want some dinner? We just finished and there's a lot left over." I had to stifle a burp, I was so full from the Arby's.

"No thanks, I grabbed something on the way." She hugged me when I got to the door. Laura hugged me the very first time I met her, when I was a gangly freshman, and she's hugged me every time since. She's an indiscriminate hugger. I had a grade school teacher who was like that—my favorite teacher, in fact.

Laura D had been the Channel 3 evening news anchor in Kalamazoo for nearly three decades. After I graduated from Three Rivers she retired, although there was a rumor she'd been forced out in favor of a younger face. If that's what happened, it was a terrible mistake because Laura had a perfect face for TV news—handsome, fearless, a few creases to show experience. Her face showed far less age than her birth certificate.

"How was your trip to Australia?" she asked.

"A real corker," I said with a wink. "The Great Barrier Reef was incredible."

"I'll bet. It's at the top of my travel list, if I can ever get what's-his-name away from the pool."

"Speaking of what's-his-name...."

"Sitting on the deck, reading the newspaper," she said, pointing with her head. "Come on through."

As I walked through behind her, I noticed what I always notice. The house had to be 100 years old, but it was in perfect shape. Neat as a pin. I'd spent a lot of time there during college –every winter break I stayed with Laura and Coach D while the dorms were closed and I trained by myself.

"Hey Coach, are you getting younger?" I announced myself with flattery as I went through the screen door onto the deck. He put aside the paper, got up and gave me a strong handshake with his other hand on my shoulder.

"Doyle, you rascal." He let out one of his big hearty laughs. "Why'd you come all the way over to Three Rivers? Don't you have anything better to do?"

"What could be better than this?" Coach and Laura had a botanical back yard with big old oak and maple trees, lots of shade, and flower gardens all around the deck.

Coach D looked good for 68. He already had a tan, and it was only May 1. I wondered how he ever became a swimmer. His giant head, thick neck and burly chest made him look like he'd sink if you dropped him in water. Maybe it was the hands—his potholder mitts were like massive swim paddles. He'd been a decent swimmer back in the day, but not great. He swam at Kenyon, a Division III swimming powerhouse in Ohio. He got his PhD in math from Ohio State, then moved to Michigan. He was 28 years old when he became coach at Three Rivers, and 40 years later he was still going strong.

The three of us chatted for a while before I told him why I came. He said he was cutting back his teaching load, that he and Laura were going to do some traveling and spend more time with their grandkids. I shot a glance at Laura when Coach mentioned traveling, and she smiled at me. After a while, Laura went inside and I introduced the main subject.

"I did okay at the Worlds," I said, "but I'm kind of disappointed I didn't do better. I was hoping for a breakthrough. So now I've got a big decision to make. Should I keep on swimming for another year, take a shot at the Olympics, or is now the time to hang it up and go to med school?"

Just then it seemed like a light bulb went on above his head. "Oh, hang on," he said. "I forgot to tell you something. I worked out a deal with Adrian." Adrian Alonzo was the Athletic Director at Three Rivers. "I'm going to phase out of coaching in the next two years. I'm getting an assistant coach, who'll then be in line to take over from me in two years."

There was a pause of approximately the length of the elevator ride with Camille in Brisbane. He was looking for a reaction, and I was looking for... shoot, I don't know what I was looking for. I was frozen. He leaned forward in his chair, toward me, and broke the silence.

"You interested?"

Take that, Archie! Something fell into my lap, just like things are always falling into yours. Heck yeah, I was interested. A job and a future in the sport I love, following in the footsteps of a man I admire—who wouldn't be interested?

"Yeah, I'm totally interested."

"Are you really?"

"Well…." Hold on a minute, I said to myself. You're not Archie; you can't have everything. If you take the job, you can still have Molly, but you can't have med school. You can't have the Olympics.

"You'd make an excellent coach, Doyle. You know more about swimming than anyone I've ever coached—more than I know. You have an analytical approach to life that would make you good at it."

Coach D had been leaning toward me with his elbows on his knees. He straightened up, and his barrel chest seemed ready to burst through his shirt. He always kept the top two buttons undone. I couldn't help focusing on the third button, which was straining mightily to hold the garment together. I was afraid it was going to pop off and hit me in the eye.

"I'm not sure…," I stammered. "Maybe I should…." I needed to think. I was stalling.

"Well, let's talk it through." He eased back in his chair. "What are the options?"

"One option is to keep swimming. I think if I do that, I have to give up everything else. It's not worth going after it without total dedication."

"You're probably right about that. That makes it tough." Coach Dewey hadn't been a good enough swimmer to have an Olympic dream.

"There's no guarantee I'll make the Olympic team. My chances of winning a medal are slim, and a gold medal is a long-shot. I could get injured, there could be a boycott, the whole thing could end in…you know, disappointment."

He looked at me like he had already calculated the odds. "You've had disappointments before and handled them well. And you know you do your best when the odds are against you." He wasn't going to pretend that the odds were good.

"The next option, I guess, is med school. I was accepted at Cal and SM and deferred both of them for a year. My dad thinks I should enroll." The word "enroll," in my dad's voice, echoed through the caverns of my brain.

"Great schools," he said. "Good options. You don't sound thrilled about it."

"No, don't get me wrong. I'm thrilled I got into those schools. There's a lot about being a doctor that sounds good to me—helping people, using science in practical ways, being physical and intellectual at the same time." He smiled, and there was a slight chuckle in the smile, as if what I said had confirmed his suspicions. I mirrored his smile, absent the chuckle.

"Then what is it about that option you *don't* like?" This was typical of Coach D. He was an excellent cross examiner. Like a good math professor, he wanted me to consider every angle.

"Nothing. I just…I love swimming."

"Really? What do you love about it—the 5 a.m. workouts? The pain? The boredom? The chlorine?"

"Yeah." We looked at each other like we both knew I was crazy. "And the chance to be great."

In Michigan, we have several kinds of trees that are either pathetic or average-looking for 51 weeks of the year. In early May, very briefly, they erupt in blossoms of pink and red and lavender and white. After a week, the flowers drop off and the trees become ordinary again. The Deweys had a magnificent pink crab tree at its peak, and two dogwoods about to burst. My vision blurred as I gazed into the deep color of the crab tree.

"So," I said, "if you were me, what would you do?"

He looked at me hard, with no trace of a smile. It looked as if I'd asked him a really hard question, the answer to which he knew but didn't like. "I'd take the job."

The steadiness with which he said it surprised me. He was totally serious. It was my turn to say something, but I was a long way from knowing what to say.

"You know," he continued, looking me square in the eyes, "there's not a lot of money in coaching, but there's a lot of satisfaction. You see kids grow into men. I saw that happen to you. If I had it to do over again, I'd do it exactly the same way."

It was convincing. I had no interest in money. Satisfaction was a word that moved me. Whatever I chose to do, in swimming or in life, I wanted to be satisfied in the end. And here was a man who had done it.

By coaching, I could still smell the chlorine. I could stay in Michigan, near home…near Molly. And maybe, just maybe, I could be great.

We both stared westward. The sun was diving toward the horizon. The silence wasn't awkward. I felt a comfort, a peace. It was coming together. "Coach," I said, "I'd be honored to be your assistant."

His face lit up like a scoreboard. "Hey hey! Laura, come out here!" He let out a big Yogi Bear laugh, which made me laugh. "Laura!"

Laura came through the screen door laughing. I'm not sure she even knew what the laughter was about. She was carrying a tray with three plates of cherry pie, one of them à la mode, which had my name written on it. "Michigan cherries," Laura said. Homemade pie, I knew. Coach D gave Laura the news with an enthusiasm that heartened me. We chatted and ate until the sun submerged.

As they walked me through the house and toward the Taurus, I remembered a vision of my swimming past—of Coach Dewey at Three Rivers, sitting on a starting block watching me swim, just the two of us in that dank, decrepit natatorium. The TR pool had gargoyle statues built into the corners, just above water level. The lights lacked candle power, and a third of them were burned out most of the time. It occurred to me for the first time that Coach Dewey enjoyed watching me swim. It also occurred to me that the man had made some big sacrifices for me.

"Coach," I said. "One more thing. I just had a flashback about all those early mornings at the pool when it was just you and me. Me swimming back and forth, you sitting on the starting block watching me. Remember that?"

"I remember it very well."

"You didn't have to do that," I said.

"I know."

"Anyway…" I was trying to think of something eloquent to say. "Thanks."

Another crushing handshake from Coach D, a hug from Laura, and off I walked toward the Taurus. As I was opening the door, something occurred to me.

"Coach," I called out. "I haven't talked to Curtains yet. I'll break the news to him tomorrow morning." He waved to show he understood.

I was back on the road. Same road, different direction.

The thought of Curtains was a reality check. For half an hour, I'd felt like I was on top of a wave—a decision made, a future settled, good times with good people. As I drove, I started to think about one more tough thing I had to do—tell Curtains. He would take it hard.

And it wasn't just the telling that quaked me. There was also the reality of ending my swimming career. The end was getting closer, like the finish wall coming into view on the last lap. The euphoria I felt upon entering the Taurus slowly drained away. By the time I got home, my hands were sore from squeezing the steering wheel, my lip bleeding from being bitten repeatedly.

I tried to watch a movie, but my favorite channel, Classic Movie Central, was playing a 1930s comedy I couldn't get into. I pulled my highlighted paperback *Ulysses* off the shelf, but it required too much thought to get past the first page. My brain was sore.

I turned off the light at 10:00, but despite being dog tired from the Australia trip, I couldn't get to sleep. My mind replayed random scenes from my swimming career. There was the time I forgot to tie my suit before my race when I was 12 years old. As soon as I hit the water I could feel the suit sag down. At the first turn, I figured I'd reach down and pull it up kind of nonchalantly, so nobody'd notice. It wasn't so easy to pull up, and it kept slipping down. I had to repeat it on every turn. I fell further and further behind, but I'd been taught almost from birth that no matter what happens, you finish the race. As I came to the final wall, in last place, I heard a thunderous roar from the crowd. Everyone was on their feet. Girls had come running from out of the locker room to see my bare moon. I didn't know what all the fuss was about. Everyone has one.

I vividly remembered the moment of my shoulder injury. I wasn't doing anything unusual, just pulling with paddles, and I felt a pop. I heard it before I felt it, which is weird because you don't hear so well with water in your ears. I didn't even stop, just kept swimming a few more laps, then got out and put ice on it. The pain kept getting worse and the doctor said he'd seen "dozens of these things in swimmers." I had to go to physical therapy twice a week and stay out of the pool. I did about a million repetitions with stretch cords to rebuild the muscle around the rotator cuff.

A song came into my head and wouldn't leave—the 1980s song *Africa* by Toto. *"I blessed the rains down in Africa…I know that I must do what's right, sure as Kilimanjaro rises like Olympus above the Serengeti."* I got a picture in my mind of Kilimanjaro, which I'd seen close up three years earlier. It was on the way home from an international "B" meet in Casablanca for people who didn't make the Olympics. We spent a few days in Kenya, skulking after animals at Amboselli Park, with Kili looming over the landscape. We climbed Mt. Kenya, the second-tallest mountain in Africa. It was a unique experience, for which I had swimming to thank.

How do thoughts come into your head? Is it just a series of electrochemical reactions, the firing of synapses? Do we have a consciousness that exceeds biology? Is there an entity beyond us, a "God" or something, that is talking to us through our thoughts? I'd been thinking the most random series of things. Was there some message I was supposed to glean? I wasn't getting it if there was.

I visualized walking into Curtains' office. I practiced over and over what I was going to say to him. It never seemed quite right. As the night wore on, I developed a dread of what was coming. It would be the hardest thing I'd ever done.

I may have fallen asleep briefly during the night, but I was wide awake when the sun came up. I dragged myself out of bed, threw on the clothes I'd dumped on the floor, and left for the pool. I needed to talk to Curtains before everyone else showed up for practice.

"Doyle, how are you feeling? You look jet-lagged."

How did Curtains know that without looking at me? I had entered his office through the door directly behind him while he was pecking at his computer. He had his reading glasses on, and his face was about six inches from the screen. He was right about the jet lag, though.

"A little sleepy, I guess."

Curtains has extra-sensory perception. He sees you without looking. He knows what you're thinking. He can tell your future. But he's not like God or anything. He can only do one thing at a time. When he's looking at that computer screen, it's like he's looking through it, into the guts of the machine. He won't let anything distract him. I know from experience that when you come into his office, you wait until he's ready to talk. Then you get his full attention.

I poked around the office. Cluttered would be an understatement. There was no attempt at decorating. He had an assortment of knickknacks, posters, photos and notes stuck all over the place. One photo was of Curtains and the President of the United States, taken at the White House. There was a presidential seal on it, and a handwritten note. Curtains had push-pinned it to a cork bulletin board, no frame, edges curling.

His real name is Aleksandr Kurtenska. He was born in the Soviet Union and moved to Communist Romania as a teenager. Shortly after that, he escaped Romania by swimming across the Danube River at night. His parents didn't make it out. Curtains found his way to the United States and his swimming ability attracted the attention of a few college coaches. Coach Don Jackson allowed him to walk on at Southern Michigan, so he enrolled and joined the team. By his senior year, he was captain of the team and had earned a scholarship. He was an NCAA champion backstroker.

Curtains will talk about his swimming career at SM, but he doesn't like to talk about his life before that. When I learned about his escape from Romania, I was intrigued and asked a lot of questions. He gave a couple one word answers and changed the subject. I've learned from other people that it's not a subject you should bring up. It leaves an aura of mystery about him.

I glanced at Curtains and his face was practically pressed against the computer screen. His fingers were flying. I knew he was working on something important, something inscrutable to the average person. It was going to be a while.

I walked over to a small table and picked up an old copy of *Swimming World* magazine. The SM team was on the cover, the captains holding the NCAA championship trophy, Curtains soaking wet from having been thrown in the pool. It was the last Southern Michigan team to win the NCAAs. I would have been on that team if I'd gone to SM.

I went to high school two miles from the SM campus and met Curtains when I was 14 years old. He came to watch the state high school meet my freshman year, when I set two state records, and for the next three years, he and I both talked as if my going to SM was a "when" instead of an "if." He didn't even technically recruit me; he just assumed I'd be going to SM. After the injury my senior year, he wasn't able to offer me a scholarship. He was apologetic, and I understood. I went off to Three Rivers.

During the summers when school was out, Curtains coached a club team in Huron Springs called Team Jaguar. At the end of my freshman year of college, he invited me to join Team Jaguar, and I trained with Curtains every summer after that. It was pure long course training with the elite swimmers at SM and others who came from all over the country to train with Curtains. Right after I joined Team Jaguar, Archie signed a letter of intent with SM and also joined Team Jaguar. We became teammates the following summer and whaled on each other in practice. We went 1-2 in three events at the summer nationals. That was when I named him "Archie."

I put down the magazine. A machine at the corner of Curtains' desk came to life with lights and sound. Curtains reached over and grabbed some pages off the printer. It was a sign that he was about ready to talk. I wheeled over the only other chair in the office and sat down.

Curtains swiveled his chair, took off his reading glasses, and looked at me. Looked *into* me is more like it. Hard, for several seconds. I had prepared a small speech, but his stare froze me. He spoke first.

"I think you can go 3:36."

Good thing I didn't have coffee in my mouth, or I would have spewed it. It was the last thing I expected him to say. The number he announced sounded absolutely preposterous: three seconds under the world record, six seconds under my personal best.

"*Really?!* What makes you think I can go 3:36?"

He handed me the papers. There were four sheets filled with numbers, equations, and graphs. "I was looking at times from your lactate sets and T-30s. There is a trend I did not plot before. One more year of pure long course training and you will be there."

A lactate set is six all-out swims—100 or 200 meters each—on eight minutes. You kill yourself and take your pulse, which should be above 200. You do that six times. A T-30 is a thirty-minute swim which Curtains uses to determine your anaerobic threshold. He plugs these numbers into macros built into a spreadsheet to predict race times. He has been collecting data and adjusting formulas his entire career.

He hadn't just picked a number to wow me. When he said "I think," it didn't signify a hunch. It was a glimpse. Curtains doesn't predict the future, he calculates it with numbers.

"Suppose I *can* go 3:36. Do you think that answers the question of whether I should go for it?"

Curtains paused for a second like he was choosing his words carefully. "All I am telling you is what you are capable of doing. You should know I think Archie can go 3:36 as well." Curtains has only a slight accent, but you can tell he's foreign because his English is completely devoid of contractions. And he drops some of his articles when he's excited.

"So even if I go 3:36 I might not win?"

"I cannot say who will win. I cannot say what Australians will do. Guy from Brazil may make a big drop. Look, 3:36 is *damn fast*, and you will have to work your butt off to get there." He used his reading glasses to emphasize the point "damn fast," and they came within an inch of my face.

Curtains has written three books on the science of swimming. In one of them, he wrote that "the pinnacle of sport and life is never achieved without sacrificing something important." He believes that life's best rewards, the ones most savored, are the ones that are hard-earned. So I knew exactly what he meant when he said "you will have to work your butt off."

"Tell me a little more about the game plan for 3:36."

"First off, you have to drop the 200 fly."

"Where does that get me? Fly training is good for my strength, which will help my freestyle."

"You will still do plenty of fly in practice, I promise," he said with an evil smile. "To go 3:36 in the 400, you have to be focused on that event, build everything around one goal. At Trials and Olympics, you will not have to swim all those 200 fly races before you swim the 400. It takes something out of you." In international races 200 meters and under, you swim semifinals in addition to prelims and finals.

At one time I was in the top ten nationally in four events and I considered the 200 butterfly to be my best event. It is, in my opinion, the manliest event in swimming. It isn't the longest event and it doesn't require as much versatility as the individual medley—the "IM," in which you have to be good at all four strokes. The 200 fly is a sheer muscle race. Technique and timing are important, but in the last 50, it's all strength. Shoulders, upper back, delts, lats and triceps. Those are my good muscles. The thought of giving up the 200 fly was not something that sounded good to me.

I leaned back, and my rolling chair scooted backwards. I flailed my arms to catch my balance, then I started walking the chair back towards Curtains.

"Okay, what else?"

"I want you and Archie to push each other mercilessly in practice."

I flashed back to Curtains' statement in Brisbane about Archie needing to work harder. It occurred to me that Curtains might be interested primarily in Archie, not me. Maybe he just wanted to use me to get the best out of Archie. Thoughts like that crept into my head every once in a while. The world was Archie-centric, and I understood why people wanted to hitch their wagons to him. Occasionally, I got tired of it.

Curtains stood to gain personally by Archie running the table in Paris. It'd put him at the pinnacle as a coach. But I had a lot of faith in Curtains. He wouldn't use me just to push Archie. Would he?

"Coach, I gotta be honest with you. When I came in here, I was ready to tell you I was quitting. I have good options out there." He knew about the med schools, but not about the Three Rivers job. "You know me pretty well. What should I do?"

"I know you well enough to know that *you* must make this decision. I can tell you my preference, from my perspective."

"Okay, I'll take that."

"I am coach of a team with 24 swimmers. Many of them have a real shot at making the Olympic team. One year from now, I want all my swimmers to achieve maximum potential. I want them to push each other like competitors in practice, but pull for each other as teammates. I need leadership. You can do great things for this team beyond what you do for yourself. And also..." he seemed to be weighing his words "...Archie has a tough road ahead and needs someone to bring out his best. Like four years ago."

Archie had always been good, but he rose to the top the summer he started training with me. I knew that the second time around would be harder for Archie. Everyone would be gunning for him. He was fresh out of college with time on his hands and money in his pockets. There would be more pressure on him, more temptations. It would be good for him to have me by his side.

Some coaches yell at swimmers to motivate them. Some give passionate speeches, and others don't try to do any motivating at all. Curtains fits his motivation technique to each individual swimmer. He gets Archie fired up by making him mad. In my case, knowing I'm a numbers guy, he threw out a number. And he also knew the leadership angle would appeal to me, because it blunted the age factor. I was old for a swimmer, but age is an asset when it comes to leadership. Finally, he knew Archie and I were tight and that I was in the best position to help Archie achieve his lofty goals. That role appealed to me.

I scratched my head. I rubbed my chin. I straightened my glasses. He was looking at me, expecting something, and not words. What was he looking for? Understanding? Recognition? Commitment? He seemed to be examining my skull for steel plates.

I told Curtains I'd take the rest of the day to think about it, and he was fine with that. The Decision was unmade. It now seemed even bigger than I thought it was. Harder. Murkier. I left his office and walked up into the spectator stands overlooking the pool. There wasn't enough light to read the papers he'd handed me, and I didn't need to. I knew how he did things. There were no mistakes.

I sat on a bleacher with my elbows on my knees as I stared down at the empty pool. To a swimmer, an empty pool is the picture of serenity. That's probably because of the contrast from our usual view—underwater, churning, feeling the pain, trying to beat somebody.

A pool is nary more than a box of water. Did you ever wonder about the human affinity for boxes? We live in box houses and sleep in box rooms on box springs. We work and go to school in box buildings. We drive boxes on wheels. We entertain ourselves with idiot boxes. We start life in a box of water, and wail when we're pushed out of it. Even when we die, where do they put us? Open water swimmers say it's unnatural to swim in pools, but I say it's part of the human condition.

The pool was beckoning me. I decided I needed to get my head inside the water. I went into the locker room and changed into my baggy Speedo. It was still half an hour before the start of morning practice, and no one else was around. I dove in and glided underwater until I came to a stop, then floated on the surface for a few more seconds. In water, with air in your lungs, you're virtually weightless. I relished the weightlessness in my body while my mind took all the weight. I took a stroke, then another, then just kept going for two hours. I didn't stop; I didn't look at the clock. When the other swimmers came, they got in other lanes and left me alone. I swam along without counting strokes, or watching my technique, or worrying about pace. My mind was free. And yet shackled.

The number 3:36 drifted through my mind. It was a fascinating number. I divided it in two, in four, in eight, and noticed how easily divisible it was. I visualized it on a scoreboard, next to my name. I could see it on paper, in my handwriting. I could hear people speaking it—Curtains, my dad, me. It was a number that sounded good, a number I could be proud of, a number that signified greatness.

I wanted to get clear of the locker room before the rest of the team came in, so I threw my clothes on helter skelter, gave my hair a five-finger comb job and bounced out the door. I achieved my goal—I saw no one. I walked home and took a nap. I slept a long time, through lunch, well into the afternoon. When I woke up, the digital clock next to my bed said 3:36. I bounced out of bed and looked at the clock in the living room—it also said 3:36. It was a sign.

I called Coach Dewey and begged his forgiveness. He told me he'd have to hire somebody else, and had somebody in mind, somebody I knew. He struggled with it a little. I could hear the disappointment in his voice. He made me run through the factors, and said "uh-huh" when I ticked them off. I was embarrassed to tell him that a number had played an instrumental role. But being a numbers guy himself, I figured he might get it.

"Curtains was looking at the lactate times and T-30s and he came up with a number he thinks I can do in the 400."

"What is it?"

"3:36."

There was a short pause. "Sweet."

"I beg your pardon?" I thought I heard him say "sweet."

"I said 'sweet.' If you go 3:36, that would be sweet."

You just don't expect a 68-year-old gray-haired math professor to use words like "sweet." Of course, hanging out with 18 to 22-year-olds all day long can do that to you.

"Sweet," I echoed. Then I just laughed. He laughed. At me or with me, I don't know.

I took the word "sweet" as another sign. A ratification. I felt relieved, adrenalized. I called home and spoke to my mom. It was a short conversation. "I'm going to keep swimming, Mom." She said that was great, she and my dad had talked about it, they were going to support me either way. I knew that wasn't just mom talk. Now that the decision was made, my parents would be my biggest fans.

I called Molly, but she was at work. I gave her the news real quick-like, knowing she had no time to talk.

I needed some music, so I scrolled through all my playlists looking for "sweet" songs. Nothing suitable popped up. I strutted around my apartment, strumming air guitar and singing from memory, songs by Neil Diamond, Lynyrd Skynyrd, Gwen Stefani, even John Denver. Yeah, I thought. It's going to be so sweet when I swim that 3:36.

CHAPTER 6

Swimming at the top level is like a job. Here's how it dominates a swimmer's life:

Swim practice takes two and a half hours—three and a half if you count getting there and back, showers, getting dressed and undressed. Most days you do that twice, occasionally three times. Then there's weight training. Some people run or bike or do other dryland cross-training. Swimming is six days a week, and some lunatic coaches add a practice on the seventh day. Add it up, and the time commitment is 40-50 hours a week. Maybe 60 for the truly committed.

In most jobs, you get a paid vacation. Swimming is year-round. When the short-course season ends, the long-course season begins. If you're training for the Olympics, there's no chance to take a real vacation. What are you going to do, anyway? You can't do anything dangerous, like snowboarding. I went snowboarding once when I was in high school, just for a day. I only skipped one practice. I didn't think my coach would find out, but he did, and he practically popped an artery.

The amount of heavy partying you can do is limited. There's little time, you're tired, and there's a workout almost every morning. Every workout counts, and if you show up hung over, or start puking in the gutter, everyone knows. For elite swimmers, there are random drug tests which can take place at the pool or even at home. You don't have time to watch much TV or blog and tweet on the internet, so you're "out of it" in social conversations.

You definitely take this job home with you. You take the smell of chlorine everywhere. Your eyes get bloodshot, which makes you look like you've been smoking dope. Chlorine makes your skin itch and burn for hours after you exit the pool. Most swimmers, at one time or another, get a painful ear infection called "Swimmer's Ear." You get water stuck in your ears all the time, and then your hearing ebbs.

Many jobs are sedentary and physically unchallenging. In swimming, at every practice, twice a day, you inflict as much pain on yourself as you can stand. The whole idea is to make it hurt. You elevate your heart rate and blood pressure. You starve yourself of oxygen. You tax every muscle in your body. Every serious swimmer experiences some level of shoulder pain. Breaststrokers get groin injuries from kicking like frogs.

Some jobs are boring and repetitive. Swimming is drudgery. You stare at a black line on the bottom of the pool and count strokes. Thirty-two strokes per 50 meters. Ten thousand strokes a day. Three and a half million strokes a year. Swimming is relentless. It dominates your thought life in and out of the pool. It affects how you eat, sleep and dream.

Swimming is one of the most popular participation sports in America.

A rchie didn't say anything when I showed up in the locker room the morning after making The Decision. He gave me a knowing look and went about his business. Archie knows I have him beat in book smarts, but he thinks he has more street sense than I do. His look said "I was way ahead of you on this one but I'm glad to see you finally saw the light."

There isn't usually a lot of talking at the start of the morning workout. Curtains was down at the shallow end, passing out sheets with the workout sets written on them. He was teasing people about their hair and the holes in their suits. When he saw me he said "good to see you, Doyle." He knew what my presence meant.

I was eager to get in the water. All night and morning, I'd been second guessing myself. I felt anchorless, like driftwood, tossing back and forth from one option to another. Did I make the right decision? Only time would tell.

Of course, the rightness of the decision was somewhat within my power. Having decided to keep swimming, I knew I'd have to train harder than I'd ever trained before. Everyone on the team had the same thing in mind—this is the year; it's now or never. Curtains, I knew, would play his part and write up some insane workouts. I was anxious to get to it.

I joined my usual lane, with the usual guys. I got back in the social flow right away. The main set that first day back was pretty intense—twenty 200s on short rest. "I'll go last," I said. I didn't want to blow out my shoulders after the time off. Archie splashed me and called me a wuss, but he knew it would be crazy for me to jump right back in. He was a couple days ahead of me in getting back into shape.

At Team Jaguar, and at most other teams, there was a rigid caste system in practice, with the castes separated by lane markers. Lane 1 was the "animal lane," populated by the people who did the most yardage every day and attempted the most arduous sets. The people in the animal lane were given the highest respect. You had to earn your way into Lane 1. A new person never started there.

Lane 2 contained the animal lane wannabes. They were the hungriest swimmers in the pool, and they'd mow you down if you had a bad day. The middle lanes were for the stroke specialists, and Lanes 7 and 8 were for the sprinters. It's a general truth, widely known in swimming circles, that sprinters are allergic to hard work.

I became a fixture in the Team Jaguar animal lane about two weeks after joining the team. Archie also moved in quickly after he joined the team the following summer. Other people moved in and out over time, but a third stalwart ultimately emerged—John "Crack" Buchanan. Like the classic D-man that he was, Crack swam at the same pace in the 1500 as he did in the 200, which meant he was only decent at the 200 but awesome at the 1500. He was a grinder. He liked to do long, hard, boring sets and swim hard the whole way.

Crack was the toughest character on the team, and he liked to look that way. He kept his hair clipped at low stubble and a circle of facial hair around his mouth. A barbed-wire tattoo encircled each arm above the bicep. He drove a murdered-out Dodge Charger—no hubcaps or chrome, black-tinted windows, the body spray-painted a dull, flat black color. Like Crack, his murdered-out car had no shine, no reflection, no bling at all.

Crack's nickname referred to the anatomy exposed by his low-riding swimsuit. Half the team could have been named "Crack."

I usually led the animal lane, but Crack was in better shape than I was. I let him take the lead my entire first week back. Every lane has a leader. In practice you swim in circles, which means you take off one at a time, ten or twenty seconds apart, staying on the right-hand side of the lane both down and back. The leader does more than set the pace—he sets the *tone* for the whole lane.

It didn't take long for me to get back into shape, and I took over the lead during the second week. I was exactly where I wanted to be—needed to be— leading the animal lane on the best team in the world.

The third week was exceptionally grueling. On Thursday, we went 10,000 meters in the morning. In the afternoon workout, we finished the sheet, giving us 8,000, and we figured we were done. Curtains had other ideas.

"Boys and girls, I have a special treat for you this afternoon. We have another set. I want Archie to take Lane 1. Doyle, you move over to Lane 2. Crack, Lane 3. Caruso, 4. Moses, 5." Caruso Tucker and Moses Weinberg were longtime Jaguars and SM students. Each had a decent shot at making the Olympic team.

"Brook and Vivian, you got 6 and 7." Brook Larkin and Vivian Li were the two best women on the team. "Anybody want Lane 8?"

"I'll take 8," said Pablo Zumaya, a 200 butterfly specialist.

"Perfect," yelled Curtains. "Everybody else, go home. You are done." Pablo hit his head with his hand like he could'a had a V-8. The sprinters whooped and hollered all the way to the showers. We chosen few went to our lanes.

"Here is the deal," Curtains started. "We are going to do ten times 200 butterfly on 2:45." Groans. "I do not want you to break stroke and you must make the interval. And I want two-hand touches." Louder groans.

Ten 200s butterfly is the nuclear option in swimming—the ultimate punishment, a powerful deterrent. It's about the hardest set imaginable. Butterfly is an incredibly dissipating stroke. Even one 200 is hard, but a set of ten is almost unthinkable.

"One more thing," Curtains yelled. "Guys, whoever wins the most repeats gets to sleep in tomorrow. Viv and Brook, same deal between you two. Figure out your strategies. Take off in two minutes." Curtains then left, as if he wanted to avoid hearing any griping.

"This sucks," snarled Archie as he smacked the water in disgust. He probably thought about leading a revolt—he'd done it before.

Everyone else looked to be deep in thought. I knew Archie had the speed to beat us anytime he put his mind to it, but he could never swim hard on all ten repeats. Crack would go nearly the same speed on every swim. Moses would go for it once or twice. Pablo Zumaya would be tough and hard to see on the other side of the pool.

Curtains re-appeared two seconds before the start of the set and for the next 27 minutes he walked up and down the deck alongside Lane 1.

On the first swim, all of the guys bagged it. Nobody was under 2:30. Archie was almost 2:40. Viv and Brook beat us all. Crack got credit for the win by touching out Pablo.

"Come on, you guys, the *girls* are beating you." Curtains was going to get an earful from Brook at the end of the set. She couldn't stand it when Curtains called the women "girls." But no one was going to waste a single breath talking before the set was over.

On the second swim, all the guys took the first 150 easy, but Pablo and Caruso picked it up on the last 50. Pablo took the win. I was still holding back. Curtains didn't look happy.

I had decided beforehand to try to win the third and fifth repeats, then take stock of how many more I needed to win. Just my luck, on the third one, Archie also decided to get in the game. He was ahead of me at the 150 and we were way ahead of the pack. I could have decided to ease off, bag the last 50 and save up for later, but instead I notched it up a gear. If I was going down, it would be in flames. Archie and I sprinted home, which is almost impossible to do in a 200 fly. I could see Archie tightening up. I touched him out.

"Crap!" Archie yelled. He hadn't even touched the wall yet.

"This is what I am talking about!" yelled Curtains. I wasn't sure whether "this" referred to the fast time, the competitiveness, or the misery we were going through. It could have been all three.

Pablo won the fourth repeat and I won the fifth. Archie was fuming after the fifth swim. He had no wins yet. Pablo and I were in the lead with two each. Archie, however, let his distaste for losing motivate him to a new level. He won the next three repeats. Crack won number nine.

The set was taking its toll. There's no such thing as taking it easy with butterfly. Even on the swims I didn't try to win, the pain grew throughout my arms and shoulders. Everybody was turning red, and I could feel the heat in my face. Every precious second of rest was consumed with gasps for air.

I needed to win number ten, so I pushed off as hard as I could. I shot an underwater glance at Archie just before the breakout, and I could see he wasn't in the race. No surprise there. He was already guaranteed a tie for the most wins. He figured that if there was a tie, Curtains would allow two people to skip the next morning practice. I know how Archie thinks.

It became a battle among Crack, Pablo and me. Whoever won would tie Archie for the most wins. Crack took it out the fastest, but I knew he wouldn't have the speed to bring it home with Pablo or me. I saw both of them on the last turn—we were all even. On the last pushoff, the arch of my right foot cramped up. I can make a cramp go away quickly if I can stop and stretch for a few seconds, but I didn't have that luxury. My foot was useless on the last lap— *both* feet were useless because butterfly requires the feet to work in tandem. All I could do was drag my feet and muscle it home with arms and hips. It was the purest agony I'd ever felt.

I touched at 2:10, but I couldn't tell whether I had beaten Pablo because he was swimming over in Lane 8. I looked at Curtains, who said "you got it, Doyle. Nice swim."

"Yes!" I gasped. I tried to shove my fist in the air, but my arm muscles were so tight the fist only went halfway up, then it splashed down on the water. Archie cruised in about 30 seconds after I finished. I floated on my back for a couple seconds.

Curtains then made an announcement. "Vivian, nice set. I will see you tomorrow afternoon. Archie and Doyle, you will have to do a swim-off. One 200 fly for all the marbles. Leave on next top." We had 50 seconds. I went to work massaging my foot and stretching out the cramp.

Archie was indignant that he and I had to swim another 200 fly. He had enough outrage for both of us, so I let him do the arguing.

"Coach," said Archie, "we both won. It's totally bogus to make us do another one."

"You do not have to do another one," answered Curtains. "Think of it as an opportunity. If you choose not to swim, you lose. I said only one guy would get out of tomorrow's practice."

"You said 'whoever'...." Archie was exasperated. It was an ambiguous word.

"Fifteen seconds," yelled Curtains. He wasn't going to change his mind.

Curtains was stoking Archie's fire. Anger was a motivator for Archie, and outrage was even better. He had juice in his veins.

We set our goggles and pushed off. Archie shot ahead immediately. He dolphined longer than I did on the first two pushoffs, and was a full body length ahead at the 100. Archie kept his stroke through the third 50, but when he pushed off the wall on the last turn, there were no dolphins in Lane 1. He was still almost a body length ahead, but I knew he was dog tired and I could make up some ground. I pulled even and then I, too, felt like there was a piano on my back. Elton John was jumping up and down, pounding on the keys, playing *Funeral for a Friend*. In the last 10 yards, my arms were barely making it out of the water. Archie died worse than I did, though, and I touched first.

"Better luck next time, Archie," Curtains hollered. He was beaming. "Great swims, both you guys. Two-hundred cool down and get out of here. Doyle, you get to sleep in. Enjoy it." With that, Curtains disappeared into his office.

After Curtains left, Archie let loose a torrent of curses that would've made me blush if I hadn't already been red from oxygen debt. I knew better than to talk to him at a time like that. I pushed off and swam an easy 400, mostly backstroke so I could breathe at will. Then I headed for the showers. I walked slowly down the pool deck, shuffling a little because my foot still hurt, rubbing my sore neck, shrugging my shoulders to release the lingering lactic acid. On my way past the women's locker room, I paused at the doorway and shouted in.

"Viv!" I waited a few seconds but there was no answer, so I shouted louder. "YO, VIV-EE-AN!" I heard a little scream and a couple of giggles inside the women's shower room. Vivian came to the doorway a few seconds later. She still had her suit on.

"Yeah, Doyle," she said. "What's up?"

"Well, we both get to sleep in."

"I don't think Curtains wants us to do it together," she deadpanned.

"True. Want to come over tonight and watch *Philadelphia Story*? You bring Sam, I'll get Molly. I've got frozen pizzas."

"*Philadelphia Story*, who's in that?" Clearly, she hadn't seen the movie yet, so this was going to be great.

"Cary Grant, Jimmy Stewart, Katharine Hepburn."

"Ooh," she said. "It's a deal. Eight o'clock okay?" The movies start at 9:00.

"Eight sharp. See you then."

I continued on to the men's showers. Even before I got there, I could hear the golden voice of Caruso singing the "toast" aria from *Carmen*. "*L'Amour! L'Amour! Toreador, Toreador, l'amour attend!*" He turned off his shower and when he saw me, he said "great set, man." Caruso was my next best pal on the team, after Archie.

"Thanks. Not so bad yourself. Sorry you won't get to sleep in."

"Not much chance of that," he said.

As I got under the hot water, I thought about what Caruso had just said. It dawned on me that he had swum that whole set without *any* hope of winning. Here I was swimming in Archie's shadow, and Caruso, an excellent swimmer, was nowhere near the shadow. He was in *my* shadow; to him *I* was great. The chance to beat Archie, to win the set, to obtain the reward—those things had given me the motivation to get through the set. I admired Caruso for gutting it out without that motivation. I started to wonder, what *does* motivate a guy like Caruso?

Caruso's father was a prominent neurosurgeon and expected Caruso to follow in his footsteps. Caruso could have taken that path. He was a straight-A student. He wanted to make his own path, however, and chose literature and music as his dual undergrad majors. He was planning to apply to Harvard, Yale and Stanford law schools, and he would probably be accepted by all of them. If I had to guess his future, I'd have said Supreme Court Justice, or maybe Senator. He was smart and talented and didn't need swimming medals to build his self-esteem. Swimming wasn't even his greatest talent, as his singing proved.

I turned off my shower just a few moments after getting in it, which was uncharacteristic of me. I walked over to the lockers, where Caruso was putting on his underwear.

"Hey, Caruso, can I ask you something? How did you get started in swimming?" He looked at me like I had asked him a highly fascinating question.

"Man, that was a long time ago. I was eight years old. My sister was 11. We used to go out to our country club and play pool games all day long. Marco Polo, Pom-Pom, Sharks & Minnows, that kind of stuff. We were both on the country club swim team, but when the summer ended, that was it for me. She joined the USS team that fall and started swimming year-round. She was getting faster and was really excited about it. She had this tight group of swimming friends, all with the green hair. Those older girls looked so cool to me, even though I wasn't interested in girls at the time."

Swimmer hair is easily recognizable. In addition to chlorine, which removes color from the hair, pool water contains just enough copper to provide a faint green tint.

Caruso continued. "So I asked my mom and dad if I could join the USS club the next year. My dad gave me this long talk about commitment and hard work and time management, but I didn't listen to any of it. I just wanted the green hair. Anyway, they let me, and the rest is history, I guess."

Green hair envy. Not exactly what you'd expect from a future Supreme Court Justice.

"Any chance you'll keep swimming after the Olympics?" I threw in the assumption that he'd make it, hoping it would encourage him.

"Nope. I'll swim my last race either at the Trials or in Paris. I'm actually kind of anxious to start the next part of my life, you know? This has been a great ride, and the coming year is going to be fantastic, but…." He kind of trailed off there.

"So what is it that's kept you going in the sport?"

"I love this sport to death," Caruso said. "I love my teammates. There's no feeling in the world like being on the starting blocks in a relay in the NCAA finals. Every member of every team is cheering for you or against you. Your teammates are depending on you. If you win, you're a hero. If you lose, you're a goat. Where else you gonna get that?"

Caruso uses words like "gonna" and "nope" like a regular guy. I bet he does that on purpose to relate better with slugs like me. I'll read some of his Supreme Court opinions in a few decades and see if he's dropped that practice.

"Cool," I said, ever the erudite linguist. "You and I are going to Paris together. I want to be there when the French hear you sing opera in their language." I made a mental note to ask Caruso to explain *Ulysses* to me.

I went back to the showers. Archie was in there. He had swum a lot more than 200 to cool down, and I think it had calmed him as well.

"Dude," he said, "great swimming out there." He was yelling it, because his head was in the water flow, and it's like wearing headphones. You don't know how loud you're talking.

"Thanks, man. You too."

"It feels good to be done with it," he yelled. "But I'm gonna kill that little Russian bastard."

Archie was 6-5 and at the peak of his mojo. Curtains was 5-9 and old. I'd have put my money on Curtains in an ultimate fight, though, because of his caginess.

CHAPTER 7

Swimming is a team sport to a greater extent than most people realize. The public's view of swimming is overly influenced by what happens at the Olympics every four years. There are no team scores at the Olympics. There is no team winner. The swimmers who get idolized are the individuals who win the most gold medals.

The image of the stoic swimmer, facing a black line on the bottom of the pool day after day, also contributes to the perception of swimming as an individual sport. Swimmers themselves sometimes feed this image. "It's just me against the clock." To a large extent it's true that swimming is an individual sport.

There are, however, important team aspects of swimming that are below the public's radar.

The primary team aspect of swimming is social. Swimmers spend more time with their teammates than with their families. Teammates become a second family. Because swimming leaves no time for a normal social life, your fellow swimmers are your social life. Swimmers are bonded by mutual suffering. And while most of the time in practice you have your face in the water, there's time to talk between sets and after practice. My sister joined the swim team for social reasons. Caruso got into it to join the Fellowship of the Green Hair.

Pushing and encouraging your teammates in practice is a big part of swimming. Those mornings I spent alone swimming at Three Rivers were hard, and although I got the work in, the quality was only so-so. You race your teammates in practice. Sometimes you keep going because you don't want other people to see you flake out. Because the sport is so mental, you have to tell yourself constantly that you're on the right track. It helps to see your teammates doing well with the same training you're doing. At my high school, the team had won several state championships and produced numerous All-Americans before I arrived. I knew those swimmers had been on the same path I was on. I knew where that path led.

Relays are the ultimate team experience. In a relay, there are four swimmers who rise and fall together. When I entered high school as a freshman, I was already a pretty good swimmer. In my freshman class there was a kid named Barry East who had never been to a swim practice or a meet. He barely knew how to swim, and came out for swimming just because there were no roster cuts. He stuck with it and worked really hard. He became known as "Beast," partly because of his approach to the sport, and partly because that's the way his name appeared on the roster—first initial, last name. By the time he was a senior, Beast was good enough to be on our relay at the state meet. We won the state championship, and our relay earned an All-American honor. Beast has that for the rest of his life. He has become part of the lore of my high school team—the guy who came in as a non-swimmer and left as an All-American.

There's a reason why most swim meets begin and end with relays. Relays count for more points than individual events, and often determine the outcome of the meet. Many a swim meet has come down to the last relay with everything on the line. I have swum a few of those and the adrenaline runs through your veins like a roller coaster car. When you win one, your teammates are insanely happy, your parents are hoarse, and your coach gets thrown in the pool.

Winning a team championship at the highest level is the greatest thrill in swimming. The atmosphere at the NCAA finals is electric, especially when the team race is close. I have had friends who won Olympic gold medals and who also won NCAA team titles. They uniformly swear that while the former got them more publicity, the latter brought them more satisfaction.

Three knockout women appeared at my door at 8:05 p.m. "May I help you?" I asked.

"Get out of our way, Doyle, we can smell the food." It was Vivian. She pushed past me as I leaned on the door looking nonchalant. Sam tried to tickle my ribs as she entered, but I'm impervious to that sort of tomfoolery. Molly came in last, and she stood on her tiptoes to hug me.

I closed the door and thought about having three young women alone in my apartment. That would be a dream come true for Archie, like a Great White cruising through a seal rookery. Of course, these women wouldn't go near Archie's pad. They come to mine because I watch old movies. I'm harmless. Sometimes I rue it, but at least I get to enjoy their company.

Beauty comes in all shapes and sizes. It was a warm evening and all three women wore t-shirts and jeans. Molly was wearing the Jackie Robinson Dodgers shirt I'd gotten her, the one that took me forever to find due to her unusual size: child's large. Vivian was wearing a plain shirt with sleeves so short they showcased her exquisite arm muscles. She had her hair down and brushed, which we didn't often see at the pool. Her hair was long, luxurious, and jet-black. She protected it meticulously with swim caps and never allowed it to touch chlorinated pool water.

"Sam"—Samanda Moore, Viv's roommate—was an SM student and avid non-swimmer. Sam was a head taller than the other two—almost as tall as me. Her skin had the color and shine of the lines on the bottom of the pool. She looked like a woman I'd seen in Kenya, only Sam wore jeans exclusively, and the woman I saw at the market in Nairobi was wearing a black-and-gold kanga. I did a double-take on the Nairobi woman. What caught my eye was her bearing. She comported herself like a queen—back straight, chin up, slow fluid movements. Sam had that same royal bearing, even in jeans.

I had a pair of pizzas in the oven and had just started tossing a salad when the women arrived. It was near the max for me as a cook. I shooed the women out of my kitchen and started hustling to get everything together.

They took a look around, as they always do. It makes them feel like decent housekeepers to see my place. My apartment was decorated in "swimming chic." Wet towels and swimming gear hung on hooks. The walls and shelves contained doo-dads, posters and photos from my swimming travels.

I overheard Molly and Sam talking about my photo of Mt. Kenya. It really is a cool photo, taken at sunrise, which required a lot of effort and planning. Mt. Kenya has two peaks. You climb one and photograph the other.

"It's Mt. Kenya," Molly told Sam, within my hearing. "He went there on the way back from a swim meet."

"It's so beautiful. Don't you wish you could go there?"

My head swelled. I savored their jealousy of my travels.

The focal point of my apartment, on the wall behind the TV, was a large poster of Archie wearing a Speedo and his four medals from the last Olympics. It was the standard pose popularized by Don Schollander in 1964; Mark Spitz sold a few just like it in 1972 with his seven golds. Most of the male swimmers, if they had any posters at all, had the Camille Cognac limited edition. My poster served a different purpose. It wasn't a decoration.

The women did most of the talking during dinner. I was really packing in the food, and that takes a lot of concentration. I wanted to make sure the TV was on before 9:00. I didn't want to miss John Castle, the host, whose job was to introduce the show and give historical tidbits about the actors and the movie. At 8:58, I moved to my reclining chair, grabbed the remote and bunkered in. Vivian came out to get her favorite spot on the couch, while Sam and Molly started cleaning up. Hey, I was going to do that. At precisely 9:00, I yelled out toward the kitchen, "Leave it! John Castle's coming on." Molly and Sam ran in.

I'm an evangelist for old movies. I had seen *The Philadelphia Story* three times already, including twice with Molly. I was most interested in how my protégées, Viv and Sam, would like it.

Vivian's name had given me the hook to introduce her to old movies. I told her she reminded me of her namesake, Vivien Leigh, the star of *Gone*

With the Wind. She thought I was making fun—Vivian Li is 100% Korean. "Your eyebrows are identical," I said, and they were—dark, full, and capable of expressing any emotion by themselves. I didn't tell her what it really was. Vivian's personality matched Scarlett O'Hara's to a T. She had to see that for herself. I lured her in with a special showing of *GWTW* from my DVD collection.

Vivian was born in Korea and grew up in a mansion on Lakeshore Drive in Grosse Pointe. Her parents pushed her hard at a young age, both in swimming and at school. When she was 14, she announced she was going to quit swimming, which came as a shock to her parents because she was so good. She was sick of it.

After her parents got over the shock, they negotiated a treaty whereby Vivian agreed to keep swimming and her parents agreed to back off and become mere spectators. She had to get herself up in the morning and arrange rides to practice. Swimming became "hers" and not "theirs." It was a breakthrough. It taught her to be dependent on her teammates and grateful for their help. During her last two years of high school, Viv was the one giving rides, to and from practice, to the younger swimmers. She developed a new love for the sport.

Swimming toughened her and broadened her. "I don't want to be some princess who has everything handed to her," she once told me. She earned the reputation of being intense, sometimes even fierce. Curtains, who knows the entire history of swimming from ancient times, told her about how few Korean swimmers had won Olympic medals. He told her how she could honor her homeland with her swimming. It put fire in her guts. Sometimes the fire leaks out.

Viv loved the part of *Philadelphia Story* where Hepburn's character, Tracy Lord, realizes she's been too much of a "goddess" and vows to change. Viv lived that transformation herself. She's no longer a goddess. Goddesses don't visit the pain threshold every day.

Samanda enjoyed the parts of the movie where the bluebloods get their comeuppances. She grew up in the housing projects in inner city Detroit.

Watching the movie, she didn't seem to have contempt for the socialites in tuxedos and ball gowns. Instead, she seemed amused by them, as if watching a different species of animal. Sam and Vivian are about as different as people can be, and yet they became friends. They met in a philosophy class at Southern Michigan and clicked right away. Sam and Molly went to the same church.

We watched the movie quietly until the scene where Hepburn dives off a diving board and swims a few strokes across a pool. That produced some scathing banter. Viv shouted "get your elbows up," and I said "get some shoulder roll."

"Wrist flopper!"

"Backhanded giddywopper!"

Sam, who'd been sitting on the floor, stood up in front of the TV. "Uh-uh," she scolded, wagging her finger. "No you ain't! Keep your swimming obsession to yourselves."

She was right. Swimming owned us. We apologized.

I already knew Molly's favorite part of the movie. Grant's character Dexter Haven gives Tracy Lord a wedding present: a model boat patterned after the "True Love," a ketch the two of them had sailed together. Tracy looks at the model boat and says "My, she was yar." Then she explains what "yar" is: "Easy to handle, quick to the helm. Fast, bright, everything a boat should be." Later in the movie, Tracy promises to be more "yar" herself. Molly and I have worked "yar" into our inside vocabulary.

When that part of the movie came, Molly turned and smiled at me. I smiled back and we both laughed. Sam said "pipe down up there" and hurled a pillow in Molly's direction. Molly blocked it to the side like a hockey goalie and it landed in Vivian's lap, sending a bowl of popcorn flying. Molly and Viv erupted in laughter.

I don't know what came over me, but I leaned over from the recliner to the couch and put my hand on Molly's. She looked down at my hand. After about five seconds she put her other hand on top, making a hand sandwich. We both resumed watching, and she seemed content and comfortable. But the stretch and lean hurt my shoulder, so I had to withdraw.

The four of us clowned around for half an hour after the movie ended, and then it was time to walk the women home. Huron Springs is a pretty safe place, as college towns go, but it was after 11:30 and pitch dark. We walked together to Molly's place first and dropped her off. It was a beautiful night and lots of people were strolling the sidewalks. As we walked on, Vivian put me in the hot seat. "So Doyle, how come you and Molly aren't a couple?"

Before I could answer, Sam jumped in. "Yeah, Doyle. Molly's shy, but she really opens up around you."

"Yeah, Doyle." It was Viv again. "We like to see her laugh, okay?"

Sheesh. I was surprised by this onslaught, because I thought everyone knew—I had decided to keep swimming, which meant I couldn't get serious with Molly. Wasn't that obvious?

"I don't know if I'm good enough for her," I blurted. Whoa, where did that come from? Actually, I knew. Archie thought it was the other way around. Molly wasn't good enough for me; I could do better. That's bull. Whatever Archie says about women and me, I'm bound to believe the opposite.

Vivian, who was walking in front of me, stopped and wheeled around. Her long black hair almost whacked me as she turned.

"*You* are a *complete* nerd!" she shouted, practically shrieking the word "complete." She said it with such finality, I couldn't argue. Only I wasn't sure if she was agreeing or disagreeing with me about being good enough for Molly. "You know what you are?" she said. "You're a tiger in the pool and a pussycat on dry land."

That phrase plunged through my skin and into my heart. I guarantee you this: no guy in the world wants to be described with that word or any part of it. I felt my face flush. I started to sweat.

"Yeah, Doyle," Sam piled on. "You need to go see Molly's father."

We were right in front of their apartment building, under a street light. It was embarrassing being scolded in full view of their neighbors and other passersby. I scrambled to save some face.

"Look," I pleaded. "Molly told me I was obsessed with swimming. Sam, you used the exact same word. I admit it, okay? Maybe it makes me a complete nerd. Maybe it blurs my vision. I just don't think it would be a good idea to get serious about anything other than swimming right now. Right or wrong."

I could read Samanda's face. It was saying "wrong." But Viv seemed to get it. She backed off. Thank goodness, because it was starting to become a tiresome ritual for women to block my path.

They let me go. We said some awkward good-nights and I turned for home.

I got back to my apartment thinking I'd be exhausted after a tough day of swimming. The discussion on the street, however, had gotten my propeller turning. The words echoed like sonar pinging in my ears. Yeah, Doyle—exactly what is the matter with you?

Here are the reasons I am a nerd: 1. I wear glasses. 2. I'm not a serious party animal like the other swimmers. 3. I'm not good with women. 4. I briefly owned a pocket protector in college. Several of my fellow math students had them.

Here is the reason I'm not a nerd: 1. I'm a major jock.

I strongly disagree with Vivian's characterization of me as a *complete* nerd. I'm only a partial nerd. I'm a jock-nerd.

Then again, maybe Viv didn't mean it in the classic sense. Maybe she just meant that I'm an idiot for thinking I'm not good enough, or for being a coward, for making up some lame excuse to avoid going to see Molly's father.

Hamlet's curse was the inability to make a decision. Mine is the inability to cut through ambiguity. Or to figure out women, I'm not sure which.

To top it off, I got a text from Molly well after midnight, wanting to know if I could meet her at Brewhaha the next morning. We set it up for right after morning practice. I wasn't planning to swim, but I was scheduling based on habit. The late-night text from Molly puzzled me. Usually I'm the one who initiates. What did she have in mind?

I slept in fits and starts. In the morning, I went to swim practice at the usual time. So did Vivian. Archie was passing out fake workout sheets that said:

1. Swim until you are dead.

2. 200 cool down.

Archie had even imitated Curtains' unique European cursive. Curtains laughed at the fake sheets, but he sure wasn't happy to see Viv and me. "Get out of here, you two. I told you to sleep in. I want everyone to think you got rewarded for winning the fly set last night. I want them to be jealous of you."

Viv and I protested that we were already awake anyway, but Curtains insisted, so we left the pool. We went upstairs to the weight room and did weights for a while, spotting for each other. Viv attacked the weights like she attacked everything: furiously. She was wearing shorts and no top over her Speedo. She pumped and grunted and sweated while I just did a few light reps. I felt distracted. There were windows in the weight room that allowed me to look down at the pool. I spent a lot of time at the windows, watching my mates go through the sets. I wanted to be down there with my head in liquid.

Why did Molly want to meet me? Maybe Sam had called her after the walk home. I replayed the street light scene in my mind. What did I say? Why did Sam look so disgusted with me? Thinking back, I realized that Molly and I hadn't really discussed what my decision to keep swimming meant to "us." Between her schedule and mine, there hadn't been a good time. There was nothing unclear about it to me, but maybe it needed to be tidied up with Molly.

I stopped by to see Curtains on deck after I got dressed. The swim workout was still going. I told him I thought the 200 fly set—which Archie had dubbed "the fly set from hell"—was good for us, but that Archie was going to be mad at him for a while. I told him about Archie's vow to "kill that Russian bastard." It made Curtains grin.

"Good," he laughed. "Tell him to bring it on. I am ready." Then he quieted down. "I am not here to make friends, you know. There is more talent in this pool than any other pool in the world. All these swimmers and their families have put their trust in me. The country has put its trust in me. If I think it would be best for this team to swim butterfly all day long, that is what we will do and I will handle the grumbling." He smiled at me. "Actually, I like the grumbling," he concluded, as if he had just discovered something interesting about himself.

"Any other surprises coming up?" I asked.

"Next Friday," Curtains said. "Full technique analysis with video through the underwater window."

The real work in swimming is performed below the surface. To fully analyze a person's stroke, to catch flaws, to see what makes him tick, you have to watch from underneath.

"Is this for everybody?" I asked.

"No. Just a few of you."

"Do I have time to groove a new stroke between now and then?"

"No, but see if you can get Archie a new attitude."

After leaving the pool, I headed for Brewhaha. When I arrived, Molly was sitting at a table, thumbing her phone. She'd gotten there ahead of me, for once.

"What up, Moll?" She looked up, then stood up, smiling, and we hugged.

We got some coffee and crumpets, and returned to the table. Molly's hair looked different, yet again—no flip this time. It was pulled into a knot in the back. She was wearing earrings and a necklace with her gray skirt and black blouse. It was a smart, professional look. No smock, no band-aids in sight.

"So," I said, "you interviewing or something?" She sure wasn't going to class looking like that.

"Nope." She took a sip of cappuccino, and it looked like she wasn't going to fill me in. Maybe it wasn't anything. Maybe it was another attempt to find a style.

"Well, you sure look nice." Pause. "Ma'am."

It made her smile, but it was an uneasy smile.

"How's the swimming going?" she said.

"I crushed Archie in a fly set yesterday. That's kinda why we had the movie night—to celebrate." I'd assumed that Viv and Sam had filled her in—evidently not.

"Feeling good about your decision?"

"Oh yeah." I didn't tell her that I was still unsure it was the right one. I kept thinking about what I was giving up. I had written letters to both med schools, asking for another deferral, and I hadn't heard back yet. I was still giving myself pep talks—trying to stay determined not to look back, not to waver—at least outwardly.

"Good."

The conversation was bloody awkward. I wasn't telling Molly everything, and she sure wasn't being open with me, either. I couldn't stand it. We were both pretending. It was time to address the issue head on.

"Moll, I'm sorry about how the decision came down. I should've talked it through with you more. I thought…."

"It's okay," she said, with a look that said it was not okay. "We're not attached, right?" The word had significance. In swimming parlance, a swimmer who has no team is listed in the heat sheet as "unattached." An unattached swimmer is pitied.

"I'd say we're…." What exactly were we? She was like a pal, a good friend, but more than that—like a teammate. Yeah, that's the ticket. "…we're teammates."

Her wry smile returned, but her brow was furrowed.

"*Teammates*, Doyle? Is that what we are? What kind of team are we on?"

"I don't know…the winning team?"

She stiffened in her chair. "You're not the only one who has to make decisions, you know." Her voice was suddenly stern. "Let me come right out with it: what do you expect me to do here—wait for you? Because I've been waiting. I don't even know what I'm waiting for, and I don't see an end to it."

"It's only another year. Through the Olympics."

"Oh, is that all it is? And then what, med school? Are you going to be less committed to that than to swimming?"

I took off my glasses. I wasn't seeing clearly. There was a spot on one of the lenses—a *damn* spot. I wiped and wiped at it with a napkin and it wouldn't disappear. Molly was being tough with me and she seemed like a different person.

"I have to swim my guts out, Mb. We can be friends, hang out, maybe more, but serious dating? I don't think I can do it. It wouldn't be fair to you."

"What do you mean, 'maybe more'?"

"I don't know—like what everyone else does." There was a whole spectrum out there. Casual dating, friends with benefits, that sort of thing.

She was instantly in full sob. I didn't have time to get the napkins to her. She put her hands on the table, stood up, and walked briskly toward the door. I was stunned. I got up and ran after her. I caught up to her on the sidewalk. I got in front of her and she stopped. I said "I'm sorry," and reached to hug her, but she stiff-armed me. She was making no attempt to stop the tears from falling onto her blouse.

"How could you think that, Doyle?"

"I didn't think it, I just said it. I'm an idiot."

She pushed past me and started walking again. I was flooded with guilt. I'd insulted her. Because of where she'd been, Molly couldn't afford to mess around. She could never be like everyone else, even if she wanted to be.

I caught up with her again. Now she looked irritated. She was still crying.

"You're not an idiot, Doyle. That's the problem. You know things. What hurts the most is, I thought you knew *me*. I thought we were on the same page."

Those words cut the deepest. I knew the importance of being known. I remembered the futility I'd felt in the Detroit Diner in Brisbane, trying to explain to my parents why I was driven to swim. They didn't get it—they didn't get *me*—and it hurt. I was on the other side of it now, but I knew exactly how it felt.

In the 1948 movie *Letter From An Unknown Woman*, Joan Fontaine loves a concert pianist who lives in her building. Over the years she learns everything there is to know about him, and is willing to give up everything to be with him. But he's not interested in knowing her, he's only interested in seduction. When she realizes it, she sinks into despair and loneliness.

Molly and I had watched that movie together and she blubbered like a baby. There is a wrinkle in the cosmos when you know somebody who doesn't know you back. One of man's deepest desires is to know and be known, to seek and be sought, to understand and be understood. It's written in human DNA. It is, perhaps, the image of God.

And the thing is, I *did* know the page Molly was on. The morals, the principles, they were fine with me. They fit her. They even fit me. That part was okay. But I wasn't ready to jump to the end of the spectrum with her. Not yet. It was too far, too much work, too much commitment. That's what my gut was telling me.

While I was thinking those thoughts, the clock was ticking. Molly had been looking at me, waiting for me to say something, but I felt powerless. I'd been stricken dumb. My tongue was twisted and useless.

She walked away. It was clear she didn't want me to follow her this time.

I've learned the hard way that there's a five-second rule with women—like when food falls on the ground or you drop your underwear on the wet locker room floor. You have a chance to recover from your errors, but you have to act immediately. This time, my failure to do anything—to say anything—turned my dropped food into poison.

Was it, indeed, my gut that kept my mouth shut? Or was it the void where my spine should be? Vivian would know, and she'd be happy to tell me, but I was afraid to ask her. Actually, I knew what she'd say. She'd already said it. The phrase she had stabbed into my heart took another twist.

I walked back inside the coffee shop to pick up the remnants. Every single person stared at me. It was obvious what side they were on. I was on that side too. I hated myself. I swept everything into the trash.

It started to rain during my walk home. Rather than run, or dash inside somewhere, I slowed down, thinking it'd be a kind of punishment. I thought about Molly, how I'd hurt her. She'd probably gotten caught in the downpour herself, and with her nice clothes, too. It would have added injury to the insult I'd inflicted. I repeatedly visualized her face as I'd last seen it—puffy and wet, angry and sad. I thought about her father, how embarrassed I'd be if he found out what I'd said. I wanted to text her, to tell her over and over again how sorry I was, but I'd probably just mess that up too.

I decided to give it time. Time is supposed to heal all wounds. In this case, it ate away at my stomach lining.

CHAPTER 8

Man was made to swim. Swimming is a natural sport, performed in harmony with nature.

There are those who say that if man was meant to swim, he would have been given great big flippers like dolphins, or gills like fish. There's no question about it: man is not the best swimmer on earth. I've been swimming with all kinds of fish, sharks, seals and dolphins. It's a humbling experience. With just the flick of a fin, they can leave you eating bubbles.

I almost drowned once. I was body-surfing in California, trying to catch the biggest wave I could. My favorite part of body-surfing is right when the wave curls and I'm at the top. At that moment, I'm on the edge of being thrown downward and thrashed by the wave, or riding just ahead of it at twice the speed of regular swimming. I've had plenty of both experiences. One time the wave sent me downward and crashed over me. Amidst all the turbulence, I couldn't tell which way was up. I struggled in three different directions before I finally saw some sunlight through the water. I came up gasping, relieved, utterly in awe of the power of the wave. Then another one came and crashed on top of me.

The humbling, to me, is part of the harmony with nature. Man isn't meant to be arrogant. Everyone has moments of arrogance, some more than others, and we don't enjoy being humbled. But it's part of the ride. The moments of triumph in life are best viewed in contrast to the humblings. Every swimmer who thinks he's something special needs to swim with dolphins or ride the waves at Malibu.

There is another sense in which swimming and nature are in tune with each other. Swimming has symmetry, like nature. The arm and leg movements are balanced about the body's centerline, the same amount of roll to each side. Swimming has a relentless rhythm, like the ocean waves, like the beating heart. One stroke after another after another, day after day. Swimming has a beauty, an artistry. I have heard it compared to ballet and poetry. It has rhyme and meter.

Swimming, like nature, also has a built-in decay mechanism. Things get old, slow down and die. Swimmers intentionally use every ounce of energy in a race and sputter in on fumes. That's how the best swims are made. Oxygen debt produces lactic acid in the muscles, which degrades the ability to do more work. It can't go on forever. In swimmer parlance, someone who is overcome with pain, slowing down and losing ground, is "dying."

In swimming, as in nature, there is a great deal of order. The planets orbit the sun, the moon orbits the earth, and radishes grow from radish seeds. It's predictable, measurable, quantifiable. Almost everything in swimming is mathematical, from times to distances to heart rates to stroke technique.

And yet, there is a little bit of chaos among all the order. Nature has its hurricanes, its mutations, its freaks. Swimming has turbulence, drag, missed turns, and fatigue. No one has the perfect stroke. No one has ever swum the perfect race.

The chaos keeps us wondering, searching. It keeps us on our toes.

I continued punishing myself for a week after my Brewhaha waterloo. The most readily available form of punishment was swim practice. It always hurts, but I wanted more than the regular pain. I wanted excruciation.

Swimming is performed in color. Curtains developed a system, which is now used in some form by almost every club, of color-coding the sets. The spectrum goes from white to purple. White sets are "aerobic" and purple sets are "anaerobic." Red is in the middle of the spectrum and is the dividing line between aerobic and anaerobic—the "anaerobic threshold." Aerobic sets build cardiovascular and circulatory capacity. Anaerobic sets build muscle. You need both. We cover all the colors every week. Occasionally we'll do a "rainbow set" where you start white and end purple. Like water coming to a boil, a rainbow set starts slowly and ends in chaotic intensity.

During my penance week, if Curtains asked for white I gave him pink. If he asked for blue I gave him purple. I went the extra mile. Curtains could see it in my face—the determination, I'm sure, but mostly the color, which can't be hidden. He asked me what was going on and I shrugged it off. I don't think he minded.

It took forever for technique analysis day to arrive. I was anxious to find out where I stood. I needed some good news. Swimming was, by my choice or ineptitude, all I had left.

"Here is the game plan," Curtains announced. "Go in any order you want, one at a time. Swim 40 lengths, flip your turns, do not stop until the end. If you swim a stroke other than freestyle, do that for 10 lengths and freestyle for the rest. Archie, do some backstroke. Doyle, all freestyle. When you are done, join the main workout."

Curtains then left to go to the underwater window. The window was cut into the side wall of the animal lane, about 3/4 of the way down the pool. You had to open a door and descend some stairs to get down there. While we waited for him to get set up, the rest of us turned to Kelton Murray. Kelton was the king of the sprinters at Team Jaguar, the only African-American on the elite squad. He was one of the summer-only swimmers who went away to school—in his case, Harvard.

The idea of Kelton swimming 40 lengths straight was fairly humorous. "I'll go first," he said, as if there was any doubt. "I'll show you how it's done."

Kelton dove in and sprinted four lengths. He really tore it up. His amazing six-beat kick created a foamy roostertail that followed him as his arms churned. It didn't look pretty, but it looked fast. When Kelton finished his four lengths, he hopped out of the pool and headed for the showers.

"So long, suckers," Kelton called out with a wave of his hand as he disappeared into the shower room.

Archie went next. I have watched Archie swim *ad nauseum*, but this time I focused on specific aspects of his technique. He has a long, powerful arm stroke in freestyle. His hands catch water early in the underwater stroke, with his elbow higher than most people's. If there is such a thing as beauty in a swimming stroke, this is it. It looks effortless. It reminds me of film clips of famous baseball players. Willie Mays makes this incredible catch, running full speed, arms flailing, legs pumping, cap flying off. In the clip of Joe DiMaggio, he just appears out of nowhere, taps his glove and makes the catch. Archie is the DiMaggio of swimmers. Kelton is Willie Mays.

I watched Vivian, Brook and Crack take their turns, then I got in. For some reason, I was nervous.

The first few times I passed the underwater window, I could see a shadow of Curtains in the window next to a video camera on a tripod. He had seen so many people swim over the years. Curtains told me one time that swimmers' stroke techniques are like snowflakes. No two are exactly the same, but at the elite level, they're very similar. I wondered what Curtains would see in my stroke. What was unique about me? What baseball player would I be compared to?

I finished my 40 lengths and joined the workout. I let Crack lead the rest of the day. I couldn't get my mind off the shadows in the underwater window, or Mays and DiMaggio.

At the end of the workout, I asked Curtains if I could come early to the evening practice to watch the films and get his assessment. He hesitated at first. His plan was to watch film over the weekend and give the feedback on Monday. I insisted politely. "All right," he relented. "I will look at your film first. Come half an hour early tonight."

I was there an hour early.

In the half hour of waiting for Curtains, I sat in the bleachers, staring down at the calm water. The empty natatorium felt like a church to me. There were talismans of faith in every sector—championship banners, school colors, record boards. They evoked reverence. Great swimmers had swum in that pool, saintly coaches had coached there. There was a lot of sweat, including mine, in that water, making it holy in a way. We'd all been baptized in it.

As I sat there, I tried to answer the question, "why is Archie better than me?" I had tried *not* to think about it in the ready room in Brisbane, but now I was ready to analyze it. Maybe I could come up with a solution.

Archie is two inches taller than I am. He has bigger hands and feet and longer arms. Arms are levers, and the longer the levers, the more power you get. Hands and feet are paddles, and bigger paddles mean more displaced water. There's nothing I can do about those things. These days, greatness in swimming is determined largely by genetics.

Archie has extremely flexible ankles and knees, almost to the point of weirdness. We had an ice skating party after practice one winter and Archie was absolutely comical. He had never been on skates. He couldn't stay vertical and could hardly move an inch. His ankles were too floppy—a disadvantage in skating, but a great benefit in swimming. I made a mental note to ask Curtains about flexibility exercises.

Archie has the fastest recovery rate of anyone on the team. There are several ways to measure this, the easiest of which involves taking heart rates immediately after, one minute after and five minutes after a hard swim. Archie is in a class by himself—no one else has recovery numbers anywhere near his. His ability to recover quickly enables him to swim at peak level in multiple events back to back.

Okay, so Archie had some advantages over me. I already knew that. What could I do to overcome them?

I couldn't think of a single physical advantage I had over Archie, but I had a different work ethic. I beat him most of the time in practice. It has always been my philosophy that hard work can overcome any disadvantage in swimming. I was still holding on to that philosophy, despite my 2-28 record against Archie.

I remembered that there was one other thing, one more difference between Archie and me. Archie thought I had something that he didn't have. He didn't know what it was, and neither did I. I made a mental note to try to figure out what it was. Even if I didn't know what it was, could I parlay this into some kind of psychological advantage?

I'm constantly making mental notes. Most of them find their way to my mental trash can.

Curtains came right on time, and we went into his office. He had a TV and a DVD player in his office. As he was hooking them up, I asked him to give me the bottom line.

"Bottom line, Doyle, you got one good hand."

"Which hand?"

"Your right hand is perfect. No bubbles."

Bubbles?!

This was a new concept to me. All my life I'd been taught to look at hand *position*, but I had never thought about bubbles. It made sense, though. Bubbles are visible signs of turbulence and drag.

"Okay," I asked, with more than a little trepidation, "what about the left hand?"

"You got a bubble on your left thumb." Curtains left that hanging while he completed the video setup.

A bubble on my thumb. It sounded devastating. Maybe nobody had yet compared me to a baseball player because the comparison would demoralize me. Obviously, I was Dave Dravecky, All-Star pitcher for the Giants. Dude got cancer in his pitching arm and they had to cut through muscle to get the cancer out. He made one of the most amazing comebacks in all of sports and returned to the mound a year later. In his second game back, he threw a pitch and the next moment he was on the ground, writhing in pain. His arm had broken in half when he pitched the ball. You could hear the crack in the stands, and you can hear it on the video. The cancer had come back, and eventually his arm was amputated.

That's me, I moaned internally. Dave Dravecky. Bum appendage. Low on luck.

Just as I was wondering if I had some kind of thumb cancer, the video started playing.

I couldn't see what he was talking about at first. I thought my left hand looked pretty good on film. Curtains had asked the video man to zoom in at certain points and now, in the playback, he put it in slow motion. Finally he hit Pause.

"There," said Curtains, pointing to the TV screen. It was unmistakable. Right at the tip of my thumb. It seemed huge on the TV screen, though in reality, it was probably pretty small. I measured it instantly in my mind. It was slightly elongated, a little thinner than my thumbnail and half as long. Half an inch by a quarter of an inch. One-eighth of a square inch.

It's hard to describe the feeling I had when Curtains pointed to the screen and said "there." Though I've never been in the situation, it might be like a beauty queen on the morning of the pageant, having someone point out a zit on her face. Right…there. Zits can be covered up with makeup and airbrushed out of photographs. This was a little different.

"So," I said, "maybe it was a random thing, just on that one stroke."

"No," he answered immediately. "It is there on every stroke. Why do you think I had the cameraman zoom in?"

"Did you zoom in like this on the others?" I asked.

"Most people have bubbles. Some people have them all over the place. You got one. It is not that bad."

I was dying to know: "Does Archie have a bubble?"

Curtains sighed and looked for an instant like he was going to BS me. He does not, however, have the BS gene in his DNA. Maybe he was just annoyed at my question. I couldn't tell. His sigh was ambiguous.

"Archie has no bubbles. Cleanest stroke I have ever seen. No other swimmer has zero bubbles."

This was worse news than the zit on Miss America's face. One more difference between Archie and me. One more disadvantage to try to overcome. One more gift for Archie.

I was no longer watching the TV. That wasn't me swimming up there. That was Mr. Bubble, Mr. One Good Hand.

"What's causing this bubble on my thumb, and what can I do to get rid of it?"

Curtains thought about it for a second. "I do not know," he finally said. That was unusual for Curtains. "It could be from angle of entry. It could be from pitch angle on the glide. We can look at those things. We have to be careful. We may create new bubbles."

Maybe it was no coincidence that the bubble was on the left.

"Do you think this is related to my shoulder injury?"

"No way," Curtains responded, with his usual finality. "I have been watching you swim for a long time. Your stroke was the same before and after the injury. You have probably had this bubble your whole life." Pause. "You and that little bubble have had a pretty good career."

"All the same, I'd like to get rid of it. And burn that tape, would you?" I had seen enough, and I didn't want other people looking at my zit.

At practice that evening, I varied my breathing pattern so I could look at the bubble. I couldn't see my left hand underwater when I breathed on the right, my usual side. My head would be turned to the right when my left hand entered the water, which was when the bubble appeared. But by breathing on the left, I could see my left hand clearly.

The bubble was there, on every stroke, just for an instant on the forward glide. It wasn't special effects. Three times I stopped, blew out all my air, sank to the bottom and watched Archie swim over me. He looked every bit as much like DiMaggio under the water as he did above it. He was utterly bubbleless.

At least now I knew what it was that I had and Archie didn't. For the millionth time, I started raging on Archie and had to talk myself down. Archie couldn't help it if Jupiter aligned with Mars the day he was born. The bubble was my problem, not his. That's what I tried to tell myself.

Through the rest of the workout, I swam last in Lane 1. Brook and Vivian beat me silly in the next lane. Curtains cut me some slack and didn't yell at me. The last set was a kicking set, and I did something unprecedented. I kicked the first length away from Curtains, lurked at the far end for a few seconds, then made my break for the showers. Curtains was watching the sprinters, so I don't think he saw me. I needed that hot waterfall on my head.

I must have been in the shower for 15 minutes, because I was still standing under it with my eyes closed when the first wave of swimmers came in after the workout ended. Their laughter and backslapping subsided when they saw me. Nobody said a word, but Kelton gave me a knowing look. It was a look of approval.

I got dressed and walked home. After dinner, I sat back in my recliner. Thoughts swirled. Where did this bubble come from? Is it something genetic? Maybe my thumb has some peculiar shape, unique to me, that cannot be changed. Or maybe it *can* be changed. Maybe I could break my thumb and change its geometry.

Swimmers sometimes face tradeoffs. Would you sacrifice your long-term health for short-term success in swimming? This is typically asked as a hypothetical on the use of steroids or other drugs. Fortunately, most swimmers answer "no" when the topic is steroids. In other situations, the answer isn't so obvious. Many a swimmer has been told that she risks permanent shoulder damage if she keeps swimming. Some people faced with that choice choose to keep swimming. If I knew that breaking my thumb would bring me a 3:36, would I do it? I'd sure think about it.

I held my hands out in front of me for several minutes, comparing the thumbs. There was no obvious difference. I probably couldn't blame my ancestors. I noticed that my thumbnails were a little long. I got the nail clippers and pared the left one back. A little more, a little more. It started to hurt, and I stopped when I saw blood.

The clipping eased my mind a bit. I would have to wait until the morning to see if it made any difference. I drifted into a daydream. In my second grade class a kid named Tommy Dieterle pulled on the ponytail of the girl sitting in front of him and she shrieked. The teacher came over with a ruler and gave Tommy a good rap on the right hand. "But Mrs. Sterling," Tommy protested, "it was the other hand that did it!" Tommy had a bad hand.

At least you *have* a left hand, I said to myself. There was a homeless guy who begged for money at the freeway off-ramp. He held up a sign that said "God Bless You." He held up the sign with his right hand, because he didn't have a left hand or forearm. I made a mental note to take that guy a meal.

Sleep was hard to come by that night. I rolled from side to side. The thoughts kept swirling. I must have fallen asleep at some point, though, because I had a dream. It was one of those disturbing dreams produced by anxiety. I was trying to go see Curtains. I had to get there. It was urgent. When I got off the subway, I realized I'd gotten off at the wrong stop. I had gone too far. I got up to street level and nothing looked familiar. I started walking, block by block, trying to get back to the pool. Everything looked strange. I didn't seem to be making any progress. I couldn't get to Curtains. I was lost.

I woke up sweating. The sweating was no surprise, because it was summer and my apartment had no air conditioning. It was dark, and I felt disoriented. I reflected on the dream. Huron Springs has no subway.

I checked the digital clock next to my bed. It was 3:36 in the morning. In disbelief, I got up and looked at the digital clock in the living room. It also said 3:36. No, no, no. This can't be.

Those same clocks, with the same numbers on them, had been instrumental in my decision to keep swimming. How happy I was to see them just a few short weeks before. Now, they represented all that was bad in my life—having a bubble on my thumb and being a pussycat on dry land.

The clocks were mocking me. In your face, Doyle! You can't swim a 3:36 with a bubble on your thumb. I made a mental note to replace the digital clocks with analog.

PART II

CHAPTER 9

Swimming trains your body. This is no revelation to anyone. The average person watches swimming only on TV, once every four years. Even the uninitiated can tell that elite swimmers have magnificent bodies. The training eliminates excess fat and builds every muscle in the body. Swimmers' muscles are large, but not grotesque; they're long and lithe.

Swimmers don't spend a lot of time looking at mirrors or admiring each others' bodies. We take it for granted. Yes, some of the women are quite attractive and the suits don't leave much to the imagination. But we see the same people every day, twice a day, in the same suits. We see them first thing in the morning with bed head, yawning, without makeup, cranky. We see plenty of skin; we're not tantalized by it.

Swimmers are healthier than average people. We don't arrive at the top of the stairs panting. We're trained to eat right. We tend to have good blood pressures, resting heart rates and hemoglobin levels—good hearts and good blood. The doctor doesn't know me. "Oh," my doctor said to me one time, "you swim? How nice. Swimming is good for you." I elected not to tell her about the pain threshold or the bone-wearying fatigue. I let her think that swimming is "nice."

You can tell how good swimming is for your body by watching what happens to people when they stop. When a swimmer has had a layoff, even for just a couple weeks, his teammates notice it right away. Maybe there isn't much of a weight gain, but there's a softness to the look.

If you retire and completely walk away from swimming, which is what most swimmers do, your body will balloon within months. You're used to eating truckloads of food, and it's hard to change that habit. When you stop burning all those calories, the body fat increases and the muscle tone decreases.

I've seen some middle-aged former swimmers who looked like they swallowed bowling balls. There are genetic and aging factors at play, but I guarantee you the round-bellies had sculpted bodies at the heights of their careers.

Stupid bubble. Why was this curse inflicted on me? Wouldn't it have been more reasonable, more cosmically balanced, for *Archie* to be the one with the handicap? Every Shakespearean character has his tragic flaw. The great heroes of the Bible—Abraham, Moses, King David—have their sins. Not Archie. He is flawless—sinless—when it comes to swimming. Somebody's thumb was pressing on the scale when Lady Justice wasn't looking. I hated the bubble; I hated Archie for not having one.

I discovered the bubble on a Friday. The next morning, I went to practice determined to get rid of it.

Curtains had an intense set planned, as usual. He liked to discourage Friday night partying. There was never a practice on Sunday mornings, so the party-goers had one night a week—Saturday—to let loose. The absence of a Sunday practice allowed the spiritual-minded to attend church and the sleep-minded to worship at St. Mattress. Curtains figured that if he gave a particularly hard workout on Saturday morning, the swimmers would be too tired to do anything really crazy on Saturday night.

The sadistic set that Saturday was ten times 800 meters on 9:20. The people in Lanes 3–6 got a slower interval, and the sprinters did something altogether different. For those of us in the first two lanes, it was an endurance test. There wouldn't be much rest for 93 minutes. It was a pure grind—the kind of set that made Crack salivate. He would go the same speed on every repeat. Archie would bag the first nine and go all out on the last one. My usual aim would be to descend my times steadily from beginning to end.

I just described three different approaches to the same set, and unless you're a swimmer, you probably thought that's all I was doing. In fact, I was describing three different *personalities*. Swim practice is a window to the soul. How you approach a tough set is how you approach life. Those who cheat in practice cheat on the outside. Leadership, dedication, selfishness, corner-cutting, grace under pressure, you name it—it all gets displayed in practice. Character overflows into the pool.

The day after the discovery of the bubble was an ordinary day for everyone else, but for me it was different. I was experimenting with my hands. I asked Crack to lead the animal lane, Archie went second and we spaced 20 seconds apart.

While warming up, I checked to see if cutting my thumbnail had made any difference. It had not. The bubble was still there, unchanged.

During the set, I breathed on my left so I could watch my left hand. On the first three 800s, I tried subtle changes to the hand *geometry*. I experimented with various thumb positions in relation to the hand, from tight to fully spread. On the next four 800s, I tried some changes to my hand *position*. I tried an early, slight, downward tip of the hand during the forward glide. None of this had any effect on the bubble.

During the eighth and ninth 800s, I changed the *entry angle* of my left hand. Usually my hand enters the water at a slight palm-out angle and flattens during the forward glide. For a while I tried having my hand enter flat. This produced a flurry of new bubbles, so I abandoned that right away. Then I tried a slight palm-in angle on entry—a "judo chop" stroke—and this felt ridiculous.

As I finished the ninth 800, Curtains was in a crouch above the Lane 1 gutter. I was getting less than 20 seconds rest each time. Before I could even take a breath in between the ninth and tenth repeats, Curtains was right there, in my face, not yelling but raising his voice.

"Forget about the bubble for now. Get going." I didn't even acknowledge that I heard him.

I pushed off and swam the last 800 hard. At the end, Curtains was especially complimentary of both Crack and Archie, more effusive than usual. Crack had swum a yeoman's set, and I knew Curtains didn't really like Archie's habit of bagging until the end and blasting the last repeat. Curtains was making a point, directed at me, by complimenting the other two. That's how it seemed to me, anyway, but I have a tendency to think everything is about me.

I stayed in the water after practice and asked Curtains if he'd help me with the bubble. He looked reluctant, but said "swim a few laps, just a normal stroke, and I will watch you."

I nodded okay, pushed off and swam 300 meters. When I stopped, Curtains was right above me, standing on the starting block. I had to look straight up to see his face.

"Not bad," he said. "Right hand is good. We do not want to mess that up. I have to be honest with you, I am reluctant to change anything big because we might make a new problem. I have never tried to remove a bubble before."

"Hey, if we fix it, you can write another book."

"Do not flatter yourself. This is worth only an article at best. First we will try putting your left hand into the water a little further from your head. You are a little close to the head right now."

"You're the boss," I said. I pushed off and swam another 300 meters, concentrating on widening the hand entry. It felt pretty good. At the end of the 300 meters, I stood on the bottom of the pool as Curtains again called out to me from straight overhead, on top of the starting block.

"Any effect on the bubble?"

"I forgot to look. I was concentrating on the wide hand entry."

"Well, do it again, exactly the same way, because I liked the hand entry."

I did another 300, this time making sure to look at my left thumb as well as the hand entry position. The bubble was still there. At the end of that 300, I didn't bother to look up at Curtains. It was hurting my neck.

"The bubble is still there." I said this while looking straight at the gutter.

"I thought so," he said. "Here is another thing. I want you to try doing a catch-up stroke."

"Are you kidding? A catch-up?"

"I am not kidding. Try it. What have you got to lose?"

"Okay." I pushed off.

It wasn't radical, but it was non-traditional. A catch-up stroke is where the timing is asymmetrical. The normal stroke has a constant beat, one arm recovering, then the other, one second apart. In a catch-up, one hand enters and the other enters shortly after it, then there is a longer delay before the first hand enters again. Instead of 1-2-1-2-1-2, the rhythm is 1-2..., 1-2..., 1-2. Some describe it as "loping." Janet Evans swam this way and it worked for her—the 400 free world record she set in 1988 lasted 18 years. To me, though, the catch-up seems unnatural. I like symmetry.

The catch-up takes a lot of concentration. It requires a rhythm. At first, I could only do it for half a length at a time. By the end of 300 meters, I thought I was doing it pretty well. It felt kind of neat. I was being won over to the catch-up idea.

"Never mind," said the voice from above. "It looks ridiculous. You stink at it. By the way, did you look at your thumb?"

"Of course not," I said. "I forgot to look again. It's kind of hard to do catch-up and anything else at the same time."

"Can you walk and chew gum at same time?"

"Probably not. I'm going to do another 200 catch-up and look at the bubble."

I was assuming that the bubble would still be there. I pushed off. I had a lot to think about this time, with both the catch-up and the bubble. Curtains wasn't standing on the starting block at the end. When I finished, he was ten feet behind the blocks, reading a piece of paper, thinking about something else.

"Get out, you are done. Catch-up is not for you."

It didn't work anyway, but I disliked the implication that I was a failure at the catch-up. I wanted to conquer it, even if it didn't cure the bubble problem.

"So, what, are we just going to give up?"

"It is just a little bubble. Most people have many bubbles. We are not going to ruin a pretty good stroke getting rid of it."

We were giving up.

It didn't sit well with me. The genius Curtains couldn't solve my bubble problem. He was supposed to be this swimming science guru. Would he have worked on it harder if it were Archie's problem? The thing that blew me away was his attitude about it. I had sacrificed a lot to make swimming my sole priority. Couldn't he at least *sound* more intense about it?

I swam another 400 so I could get a thorough look at the bubble and try to curse it out of existence. It refused to go away quietly. As I swam, and thought about what Curtains had said and his lack of apparent worry, my frenzy slowly waned. I had to accept it. There was nothing more to do.

The bubble was here to stay. I could whine, I could appeal, I could curse, I could hope, I could pray, but the bubble would be there the rest of my life. It would be an eternal reminder of my station in life—a little lower than the angels.

I needed a long, hot shower, but I didn't have time. When I hit the locker room, the rest of the guys were clearing out. The testosterone was flowing. Everyone was talking about their plans for the weekend, where the parties were going to be, what girls were worthy of being conquered, etc. I grabbed Archie as he was bouncing out the door, and confirmed that he was going to pick me up at noon outside my apartment.

At 12:11 p.m., after I had been waiting outside for exactly 11 minutes, Archie pulled up and I hopped in. He calls his car "the Jag-you-arrrr." After his last NCAA season ended, Archie was allowed to sign some big endorsement deals. The Jag is his one major ostentation. It has a pouncing jaguar hood ornament. I like the soft leather seats, and Archie likes the sound system. You can feel his car coming before you can see it.

Archie is asked to attend a lot of charity events. He turns down most of the invitations, but he favors the ones that have something to do with swimming. He had agreed to appear at a Special Olympics swim meet in Lansing, and that's where we were headed.

Archie always brings someone along with him to charity events. He doesn't like being alone, and he wants to share some of his celebrity with his friends. He always asks me first. He thinks I deserve more recognition than I get, and he's trying to help me get some. In fact, helping me "get some" pretty much describes Archie's mission in life—that, and winning gold medals.

When Archie picked me up, he had no shirt on, no shoes, a backward baseball cap and sunglasses. He could have been almost any 22-year-old. Except for the Jag.

The Jag burned no rubber as it peeled out. If my Taurus had accelerated like that, if indeed it were capable of such acceleration, there would have been some major screeching. In about three minutes we were on the freeway, and that's when he really opened the throttle. I was with Archie once when he was stopped by the police. He smiled at me and said "watch this." When the cop appeared at his window, Archie flashed his gold medal smile and the guy said "are you—?" Archie nodded. "Can I get your autograph for my son? He's a swimmer." Archie pulled a photo card out of the center console, wrote a note with the kid's name, signed it and handed it over. "Sorry to inconvenience you," the cop said, and off we sped on our merry way.

Archie had the music up loud and I didn't care. I was thinking about the fact that I had a bubble and he didn't; he had a Jag and I didn't. He broke the noise with a question.

"What was the deal with you and Curtains this morning?" he shouted.

"Curtains and I looked at the video and we discovered a flaw in my stroke. I have a bubble on my thumb." I felt silly shouting back.

"A bubble on your thumb." Archie bobbed his head to the beat. "Doesn't sound too serious to me."

The most common reaction people have to me is that I'm too serious, too analytical, I think too much. I get told to "lighten up" fairly frequently, especially by Archie, who is as light as they come. I'm used to it.

"I don't really know how serious it is," I said. "It's pretty obviously there. I tried a few things this morning to get rid of it. Nothing worked."

Archie looked over at me and must have seen something on my face. He reached down and turned off the stereo, showing respect for my concern.

"I think you have an awesome stroke," he reassured me, though I doubted he had ever really studied it.

"Thanks," I said, smiling to wipe away whatever was on my face. I turned the music back on and we jammed for a while. Unfortunately, I am incapable of just jamming. My mind wandered, as usual, in the general direction of the future. With a bubble plaguing me, should I rethink my decision to keep swimming? Should I dedicate something less than my whole life to the sport? Should I move on with my life? Then my mind started wandering out loud. I turned toward Archie and shouted over the music.

"Do you ever think about life after swimming, Arch? Like, what are you going to be doing 30 years from now?"

"Good question, Bro." He turned down the music and made his face look all serious. "First things first, you know? I have this talent, or gift, whatever you call it. Now is my time. I want to ride it. I don't know when it's going to end. I'm starting to make some money, you know?"

"I'm actually not worried about you missing any meals. I guess what I'm asking is, what do you want to do with your life? What are you interested in?"

He gave me the big cheesy smile from the poster. "Man, I'm interested in going fast."

That was the stock answer, the Greg Norman answer, the media consultant answer. I'd heard Archie say it a million times. I realized I was asking too much of him. He was incapable of thinking 30 years out, and he didn't need to. Not like I did. And the thing about going fast, well, that is what he was doing in swimming, in driving his Jag, in dating women. It pretty much described his life. I had another fleeting moment of empathy for him. I suspected he was peaking early, taking his life out like Jack the Bear. After swimming, things were going to slow down for Archie.

"Okay, here's what I really mean: what is the meaning of life?"

We both laughed out loud when I asked that. It was a joke, because we both know Archie doesn't like the deep stuff. If I need a dose of that, I talk to Molly. Archie likes to talk about going fast. It is, to him, the meaning of life.

Who determines the meaning of life? If a person can pick his own meaning, then going fast is a good meaning for Archie. Is it the same meaning for everyone? Am I a little less important to the cosmos than Archie because I'm not quite as fast? Is he the pinnacle of humanity? Are all other people lesser beings because they're slower? I flashed back to the movie *Chariots of Fire* where the 1924 Olympic 100-meter dash runner, Harold Abrahams, says "I have ten lonely seconds to justify my existence." Please, let it not be so. Let there be more purpose to life than going fast. In the meantime, let me go fast.

We arrived at the outdoor aquatic center in Lansing. Archie parked his Jag across two spaces, away from the other cars. He took off his cap and ran his fingers through his thick mop of blond hair. He never combs it except for photo shoots, and even then the stylists don't do much. Women think his unkempt hair is sexy. I know this because my sister, of all people, told me. You don't want to hear stuff like that from your sister.

Archie tossed his cap into the back seat, grabbed his "USA Swimming" shirt and put it on. It was an old school shirt, just a simple red t-shirt with the letters in navy blue, outlined in white. It had the Olympic rings on one sleeve and the logo for United States Swimming on the other. He pulled one of his gold medals from the back seat and stuffed it in the pocket of his cargo shorts. He was now Hunter Hayes, Olympic Champion.

It was one of those Michigan summer days when everything looks high definition. There were only a couple wisps of white cloud in the sky, just to highlight the blue. As we strolled across the parking lot toward the pool, we could hear cheering mixed with splashing, the trademark sound of Michigan in the summer. The sound told us the meet was in progress. We were late. We were always late. As we entered the gate and walked onto the pool deck, Archie was swarmed by several young swimmers. A couple of them came up to me, but it was hardly a swarm.

We stayed at the pool in Lansing for about an hour. Archie was at his smooth best, handing out medals, posing for photos, and he even shed his t-shirt and cargo shorts, revealing a Speedo underneath, and got in the water with the kids for a sort of "clinic." They utterly adored him, and a bunch of them followed us out to the gate as we exited. By the time we got to the Jag, Archie had stuffed the medal in his pocket and removed his shirt. As we hit the road, I felt compelled to give Archie some props for what he'd done.

"You were good today, Arch."

"Thanks. And thanks for comin' with me."

"No, I really mean it. And what I mean is, not only is that a good thing you did, to sacrifice your time and all that, but you did it well. You were good at it. It's like you were born to do it."

Oops, I overstepped again. Archie was tired of hearing about being gifted. As he had told me before, it was a burden to him, a responsibility.

"Just trying to give something back," he said, closing off the discussion.

Archie was used to hearing praise, but that wasn't my role. I guess I couldn't help myself. I understand Archie better than he understands himself, but occasionally even I can be amazed. Archie's performance at the Special Olympics made me forget how much I'd hated him earlier in the day for not having a bubble. He had totally redeemed himself.

I decided to do him a real favor by changing the subject to something he liked to talk about.

"Hey, how fast will this buggy go?" This time I got the wide, genuine grin instead of the cheesy poster smile.

"She'll do about 20 knot," he said, perfectly imitating old Norman's boat captain, Will. Then we both said, in unison, "if we fang it."

Archie turned on the stereo and we bobbed our heads to the beat for a while. He floored it for a stretch, but there were too many cars on the road to really open her up.

After a few miles, Archie shouted over the music. "You goin' to Crack's party tonight?"

I wasn't planning to go. Crack was insane on Saturday nights. He was an absolute grinder in every aspect of his life. The only time Crack ever let loose was on Saturday nights, and even then it was a grind. He swam hard, he studied hard, and on Saturday nights he partied hard. A Saturday night party at Crack's meant beer by the gallon.

I always felt like a foreigner at Crack's parties. I don't like beer, or the loss of self-control that goes with it. The other guys drank it from bottles and steins and hoses and funnels, or straight out of the tap, however they could get it. So I stood out, with my half-nerdiness, my eyeglasses, my slide rule mentality and my root beer. The music was too loud for me and most of the guys were too wasted to engage in any sort of intelligent conversation. The women on the team never went to Crack's parties because the guys usually ended up fighting, or shouting at each other during video games.

"Yeah, I think I'll come for a little while," I said.

Archie smiled at that. Maybe that's why I said it. I felt bad for putting an extra burden on Archie's shoulders. I had meant to encourage him and let him know he was doing something valuable with the charity work.

I went to Crack's party and stayed to the end. I could have found another way home, but I waited for Archie to leave. I'd kept my eye on him through the night, and could tell he was pouring it in. By the time we were leaving, he was sloshed.

I put my arm around his shoulder. "Let me drive, man."

"Why?" He looked at me like he couldn't focus on my face. Then he turned toward Crack and laughed.

"Seriously. You're trashed. You can't drive." I held out my hand.

He pulled the keys out of his pocket, dangled them over my hand, then grabbed them back in his fist. "I'm NOT wasted," he said, followed by a burp. "YOU are!" He put his finger on my shoulder and pushed. When he and Crack shared another private chuckle, it felt like they were mocking me.

"Whatever," I said. "I'm walking home." My place was almost two miles away, and it was 2:30 in the morning. I started to leave.

"Doan worry," Archie called, "the Jag-you-arrrr knows the way."

I walked downstairs and out the door of Crack's building. There was a mist in the air and it braced me. I walked with my hands in my pockets. After half a block I turned back to see Archie tumble onto the sidewalk. The keys hit the pavement, and the Jag's car alarm started whooping. Archie was crawling on all fours, looking for the keys. I could see them. I thought I had a chance to get them before he did. I ran toward them. Unfortunately, he got there first.

"Found 'em! Hey Doylie—you want a ride?" I could barely hear him above the noise.

"Turn the alarm off." He fumbled the keys and pushed several buttons on the remote before the noise abated. I pulled him to his feet.

"Thanks, man." He walked toward the car. "C'mon." I don't know why, but I followed him. He got in the driver's side and I got in the passenger side.

"Arch, really, don't turn the key." He started the engine.

"I'll be fine. Fine fine fine. You're always worrying about me." He peeled the Jag out of the parking space. I was worried about ME.

I buckled my seatbelt hastily while Archie floored it. He blew the first two stop signs—didn't even hesitate; probably didn't even see them. He weaved the Jag across the centerline repeatedly, and after he got onto the main drag, he did a hard, squealy U-turn. Fortunately, there were no other cars on the road.

Well, there was one car. We passed a police cruiser that was parked at the side of the road at an angle, with its lights off.

"Did you see the cop car?" I said. He shook his head. But he kept looking in the rear view mirror.

"Shit."

"Pull over, Arch. Maybe you can talk your way out of it."

"No way, man. They let me speed, but this is different. I already have a wet reckless."

I didn't know that. He'd get his license yanked and it'd be news. His mug shot would be plastered all over the internet and the tabloids. I felt sorry for him, and especially sorry that I hadn't succeeded in stopping him. I also felt panic. The situation was dire.

Meanwhile, Archie seemed to have been sobered by the adrenaline rush. He made a hard turn onto a side street and turned off the headlights. He worked the side streets like a maze until he hit Route 17, the main highway out of town. Then the lights came back on and he floored it. I gripped the arm rest.

"Does this thing have side air bags?"

"She's got everything." His jaw was clenched.

"What's the plan?"

"I know a place we can hide. Five miles out, off Dancer Road. An old abandoned shack."

There were no longer any street lights. The scenery became increasingly rural, with light coming only from the half moon and the porch lights of the occasional farm house. We turned down a dirt road and all light ceased except our headlights. After half a mile, I noticed a dark shape in the road ahead.

"Do you see it?"

"Yeah, what is it?"

"An animal!" I yelled.

Archie was going too fast to stop. The critter came into focus. It was a giant striped raccoon, right in the middle of the road, frozen by the headlights, staring at us. I thought to myself "we're going to kill a raccoon," but at the moment of truth, Archie swerved. My head conked the side window. We careened through the ditch. Tree limbs swiped the window next to me, Archie yelled a stream of obscenities, and we bounced until we hit a culvert.

I felt my head and found a spot that made me wince when I pushed on it. My first coherent thought was "thank God I'm alive." I turned toward Archie but he was already outside the car. When I unbuckled and got out there, he was examining the damage. He had his hands threadlocked on top of his head.

"Oh no, oh no, oh no."

"They can fix it, Arch."

"She'll never look the same!"

Just then I saw a pair of headlights coming our way down the dirt road. There were no gumballs flashing but it was, indeed, the cop car. It stopped in the middle of the road, and two of Huron Springs' finest got out. The lead officer walked completely around the Jag, shining his heavy-duty flashlight on it, before saying anything. He kept pushing his cop hat up and down on his forehead. Twice, he whistled. When he was done looking at the car, he came up to me and shined the flashlight in my face.

"Driving a little recklessly back there, weren't we?"

"Yes sir," I said. I've always been respectful to cops. Plus, I was almost paralyzed by the weight of authority. My head was throbbing.

"Have anything to drink tonight son?"

"No sir. Just pop."

"Pop?"

I nodded. I finally got a glimpse of his name badge—Officer Duane Riske. "Well," he said, "why don't we just see if that pop registers on the intoxilyzer?" He never even asked who'd been driving, and I was too scared to volunteer anything. The second cop produced the intoxilyzer, and I turned it around and looked at it from a bunch of different angles trying to figure out how it worked. "Just blow," Riske said. "Into the tube." I blew. Riske pressed a button and looked at it, handed it to the second cop, they both looked at it for a while under the flashlight, then Riske shook it like a thermometer.

"Blow again." I blew again, and the scene repeated itself. They looked disappointed. It finally occurred to me that we might beat the whole rap if we let them think I was the driver. I decided not to fink.

Officer Riske walked over to where Archie was sitting, on the hood of the Jag. He shined the flashlight toward Archie, who turned his face away. Riske kept shining it, and finally Archie turned into the light and flashed the million-dollar smile.

"Are you...?" The whole rigamarole started, and by the end Archie had signed two autographed photos. The cops were happy.

"Here's what we're gonna do," Officer Riske said to Archie. "Your friend here"—he had his pencil out and pointed it at me—"busted a whole lot of laws back there. We could be talkin' jail time. Mighta been trying to outrun us, I don't know. But he's clean, so we're gonna let him off easy. Give him a moving for running a stop sign. That's all." He turned toward me. "But I hope you learned a lesson."

"Yes sir, I did. I learned a lesson." I'd learned a bunch of lessons, not one of which was what Officer Riske had in mind.

We were able to get the car moving, and the cops helped us push it out of the ditch. I drove, of course, and Archie let me. We waved to the officers as we slowly crept toward home. The car made all kinds of funny noises, and Archie seemed mostly concerned with the noises as we drove. But as we stopped in front of my apartment, he looked at me and said "Wow. What a bro. I owe you, man." He gave me a hearty handshake on the way around the car, before getting in the driver's seat. He winked at me as he drove off.

I'd done something nice for Archie. I felt good about that. I didn't feel so good about the ticket in my pocket, which would cost me money I didn't have, not to mention raising my insurance rates. And I wondered if Archie even got it—was he going to change his ways, or was this just another confirmation to him that he could get away with anything? And what about me—wouldn't it be better for me if I let him go down? He had every advantage over me, including a bubbleless thumb. Why should I bail *him* out?

CHAPTER 10

Swimming trains your mind. This may seem counter-intuitive, given the mind-numbing boredom of watching a black line for five hours a day. You'd think swimming would deaden the mind. The opposite is true.

In some ways, the boredom itself works the strengthening. Just like a muscle, the mind responds to repetition. Something long and difficult becomes easier to do the second time around, and easier still the third time. Why? Because you're familiar with it. You know it won't kill you. Swimmers, therefore, are not reticent to take on hard tasks in real life. They will handle the hot potato; they'll draw enemy fire. The boredom and the mental effort required to perform hard sets toughens your mind.

There is a sharpening to go along with the toughening. You don't turn your mind off when you swim. In fact, you're required to engage it on several levels at once. Proper stroke technique is complex and nuanced. You have to monitor and adjust constantly. You check rhythm and pace; you keep a clock and a counter going in your head. Race strategies must be planned and implemented carefully. Your brain has to multi-task.

Swimmers must be observant and make decisions on the fly. Adjustments are often required based on small, fleeting pieces of evidence—a splash in your peripheral vision may mean someone is racing you across the pool; a small tinge of new pain in your shoulder may signal the need for a stroke modification. If you lose focus, you may miss the wall on your flip turn. Continual concentration is mandated.

Every lap and every stroke trains the mind as much as it trains the body. Mental toughness is a premium attribute. When the race is on the line and your muscles are full of lactic acid, the mind is what pushes you through the pain and enables you to bring it home. You have to be able to tell yourself that you trained harder than the guy you're racing. In a world governed by hundredths of a second, the mental edge is crucial.

In June I received a letter from Cal. My place in the fall med school class was no longer being held for me. I could re-apply if I wanted to be considered for the following year. Southern Michigan was only a little less formal: my acceptance could not be deferred again, but my application would be held for one more year. Coach Dewey hired Joe Salazar as his assistant at Three Rivers. Thus, all my bridges had been duly burned. Even that analogy was inadequate—I was not on one side but *in* the creek, without a paddle *or* a boat, with no option but to swim.

It was a lonely summer. I'm okay being by myself, usually. I don't need to party, I can cook for myself and I like to read. But this was a self-imposed exile. The discovery of the bubble and the failure to eliminate it meant that I had to double down. I withdrew into a very tiny world of swimming and subsistence. I spent more time at the pool, doing extra laps and weights. I hosted no movie nights; I stopped going to parties at Crack's; I left Molly alone.

Water, I decided, was the solution to all my problems. "Drink more water" is the only prescription I've ever gotten from the doctor. Water clears my mind. Water offers the promise of redemption. Water can wash away sins.

So I swam. I poured myself into that one pursuit.

Our summer season wound down and we began preparing for the Long Course Nationals in Omaha. "Long course" refers to the 50-meter pool in which the event is held. "Short course" events are held in 25-yard or 25-meter pools. The Olympics are long course. In the year before the Olympics, the Long Course Nationals provide a tune-up for the stars and a chance for new talent to emerge. It's the crowning event of the summer season.

Ordinarily, Team Jaguar would peak for the summer Nationals and try to win the team title. With the Olympics a year away, however, Curtains elected to rest us very little, knowing that we wouldn't swim our best times. He didn't want to sacrifice the training time. He planned for us to be hard at work doing 20,000 meters the day after the meet.

The Nationals were the first test of my new status as a pure 400 freestyler. I would've had a chance to make the finals in the 200 fly and the 200 free, but Curtains wanted me to concentrate on the 400 free. The only other event he allowed me to swim was the 800 free relay, which came *after* the 400 free.

The strategy for Archie at Nationals was the complete opposite of the strategy for me. Archie's goal was to win a chest full of medals in Paris, which would require him to swim a grueling schedule of multiple races every day. To better simulate the Olympic schedule, his five individual events would be loaded into *two* days in Omaha. On the third day, he had three individual events and a relay, which meant that, adding prelims and finals, he would be swimming seven times in one day.

The day before we left for Omaha, at the afternoon practice, there were no lane markers in the pool when we arrived. That was odd, and we all knew something was up. When we congregated at the starting end of the pool, with our suits on, Curtains came out of his office and announced that we were going to have a talk. He ushered us to the stands, then he disappeared.

When Curtains returned, he had someone with him. It was a tall, lean man whom I estimated to be in his fifties. As he approached us, I noticed his spectacles, which made him look smart. He had graying hair and was wearing a lab coat with a caduceus on the left breast.

"Okay, everybody, listen up," Curtains began. "This is Dr. Nate Sensibaugh. He swam for me many years ago when I first came to Southern Michigan. He came here to swim for Don Jackson as a walk-on. Nate was not too happy when I replaced Coach Jackson, but he did everything I asked. When he was done swimming he went to medical school and graduated top of his class. Now he does heart surgery at SM Medical Center."

"Let me tell you one thing about Nate, then I am going to let him talk because he is much better. When Nate was a junior—it was my first year as coach—he almost won the conference title in the 1650. His teammates elected him captain for the following year. That year he was captain, we won the conference team title, first time in 15 years, and we won it by one point. Nate was the best captain I ever had. I am proud to have coached him."

We all scrutinized Dr. Nate as he prepared to speak. Curtains had talked him up, but clearly this was not the best *swimmer* Curtains had coached. None of us had heard of him. His name was nowhere to be seen among the record boards and walls of plaques at the SM pool.

Dr. Nate started by thanking Curtains for his kind introduction and saying what an honor it was to have swum at SM. He explained that none of the swimmers had liked Curtains at first, because they loved Coach Jackson and Curtains' ways were different. But they came to appreciate his novel training theories and by the end of the first year, they all thought he was going to be a great coach. Now, he said, all of Curtains' former swimmers would take a bullet for him.

After the love fest was over, Dr. Nate got down to business. He told us there were lots of parallels between swimming and heart surgery.

"Right before you dive in, you put on a cap and some pretty funky eyewear."

He pulled a pair of glasses from his lab coat pocket. They were large black-framed nerd glasses with little microscopes attached. I heard a few chuckles. Freddie Boxer was sitting next to me and his goggles hit the floor when he laughed. He'd been chewing on the strap.

"We also like to blast out music before we get into a patient's chest, just like you guys do before a race." I saw Archie smile, perhaps imagining a surgical team in scrubs doing hip-hop moves.

"A surgeon is part of a team that includes several kinds of doctors, nurses, and assistants. Everyone has a role, and everyone depends on everyone else. The surgeon is like the anchor-man on a relay, finishing the job that has been set up by others."

"Finally," he said, completing his list of parallels, "in heart surgery, as in swimming, there are two nemeses." My ears perked up.

"In swimming, the guy in the next lane is one nemesis, and the other one is a box on the wall that spits out numbers. In heart surgery, you're constantly fighting against blood, which gushes out as soon as the chest is cut open. It gets in the way, and too much blood loss can kill the patient. Blood is the first nemesis. The second nemesis is a box that spits out numbers: blood pressure, heart rate, hematocrit, platelet count. Those numbers tell how the patient is doing—how much gas is left in the tank."

I could see a couple swimmers getting queasy over the thought of blood gushing all over the place. I thought it was cool. Through most of his talk, Dr. Nate kept his hands in the pockets of his lab coat. Occasionally he would gesture with them, and when he did I examined them closely. They looked average to me. I expected them to be extraordinary.

Dr. Nate said he was going to tell us one story to illustrate what swimming meant to him.

"I usually do two heart surgeries in a day. One day a couple years ago, after completing my two scheduled surgeries, I was called in for an emergency procedure. The patient was in bad shape and we had to operate right away. We had a good team in there, and we fought for five hours to try to save him, but he didn't make it."

He paused for about twenty seconds while all the swimmers shifted in their seats.

"It wasn't the first patient I'd lost. We'd done everything we could. But I was demoralized. I was sitting on a stool in the scrub room with my head in my hands when the resident came in and told me the family of the patient was in the waiting room. I told him I'd talk to the family. A kind of full-body hurt came over me and I recognized it. It was just like how I felt in the 1650 my senior year in the conference finals. I thought I had a chance to win that race, but after 500 yards, I could tell it wasn't my day. The leaders were way ahead of me and my arms were already heavy. I felt like backing off, but I told myself to keep going, to fight to the end."

Dr. Nate only got sixth place in the 1650, his time was slower than the previous year, and he felt like crap. He couldn't move for five minutes. No one congratulated him.

"As I sat in the scrub room, I tried to summon the mental strength I had built during my swimming days." He went home 22 hours after he'd awakened, having done three surgeries back-to-back.

"I couldn't have gotten through that day if I hadn't been trained as a swimmer. The mental toughness I got from swimming has served me well in my profession. That was the first time it dawned on me, but now I realize it's been there with me every day."

Curtains explained that Nate had passed a guy on the last lap of the 1650, which proved to be the difference in SM winning the conference title.

We swam an easy thousand and hit the showers. There was a buzz in the locker room about Dr. Nate's speech. A couple guys had missed the point. In the past, Curtains had brought in Olympic swimmers who'd talked about their great swims. This guy wasn't even a great swimmer, and he hadn't talked about how to swim a great race. Sixth in the conference—who wanted to be like that?

Maybe I missed the point too. I came away motivated, but my motivation was in a different direction than Curtains had intended. I wanted to do something noble with my life. It stayed on my mind throughout the trip to Omaha.

We arrived in Omaha on Wednesday, the day before the competition started. That gave us time to get used to the pool, the heat and the time zone.

Team Jaguar was an impressive group. We had 33 swimmers. When we traveled to and from the pool, Curtains liked us to wear our Team Jaguar warm-up tops—lightweight jackets, royal blue with black lettering and white piping. On the back was a pouncing Jaguar that looked like Archie's hood ornament. When we traveled as a group, we looked fierce.

We also had team t-shirts. There's a tradition in swimming that goes way back. Longtime coaches are revered, and the tradition is to make a slogan for your team that incorporates the coach's name. The team in Coronado, California, coached by Mike Troy, had t-shirts with the slogan "For the Love of Mike." Indiana University honored its coach, Doc Counsilman, with the phrase "What's Up, Doc?" Our t-shirts were old school—"Team Jaguar" with a small pouncing jaguar on the front, and "It's Curtains for You" on the back.

We went straight from the airport to the pool for a warm-up. The pool wasn't crowded until we got there, and we took over four lanes. It was a blazing afternoon, with no clouds and little shade at the pool. Our swim was short, but because I wasn't swimming the first day of the meet, I warmed up a little longer than everyone else. I finished up and started walking to the locker room.

"Oh Doy-al!" It was a singsong female voice. I turned and stared straight into the sun, ruining my chance to figure out who it was.

"Doyle!" Same voice.

I turned a little to the left, blinked hard, and there she was. It was Camille, sitting in the third row of bleachers, wearing a bikini and sunglasses. She was reading a book—*Ulysses*, the same book she'd showed me in Brisbane. She appeared to be about halfway through it.

"Camille," I said, squinting. "You look hot."

"Thanks," she beamed. But I hadn't meant it that way.

I remembered the ambiguity from Brisbane—had she been interested in a romantic hook-up, or did she want some intellectual talk? The ambiguity was still present. There was the book. There was the bikini. My eyes settled on the bikini.

She set the book on the bleacher and walked down the steps. The shark tattoo, on her left hip, was coming toward me.

Camille didn't stop when she got to me. She put her arms around my shoulders and clenched me in a bear hug. I wasn't sure where to put my hands, and they came to rest on her bare hips. Oh my goodness. The touch had power. The smoothness of her skin, the curve of her hips—they filled my mind.

In the 1964 movie *Sex and the Single Girl*, Natalie Wood instructs Tony Curtis: "One of the ways to control a woman is through the power of touch." I definitely saw the link, but it was working the wrong way. I could feel control slipping through my fingertips.

"Great to see you," she said. "I haven't seen you since Brisbane." Her lips were speaking into my neck.

"Good to see you too," I mumbled.

I think of myself as having some internal strength, some kind of character, the ability to resist things that other people instinctively succumb to. I'm an analytical person who assesses all the facts and doesn't make rash decisions. I'm calm, not emotional. I've had relationships with women, but not slobbering head-over-heels devil-may-care infatuation. I'm stronger than that.

All that stuff I think about myself—true or not—Camille melted it with the heat of her breath on my neck, which oddly had the effect of sending a shiver down my spine. Control wasn't so important anymore, because the bubble on my thumb had rained chaos on my world. I had blown it with Molly. Where was it getting me to be such a straight-arrow anyway? Maybe I needed to be more out-of-control. Maybe having a fling with Camille would be more than fun—maybe it would save me.

I was willing to give in, to become fish food.

We unclenched, and she kept hold of both of my hands. We were eye to eye. "Why don't we hang out while we're here?" she asked.

"Okay," I submitted.

"Awesome," she said. "How 'bout tonight?"

I saw the Team Jaguar mob clearing the locker room and heading for the vans. I couldn't think clearly. The hips, the lips, the eyes, the shark—they made me stupid. I couldn't think of how to seal the deal. She saw me looking toward the team, and spared me the burden of thought.

"Tell you what," she said. "Your teammates are waiting for you. Why don't we catch up after your 400 free on Friday night?"

"Yeah, that sounds good." She let go of my hands.

I was high on a cocktail of adrenaline and testosterone. I felt nervous, too, like when I was 11 and entered a store with my friends, intending to shoplift some CDs—a crime I was never able to pull off. I jogged off down the pool deck toward the locker room. You're not supposed to jog on pool decks, especially when you're not paying attention. I hit a slippery spot and my right foot shot forward. I caught it and balanced myself with a Charlie Chaplin windup. I skidded for about a meter and stopped. There are some well-known stories of swimmers' careers ending with freak accidents. But hey, I was on a roll, and I acted like I intended that skid all along.

Archie entered the locker room right behind me, already dressed in his sweats. He snapped my Speedo with his towel, and I turned to see him grinning like a lawyer at a crash scene.

"Wasn't that Camille Cognac kissing your neck?"

"She wasn't kissing it, really…."

"Looked like it to me. I told you, man, you're in! All you gotta do is grab it."

I was not oblivious to the implied insult—Archie acting like my big brother, like he knew the ropes and I didn't. But I didn't care. All that was behind me. I had made my decision.

"I know, Arch. Don't worry, I have a plan." I made like it was *my* plan.

His eyes doubled in size and his jaw hit the floor. He put his arm around my shoulder and we marched out of the locker room together—comrades in arms, two warriors in the conquest of women.

Finally, I was on an upward path. Sure, I had suffered some setbacks, but I was on the verge. Some great things were about to happen in Omaha.

On the first day of the meet, I had no events to swim, so all I did was warm up and watch the races. With the exception of the sprinters, our team looked sluggish on the first day. In the men's 400 IM, five of the eight finalists were from Team Jaguar. But the winner was Jesse Vallejo, a teenager from Puerto Rico who trained with the Marlins in Texas. We hated to lose anything to the Marlins, our team's arch nemesis.

I watched the 400 IM intently, because Vallejo was also swimming the 400 free. He was on the rise. I knew I'd have to beat him ten months hence to make the Olympic team, and it would be tough.

The second day of the meet was a big day for Archie and me. We both had the 400 free, prelims and finals, and Archie also had the 200 butterfly and the 400 medley relay. I didn't feel great in my preliminary heat and swam a lackluster time. But I made it into the finals, which was all that mattered. Archie and Crack also made the finals. After Archie swam the prelims of the 200 fly, we went back to our hotel to rest up.

The air that night was thick, not with tension but with humidity. It was the hottest night of the meet, the hottest night I could remember. I was sweating as I stood behind the Lane 7 starting block, wearing only my suit.

The finals of the 400 started with the usual electronic beep. I instinctively moved over to the lane marker next to Vallejo. Vallejo went out fast—too fast, I hoped. At the 100, he was a full body length ahead of me. Not to worry, though. He was still in sight and my strategy was to go out behind him. The first 100 took more out of me than usual, though. I wondered if Vallejo was setting some kind of blazing pace and making me go out too fast.

At the 200, I had fallen two body lengths behind, and I was really hurting. That seemed strange to me. I relaxed out of the turn and started to build the next 50, but it felt labored. The third 100 is when I'm supposed to make up ground.

I remembered *Radar Love* and tried to sing it in my mind. Unfortunately, I could only muster *Mamas, Don't Let Your Babies Grow Up To Be Cowboys*. I had heard that song on the radio earlier in the day.

As I turned at 250 meters, Vallejo was still increasing his lead, and the guy in Lane 8, whom I'd never seen before, was also ahead of me. I took a few breaths on the left side to see what was over there, and I noticed that Archie, in Lane 4, was also well ahead of me. I shot a glance at my left thumb. The bubble was there, big as ever, reminding me of my mortality.

By the time I hit 300 meters, I was dead tired and it was clear that several people were going to beat me. It occurred to me that nobody would really care if I finished fourth or sixth or eighth. That's a really bad thought, though. Even thinking it violates one of the fundamental principles of the sport. Every race matters. The effort matters. You have to do your best every time. I shook off the thought, but my body was in rapid decline.

I muscled my way through the last 100, dying like a dog, falling further and further behind. I drove for the wall and finished as hard as I could, my arm dragging across the surface on the last stroke. After hitting the wall, I slumped in the water and floated on my back. I lacked the power and energy and will to do anything.

I felt murdered-out.

When I was finally able to look at the scoreboard, it confirmed what I already knew—last place by over a second. Even Crack beat me. My time, 3:51.55, was embarrassing. Archie won, and Vallejo was a close second. I leaned across the lane marker and shook Vallejo's hand.

"Great swim," I said weakly.

He thanked me and popped out of the water, fresh as rain. I had to swim under the lane markers to the side of the pool to get out at the ladder. I limped over to the warm-up pool and plopped in. After I swam one length, Curtains was there, leaning down, his face near mine.

"What the hell happened out there?"

"Way to take the words out of my mouth," I said. I was hoping he had the answer, not the question.

"You looked like crap from the beginning."

"Tell me something I don't already know. The question is, why did I *feel* like crap from the start?"

"We only rested five days. You are probably just tired from all the hard work."

"Archie and Crack have been doing the same workouts and they both kicked my butt." I was getting more and more irritated.

"Everybody is different," he said, ambiguously. "Maybe you are coming down with something. Do you feel sick?"

"No. Other than the bubble on my thumb, which we didn't fix, remember? I'm sick of that."

"It is not the bubble; stop focusing on that."

I spat into the gutter. He leaned down even closer to my face.

"Nobody cares about this meet. You have been working hard and that is what is important. A 3:51 right now does not mean anything."

"So you still think I can go 3:36?" I said it sarcastically.

"Absolutely."

Dead silence. We stared each other down.

I thought he might've been lying. I really did. I knew it would be very unlike Curtains to do that, but frustration had displaced logic from my mind. Maybe Curtains would do it out of sympathy for me, just once. Because let's face it, 3:36 was out of the question. Curtains must have known that. How could he not see the futility of it all?

Curtains set his jaw and gave it to me. "Listen, Doyle, you are on track. I have been doing this for a long time; you better not doubt me. Three thirty-six will take every ounce of dedication you have. So get your mind ready for it. Right now."

He stood up and walked away abruptly. He was mad. He had never been mad at me before. I bet he was reading my mind when I was thinking he was a liar.

It was a moment of truth for me. I felt stupid for deciding to keep swimming in the first place, for ever believing I could do a 3:36. I was dragging Curtains and the team down. I felt like a poser. And yet, who was I to doubt the great Curtains? How could I disrespect him like that? How could I let him down? I needed to run after him and apologize. Only I didn't feel like it. I let go of the gutter, blew out my air and dropped like a rock to the bottom of the pool. When I resurfaced, Curtains was long gone.

It hung over me the rest of the meet like a chlorine vapor cloud. Curtains was mad at me, and it was the worst feeling in the world. I was mad at him, too. We avoided each other.

The rendezvous with Camille did not go down. I didn't forget. I was mired in self-pity and embarrassment. She wouldn't want to hook up with a last-place finisher anyway. I saved her the trouble of rejecting me. I failed to show up. I scratched.

On the third day of the meet, a driving rain storm delayed the prelims by two hours, which further compressed Archie's ironman schedule. I had only the 800 free relay at night, so the rain made no difference to me. Archie made it into the finals of all three of his individual events: the 200 free, the 100 breast and the 200 back.

At the finals that evening, there was a buzz in the crowd about Archie swimming four events in less than two hours. It was an audacious program. He was the premier swimmer in the world, and everyone knew he could do well in virtually any event, given enough rest. But this schedule intentionally put him in races where he would *not* be well rested. He would still be breathing hard at the start of his second, third and fourth races. He was attempting to raise the physical and mental bar to an unprecedented height.

To everyone's amazement except mine, he pulled off a sweep. Archie won the 200 free and the 200 back, as expected. In the breaststroke, which he had never swum before at a major competition, he came from behind and touched out the American record holder.

In the 4 x 200 freestyle relay, Team Jaguar had been untouchable for five years. This year was possibly our best year ever. I swam the leadoff leg, followed by Caruso, Crack and Archie. I muscled out an average swim and gave us a slight lead, which Caruso expanded and Crack held. Archie has never lost a lead. I was amazed at how much he still had left after three prior swims. He looked powerful, with long strokes and a big kick. His split was faster than the world record, although it doesn't count unless it's leadoff. Our relay broke the club team record.

Archie got a lot of pats on the back after his four-swim evening in Omaha. I grabbed the van keys from one of the assistant coaches and invited my relay mates to Anthony's, a great steak place in downtown Omaha. We had to wait for Archie to do a press conference. Crack, Caruso and I stood in the back of the little room making gang signs at Archie while he answered questions. Once again, I was in awe of Archie. He sounded intelligent, humble and articulate. He made it look effortless.

Near the end of the press conference, Archie pointed us out in the back and said "I want to give a shout to my teammates on the relay, who are standing in the back right now." All the media heads in the room turned in our direction. We stopped making gang signs. "Thanks, guys, for giving me a lead. I love you guys."

I had never heard Archie use the word "love" about people before. He loves hip-hop, he loves to go fast, he loves his Jag. He throws the word around loosely, but he really sounded sincere this time. I believed him. I got a lump in my throat.

Archie loves steak. I was hungry but I couldn't finish a whole steak. Archie had two. He deserved them. He had to sign a few autographs and pose for a couple photos at the restaurant. The swim meet was the biggest sports news in town, and we weren't exactly incognito with our Team Jaguar jackets. One of those jackets had been seen on Sports Center.

The final day of the Long Course Nationals was anti-climactic. I was done swimming, and Archie had only one relay—the 4 x 100 freestyle—at night. The Marlins had pulled away from Team Jaguar and sewn up the team title. It was a good thing Archie didn't have multiple races, because I think the steaks weighed him down. Crack had his most important event, the 1500 meter free, that evening, and he looked like his blood was still beef-positive. He was having a good meet, though, and although he didn't swim a personal best, he won the event.

After the meet, as we loaded into the vans to head for the airport, I spotted Camille across the pool deck. She saw me and waved. I had successfully avoided her since the day before the meet. I felt a tinge of regret, and went over to apologize. She was standing with three of her teammates, all guys.

"Hey," she said, "it's cherry. There'll be other meets."

It seemed like she was okay with it, though I hoped she was at least a little disappointed. I gave her sort of a light hug, and as I did, she pecked me on the cheek. "Thanks," I said, not being really sure what I was thanking her for—understanding? Flattering me by being interested? I started to back away, then said "Camille, can I talk to you alone for a second?" She nodded, and we went behind the bleachers.

"I didn't want to say this in front of those guys," I began, "but the reason I didn't show up after my 400 free is that I swam like such a slug. To be honest, you're so gorgeous, and such a star, I can't figure out why you'd want to bother with me."

Her answer was a kiss. She put it right on my lips, and I welcomed it. It wasn't a long one, and when it was done, she put her head on my shoulder and squeezed me with her arms. I squeezed back. It felt good.

"You're a fox, Doyle," she said into my shoulder. "A catch. Don't ever forget that."

"Wow." And what I meant was: really?

I wasn't prepared for any of that. She didn't sound like an experienced woman looking for the next liaison. I had misjudged her. I wanted to talk about what made me a catch, but there was no time. We relaxed the hug, and I put my hands on top of her shoulders. "Camille, I gotta run, but…really, I'm glad we talked." I kissed *her* this time. It was nice.

"Catchya later," she said, smiling.

I backed away and waved. My mind took a snapshot of her waving back. She was wearing her team sweats, her hair was wet and combed, there was no sign of any makeup. She didn't look like a predator. She looked more desirable than ever.

I jogged back to the vans, and heard my name being called as I approached. I bounced into a loaded van, taking the last seat. I must have been smiling still. Archie noticed.

"Dude, we been waitin'. Who you been foolin' around with?"

"I was saying goodbye to Camille."

"Whoa-ho." He punched me in the tricep. "Arright!"

I did feel pretty good. It wasn't anything close to what he thought it was, or what I originally thought it was going to be. I had, in fact, chickened out of that. But it was still good. Better, perhaps. It's not true that 20-something guys are interested only in sex. We're quite interested in that, of course. But some of us want more than that, and I discovered that I'm one of those guys. It felt better with Camille when it wasn't about a fling. I'm not a flinger. I told you, I'm a bit of a nerd.

Still, I was a long way from figuring out Camille, or any other woman. It was way too hard for me. And while the thing with Camille felt good, it was going to be months before I'd see her again.

We took a late flight back from Omaha. I don't sleep on planes. The lights went down, and every other person on the plane started snoring, which annoyed me. I closed my eyes and put my headphones on. I scrolled through my music and found *Radar Love*. I played it three straight times, hoping it would be in my brain the next time I needed it.

What I couldn't get *out* of my brain, though, was that I'd swum like crap, I had an incurable bubble on my thumb, and I had alienated Curtains. When your world is focused on a single thing, and it turns out you stink at it, there's a noticeable lack of harmony in your life. I had reached a new low. I tried to comfort myself with the thought that things couldn't possibly get worse. There had to be something better around the corner.

CHAPTER 11

Times in swimming are measured to the hundredth of a second. You cannot discern a hundredth of a second with your eyes or ears. It's an infinitesimally small amount of time, less than the twinkling of an eye. It can be critically important.

Before 1960, times were measured in tenths of a second with hand-held stopwatches. Because of the high potential for human error in this type of timing, it was common to have three timers in each lane, and the middle time would be chosen as the official one. There was also a "finish judge" who would eyeball across the finish wall and call out the lane numbers as swimmers finished. There were many heated controversies, and occasionally the finish judge awarded first place to a swimmer with a slower official time than the second place swimmer. The results would be posted with the notation "judge's decision." In the 1960 Olympics, the timers had Lance Larson as the winner of the 100 free, but the judge ruled that John Devitt had won. Devitt was given the gold. The controversy paved the way for electronic timing.

Touch pads on the walls and electronic "beep" starters came into play in the 1960s. They didn't end the controversies. In the 400 meter individual medley in the 1972 Olympics, Tim McKee of the U.S. and Gunnar Larsson of Sweden swam the same time down to the hundredth of a second. The timing system in Munich had been programmed to pick a winner down to the thousandth of a second. The machine picked Larsson, and he was awarded the gold medal. Although the results of that race have never been overturned, the ensuing controversy caused a re-examination of just how accurate the timing systems could be. There is no such thing as perfect accuracy. The wise owls at FINA, the sport's international governing body, decided that the systems were accurate only to the hundredth of a second. Thus, in ensuing Olympics, if two swimmers tied to the hundredth of a second (such as in the women's 100 free in 1984 and the men's 50 free in 2000), the race was declared a tie and two gold medals were awarded.

After my freshman year of college, I swam a 1:46.83 in the 200 meter freestyle at the Long Course Nationals. The time put me seventh in the world rankings for that year. The next summer, I was at a meet in Spain, in the ready room before another 200 freestyle race, and the guy sitting next to me introduced himself. I said "I'm Doyle," and immediately he said "1:46.83." I asked him how he knew, and he said he was 1:46.84, one slot down in the world rankings. Most people, when they look at the world rankings, only look above their names and not below. When this guy told me he was 1:46.84, I felt a little bit taller. Then I beat him.

One one-hundredth of a second can make a big difference. Swimmers will do almost anything to shave a hundredth or two off their times.

Some people say that every person has a predetermined number of heartbeats, and when you reach that number, you die. You have a set number of seconds to live, and when your time is up, it's up. I guess some great measuring device somewhere determined that Coach Dewey had reached the finish wall. He passed away, unexpectedly, in his sleep.

I was in the middle of a brutal set in the morning practice on August 24 when Curtains stuck his hand in the water to try to stop me. I didn't know what was going on, so I kept swimming. Five seconds later, a kickboard landed right in front of me and my arm hit it. Curtains had thrown it at me. I stopped and looked at him like "what!" He motioned me to get out. I got out.

"I just talked to Laura Dewey," he began. He put his hand on my shoulder. "Coach Dewey had a heart attack. He…passed away."

Coach D was old, but not that old. I knew he'd had surgery and was taking heart medicine, but I didn't think it was that bad. Lots of old people have heart problems. He'd been a swimmer his whole life. Swimmers are healthy. Rugged.

I stood there looking at Curtains, blinking the water out of my eyes. I was waiting for the rest of the story. Sometimes there's good news and bad news and you get the bad news first. It took me a minute to realize that there was no good news. It hit me hard. I started to shiver. Curtains noticed, stepped into his office, grabbed a towel and tossed it to me.

"How? When?"

"I do not know details," Curtains said. "It happened during the night, at home. He was already gone when the paramedics showed up."

"Poor Laura," I stammered. I slid the goggles off my head and dropped them to the pool deck. I toweled off my hair and draped the towel over my shoulders.

"She sounded pretty good on the phone," Curtains said quietly. "She wants you to call her."

I thought about that for a few seconds. No, I'm just going to go out there. Right now.

Curtains read my mind again. "You are done for the day here. Take as much time as you need. Take a few days. Go to Three Rivers."

"Thanks, I think I will."

"Maybe I will see you out there then."

I walked slowly to the showers, thinking about what I was going to do. Right before I got to the door, I looked back to see Curtains crouching over Lane 1, talking to Archie and Crack. They saw me look, and they waved to me.

When I got to the showers, my instinct was to turn the handle to the very hottest temperature and just soak. I really felt like doing that. Maybe all day long. My mind took over, however, and reminded me that Laura wanted to talk to me. There was an urgency to be with her.

I skipped the shower, pulled on my jeans and saddled up the Taurus. Destination: Three Rivers.

I don't know why people do this, but they do. When someone dies, you "go there." You don't really know what you're going to do there, but you go. When I was a kid, an old guy down the street named Izzy Wolverton passed away. I always thought Izzy was a mean old cuss. My parents didn't like him either. But my mom baked a pie and we walked over there. People came and went all day long to pay their respects to Mrs. Wolverton. I didn't really get it then and I'm not sure I will ever get it. I felt a pull toward Three Rivers.

When I arrived at Coach D's street, there were cars parked everywhere. The front door was wide open and I walked right in, waving to a couple people I knew who were sitting in chairs on the porch. There were dozens of people inside, all talking to each other. Some were eating food that people had brought. One woman was on the phone, writing down messages. Another woman came up to me and introduced herself as Sue from next door. When I gave her my name, she took my hand and said "right this way." She was acting as some kind of gatekeeper.

Sue pulled me through the house, explaining along the way that people had started arriving early in the morning—neighbors, faculty, TV3 staff, people from church, former students and swimmers, even parents of swimmers. "They all want to help, they all want to honor Coach."

We went out the screen door and onto the deck. Laura was talking to someone else and when she saw me, she came over and threw her arms around my neck. She didn't say anything, but she sobbed for about thirty seconds.

She stopped crying as abruptly as she'd started. She unclenched from me, wiped her tears away, and it was like she had never been crying.

"Doyle, I'm so glad you came."

"I'm sorry about Coach. I'm going to miss him like mad."

"I know. Me too." She launched another short bout of tears, and I put my arms around her this time. I could tell that she'd been doing this for a while—going from person to person, hugging, crying, cutting it short.

"Is there anything I can do?"

"Yes, there is," she answered quickly. "Two things. Would you do Coach the honor of saying a few words at the service on Friday?"

"Umm...I'm really bad at speeches." What I thought was: ain't no way that's gonna happen. I was the kid who never raised his hand in class, who abhorred speaking publicly.

"Please, Doyle. I want you to do it and Coach wanted it too. We talked about it."

"You and Coach talked about...what?"

"After his surgery four years ago we talked about 'what ifs'—what if he died? We made...arrangements. We talked about memorial services."

"And my name came up during that discussion?" She nodded. I have to admit, I was creeped by that thought. "Well, I'll think about it. What was the second thing you wanted me to do? Whatever it is, I'll do it."

"Oh...yes...what was it?" Just then Sue arrived with someone Laura had to greet—an elderly gentleman. Another hug, another sob. I waited. After a couple minutes she said "excuse me" to the old guy and pivoted toward me.

"I'm in no hurry," I said, "but...was there a second thing?"

"Mmm. There's a box."

"A box?"

"Coach had some swimming mementos in a box. I don't know the meaning of the things he put in there, and I thought perhaps you could explain them."

"I understand," I said. "I'll take a shot at it, but I'm not sure I'm the best person for this."

"I think you are. You're always looking for meaning. Coach liked that about you."

"Okay. Where's the box?"

"You'll have to forgive me, I'm a wreck right now. There's just so much going on."

"No problem," I said. "Tell you what. I'll take the box, go hang out on campus for a while, and I'll come back tonight and we'll go through it. After things have settled down."

She went away and returned with the box. It was a shoe box. She told me to get some food. I took the box, grabbed a sandwich and hopped in the Taurus. I could have walked to campus, but I knew there would be plenty of places to park. It was summer, and half the faculty was at Laura D's house. I parked at the bottom of Chapel Square, the main grassy knoll on campus where I used to hang out during my college days. I took a towel from my swim bag to spread out on the grass for my picnic.

I had forgotten how pretty The Square was. The campus dated back to the 1830s and grew outwardly from The Square. The trees had seen ten generations of students come and go. Grass covered The Square, with the exception of two paved paths that crossed diagonally. The grass sloped up a gentle hill, on top of which sat Staunton Chapel. Three Rivers was founded as a religious school, but like most such colleges, it lost its religiousness decades ago. The chapel was used for weddings of Three Rivers alumni, as well as concerts and the occasional funeral. Coach D's memorial service was going to take place there.

As I started my picnic, I noticed there were no students criss-crossing The Square. When school's in session it's a lively place, full of determined people walking to their classes, lazy people taking naps, playful people tossing Frisbees, passionate people making out. Now it was empty, quiet.

I finished my sandwich in about two minutes. After I brushed away the crumbs, I reached for the shoe box and opened it for the first time. There wasn't much in there. On first glance, it looked like there were a couple old photos, some handwritten notes, a medal, a couple ribbons, two newspaper clippings and a stopwatch. It was an odd assortment of artifacts. I knew, for example, that Coach D had earned a few All American certificates that weren't in the box. He had received some nice coaching awards that weren't there either. The medal hung from a red ribbon, signifying second place, and the other ribbons said "Heat Winner" so they didn't seem very significant. The clippings weren't about him.

I closed the box after a cursory perusal. It was going to take some thought. I wasn't up to any heavy duty thinking right then, so I leaned back and put my hands behind my head. The leaves on the trees were fluttering eastward, like backstroke flags in a steady breeze. I drifted off into a light nap. When I woke up, the sun had given way to clouds. I picked up the shoebox and the towel, and headed for the Taurus. I dropped off the box and grabbed a suit and a pair of goggles. The Three Rivers pool was only two blocks off The Square. I walked it.

I wasn't looking for a workout. I just wanted to take in the sights and smells of the old pool. When I got to the building, the door was locked. I could tell there was nobody inside, and why would there be? I walked around the building, remembering the time when I was a freshman and a couple of the seniors decided they wanted to take a "midnight swim" on a Saturday night. They rousted me out of bed and accumulated a gang of ten teammates. We got to the pool building, which was locked, and figured out a way to force open a window. I was elected to crawl through the window and let everyone in. I was scared walking through the dark building and relieved when I got to the door and saw that the others hadn't ditched me. We splashed around in the pool for about an hour; I thought it was kind of lame. We didn't do any damage, and sneaked out quietly at the end. Somebody had seen us, however, and reported us to Campus Security, who reported it to the administration, which came down on Coach Dewey. He read us the riot act, and I felt ashamed, like I had let him down.

After finishing that lovely reminiscence, I came to a door that was locked but wasn't completely shut. I opened it. Sorry to let you down again, Coach. I pulled the door open and the scent of chlorine filled my nostrils. I went in.

On the way to the locker room, I walked down a long corridor lined with framed All American certificates. They dated back to the 1950s and went past my time. I looked at the names as I passed: guys whose records I had broken, teammates of mine, guys who had beaten a couple of my records.

I put on my suit and walked through the shower room to the pool. I took in the full panorama before diving in: lane markers rolled up on a giant spool; a pace clock with black and red hands on the wall; a record board; black and red backstroke flags; one and three meter diving boards. I absorbed the scene as if I would never see it again.

I just swam. There was no purpose, no meaning to it. Thoughts floated in and out of my head. I remembered the night we beat Kenyon in a dual meet, a huge upset, and we threw Coach D into the pool. I remembered Senior Night, my last meet in the pool, when my parents came and got flowers presented to them and hearty hugs from Coach D. My mom was crying.

I don't know how long I swam. I didn't count laps or strokes, or look at any clocks. At one point, I noticed there was another person with me, not in the water but sitting on a starting block. I stopped. It was Joe Salazar, the new assistant coach. He had graduated from Three Rivers two years before I started there, but I'd seen him a few times.

"Hey, Joe," I said, as I reached up to shake his hand. He was smiling, so I was pretty sure he wasn't there to kick me out.

"Great to see you, Doyle. I was looking for you up at Laura's house. She told me you'd be down here."

"It's good to be here," I said. "I just wish it were for a different reason." The smiling stopped.

"Yeah. What a great guy. Hey, feel free to swim as long as you want. Sorry to interrupt you. I really just wanted to say hi."

"I think I'm done." I could tell he had more on his mind. I got out of the pool and grabbed my towel. "Congratulations, by the way, on being named Assistant Coach. I guess you're the head coach now."

"Yeah," he said. "I was called in to Adrian's office this morning and that's who told me the news about Coach D. He said I was a little young to be a head coach but he has a lot of confidence in me. So I have the interim job. I'm daunted by it, frankly, and I could use a lot of help."

"You have my complete support," I said. "I'm just down the road, and I'll help you any way I can."

"Do you want to do some coaching?"

And there it was. He was asking me to be his assistant coach. Since turning down Coach Dewey's offer, I'd grown a bubble on my thumb, tanked in Omaha and made Curtains mad. I had a chance to reverse what looked like a bad decision. I should have taken some time to think about it.

In *Moby Dick*, Captain Ahab's pursuit of the white whale becomes more and more irrational the further he goes. Every pitfall seen by the crew as an omen of doom, Ahab sees as confirmation of his destiny—his obsession becomes all the more resolute. He vows to follow the whale not just around the Horn but "around perdition's flames before I give him up." No logic can account for it; it cannot be explained. I was tethered to a whale myself.

"Boy, I'd love to. But I—I can't, Joe. It's probably not very smart of me, but I have all my eggs in one basket and I need to keep them there."

"I totally understand," he said. "I'd give my right hand for a shot at the Olympics."

When I drove up to Laura D's house that evening, there were more cars than ever. I decided to drive around a bit, go down to the river, examine the contents of the box a bit more, and come back later. I did that, and when I arrived back at about 9:00 p.m., there was no crowd of cars. A few people were just leaving, and I caught sight of Curtains.

"Coach," I called, and several people turned and looked at me. "Curtains," I said, and he walked toward me. It was dark out.

"Did I miss a tough workout?" I asked him.

"Do you know what, Doyle? I just spent two hours in that house, and everybody was talking about *you*. I did not know you were such a celebrity." He knew. I was a very minor celebrity and only in Three Rivers. Even in Kalamazoo no one knew me.

"They're probably wondering what I'm going to say on Friday. Got any ideas for me?"

"No, I am no good at that stuff. You will do fine. Tell a joke."

Curtains was being nice to me, which made me feel worse about my prickliness in Omaha. I needed to make amends, but it would have to wait.

I proceeded inside with the shoe box. Laura met me just inside the door and gave me another hug, this time without the sobbing. She looked exhausted.

"Your timing is good," she said, "the last few people just left."

"Must've been a rough day."

"Oh my." She took a deep breath and let it out. "I'm looking forward to tomorrow." I knew from Sue, the gatekeeper, that Laura's daughters and their families would be arriving throughout the next day. They all lived out-of-state.

We sat down in the living room and she insisted that I sit in Coach D's favorite chair, which also creeped me out a little. She sat near me, on a couch. I had the box on my lap, but I could tell that Laura was still a bit wrecked. I wanted to help her get through it.

"I thought about the speech," I said. She looked at me expectantly. "I'll do it."

"Good." She put her hand on her chest, just below her neck. "Thank you. That's a load off my mind."

"I wouldn't expect too much. I don't have any idea what to say or how to say it. But I'll work hard on it."

"I hope it's not a burden on you. I hope it's…meaningful to you."

"I'm just worried that my words won't measure up. Coach D was like a…." I started to choke up. "He was like a second father to me." It made her cry, and this time it was unchecked. I knew what to do. I reached across and held her hand until she was done.

"We never told you this, Dear, but we wanted you to marry one of our daughters." She sighed. "They were too old for you." We both got a chuckle.

She looked at the box and I felt like she was ready. I opened it. She had already seen the contents, and was just waiting for the explanation.

"I haven't come up with a unifying theme," I started. "I don't know what criteria he used to select the things that went in this box. I have some ideas on the individual items, though, and maybe we can take them one by one." She smiled and nodded.

I pulled out the medal attached to the red ribbon.

"This looks really old to me. It's for a second-place finish. The swimmer on the medal is a male. I'm guessing that this is a medal awarded to Coach for one of his swims when he was a kid. Why he saved this one, I don't know. Maybe it was his first-ever medal. Or maybe it was a memorable swim for him, like the first time he broke 30 seconds in the 50 free."

As I displayed the medal, I could feel something rough on the back. I turned it over and there was some engraving, barely visible. It said "Water Wonderland." I read it out loud and explained that the Water Wonderland meet was a big summer meet in Detroit. People from all over the Midwest came to that meet. I guessed that little Bobby Dewey had broken through at that meet and turned some heads. Maybe the guy who beat him became famous.

Next I pulled out the "heat winner" ribbons. These had female swimmers displayed on them. I asked Laura if her daughters had been swimmers. I was surprised I didn't already know the answer.

"Oh yes, they all swam when they were kids. Coach was so proud of them. He was just like all the other parents, making a fool of himself cheering for his little girls. They weren't any good. They gave it up before high school."

The two newspaper clippings came next. They were both seriously yellowed. One included a photo of a soldier in uniform, wearing a medal, sitting in a wheelchair, shaking hands with the President. I showed it to Laura and asked if she knew the guy. She squinted for a second.

"That's Lawrence McKevitch. He swam for Three Rivers." I had never heard of him. He hadn't been an All American, never set a record as far as I knew.

"Well," I said, "it says here he won the Congressional Medal of Honor, which is awarded for bravery. It's a huge honor, the biggest in the military. Most of those medals are awarded posthumously."

We looked at each other after I said the word "posthumously." I was becoming increasingly sensitive to words that make women cry. I wanted to take it back, but Laura seemed okay. I moved on.

The other clipping was from the local Three Rivers paper and carried no photo. The headline was "TR Drowns Kenyon In Swim Dual." The story was only three paragraphs. That was the biggest swimming victory—probably the biggest *sports* victory—in the history of Three Rivers, and it barely got mentioned in the local paper. I was glad to see it among Coach D's highlights.

Laura remembered the night we beat Kenyon. She was there. It was the only time she could remember Coach D being thrown into the pool against his will. When we won conference championships, he expected it, brought a change of clothes, sometimes even vaulted into the pool off the diving board. No one, not even Coach D, expected us to beat Kenyon. Laura remembered being horrified when we threw him in.

"His wallet was in his pocket. He had his watch on. His reading glasses, his keys…. He had no dry clothes to change into. I made him strip naked and put a towel around himself, with a winter coat on top, for the ride home. I didn't want him wearing wet clothes in the car. He didn't care. He was so thrilled." She was laughing and crying at the same time.

All of the other items provoked memories for Laura. Except the stopwatch. That was a puzzle for both of us. I asked her if he had bought it himself, or maybe someone had given it to him as a gift. She didn't know. A lot of coaches didn't even use hand watches because of the sophistication of modern timing systems.

Most scoreboards display times and splits, so hand watches are unnecessary. Three Rivers had never gotten a nice system like that. I remembered this watch hanging around Coach Dewey's neck at swim meets. It was a non-descript old-school watch, analog.

I was about to hit the start/stop button to see if the watch still worked, when Laura said "wait." We could both see that the watch had a time on it—it hadn't been cleared. "Can you read what the time is?" Laura asked.

I had to look at it for a few seconds to decipher what it said. I wasn't used to analog. "Forty-three nine," I said. When I figured out the time, I knew instantly what it was, but Laura needed an explanation. "This is the watch Coach used to get my split on the anchor leg of the final relay against Kenyon. That was a pretty fast split for a Division III dual meet, though it would have been fairly pedestrian in Division I. The watch went in the pool with Coach when we threw him in. I guess the moment was meaningful enough for Coach D to retire the watch on the spot, without clearing it. He must have put it in the shoe box the night of the Kenyon meet. He wanted to freeze that moment forever."

The stopwatch was a succinct summary of Coach D's career. He was an old-school coach who produced swimmers and teams that were good, and one magical night they did something great. The rest of the items in the box confirmed that Coach was interested more in moments, individuals, teams, than he was in his own accomplishments.

"This has been so helpful," Laura said when it was done. "I needed this."

"Me too. Let me know what else I can do."

"I want you to take the watch."

"No, no, I can't take the watch," I said.

"You're the only person who will appreciate it, or even understand it." She was right, and it would've been a nice trophy.

"It's cool, but that watch is about Coach, not me. If I take it, people will think it's about me. *I* will think it's about me. You need to keep it." She kept it.

There was one more hug before I reached the Taurus. I drove back to Huron Springs. That night, alone in my apartment, it hit me like a tsunami. I'd been living in a stupid self-imposed exile for weeks. Coach D, who was not my equal in the pool, or probably even in the classroom, was adored by hordes of people. That's what mattered at the end of his life. What about my life? I had people who loved me, sure. But I acted like that wasn't important, like it was a distraction. And now, one of them was gone from the face of the earth.

Coach D's death left me more alone than ever. For three straight nights, my sleep was haunted by the image of Coach D, sitting on the starting block while I swam in the dungeon pool at Three Rivers.

I went to practice the rest of the week. I forgot about the bubble for a while. I pushed myself hard and put in some fast swims. During warm-ups, kicking sets and other down times, I thought about the speech—the eulogy, I guess, but that was a word I didn't use and didn't like. I talked to a lot of people about it, trying to get some useful tips. I got nothing. I had no prior experience to go on and nothing came naturally to me. Working on the speech took effort.

When Friday came, I got dressed up in my black suit and red tie. Archie picked me up right on time, for the first time ever. He didn't even know Coach D or Laura, and Archie would be a fish out of water at a funeral. He came solely as my friend. We stopped at Molly's place, which I hadn't expected. I got out to let her take shotgun, and she hugged me hard without saying anything. I got in the back seat. I guess Archie had arranged it with Molly for her to go along. He figured I needed her support. Molly didn't know Coach D either. She must have taken a day off work.

I sat quietly in the back seat, watching the familiar freeway sights while Archie and Molly chatted quietly in the front. Halfway there, Molly turned to look at me and studied my face for a few seconds. She said "How're you doing, Doyle?" She had a look of concern on her face. I don't like that look on her. I like to see her smile.

"I'm gonna need you to shout some slogans at me," I said, and her face went slowly from fog lights to high beam. She had the old glint in her eye, the old crooked smile. The guilt I'd been carrying since the fiasco at Brewhaha drained out of me.

"GO, DOYLE! YOU CAN DO IT! YOU'RE MY HERO! YOU'RE SO SMART! AND HANDSOME!"

It was just what I needed. Not the slogans but the humor. And Molly, laughing. She laughed so hard, I could count her teeth. Most people don't laugh like that on the way to a funeral.

We got there an hour early. It was a hot day and I was sweating in my monkey suit. We had planned to stroll around the campus, but because of the heat and my nervousness, I decided I needed air conditioning. Molly and Archie left me alone in a little side room off the chapel, and I sat there thinking about Coach D and my speech. There was a clock on the wall and I glanced at it from time to time. It moved slowly, like the clock in a ready room. The longer I sat in there, the more it seemed like a ready room. I was there to think, to prepare, to weigh the task ahead. Giving a eulogy weighed a lot—more than any race I'd ever swum.

When the time came, the little chapel was packed to the rafters. The balcony was full and people were standing in the side aisles. It had the feel of a championship meet. Anticipation filled the air. People had come to witness and to honor.

I sat in the front pew, between Laura and Molly. They sang a few songs, and the preacher gave a message based on Coach D's favorite Bible passage, which was in the book of Job, chapter 38. I didn't really listen. I had memorized a portion of my speech so as not to blow it under pressure and I was rehearsing it in my mind. My time came.

I started by telling a couple stories. Laura forbidding Coach from wearing his wet clothes in the car after the Kenyon meet drew some laughter. I told about Coach D sitting on the starting block while I did extra workouts. I talked about the shoe box. Then I came to the memorized part:

"Coach Dewey was a swim coach and a math teacher. Swimming is all about yards and laps and times. You measure a swimmer with a stop watch. A swimmer is defined by numbers. In math, you measure with a ruler, a protractor, a slide rule. It's all objective, fair, clean. Coach Dewey was into measuring things.

"How do you measure a man? How do you measure a life? How can we measure Coach Dewey's life? Do we have the tools?

"He generated some numbers in his life. His best time in his best event, the 100 meter breaststroke, was 1:06.5. His best finish was sixth in the nationals. He was a three-time All-American. He coached 43 All-Americans and 23 conference champion teams. He had four daughters. One wife. He lived 68 years, nine months and six days.

"Those are pretty good numbers, but they don't come close to measuring the man. I don't think Coach Dewey would want to be measured by those numbers. Or by any numbers.

"There are words that describe him better than numbers: love, sacrifice, respect, influence. Those words are hard to measure. If we tried to measure those things and add up the numbers, we would be measuring and adding for a long time. Everyone in this chapel today would be part of it, as would hundreds of people who aren't here.

"If we were able to reduce those things to a number, Coach Dewey would have a very high number. He would be a giant. A world record holder. And he wouldn't care. Because he didn't care about his own numbers, he cared about other people's.

"Coach Dewey was a sweet man. If I had him back for five minutes, I wouldn't tell him what a great coach he was or what a great teacher he was or what a great swimmer he was. I would just tell him I love him. We all do, Coach. So long."

The rest of the service was a blur, except I remember the vigor with which the organist played the last hymn. *"The love of God is greater far than tongue or pen can ever tell."* There were no hymnals in the front row, but the two women beside me knew the words and I just listened to them sing. *"Oh love of God, how rich and pure, how measureless and strong."* They belted it.

Afterwards there were lots of tears and hugs and handshakes. I met Coach D's daughters, a few other relatives and a bunch of former swimmers.

Archie had been blending into the crowd, avoiding attention. I hadn't seen him since shortly after we arrived. When it was all over, he came up to me and shook my hand. "Solemn," he said. It was his way of saying I nailed it. After shaking my hand, he put both his arms around my shoulders. It was the first time Archie ever hugged me outside a pool. I hugged him back, and we held it longer than straight guys normally hold a hug.

The crowd dwindled, as did my adrenaline. Laura stayed until the last guest had left. She came up to me and held both my hands and kind of sized me up. She was smiling. Smiling! She looked like she was proud of me or something.

"*Bravo*, Doyle."

She reminded me of the title character in *Mrs. Miniver*, whose world is rocked by the uncertainties and tragedies of World War II as it arrives on British soil. With her husband and son off in the fight, and her younger children asleep upstairs, she encounters a German soldier in her kitchen. She waits for her moment, grabs the German's gun, and turns him in to the police. Like Mrs. Miniver, Laura D wasn't decimated by difficulty. She transcended it.

I wasn't wholly pleased by the thanks and congratulations I got for my speech. I felt inadequate, like the words had not encapsulated the man, like the speech was good but not great. Maybe that was fitting.

CHAPTER 12

Swimming history is full of gutsy competitors who overcame obstacles to achieve success.

The first swimming events of the modern Olympics were held in the Bay of Zea off the coast of Greece in early April 1896. In the 1200 meter event, a boat took the eight competitors out to sea and they swam to shore. The water was cold—about 50° F—and the waves were as high as 12 feet. The winner of the 1200 free, Alfréd Hajós of Hungary, was quoted as saying afterward, "my will to live completely overcame my desire to win." The admiring Greeks nicknamed Hajós the "Hungarian Dolphin." He learned to swim after his father drowned in the Danube. At a banquet after the Olympics, the King of Greece asked Alfréd where he had learned to swim. His answer: "In the water."

The next Olympics featured an event called the Obstacle Swim. It was held in the River Seine. Swimming in the Seine is enough of an obstacle for me—it seems disgusting. Competitors in the Obstacle Swim in 1900 had to climb up and over a pole, crawl over a boat and swim under another boat in addition to swimming 200 meters. Freddy Lane of Australia was the champion. He learned to swim at the age of four after his brother saved him from drowning in Sydney Harbor.

One of the great obstacle-transcending stories in swimming comes from the 1960 Olympics. Jeff Farrell was the brightest U.S. star in sprint freestyle, the best hope to lead the Americans to success over the Australians, who had dominated the freestyle events and relays in 1956. Six days before the Olympic Trials, Farrell's appendix burst and his roommate found him on the floor during the night, writhing in pain. He was rushed to the hospital, where his coach shouted instructions to the doctors. The doctors laughed at the coach's assumption that Farrell could still swim in the Trials, because they knew it would take three weeks to recover from the surgery. The U.S. Olympic Committee and swim coaches discussed various options for Farrell to make the team without participating in the Trials. They came up with a compromise where he could compete in a special swim-off two months later. Farrell rejected the compromise. He wanted to try to make the team the normal way, and he didn't want some other swimmer to earn a spot at the Trials, only to lose it later in a swim-off. Farrell swam in the Trials with bandages around his abdomen. He qualified for the team, and in the Olympics he led the U.S. to two relay victories over the Australians.

Steve Genter suffered a collapsed lung a week before the Olympics in 1972. He underwent a painful procedure in a Munich hospital without anesthesia. He was sewn up with 13 stitches. He couldn't take painkillers because they were on the disallowed drug list. Genter was determined to swim despite the pain. During the 200 free finals, the stitches came open and blood trickled out. Genter bled his way to a silver medal, and won a gold in the 4 x 200 relay.

Tom Dolan had severe exercise-induced asthma, made worse by tracheal stenosis—a narrowed windpipe. He was a distance specialist and his best event was the 400 I.M., which is recognized as the event that determines the best all-around swimmer. Tom Dolan took "oxygen debt" to a new level. At one practice session he passed out on the pool deck. He overcame his limitations to win two Olympic gold medals in the 400 I.M. He owned the world record for eight straight years.

The ability to overcome obstacles is one of the great life lessons of sports. The heroes we love the most are the ones who have suffered setbacks along the way.

The south wall of the Don Jackson Natatorium at Southern Michigan is made of glass panels, and outside the glass is a row of sugar maples. We stared at those trees a lot—they were the only true scenery we had. In autumn, the leaves on the sugar maples turned from green to bright orange and we'd watch the transformation. The color change is the result of a reduction in the supply of chlorophyll. Swimmers can relate. Our faces change color when the oxygen supply gets low. The best color comes right before you drop dead.

The passing of Coach Dewey, the reliving of memories with Laura and the delivery of the speech released me in a way. They took my focus off myself for a while. I spent a couple Sundays with my parents out at the farm, relaxing, talking to the horses. Being less talented than Archie, and having a bubble on my thumb, seemed less important. I was free to just swim. I enjoyed every workout, and I was really swimming fast. The fact that I was beating Archie almost all the time was secondary, though I noticed it, and so did he.

Fall brought my 25th birthday. There was, as always, a birthday swim.

The birthday swim is a Team Jaguar tradition, and other teams do it too. A birthday is acknowledged by a special swim workout. At Team Jaguar, the birthday swim workout is harder than usual.

"Okay everybody," Curtains began, as the team gathered for the afternoon workout. "As you know, Doyle has his birthday today. He is 25 years old. Congratulations, old man. To celebrate, we will do 25 four-hundreds. Be sure to thank Doyle for privilege of doing this set."

There were groans all around. The set added up to 10,000 meters—more than six miles. It would be grueling and mind-numbing. There would be very little rest. Almost two hours of straight swimming.

"Thanks a lot, Doyle," Archie grumbled. Right, like I could do something about it.

I asked Crack if he wanted to lead, but he said "no way. You Da Man, man." So I led the whole set.

The birthday swim was all Curtains hoped it would be. The first ten were slow. My shoulders felt tight. My arms felt heavy. The thought of how many more we had left was painful. Like the birthday itself, there was nothing I could do about it but slog on.

As the set progressed and 15 became 20, my mind wandered. I must have been hungry, because I thought a lot about food. I imagined my teeth penetrating the sweet nougat of a candy bar. Food is the worst thing a swimmer can think about during a long set. You're a long way from getting any, so you're just torturing yourself.

By the 20th repeat, I got a second wind. My arms started feeling lighter, and I got into a rhythm. My times started descending. My mind became more focused on technique and body systems. The same thing was happening to Crack and Archie, because they were staying right with me. The last 400 was a race. It felt like I was body surfing, swimming downhill. I was on top of the water. I felt exhilarated and kept pushing the pace harder and harder.

I went 4:00 on the last 400, an incredible time under the circumstances. Archie was right behind me, having passed Crack. We high-fived each other when it was over. Nobody said anything, but we all felt like we had crossed a threshold, gotten over a hump. We were utterly depleted, yet enlivened.

The time came to make my peace with Curtains. I stopped by his office after the birthday swim. As usual, his face was practically touching the computer monitor, and he had his back to the door. I knocked, even though the door was open. He kept glaring at the screen.

"Hello, Doyle. I was expecting you." I sat down and waited until he was ready. When he turned toward me, I gave him a little speech I had prepared.

"I've been thinking a lot about Omaha, Coach, and I just wanted to say I'm sorry. I shouldn't have doubted you. I'm back on track, I think."

"Good." He smiled. "You know, I have seen swimmers who were demoralized by a bad swim and never bounced back. I have seen other swimmers who gritted their teeth and dug in when the chips were down. I always took you for one of the latter."

"I see myself that way too."

"Then here is what I want you to do with Omaha. It was a bad swim, that is all. But do not forget it. Keep it in your mouth and chew on it, get the full flavor. Never forget the taste."

"I will," I said, "I mean…I won't." All I could taste was chlorine. It has a bitter after-taste and makes your mouth cottony for hours after practice. "By the way, the bubble on my thumb—"

His reading glasses had been perched halfway down his nose. He took them off and peered into me. "You remember Boyd Watkins?"

"Yeah. Great middle-distance freestyler. I saw him on TV a few times."

Boyd Watkins had swum for Curtains at SM, finishing his career with a handful of NCAA championships and three Olympic medals.

"Right," Curtains affirmed. "He was like you. Very smart person, good student, really understood the science of swimming. He worried a lot."

That surprised me. Watkins was somewhat of a legend.

"What did Boyd Watkins worry about?"

"He had a crossover."

A crossover is when your hand, in the underwater pull, goes underneath your ribs on the opposite side instead of underneath the centerline of your body. The hand then sweeps back across at the end and finishes at the typical place, so it travels a longer path in going from Point A to Point B.

"I saw him in the Olympics on TV," I remembered, "but I was pretty young. I'm not sure I noticed anything wrong with his stroke."

"You could not tell from watching above water," Curtains continued. "His stroke looked great on top. I spent hours watching him through the underwater window. When I told him about the crossover, he became very worried. We worked on it for about three weeks. This was during his freshman year."

"What happened?"

"We worked on it, but he could not change it. We did drills designed to force him to change. He did drills fine, then when we went back to regular swimming, the crossover was as prominent as ever. So we gave up."

"He just continued with an imperfection?"

"After thinking about it, the crossover was not so bad. It seemed like too much effort, but there was a benefit that went with it. He got extra roll. Watkins had the lowest stroke count of all my swimmers. We decided it was not a disadvantage, just something unique about his stroke. From then on, he was proud of it."

I made a mental note that Watkins had won his NCAA championships and his Olympic medals *after* giving up on changing the crossover.

"So, does the Watkins story have something to do with my bubble?"

"Hell no. I only thought of Watkins because I just got an e-mail from him. He was appointed federal judge in Indiana, youngest one ever." Curtains never bragged about his coaching, but he occasionally bragged about his swimmers. Nine times out of ten, the bragging had to do with life rather than swimming.

"You said there was a benefit that went with his crossover. Is there any benefit that goes with my bubble?"

He put his glasses back on. "We will see." He said it like it was possible, like it depended on me. It gave me a drop of hope, but a gallon of confusion. And it was clear he meant it that way, because he turned back to his computer screen.

One thing I took away from the Watkins story was that you can still swim fast even if your stroke is different. In fact, some of the "different strokes" have revolutionized the sport. Before Mike Barrowman, breaststrokers swam a flat, straight-ahead style. Barrowman swam it with a lot of up and down movement, like a sine wave. Everybody does that now. David Berkoff developed the "Berkoff Blastoff" in backstroke, in which he swam most of the way underwater. Misty Hyman did the same in butterfly. FINA made a new rule to regulate the amount of underwater swimming that is allowed in those strokes. Those were folks who thought, and swam, outside the lines, and they advanced the sport.

Would the bubble be my ticket to swimming legend? The Berkoff Blastoff, the Watkins Crossover, the Wilson Bubble—no, it was preposterous. The conversation with Curtains had decreased my anxiety level, both because of the hope that my bubble wouldn't be debilitating and because I was back on Curtains' good side. But the bubble was still there.

"DEEDLY DEE?" I texted Molly, hoping for a chance to make peace with her. I was on a roll with peace.

"DDDDD****." It was a good sign.

"WHERE U @?"

"BATES."

Molly worked two evenings a week at the campus counseling clinic as part of her psychology program. Under the supervision of a senior psychologist, she counseled students with emotional problems. The clinic was in an old gabled two-story house across the street from campus. It was kind of dilapidated, with loose shutters and peeling gray paint. They didn't get the real psychos there, but Alfred Hitchcock would have loved the place. So I named it Bates Motel.

I still didn't want to show my face at Brewhaha, so I walked up the hill to Bates. Inside the door, I quickly scanned the place from left to right: a hallway on the left leading back to the counseling rooms; a makeshift reception desk in the middle with no one sitting behind it; and a waiting room with a big couch and four plush chairs. There was nobody waiting.

Molly appeared and came toward me. I got a good look at her. She had her hair pulled back in a ponytail this time. Her glasses were new; the frames were jaunty. She was wearing a gray sweater with a hypnotic pattern of colored wavy lines, and a short skirt—but no knees, darn! She had on black tights under the skirt.

There's always something reassuring to me about the sight of Molly. The glasses are reassuring. Her quirky, changing looks are somehow reassuring to me. Her upturned mouth, the opposite of my dad's, is reassuring. It was good to see her after all the time we'd spent apart, punctuated only by the Dewey memorial.

As she got close, she stopped in her tracks and said "whoa, Doyle, your hair is scary."

I'd been letting it grow and stopped bothering to comb it. It was frizzed out and tangled. I tried to smooth it with my hand, but that just created static. "Think I should get a Mohawk?"

She'd gotten close enough to reach up and touch my hair. "That won't help," she said. Her nose was scrunched. "The scariest part is the color. Or… lack of it."

We hugged. I didn't mind joking about my hair. It was a badge of honor, actually. Ruined hair meant hard work in the pool.

Molly grabbed me by the hand and led me into the kitchen, which doubled as a break room. I sat down at a table. "Tea?" she offered. I hate tea, but I answered "sherr." She poured the tea, set down two mugs, and sat in a chair across from me. I took my first sip of the tea and almost gagged. It tasted like flowers.

"It's chamomile," she said. "Like it?" I nodded.

I reached across the table and grabbed her left hand, which made her smile. "I don't know what to say, Moll. We haven't really talked about that last time, at Brewhaha, when I blew it big time. Did I mention I was sorry?"

She waved her free hand. "Water off a duck's back."

"You sure? I've really been missing you."

"I've been missing you too. But let's not do us. Let's do you. Tell me what's going on."

I was a little wary. But she'd been smiling. She seemed sort of happy-like, in a good mood. And I like to do me. So I gave her what she was asking for.

"Okay, here goes. I have a problem. A swimming problem."

She rubbed her hands together, like she knew the good stuff was coming. "And you need some reassurance," she said.

"How did you know that?"

She smiled and took a sip of tea. "I guess I know you pretty well. There are some things about you that are—" she stroked her chin like she had a beard "—predictable." Darn, I was shooting for enigmatic.

"Well, you don't know what it is that's creating the need for reassurance."

"True," she said. "Let's hear it."

"I have a bubble on my thumb."

She took another sip, probably just to make sure she didn't burst out laughing. I was glad to be amusing her again with one of my strange problems, just like in the old days.

To make sure she got the point, I added "Curtains says I have one good hand…and one bad one." I held up my left hand and wiggled the thumb to show her. She slowly grew a wry smile.

"Hey, remember *The Beast With Five Fingers*?"

"Kinda. Peter Lorre?"

"Yeah. This dismembered hand goes around strangling people. And playing the piano." She made her hand crab-walk across the table as she was saying it.

"Did you have a point?"

"Talk about a bad hand. That's all I'm saying."

"You do realize that's science fiction. My problem is real."

"Sorry." She could barely suppress her delight. "Okay, show me again."

I held both hands up, so she could compare the good one to the bad one. She put her hands against mine. My hands are 30% bigger than hers. We looked at each other through spread fingers.

"And which thumb has the bubble?" She withdrew her hands.

I took the good hand down and stretched out the thumb on my left hand. She felt the thumb, took off her glasses and moved in for a close inspection.

"Hmm…your hand looks good to me. How's that for reassurance?"

"Insufficient." She smiled. I didn't.

"Oh, I get it." She felt my hand again, and took her time doing it. "*Wow!* What a *manly* hand. So strong, so big. You can do wonders with a great hand like that."

I was smiling on the inside, but tried to continue looking annoyed on the outside. I took a sip of my tea, she took a sip of hers, and we eyed each other through the steam. Her eyebrows were up.

"Please lower your eyebrows." She lowered them slowly, one at a time.

"Okay," she said. "I think I know something else about your bubble. Let's see…Archie doesn't have a bubble, does he?" My last ounce of enigma was gone.

"Bubbles are bad in swimming, 42. It's a sign of turbulence. It means there's an imperfection in my stroke." She pondered that for a second.

"And it bothers you that Archie has no such imperfection." I gave her the stink eye and she smiled.

"Curtains couldn't fix it," I said, because she was going to get there pretty soon anyway.

"What does Curtains say about it?"

"He says I shouldn't worry about it."

I could tell that Molly was working up some general truth. She always does. She's kind of predictable herself.

"Did you ever consider the possibility that this bubble might be a good thing?"

"A *good* thing? How could it be a good thing?"

"Well, first of all, I'm clueless about swimming, as you know. I have no idea what this bubble does to you in the water. I'm talking about life in general. Maybe this 'imperfection,' as you call it, has a purpose. Maybe it can help you mature or advance as a person."

As a *person*? I'm a swimmer. That's the person I am. "Explain."

She unwrapped a bite-size cupcake, cut it into four pieces with a plastic knife, and popped one of the pieces into her mouth. She chewed slowly for a few seconds, then it came to her.

"You're a searcher, Doyle. You look for meaning."

"And the bubble…?"

"The perfect don't search."

The perfect don't search—what does that mean? It sounded vague, but there were empirical data to support it. Archie is perfect and he doesn't search. Doyle is imperfect and he searches.

If I'm a searcher, how come I never seem to find anything? And what am I searching for? I'm searching for 3:36, that's what. But Molly was clearly thinking beyond swimming.

The best part of the whole conversation was that it was the old Molly—the wry smile, the jabs, the big picture. There had been no crying. I was tired of talking about my bubble and me.

"Let's do you now," I said cheerfully.

She shook her head. "I don't think so."

"C'mon, how about a tidbit?"

Her forehead wrinkled. "Okay." She paused and heaved a sigh. "I was seeing someone."

"Oh." I didn't see that coming.

"It's over already. I thought maybe you'd heard."

I drained the crappy chamomile tea, including the flower dregs at the bottom. They were hard to swallow. "Listen, you don't…."

"It was a mistake, okay? And don't blame yourself for it, either. It had nothing to do with you."

"Did he…."

"He didn't do anything wrong. It was me."

Internally, I reeled. I tried not to show it, but a grenade had gone off in the inner chambers of my heart. I missed a few beats. My blood lost oxygen. My first thoughts were irrational.

I thought: I bet it was Archie. It was suspicious that he knew where she lived, that she and he had arranged something behind my back on the day of the funeral. It had seemed like an incredible act of friendship at the time, but maybe I'm just gullible. Molly isn't his type, but he'd go after anything under the right circumstances. And he's competitive, even with me—*especially* with me. He'd do it to me. He would. And now, I'll have to kill him.

"Who is this guy?" I growled. I was plotting to make it a slow death. I'd just seen a documentary on TV about a woman who poisoned two husbands by getting them to drink small amounts of antifreeze over several months' time. I had some in the trunk of my Taurus.

"You don't know him. I appreciate your concern, but I'm way over it. It lasted like a minute."

My heart pumped hard for a few beats. It was catching up. Okay, it wasn't Archie. But it was serious. It was wrong. It changed my image of Molly. She'd been the solid one, the one with principles, the one with faith. Those very things were what I'd negligently disrespected at Brewhaha in May. And now, she'd violated them herself. I was disappointed in her, maybe even mad. Even her nonchalance troubled me. The old Molly would've been in tears by now.

The kitchen at Bates had two framed posters with flowers spelling out the words "Love" and "Peace." They were designed to soothe the psyche, just like the chamomile tea. They had the opposite effect on me.

"Want to talk about it?" I was restraining myself, but I could hear the edge in my voice.

"I really don't think you're qualified to counsel me." She craned her neck around to look down the hallway toward the counseling rooms. I got her point: she'd been professionally counseled. It was beyond me. But that only confirmed how serious it was.

"Look," she continued. "I don't want you to worry about it, so I'll tell you a couple things to ease your mind. This thing happened when I was… hmmm…out of touch with God." Ever since I'd known Molly, she'd always talked like she and God were next door neighbors. She'd been through a lot, though, and I knew she'd struggled with God over her mother's illness. "I guess I had a bubble of my own to deal with."

Yes, it was beyond me. I'm a dunce with God things. But I knew all about bubbles. My viewpoint shifted. Instead of being upset with her, I felt sorry for her. I'd had the napkins poised. I reached across the table and put them into her hand. It made her smile.

"Hey," she said, "I didn't want to do me in the first place. It's all good now. I'm teaching Sunday School, I applied to a PsyD program, and I cleaned out my purse. So I got all that going for me."

I thought about arguing. I thought about drilling down. I wanted to find out more. But she was keeping it short intentionally. I decided to play her light-hearted game, even though my heart was anything but light. I decided to honor her wishes instead of mine.

"And you look fabulous," I said. She really did.

Two other people, both women, came into the kitchen. They greeted Molly by name and said hi to me. Molly and I sat silently while the two women got their tea. A new thought came to me: it was my fault. She'd said it had nothing to do with me, but she was obviously protecting me, trying to avoid weighing me down. The fact is, I'd left her vulnerable. I'd disappointed her at a critical time. The whole thing could've been avoided if I hadn't been a pussycat.

The two women were lingering, and I was getting impatient. Molly read my face. I think there's a class on that in psych school. She made a "let's get out of here" gesture with her head. We stood up and took our mugs over to the sink. She walked me to the front door.

At the door, she put her hands on my shoulders, looked up into my eyes and said "by the way. The thing about you being a searcher—I like that about you." She got up on her tiptoes and gave me the slightest brush on the cheek; a barely perceptible kiss. Our glasses frames clinked. My face immediately turned volcano-hot, like at the end of a rugged set.

It brought things into focus for me. I'd gone through a swirl of thoughts and emotions—I'd blamed her, blamed the guy, blamed myself. In that tenth of a second after the kiss, I got to the bottom line. I asked myself: is she less desirable because she dallied? Am I less interested because she had a bubble? The answer was clear: no.

"Holy Moly…can we talk about doing us?"

"No way, Doyle!" She was laughing. "You go off and do your little swimming thing. When you're ready, if you ever are, well, we'll just see if I'm still available."

"Little swimming thing" was one of her pet phrases, an elbow in my ribs. I got it. She wasn't going to invest in me, and she wasn't going to distract me from swimming. The light-heartedness had replaced the Batman band-aids. It was her new veneer of protection.

It deflated me. This is why I was never good at romance. It's complicated. It's not enough to be right for each other. You can't just be at the same place, you have to be there at the same *time*.

Molly said "tootle-oo" as I walked away in the wrong direction. I was off my feed again. I looked down at my hands and remembered the feel of Molly's hands against them. It was a good feeling. Something had passed through her hands into mine, something immeasurable, like the eyeball energy transfer between old Norman and Archie. I was too focused on my bubble to notice it at the time, but as I walked away from Molly I felt it again. It made me smile.

I thought about what she'd said about my bubble—that it could have a purpose, it could be a good thing. Curtains had suggested something similar. I couldn't get my mind around it. I could see, of course, that I didn't have it as bad as the beast with five fingers, or the armless guy at the freeway off-ramp.

Not so bad, relatively speaking, but a *good* thing? How? If some grand purpose was being served, how could it be anything but an evil purpose?

What about *her* bubble? Could that have had a purpose? A benefit? I couldn't see it.

I tried to watch a movie on CMC, but the thoughts in my head kept me from concentrating. The feel of Molly's cheek on mine, her hands on mine—they stayed with me. I daydreamed about Molly and me being a couple—about holding her hand for real, about kissing her and hugging her like a real boyfriend. It was the first time I had swum those strokes in my mind.

I thought about the unnamed guy. It was best that I didn't know him, that I'd never seen him, that I couldn't picture him in my mind, doing stuff with Molly. I wondered what else had happened, what else she'd done during her dark period, what she'd said to God. As I drifted in and out of sleep on my recliner, in front of the TV, my mind tortured me with possibilities.

The tables had turned—I wanted to do us more than Molly did.

CHAPTER 13

Swimming is a sport for everybody, young and old, slow or fast. Age group competitions start with the "8 and under" age group, and toddlers have competed in these events. Masters swimming competitions are for the elderly, beginning at age 19. FINA keeps world records for masters, and there are records held by swimmers in the 100-104 age group. The number of competitors is small, but the competition is fierce in that age group.

In swimming, you know exactly where you stand. Performances are measured objectively and the results are there for everyone to see. In some sports, players who deserve to see action ride the bench because the coach doesn't notice them, or plays favorites. Not in swimming. Some sports pivot heavily on subjective calls made by human referees which are sometimes erroneous. This rarely happens in swimming.

There are all kinds of targets for swimmers to aim at. There are world records, national records, state records, varsity records, meet records and pool records. In addition to records, there are also qualifying standards, or "cuts," for various events. All of these are objective measurements of achievement, and there is always something within reach.

The universal standard of individual achievement is the "personal best." All swimmers know their personal best in their favorite event. Beating your PB is a lauded achievement. There are also goals that a swimmer can set, which may or may not correspond to records or cuts or PBs. Some of the greatest performances in history were swum by people whose goals went beyond world records.

There was a kid on my high school team named Bruno who was a terrible swimmer by most standards. I watched him underwater one time and his stroke was a disaster. Bruno was about 4'6" tall, his growth having been stunted by a childhood disease. The first time Bruno swam the 50 free, he took about 100 strokes per length and didn't even break a minute. He listened as the coach told us all to set goals that seemed just out of reach, slightly audacious. He set a goal of 40 seconds in the 50. The fastest swimmers in the state were swimming the 50 in about 20 seconds. Bruno swam the 50 in every meet, because he couldn't swim anything else, and his PB kept coming down. Everyone on the team knew Bruno's goal time. When he went 39.96 at the conference meet, he got the loudest cheer of anyone at the meet, and was the happiest kid in the pool. He came in last in his heat, and the guys on the other teams had no idea what the cheering was about.

Swimming is a sport in which physically-challenged folks can participate. There was a blind swimmer on one of the high school teams in our state. He had a teammate at each end of the pool tap him with a pole when it was time to do a flip turn. His flip looked like everyone else's. There have been deaf swimmers who made it to the Olympics. At the start, they watch for the strobe light, or if there isn't one, they watch the other swimmers and go when they go. I've seen a swimmer who had no legs compete very effectively. Her turns were a little unorthodox, but fast.

Swimming is available to people of all social classes and ethnic backgrounds. Anybody can join a swim team at a YMCA or a local municipal pool. Minorities have accomplished great things in the sport, including Olympic gold medals. I wish Team Jaguar had a dozen Kelton Murrays. The clock does not discriminate.

A new freshman arrived in the fall and made an immediate impact. His name was Desmond Walker, and he told us most people called him Des or Desi. His mother was Jamaican and his father was British. His skin was darker than mine, but lighter than Kelton's. His parents had moved to the States before he was born and raised him in the suburbs of Philadelphia. Before coming to SM, he was the second-fastest high-school kid in the country in the 500-yard freestyle.

Desmond Walker's most notable feature was his hair. He had loosely-stranded ropes coming out of his head and flowing in every direction. He never brushed it and it appeared unaffected by chlorine. Curtains told him it looked like his hair had its own ecosystem. He had bushy eyebrows that drooped downward at the sides. The overall look was lion-like. Someone called him "Leor" and it stuck. Okay, I'm the one who named him.

Leor's immediate impact had less to do with his looks than with his swimming. He wasn't afraid to go at it with Archie or anyone else. Like most freshmen who weren't sprinters, he started in one of the middle lanes. Curtains kept moving him over. He swam in Lane 2 for two weeks, then Curtains moved him into the animal lane.

We swam long course all fall. We did lactate sets once a month and you could see a progression in the times. Archie, Crack, Leor and I always did six 200 freestyle swims on eight minutes in our lactate sets. We all dropped our averages by a few tenths each month. I had the fastest times, then Archie, then Leor and Crack. Curtains was plotting the data on a graph. It looked impressive.

Leor was wet behind the ears and we figured it would be fun to haze him. He always wore his suit kind of loose and low. One day, after warm-up, Archie and I plotted a move. I grabbed Leor and held him, while Archie removed his suit and hurled it up on the deck. Leor just laughed and didn't even struggle. The best part of the plan was that Leor would have to humiliate himself by getting out and walking across the deck naked in front of everyone to get his suit. But he didn't get out. He swam the whole rest of the workout without a suit. We insulted him mercilessly and he just took it.

"Hey Leor, did your mom smoke dope with Bob Marley?" Archie taunted.

"Yah, mon," answered Leor, with a fake Jamaican accent. His mom had been a runner on the Jamaican national team. The kid had good genes.

Fall eventually gave way to winter. By mid-December, most people in Michigan are already sick of winter and ready to escape to somewhere warm.

The Michi-gander is a migrating snowbird. The top college swim teams in the north take winter training trips. The schools that want to save money send their teams to Florida. Curtains put Southern Michigan into the big time, so the team goes to Hawai'i. Archie and I were invited to tag along. We left the day final exams ended at SM, a week before Christmas. This was a trip only for the men; the women's team went to Puerto Rico.

On the way to Hawai'i, we stopped in Los Angeles and spent one night there. One of Curtains' friends was the coach at Mission Viejo, so we trekked down there for a workout. The club swimmers at Mission Viejo were all tan, and we were blindingly white, except for Leor. We swam a combined workout with the Mission Viejo team, and after about 7,000 meters, Curtains made a bet with the Mission Viejo coach. He would match Leor against any Mission Viejo swimmer for a 200 free challenge match. The winner's team would get to skip the rest of practice. You'd think it would be unfair, a club team against a college team, but Mission Viejo had the high schooler who had beaten Leor in the 500 the previous year. His name was Brett Mayhew, nickname: "Mayhem." It was Mayhem against Leor.

The Mission Viejo swimmers lined one side of the pool and we lined up on the other. The two swimmers stood behind their starting blocks. Mayhem looked fierce, like he was trying to psych Leor out. Leor's droopy eyebrows made him look totally relaxed. He just stood there while Mayhem stretched and hyperventilated and pounded his starting block with his fists. Our side took up a chant: "Lee-or, Lee-or, Lee-or." He nodded faintly in our direction.

Mayhem and Leor swam each other stroke for stroke the whole way. In the last 25 meters, Leor found another gear and put the race away. He won by almost a full body length. His time, according to the scoreboard, was 1:51.53, an amazingly fast time for an 18-year-old at the end of practice. This kid was for real. Leor made a lot of friends that day.

We landed in Honolulu at night. We stayed in apartments near the University of Hawai'i campus in Manoa, up the hillside from Waikiki beach.

The nighttime view down toward the lights of Waikiki was hypoxic.

Our swim practices were held at the Duke Kahanamoku Aquatic Complex at the University of Hawai`i. We called it "The Duke" for short. The Duke had an outdoor 50-meter pool and a separate 25-yard diving pool. Because several teams were there at the same time, we had to get up early and still had to share the pool with another team. The first week, we started practice at 5 a.m., which was fine because our bodies were used to eastern time. We shared the pool with a team from Minnesota. Our evening workout was at 5 p.m. and we shared the pool with a team from Ohio. At both workouts, we used four lanes and swam eight people per lane. There wasn't a lot of interaction with the other teams.

Archie and I had a car and we had few restrictions other than having to be at all the practices. The team had organized trips to Pearl Harbor and a pineapple plantation. Archie and I were allowed to miss those, but we went to Pearl Harbor. The thing that spooked me about Pearl Harbor was all the sailors who drowned during the attacks. Drowning has a special significance to swimmers. Most people who drown do so because they can't swim. If I found myself in the middle of the ocean, I wouldn't drown—I'd keep swimming until the sharks got me. But many of the sailors who drowned on December 7, 1941 were good swimmers. They were trapped underwater, right under my feet as I stood at the U.S.S. Arizona Memorial. Good swimmers, wanting to breathe, trying to emerge, and yet trapped, never to breathe again. I don't spend a lot of time thinking about bad ways to die, but that would be at the top of my list.

The day after the trip to Pearl Harbor, the team drove up to the North Shore between practices to watch the surfing at Waimea Bay. Most of the guys had never seen big-wave surfing and it was pretty impressive. Zumaya and Caruso knew how to surf and wanted to find some boards and get in the water, but Curtains had given explicit instructions about that. It was too dangerous. Not in an Olympic year. We weren't allowed to jump off the rocks into the water, either, though there were teenagers at Waimea challenging us to join them.

The restrictions chafed at Archie like brand-new boxers. (Yes, *Gentleman's Quarterly* wrote that Archie wears briefs, like it was something everyone wanted to know. But that was just the author's assumption based on the fact that swimmers wear nylon briefs in practice. I'm here to set the record straight. Archie wears boxers. I told you, he likes freedom.)

Archie was itching to get into the surf. I made a deal with him that the following day, we would break off from the group and go body surfing. The team would be heading for the pineapple plantation, and Archie had already denounced that trip as lame.

Archie woke up early the next morning, and I could tell that body surfing was on his mind. We had to complete a workout first, but that was just a prelude for Archie. He loaded up a backpack with board shorts and towels. I did the same. Archie wanted to go straight from the pool to the beach.

The workout was especially hard that morning. After we swam a rainbow set of 20 x 200 meters, Curtains made a deal with the Minnesota coach. They spread the fastest swimmers across the lanes and wanted us to race each other. Three Minnesota guys made the front row, as did Archie, Leor, Crack, Moses and I. The set was three 400-meter swims. On the first swim, we all had to finish at exactly the same time, and the time had to be 4:30. On the second one, we had to finish together at 4:20 or better. The last one was a pure race.

The first 400 was more difficult than we expected because every swimmer had a different approach to swimming 4:30. At the halfway point, there was about an 8-second spread between the fastest and slowest swimmers. I was in the middle, swimming in Lane 5, watching both sides. I was afraid that Crack, who was out in front, wouldn't slow down at the end. It all came together, though, and all eight of us touched at 4:30.

We failed to achieve the goal on the second 400, as only one Minnesota guy was capable of swimming a 4:20. On the last one, my goal was to beat Archie. It proved easier than usual. Archie must have been distracted by thoughts of body surfing. He coasted in at 4:09. I flirted with 4:00, but this was not a particularly fast pool, and it was early in the morning. I was happy with my 4:05. Curtains was furious with Archie and launched some rage on him.

"What the hell are you doing, Hunter Hayes? You are the world record holder and guys are beating you all over the place. I could beat you. Hell, my grandmother could beat you." He pulled the sandal off his right foot and threw it in Archie's lane. It skimmed across the surface and floated down the lane. "My flip-flop is faster than you are. Go, flip-flop, go! You are beating the world record holder!"

The Minnesota guys didn't know what to make of Curtains, so they watched the scene in silence. It was classic Curtains, nothing new to Team Jaguar, and even Archie knew that Curtains' anger was always short-lived. But Archie was miffed that he'd been embarrassed in front of the Minnesota guys. He picked the flip-flop out of the water and took dead aim. He played the break perfectly, and the flip-flop went straight for Curtains' head. Curtains turned just as it arrived, and it hit him right in the cerebellum. The Minnesota guys looked horrified. When Curtains turned around, he was laughing so hard he almost fell over.

"Okay, 200 cool down and get out of here," Curtains yelled when he was done laughing. "Stay out of the sun today because we are going to have a whale of a workout tonight."

Archie swam down to the far end of the pool and got out. He was avoiding Curtains. I followed him. He walked right through the showers and into the locker room. He put on his board shorts. I kept following, ruing the missed shower. When Archie was ready, he said "let's roll." I didn't even have my sandals on. I grabbed them and followed Archie out.

Our destination was Sandy Beach, on the southeast side of Oahu, about 15 minutes past Diamond Head. As soon as I reached the car, before Archie could let loose with an anti-Curtains tirade, I made sure to get in an encouraging word.

"That flip-flop hitting Curtains in the head is the highlight of the trip. I have that image frozen on my corneas."

"Dude, that guy's gonna be the reason I quit swimming."

We got in the car and I started driving. I always drove the rental cars—Archie had no interest in driving a PT Cruiser.

"He's just having fun with you," I said. "Pushing your buttons. Making you mad makes you swim faster and that's all he cares about."

"I don't like it," Archie muttered. "I want to break some rules."

That last statement poisoned the air like a water-fart (they're chlorine-enhanced). We were already breaking Curtains' directive to stay out of the sun. It made my pulse quicken just to do that. But Archie pays no heed to little rules. He was planning something much, much bigger.

"What do you have in mind, Arch?" I hesitated to ask.

"Let's go AWOL for a couple days. Pick up some women."

I looked at Archie and he looked at me. I was wearing the glasses that make me look smarter.

"Right. Look who you're with here." He and I had discussed the fact that I hadn't actually hooked up with Camille.

"Are you kidding me? I can get you any babe you want." It remained one of his life's unfulfilled missions.

"Babes aren't the issue. The issue is, we're swimmers in training. You're the best swimmer in the world. I'm trying to make it to Paris. I can't go AWOL for a couple days, and neither can you."

He knew I was right, but he didn't look defeated.

"All right," he countered, "no AWOL, just babes."

"I'm not going looking for babes. I actually want to go body surfing. Maybe there'll be some women at the beach." That thought pacified him for the moment.

We stopped at a supermarket on the way and got some breakfast. We inhaled the food while I drove. When we got to Sandy Beach, it was still pretty early in the morning. The sun hadn't been up for long, but there were surfers in the water. The surfers were congregated in one spot, and there was a separate spot for body surfers. There were only two body surfers in the water, but we could see some others getting ready on the beach. Archie was anxious to get right in, so we dropped our stuff and ran down to the water.

All the other people at the beach were locals. Most of them had dark skin. They gawked at us with our pasty white skin and bleached hair. I'm sure they thought we were yahoos who'd stumbled into the wrong place and would get eaten by the waves. They didn't know we were two of the best swimmers in the world, experienced body surfers.

We body surfed non-stop for three hours. We must have gained the respect of the locals, because a couple of them came up to us in the water and asked a few questions.

"Where you guys from?" one local asked.

"Michigan," Archie answered. "We're on a swim team that's here for training."

"Where's the rest of the team?"

"I don't know, at some pineapple plantation," Archie said disparagingly. "We couldn't handle that scene."

"Cool," said the local. "You picked a good day for this scene. Welcome to Sandys."

Body surfers aren't much into talking. They're into the next wave. I appreciated this guy coming over to let us know we were welcome there.

A pod of Spinner Dolphins swam by. Archie and I swam out a few hundred meters to get a closer look, and the pod turned out to be immense—there were several dozen of them. They didn't mind us swimming alongside them. In fact, they seemed to be showing off. They breached and spun and flapped their flippers like they were playing with us. It took some effort to stay near them, but we swam along for half an hour.

Swimming with the Spinner Dolphins was thrilling, but it exhausted us. We rode a wave back in. When we got out, we flopped onto our towels to air-dry. The sun was in full flare and the beach was getting crowded, still mostly with locals. There were a few tourists sitting in their cars, some with binoculars, watching the surfers and body surfers.

One thing I love about body surfing is that the feeling stays with you on dry land. As we air-dried, lying out in the sun, with the sound of waves crashing, I was catching phantom wave rush—the imaginary feel of skimming through the water at high speed, of water flowing over me.

After about 15 minutes, we propped up on our elbows and assumed the gaze position. The waves were really rolling, each one leaving a turquoise luminescence under the crest. The beige sand and black rocks down the coast contrasted vividly with the water color. It was a grand scene.

"I could get used to this," Archie said.

I lazily turned my head his way and we glanced at each other through our shades. "Yeah."

"Do you ever wonder if it's worth it? I mean, knockin' ourselves out in a pool for hours and hours every day when we could be here?"

"I do, Arch. I weigh the pros and cons all the time."

We both stared out at the waves. Archie is not a weigher of pros and cons, he's a blinker. He goes with his gut. As I analyzed the situation, I started to worry again about Archie going AWOL. He would've been gone already if I hadn't been dragging him down. I needed to do something.

"You as hungry as I am?" I said.

"Starving to death."

We grabbed our stuff, got in the car and drove back toward town. We stopped at a roadside stand that was selling Opakapaka tacos. We ate ten of them. We finished the last two in the car on the way back to the beach.

Archie and I broke another rule when we arrived back at Sandy Beach. We immediately got back in the water. I don't know who made the rule about waiting half an hour to swim after eating. My mother tried to teach it to me but I routinely ignored it as a kid. Elite swimmers consider it to be a rule that applies to weak swimmers. What can happen? You might get a cramp, but so what? I've had a million cramps and it's no big deal. You might throw up, but who cares? Most elite swimmers have puked in the gutter more than once. You just keep going. The ocean is one big gutter. You know people are peeing in it, so what difference does a little vomit make?

We body surfed for another hour, then Archie noticed something on the beach. He didn't say anything, but he rode a wave all the way in and walked up the sand. I took the next wave and followed him. When I caught up, he was engaged in chit-chat with a pair of young women in bikinis.

"This is my friend, Doyle Wilson," Archie said as I walked up.

"Nice to meet you, Doyle," said the one in the red bikini with white polka dots. "I'm Holly, and this is Megan." Megan was wearing a brown and coral bikini. "We didn't catch your name," Holly said to Archie.

"I'm Hunter Hayes," he announced. "My friends call me Archie."

I then witnessed something rare. There was no apparent recognition on their faces. They didn't know who he was. The typical response is "Hunter Hayes, the Olympic swimmer?" Or "Hunter Hayes, the world record holder?"

"Nice to meet you, Archie," Holly said.

I was offended for Archie at the lack of recognition. How could they not know who he was? I mean, the guy had a poster. He was on magazine covers. I was thinking that these women were not worth the trouble and we should leave. I started to say something but Archie gave me a stare that shut me up. He liked the fact that they didn't recognize him.

"Doyle is a great swimmer," Archie said. "A champion." Oh no, I thought. He's trying to get me a babe.

"Well…," I stammered. "I'm a good swimmer, but not great." Archie was staring me down again. He wasn't going to tolerate me saying anything about him.

"He's great," said Archie with a glint in his eye, implying that I was underselling myself.

We sat down in the sand and chatted for a while. Archie has a good eye for women, even from way out in the waves. Megan had a Polynesian look and long, silky black hair. She was petite, a little too slender for Archie, sort of like Molly in that respect. She was from Maui and was in her first year of medical school at the University of Hawai`i. Holly was a curvy blonde, right within Archie's sweet spot. She was born in California, but spent her later childhood in Honolulu. She was a fifth-year senior finishing up a dual major in microbiology and organic chemistry.

As we talked to Holly and Megan, it became obvious that they were more my type than Archie's. I mean, they were brainy, and I like brains. Yet the more Archie tried to get them to focus on me, the more interested they seemed in him. That was fine with me. I was used to it. I just wanted to body surf anyway.

Time was running short if we wanted to do any more body surfing. I decided that I would be the one to end this talk, and I knew how to do it.

"Archie has four Olympic gold medals," I blurted out. He gave me the stare, but it was too late. I stood up like it was time to go.

"Wow," said Megan. She was the less talkative of the two women. Archie stood up, and before another second passed, we were all standing up.

"In fact," I continued, "we're here as part of our training for the next Olympics, and we have a workout this afternoon over at the Duke pool."

"Wow," said Megan, again, as she sized Archie up.

"It's been nice talking to you, Megan and Holly, but we've got to catch a few more waves and then trundle off to practice." I said this with finality to stave off any argument. The word "trundle" was particularly suave, if I may say so myself.

Archie and Megan protested, but Holly was wise to me and helped me out.

"It was nice talking to you guys, too," said Holly. "Good luck in your training, and I hope you win some medals in Paris. Both of you."

I walked off, and Archie followed me. I knew he was frustrated, so I didn't wait up to hear him gripe. I walked straight to the water and dived into the face of a wave.

With only one more hour of body surfing ahead of us, we both stepped up the intensity. We took waves more frequently. Instead of passing up waves that looked too big, we took greater chances. The last hour of the day is always the riskiest.

Archie and I have different styles of body surfing. He uses the more classic style, riding the face of the wave, cutting across at an angle, one arm streamlined ahead and the other at his side. I ride the top of the wave and take it straight in, with both arms streamlined ahead of me. I like the crest of the wave to throw me down. Mine is a shorter, faster ride.

As the last hour wore down, I noticed that Archie was no longer using his typical style. He was using my style. He was imitating me. Before I had a chance to be flattered by this, or to warn him, he swam ahead of a wave that was clearly too big to ride in the Doyle style. "No, Archie, bail out," I whispered. "Bail out." He didn't.

The wave curled and crashed, and I lost sight of Archie. I hoped he would pop out of it, but I watched and watched with no sign of Archie. I started to swim in toward where I expected him to surface. Still no Archie. I swam furiously. I noticed another giant wave coming from behind me, and I had to stop and wait for it to go by. I was praying it wouldn't crash on Archie when he surfaced. *If* he surfaced.

I resumed swimming for shore, scanning everywhere for signs of Archie. The second wave obscured my view. I felt panic enter my spinal cord. I sprinted parallel to shore and then toward it, shouting his name.

Finally, as I got close, I saw him. He was up on the sand above the receding water line, face down. I watched him roll over and sit up, turning toward me. He had a gash on the side of his forehead and blood was flowing down over his face. He was spitting out sand and blood. He looked like one of the pecking victims in *The Birds*.

At that moment—at that first glimpse of the bloody Archie—a heat of conflicting thoughts sprinted through me. If Archie is seriously injured, that will increase my chance of making the Olympic team and winning a gold medal. It will bring justice to the universe by balancing out the luck that always favors Archie. But Archie is my friend. I'm responsible for this calamity. I drove him to this beach. I was the one who broke off from the women to get back in the water. I was the one he was imitating when he almost got killed.

All of those thoughts washed through me in a hundredth of a second. What was left when they were gone was a feeling that transcended Archie and me. I saw my duty. My duty was not to Archie, or to my team, or Curtains, or my country. My duty was to the cosmos. God or nature had created this incredible swimming creature, this elegant swimming machine. Archie's talent needed to be preserved and nurtured. There were threats everywhere. I was with him all the time and in the best position to protect him.

I had been given goggles from heaven. I could see it clearly. My purpose on earth was to keep Archie from going down.

I got to Archie first, but Megan and Holly were there only seconds later. Archie seemed stunned and wasn't saying anything. Megan was sizing him up as a candidate for mouth-to-mouth resuscitation. He didn't need that. He started to get up.

"Don't move," I barked at Archie. I had heard stories of people being paralyzed as a result of body surfing injuries. I was heartened by the fact that he'd rolled over and sat up. But he had clearly hit his head, and the neck is vulnerable when that happens, so I knew we needed to be cautious. There was a lifeguard way down the beach, and I asked Holly to go get him. She ran off.

"Move your fingers," I commanded. He did. "Move your toes." He did. "Turn your head." He did, but it made him groan. I noticed he had a scrape and some blood on his left shoulder. "Lift your left arm." He did. "How does your back feel?" I asked. He said it felt fine. "How many fingers?" I asked, holding up two. He didn't answer that one—he's not a numbers guy. A couple waves had washed up while we were checking Archie out, and he had gotten over his momentary stun. He was tired of the water washing over him, and suddenly he stood straight up. He looked at himself all over, front and back.

"I'm fine," he said through a bloody mouth.

Holly came running back and announced that the lifeguard was off on another rescue. We went over to where Megan and Holly had been sitting. They had an extra towel, which they used to clean him up. They enjoyed that. The gash on his head wasn't deep, so he wouldn't need stitches. It covered a large area, though, and it was going to be quite noticeable. So was the deep sunburn he had gotten during the day. Archie is not a sunscreen user.

While I started thinking about how to explain this to Curtains, Holly was dabbing at the gash with a napkin she had soaked in contact lens solution. Archie winced at the first dab, then he held still. By the time Holly was through with him, the gash looked more like a scrape. She dabbed at his shoulder as well. Meanwhile, Megan had been rubbing aloe on the parts of Archie that looked most sunburned.

"Megan and Holly, I don't know how to thank you," I said. "I'm really sorry we have to run. We have to get to practice."

Holly wrote her cell phone number on a scrap of paper and handed it to me.

"Give me a call if we can help you guys while you're here. Or...."

Archie winked at me as I took the scrap of paper. He had accomplished his goal for the day, getting me a woman's phone number. We trundled off to our car.

As we drove off to The Duke, we planned our strategy for explaining Archie's scrape and sunburn. The sunburn was the most noticeable. I favored being forthright with Curtains and admitting we screwed up. Curtains would go vesuvial, then calm down quickly. Archie was against this approach, however. He believed he could hide the scrape from Curtains, at least for a couple days, until it had a chance to heal and didn't look so bad.

"How about the sunburn?" I asked.

"Is it really that bad?"

"Curtains will notice it a mile off."

"Pull into this strip mall," he said. "I have an idea."

I pulled in and parked by the drugstore. Archie got out of the car and headed into the store. I followed him. He bought a big spray bottle of fake tanning solution, the kind that makes your skin look orange. Outside the store, he made me spray the stuff all over him, concentrating on the most burned parts—his face, back and shoulders. He made me spray the whole bottle on him. It was supposed to work fast, which was good because we only had 45 minutes until the start of the workout.

Back in the car, Archie sat forward in the passenger seat the whole way, so as not to rub his back on the seat cushion. He was really into his deception scheme. He cared more about fooling Curtains than he did about his injuries.

"And I thought *I* was a dork," I told him, observing his uncomfortable car-riding posture.

The fake tan spray worked. Well, it covered up most of the sunburn. When we got out of the car at The Duke, I sized Archie up and couldn't help laughing. His feet were white. His shins and calves were pink. His back, shoulders and face were dark orange. We had overdone it on the spray.

We walked out onto the pool deck. Archie had a towel draped over his shoulders and a baseball cap on, as if that wasn't going to look suspicious in itself. When we got to the end of the pool closest to the locker rooms, Archie tossed his towel and cap onto the deck, jumped in the pool and started swimming. I continued walking to the far end, where the teams always congregated. When I got there, people were asking "who's in the water already?" "Is that Archie?" "What is Archie doing?" I just shrugged.

During practice that afternoon, whenever we finished a set and were standing on the bottom, Archie slouched down in the water and faced away from Curtains. I could see Curtains eyeballing him while we were swimming. We had a hard workout, and to his credit, Archie kept up. It must have been torture for him, with his scrape, his sunburn and his pain in the neck. Plus,

I noticed myself, six hours of body surfing can do a number on your energy level. I felt exhausted.

Curtains didn't say anything, and at the end of the workout, Archie slinked away just as he had arrived. He swam down to the far end of the pool, got out, grabbed his towel and baseball cap, and disappeared into the locker room.

As I started walking toward the locker room, Curtains called my name and motioned me aside. When all the other people had passed by and no one could hear, Curtains put me on the spot.

"Where did you guys go body surfing?"

"Sandys."

"*Sandys*?! Are you insane? The most dangerous body surfing beach on the island?" He spoke as one who knew.

"I'm sorry, Coach. Archie got scraped up and sunburned. I'm really sorry."

"I saw the scrape on his head. Does his neck hurt?"

I noted that Curtains was *not* mad, he just thought we were crazy.

"I'm not sure about his neck," I said. "It doesn't seem to hurt much right now, but it may hurt more tomorrow."

"It *will* hurt more tomorrow," said Curtains.

"Coach," I said, "I had an epiphany out there today."

He looked skeptical. "An epiphany?"

"Yeah. I came to a realization. I know I'm Archie's competitor, and I'm focused on beating him every day up through Paris. I want to pummel him, but I also want to protect him. I see that as one of my duties."

Curtains, who had been viewing me as a stupid kid, suddenly looked at me like I was an adult.

"I have a deal I'd like to propose to you," I continued. "Archie felt you embarrassed him in front of the Minnesotans this morning and he wanted to get even with you. That may be one thing that led to his…incident. It would mean a lot to him if he could think he has fooled you and gotten away with it."

Curtains chortled. "And the deal is…?"

"You act like you don't know," I explained. "That's your end of the deal. In exchange, I will keep Archie out of trouble the rest of this trip. And, even after the trip, I'll do my best. I'll watch out for him."

Curtains mulled it over. "Do I have to act like that tan is natural?"

"No, but he'll take enough ribbing from the guys. You don't have to mention it."

"Deal," said Curtains. I nodded and started to walk away.

"One more thing, Doyle." I turned back toward him. "When a wave takes you down, put both hands in front of your face." He demonstrated. "The hands protect the head. You cannot go in face first." It was now obvious to me that Curtains had experienced a similar incident. He wasn't the only one who could connect the dots.

"You got it. I'll tell Archie. But we're done body surfing on this trip."

"No you are not," he said. "Team is going on the last day. Not to Sandys."

The deal was ensconced, and Archie would never know. I walked along the deck, biting my nails. It wasn't just the physical danger. Archie was having trouble staying on task. He already had four gold medals, money and fame. The path to Paris was a hard one, especially for him because of the expectations. He had Curtains *trying* to make him mad. The temptation to chuck it, to go AWOL, was ever-present.

My job would not be easy. I'd have to cut Archie enough slack for him to have fun, all the while keeping an eye out for trouble. When necessary to rein him in, it would have to be subtle, and the pact could never be revealed. I had signed up to be a tightrope walker. Hey Ma, I've joined the circus.

When I got to the showers, Archie had already cleared the locker room. I wasn't about to miss two showers in one day. I took a hot one, got dressed and went out to the car. Archie was sitting on the hood. He was grinning under his threadbare Tigers cap, pulled low over his gash.

"I don't think Curtains suspected a thing," Archie said.

I looked around before answering, like I was going to tell him a secret. "You're a genius, Arch," I whispered.

The next morning, Archie was moaning when I woke up. The sunburn pain had peaked and his neck was sore. He had trouble turning his head to the left. The neck pain stayed with him the rest of the trip, but it diminished and wasn't permanent.

I called Holly and invited her and Megan to dinner two nights after the incident, to thank them for their help. Archie wanted to invite them back to our apartment, but I said no. We took them dancing down in Waikiki and had a good time that fit within the parameters of my pact with Curtains.

Once Archie's sunburn pain receded, he buckled himself down to hard work in the pool and put in some impressive swims. On the second to last day, we did an open water swim across Waikiki Bay, a little over two miles total. Several other teams swam with us, and it generated a little publicity. The publicity featured Archie, of course, and he told me he was going to try to win the race. I scoffed, because Crack and about four other D-men could eat Archie's lunch in a 2-mile open water swim. He pulled it off. I was still in the water when he finished, but Holly was there. She told me he had a big grin on his face when he emerged from the surf and ran up the beach. He waved in three directions to the spectators at the finish, posed for the photographers, and gave a TV interview.

On the last day of the trip, after a tough morning workout, we piled into cars and drove to Makapu`u Beach. There's a lighthouse on the hillside above the bay, and it was picturesque with all the hang gliders soaring overhead. Makapu`u is on the windward side of the island, and the waves weren't as big as they were at Sandy Beach. Archie and I played in the waves with the guys, but didn't do any serious bodysurfing. Up on the beach, in the hot sun, I offered to put sunscreen on Archie's back. He let me do it.

CHAPTER 14

Some people think of swimming as a sport for intellectuals. That may be because of a misperception that swimmers don't sweat. Swimmers sweat like sumos in a sauna. You don't see it because the water washes the sweat away. You feel it, though, when you're pushing your limit. Your body feels overheated, like when you have a fever. Your skin feels prickly. If you keep pushing it, you'll throw up.

If swimming is a thinking person's sport, what do swimmers think about?

In a race, your mind is fixed on matters at hand and the immediate future. Ninety percent of your thoughts relate to implementation of your pre-planned race strategy. You have already determined how fast to take it out and bring it back and where to make your move. You can't predetermine what the other swimmers are going to do, so in the race, you watch them and factor in what they're doing. If necessary, you modify your strategy. Mainly, though, you monitor your body systems and technique to stay on plan. You watch for the walls and make adjustments to hit your turns. You talk to yourself, especially when the pain comes near the end of the race. Different people say different things when the pain arrives. I say "so we meet again." I talk to pain in the second person. Come to think of it, I talk to myself in the second person. If I'm in a close race, I tell myself "he hurts worse than you do."

In practice, about 50% of a swimmer's thoughts relate to numbers. You count strokes, count laps, count repeats. If you do a set of 30 one-hundreds on 1:10, you simultaneously count up from one and down from 30. "Ten down, 20 to go." You always know exactly where you are in a set. You watch the clock. If you do a 1:02, you get eight seconds rest. Usually you try to descend your times, so you keep a running history. In longer swims, you check your splits along the way by looking up at the pace clock on the first breath out of the turn. At the end of a set, you count your heartbeats for ten seconds and multiply by six. Numbers are second nature to me, and that's one of the reasons I like swimming so much.

Another 20% of your thoughts in practice relate to technique assessment. There's a lot to pay attention to in the freestyle stroke. It's kind of like patting your head and rubbing your belly at the same time, only about five times harder. Every part of your body is involved, and the rhythms of the parts are different. Your arms are on a continuous rhythm of about one stroke per second. Your feet, on the other hand, kick two or four times in a row, then stop for a moment before kicking again—except when you're sprinting, when you use a six-beat kick. Your shoulders roll from side to side, but it's actually your hips that lead the rolling. Your head doesn't roll with the shoulders but instead turns to the side, just enough to catch air. Add all these non-synchronous movements together, and it's mind-bogglingly complex.

Twenty percent of your thoughts in practice relate to other people. Quite a bit of racing takes place in swim workouts. You watch what the others are doing and, especially at the end of a set, you pour it on to beat them. You develop mini-strategies for each set, each swim within a set, and for the practice as a whole. If someone needs encouragement, you might say a word or two in that eight second rest interval. There is always a bit of pure socializing and, if the moment is right, trash talking. If you're in a crowded lane, you have to think about passing people, or people passing you, or running into people. Of course, you also listen to the coaches and occasionally try to do what they say.

That leaves 10% of your brain free. This is the magical 10%. When people say swimming is a thinking person's sport, this may be what they're talking about. You're free to think whatever you want, or whatever happens to float into your mind. The things that are bound to float into your mind are the last song you heard, the last girl you saw or the homework you have to do that night. Some swimmers say they talk to God. I used to solve math problems. Now I think about the meaning of life.

Archie and I needed some international competition, so Curtains sent us to Rome in March to swim in the World Short Course Championships. Most Americans skipped the meet, because it came near the time of the NCAA championships. The Australians were absent as well, so we knew the competition would be marginal. But we needed to race, and being out of college, the opportunities were limited.

We were accompanied by a graduate assistant coach, Luc Riendeau. Luc had been a sprinter in college. He grew up in France and came to Southern Michigan as a walk-on. He was in business school at SM pursuing an MBA. Luc had been to Rome many times and was planning to visit his family in France after the meet.

Curtains didn't want us to miss much training, so we didn't taper for the meet. Of course, the travel alone imposed a slight taper, and the meet was six days long, so we lost eight days of normal training. Curtains told us to swim at least 5,000 meters a day, every day, and more if we could. This is known as "swimming through" a meet.

Archie, Luc and I took an overnight flight to Rome and landed the day before the start of the meet. We went right to the pool and Luc watched as Archie and I dutifully put in our 5,000 meters.

The SCM Worlds is not a big enough meet to justify a new venue. Because the Olympics are held in a long course—50 meter—pool, a short course meet has limited usefulness in an Olympic year. The Italian swimming federation spruced up the old indoor pool at the *Foro Italico* to make it suitable for the meet. Bulkheads were brought in to establish the 25-meter course. Temporary bleachers were added for spectators.

The *Foro Italico* dates back to the time of Mussolini. The walls of the indoor pool feature paintings of Mussolini-era athletes—the kind of strapping athletes that fascism was supposed to produce. There are subtle and obvious references to Mussolini all over the *Foro Italico*. As Archie and I scoped them out, I thought about how politics had influenced sports over the years. Mussolini believed that a political system could produce great athletes. In the case of fascism, he was wrong. Italy has produced some fine athletes, but it was not a dominant athletic force in Mussolini's time. Hitler believed that the Aryan race was superior in many ways, including athletics, but Jesse Owens became a fly in his soup at the 1936 Olympics. In the 1970s and 1980s, the East Germans dominated women's swimming and I'm sure they thought their communist philosophies brought out the best athletic talent. Two decades later, it became known that many East German athletes had been subjected to systematic doping. I guess if your political philosophy encourages cheating, it might have an effect on sport performance.

Americans and Australians have won the most Olympic medals in swimming over the years. Could we argue that the politics of democracy produce the best swimmers? It can certainly be argued, but I believe the best argument is that politics are inconsequential. Of course, politics can get in the way, such as when the United States boycotted the 1980 Olympics and the communist countries retaliated in 1984. South African athletes were barred from the Olympics for years because of their country's politics of apartheid.

I wondered how the Italian people felt about the big fascist athletes on the walls of the indoor pool. Italians are among the biggest victims of fascism. They have had to pay for their past.

Archie and I agreed that swimming and politics mix like oil and water.

The media darling of the SCM Worlds was Capria Diamanti, a 23-year-old Italian sprinter who was headed for a face-off against Camille Cognac in the Paris Olympics. Capria was like Camille in many ways. She was six feet tall and slender with big shoulders. She had a winning smile. Capria had been on the covers of many European magazines. Americans knew little about her, though. She didn't hold any world records, and she hadn't yet swum any meets in U.S. waters. In America Camille was "all that," but in Europe it was Capria who made the guys drool.

I noticed Archie reading the media reports about the meet. He didn't usually read those things, and he couldn't read Italian. Most of the reports had pictures of Capria. I started to be afraid, very afraid. Even in newsprint, her eyes were mythical.

The 400 free was on the first day of the meet, Monday. In short course meters, a 400 free is 16 lengths of the pool instead of the eight lengths you swim in long course meters. Your times are faster in SCM because you get eight more turns. Turns are faster than straight swimming because of the extra pushoffs. Archie and I cruised in the prelims and easily made it into the finals.

In the finals that night, I decided to employ Archie's typical strategy of starting out slowly and coming on like gangbusters at the end. At 300 meters, Archie and I were in fifth and sixth places, respectively. We were swimming next to each other and I'm sure Archie wondered what I was doing. I'm usually out ahead of him. He put on his usual spurt, and probably expected to swim away from me. I, however, stayed right with him. I felt strong on the last length. I wasn't sure where everyone else was, but I treated the last 25 meters like a sprint. I put my head down and only breathed twice. I increased my kick. I hit the wall just right.

Lo and behold, I won the race. I beat Archie by .03 seconds, improving my record against him to 3-31, not that I was counting. All eight swimmers in the final finished within two seconds of each other, and the times were slow. It was a relatively meaningless accomplishment to be the SCM world champion, but hey, I'll take it. I assumed the position—arm straight up, ending in a fist.

Archie reached across the lane marker and put his arm around my shoulder. "Way to go, man," he said. He wasn't one bit breathless. "It was us against the world and we won. *You* won."

Luc came over with the splits. My last 100 was faster than my first 100, which was ridiculous because the dive alone is worth at least two seconds. The time was well off any record, and I wouldn't be bragging about it.

Archie and I hammed it up during the awards ceremony. I grabbed his hand and we held our arms aloft, grinning the whole time like we'd done something special. As the winner, my awards included a bottle of Italian wine. My instinct was to give it to one of the meet workers, but I decided to take it home and give it to Curtains. I'd give the gold medal to my parents. Even though this meet was far less important to me than many others I'd swum in the past, it was nice for my parents that on one night, I was the best in the world.

Later that evening, Capria Diamanti broke the SCM world record in one of the 50 freestyle semifinals. Archie yelled for her during the race and applauded at the end.

When all the events of the first evening were over and it was time to leave the pool, Luc and I couldn't find Archie. We looked everywhere on deck, in the stands and in the locker room. We finally found him outside in a little courtyard, sitting with Capria.

"Doyle, do you know Capria?" Archie asked as we walked up. He turned his head to speak to her. "Doyle Wilson, World Champion. And this is Luc Riendeau."

"*Very* nice to meet you, Doyal," Capria said. It was worse than I thought. Her voice was sexier than her eyes; the accent was seductive. I even liked the way my name sounded. "And you too, Luc." Luc shook hands with her and I did the same.

"Pleased to meet you," I said. "Congratulations on the world record." Fastest woman in the world.

I could only speculate about how Archie got her alone. She must have had an entourage. Reporters and camera crews were on the prowl, and autograph seekers were everywhere—even I had signed one that night.

"Capria's family has a villa on the coast," Archie said. "She'd like us to come out and visit. After the meet, I mean." Capria was nodding.

"That's a very generous offer," I said, looking at Capria. "Maybe we can visit on Sunday afternoon. Is it far away?"

"One hour," Capria said. "It is in Santa Marinella." Her accent was killing me, and I assumed Archie had already succumbed.

"It sounds great. Will your parents be at the swim meet?" I asked, mostly wanting to remind her that she had parents. "I would like to meet them, too."

"My parents are not in Italy now," she said. "They are away on business."

That was a little sad. She had just broken a world record in her home country and her parents weren't there. I gathered that they were jet-setters and her relationship with them was not close. Obviously, her parents being away added to the danger of visiting the villa.

"That's too bad," I said. "Well, let's see how it goes. Maybe we can go to Santa Marinella for a few hours on Sunday." She looked at Archie and he winked at her. She smiled and nodded.

We had a driver named Paolo who was assigned to drive us anywhere we wanted to go in Rome. All we had to do was call him on his cell phone and he'd show up. I called Paolo. He was nearby. Archie, Luc and I said goodbye to Capria and walked over to the Piazza Lauro de Bosis to meet Paolo. He took us to a great restaurant for pasta, then gave us a one-hour nighttime tour of Rome.

On the second day of the meet, Archie had the 200 fly prelims and semis. I was done, except for swimming my 5,000, which I did early in the morning. I watched his swims, but I also spent some time sightseeing, so I wasn't with Archie constantly. Whenever I needed to find him, he was with Capria.

On the evening of the second day, Capria won the finals of the 50 free and the crowd went nuts. It wasn't a big crowd—fewer than two thousand people—but in the enclosed pool area, it was insanely loud. You'd have thought Capria had been crowned Miss Universe. Seconds after she finished, she popped out of the pool and blew kisses to the crowd. A little girl came up and gave her a bouquet of flowers. She hugged all of her competitors after they got out of the pool. She was wearing some pretty serious waterproof makeup.

There was a little band in the stands and it struck up some song I didn't recognize. There had been no music of any kind after I won my race.

On the third and fourth days of the meet, Archie was busy. He won the 200 fly and the 200 IM, and qualified for the 200 freestyle finals. His times were unimpressive. In the IM, in which no one should come near him, he almost lost to a Belgian swimmer I'd never seen before. Capria won two more events, giving her three gold medals.

After the finals on Friday night, the fifth day of the meet, Archie looked knackered. He won the 200 free that night, but he didn't mount his usual charge at the end. He just cruised in, barely ahead of an unknown Italian. His last event, the 400 IM, was coming up on Saturday. It was his best event. As we were driving to dinner after the finals on Friday, Archie complained about the pool, the meet, the other swimmers, and Rome.

"I'm gonna scratch the IM," Archie announced. There was dead silence for several seconds.

"*What?*" said Luc. He had an "are you crazy?" look on his face. Archie repeated himself. Luc said "no way."

I confirmed that Curtains would be quite unhappy if Archie scratched. "Is getting out of the IM really worth incurring the wrath of Curtains?"

"I'm tired of this meet," he answered. "I hate this pool. I'm not up to it mentally or physically."

"You can cruise the prelims," I argued, "and maybe you'll be jacked by the time the finals roll around. Besides, this is one of those mental toughness tests. Remember why you swam four races in an hour at the Nationals? You just have to suck it up."

I had a little league baseball coach who was always telling his players to "suck it up" whenever something bad happened. We were a horrible team, so there were a lot of things to suck up.

"Whatever," Archie muttered, ambiguously. He wasn't in the mood to talk. We grabbed some quick pizza, skipped the nighttime sightseeing, and turned in early.

I woke up before the crack o' dawn on Saturday morning. Something troubled me out of my sleep. I looked at the clock, which read 5:15. I switched on the light.

Archie was gone.

My pulse skyrocketed. Stay calm, I said to myself. There's no time to lose. Think fast.

We had a two-room condo and Luc was sleeping in the other room. I elected not to awaken him. I pulled on my jeans, shoes and sweat jacket, grabbed my phone and headed out quietly. I called Paolo.

"Paolo, this is Doyle. Did you take Archie somewhere?"

Paolo sounded like he'd been in a deep sleep. He flung out several sentences in Italian before I stopped him.

"The American swimmers. This is Doyle."

"Ah, Doyal," he said. "You want ride?"

"Yes. Si. Come to the condo right away. Grazie molto."

To his credit, Paolo understood the urgency and he got there within ten minutes. It seemed like ten hours. He pulled up and I got in. Usually I know where to tell him to go.

"Buongiorno, Doyal."

"Buongiorno. Listen. Did you drive Archie somewhere?" I made steering motions. "In the night…di notte."

"Som…where?" Paolo wasn't getting it, and I couldn't remember the name of that town. Santa something.

Paolo was looking at me like he really wanted to help, but he didn't know what to do. The clock was ticking. What was the name of that place?

"Santa Clara…Santa Monica…" I was thinking out loud. "Santa Marinella!"

"Si, Santa Marinella! Si!" Paolo was getting it. He was getting something, anyway.

"Did you…drive…Archie…to Santa Marinella…in the notte?"

"Si, si, Santa Marinella!" It was ambiguous to me whether he simply recognized the name of the place or had actually driven Archie there. I don't do well with ambiguity, but I decided to go for it.

"OK, Paolo. Let's go. Drive me to Santa Marinella. Adesso." Now.

"Adesso. Santa Marinella. Buono."

Paolo drove like a madman. There must be a nuance to the word "adesso," along the lines of "stat!" or "fang it!" He hit it like a bat out of hell as I gripped the arm rest.

Not only did Paolo drive to Santa Marinella, he drove straight up to a particular villa, which I hoped was Villa Diamanti. He wouldn't have known where to go—certainly not from anything I'd told him—if he hadn't already been there with Archie. Capria's parents were gone, so I suspected I'd find Archie and Capria alone inside. I told Paolo to stay put and turn the engine off.

It was just before 6:30 a.m. when I got to the villa. The prelims were scheduled to start at 8:00. The last day of a meet often begins and ends earlier than the previous days so that people can catch flights.

The front door was locked. Rather than bang on it, I went around to the back. There was a big wooden terrace and a set of steps leading up onto it. I paused for a second to consider the gravity of what I was about to do, then climbed up the steps. I tiptoed across the terrace to a set of French doors leading into the house. My heart was in my mouth. I checked the door handles. One of the doors was locked but not fully closed. My specialty.

I went through the door, into the villa, and looked around. There was just enough light to see the furniture, so I didn't bump into anything. I quickly determined that there were no people on the first floor. There was a stairway up to the second floor and a hallway at the top of the stairs. I guessed that the bedrooms were upstairs.

"Archie! Archie! It's me, Doyle."

I didn't yell it, but I said it loud enough that anyone up there would hear me. I waited. I heard no signs of life. Was this the right house? Sweat dripped from my armpits in time with my heart beats.

"Arch! Capria!"

I heard stirring upstairs. The moment of truth was approaching. I could hear the blood pumping in my ears. Finally, I heard my name.

"Doyle? What the…." It was Archie's voice. More stirring, then Archie appeared, in his boxers, at the top of the stairs.

"Come down here," I ordered.

He complied. I turned on a light and pointed to a seat I wanted him to sit in. He grabbed a blanket off the couch, draped it around himself and sat down. I sat on the couch, facing him.

"Doyle—," he started.

I cut him off. "Listen to me." I hushed my voice. "You don't owe me any explanations. I'm here for one reason only, and that is to get you to the starting blocks in time for the 400 IM."

"But—"

I cut him off again. "I'm here to keep you out of trouble. I owe it to you as your friend. This situation, to me, looks like trouble."

"But I just—"

"Paolo is out in the car. You're going to get dressed, get in the car, get over to the pool and make the finals of the IM. That's all I'm going to say."

There was a moment of silence. I tried to look resolute.

"I think I'm in love," Archie blurted.

Oh, no. That was the worst possible thing he could have said. I knew instantly it could take him down. It could be his Achilles heel. And why did he have to fall for a sprinter?

"Did you say 'love?'" I asked, but he was staring out to sea. The French doors faced west, toward the Mediterranean. The sun was rising on the other side of the villa and starting to leak color into the sky. It was a stunning view.

There was another moment of silence as we both stared westward. It was a respectful silence. I had to play it right. I had to take him seriously, not make fun of him, and yet steer him back toward Rome.

"Arch, have you been in love before?"

"No, nothin' like this. I'm totally smitten. Those eyes…that voice…." He trailed off, still looking out to sea. I was well aware of Capria's assets. Archie picked up the trail again. "I just want to be with her all the time."

I had to think about that one for a minute. I was smitten with a girl named Wendy Dickinson in seventh grade. My mom told me then that being smitten is not love. It doesn't last, and love does last. Being smitten just alerts you to the possibility of love. Many people mistake it for love and that leads to trouble. Archie was probably on target when he said he was smitten with Capria, but he'd just met her. Equating his feelings with love could be dangerous.

"I hear you, man. She seems like a terrific gal. But I mean, you gotta get to the pool."

"The *pool*?" He looked at me like I was the crazy one. "I don't care about swimming. Don't you think love is more important than a few medals?"

When he said "a few" medals, he wasn't talking about missing one race.

"Here's what I think, Arch. I think true love is more important than a few medals. I do. I also think that your feelings for Capria, whatever they are, love or not, are making you goofy. You cannot afford to be goofy right now. That's exactly why I'm here. You need a friend to bring your GQ down."

"GQ?"

"Goofiness quotient." He laughed out loud. Archie had been on the cover of *Gentleman's Quarterly*, which is what he probably thought GQ stood for. "Look," I continued, imitating Curtains to buy some authority. "Real love is strong and permanent. If this is love, it will still be there after the 400 IM. Love wants the best for the other person. If it's love, Capria will *want* you to do your best in the IM."

"Do *you* want the best for me, Doyle?"

He sounded like a drunk. Archie once told me "I love you man" at a party, but it was the beer talking. Now he was inviting it from me, but it would have been the adrenaline talking.

I looked Archie in the eyes. He knew I had gotten myself up at the crack of dawn and hustled across Italy for his sake. I had surreptitiously entered a strange villa in a foreign country. I wasn't looking out for myself.

"No, actually, I want *second best* for you. I want you to win the silver in the 400 free. In everything else, yeah, I want the best for you." He laughed again.

I wanted to freeze the moment in preposterity. There I was, 5,000 miles from home, with the best swimmer in the world, and we were talking about love. If anyone secretly recorded the conversation and put it on YouTube, it would get ten million hits. If any of our teammates ever got wind of this, Archie would never live it down. I had blackmail material on him. I could sell the story to *GQ*.

Capria appeared at the bottom of the stairs, wearing a bathrobe. I motioned her over and she came. I looked at my watch.

"Arch, it is now crunch time. I can personally testify that Paolo is a fast driver but there are limits to what even Paolo can do. If you're going to swim, you've got to get in the car *now*. Adesso."

"Adesso," Capria repeated.

"You go with Paolo," I continued. "I'll stay with Capria and explain everything to her. I'll ride into Rome with her."

I looked at Capria, who nodded faintly. Archie saw the nod. He got up, with the blanket draped like a towel over his shoulders, and went over to where Capria was standing. I turned my head to avoid seeing a rather lengthy kiss.

I took off my sweat jacket and tossed it to Archie. "I'll bring your clothes. Your swim bag is in the car. You can put on your suit while Paolo drives." I grinned, thinking of Archie running from the car to the pool, wearing only his swimsuit and a sweat jacket. He trotted off. A few seconds later, I heard the car engine start. Paolo burned rubber.

Capria and I looked in the direction of the squeal for several seconds, then turned back to face each other. It was an awkward moment. I was, as usual, left to pick up the pieces of an Archie-induced change of plans.

"Coffee?" I suggested.

"Of course."

We moved into the kitchen and made a pot together. Capria was in no hurry; she only had a relay final that afternoon. She didn't seem to be in a hurry to find out what the deal was with Archie, either. I poured the coffee and we took it back out to the living room. I was shirtless, and Capria was in her bathrobe. Her dark chocolate hair fell below her shoulder blades and looked like it had been brushed.

I sat on the couch. She sat down in the chair where Archie had been sitting and crossed her legs as if to say she was ready. I hadn't noticed anything remarkable about her legs when she wore her swimsuit. Coming out of a bathrobe, however, they caught my attention. Length was their primary attribute. I tried not to measure.

"I'm sorry to come out here like this. Archie and I are best friends, you know? We kind of watch out for each other. I couldn't let him miss his race."

She listened very intently. "It is good that you came," she said.

I finally figured out what it was about her voice. It was exactly like chocolate mousse. There was a sweetness to it, like a little girl's. There was a richness, too—a creaminess. But the dominant feature was tactile. Chocolate mousse tickles your tongue; Capria's voice caressed the ear drums in a way that made you want more.

"He seems to have some strong feelings for you," I told her.

She wrinkled her brow. That told me all I needed to know. If Archie was serious about her, the feeling was not reciprocated. She would've broken his heart.

"It was just for fun. I am not trying to steal away your Archie."

We sipped coffee and talked for half an hour. Capria was inquisitive. She asked a lot of questions about me, about Molly, my parents, my plans for life after swimming. I told her what the options were, the things I was considering. She seemed impressed that swimming wasn't my whole life, that I wanted to do something meaningful beyond swimming. Archie's name wasn't mentioned. Except once.

"You are a good friend to Archie."

"Well, I don't know about that. I insult him a lot. I hate him sometimes. I want very much to beat him."

"You came here to…to rescue him." She was smiling. It did seem pretty funny, the notion of "rescuing" someone from the arms of such a delightful creature.

"I guess I did," I said, smiling back.

"It is…dolce…how do you say it? Sweet."

Yeah, sweet.

Capria envied our friendship. I sensed that she didn't have many true friends, if any. She had people who worshipped her, followed her, helped her, and basked in her glow. Archie had those, but he also had me.

When the coffee was gone, Capria went upstairs and brought me Archie's clothes. I put on his shirt. After she got dressed, we went to the garage and got in her Lamborghini. She asked me if I wanted to drive it, and of course I did, but it was too much car for me. I didn't enjoy it the way other guys might have. I missed the safety and comfort of my Taurus.

I learned more about Capria on the drive to Rome, even though I had to give the car 99% of my concentration. The thing that drove her in life was that her parents were never impressed with her. She was an only child, and had nannies from an early age. She hardly ever saw her father. Her mother wasn't into being a mother. They didn't understand her obsession with swimming. Capria wanted to win Olympic gold medals and then become an actress. She wanted to be famous in Italy. She wanted to outshine her father, a prominent businessman who thought making money was the only important thing in life.

"I would like to ask a favor from you," I said to Capria as we neared the *Foro Italico*.

"Yes, of course," she said.

"This is going to be difficult. I don't want you to run away with Archie but I don't want you to break his heart, either. Can you part with him in a way that shows you still admire him and care for him?"

"Yes," she answered. "I know just what to do. Like a summer love, it will just end. No one will be hurt."

Capria had undoubtedly broken a few hearts. She knew how to do it gently. I trusted her.

We parked the car and went to the pool. The prelims were just finishing. Archie had qualified eighth in the 400 IM. He was no longer at the pool. I found Luc, who said Archie had run onto the pool deck just as the competitors were mounting the blocks for his prelim heat of the IM. There was a murmur when there was no swimmer in Lane 4. Archie yelled out "wait" and the starter told the other swimmers to relax. He climbed up on his starting block and the heat went off. He finished third in his heat, and made the finals by less than half a second. Luc told me Archie had gone back to the condo immediately after swimming in order to rest up for the finals.

I told Luc I would explain later. I needed to think up something that wasn't an out-and-out lie, but also wouldn't set off smoke alarms. Whatever I told Luc would be reported to Curtains. Everything was under control. I felt good about that.

Archie won the 400 IM that afternoon. It was his best swim of the meet, and it was no contest. He buttered the kid from Belgium. Capria led Italy to an unexpected relay victory, and we got to hear the band again. Archie and Capria had each won four gold medals, so they both had to answer questions at a press conference. It was pretty late when we left the pool. We invited Capria to dinner and a drive, but she told us she wanted to hang out with her teammates. That was a good decision, I thought.

We went back to Santa Marinella on Sunday afternoon. We had a wonderful time, all five of us: Capria, Archie, Luc, Paolo and me. We drank all four bottles of the wine that came with Archie's gold medals. Well, Paolo drank two of them and I didn't drink any. We watched the sun set over the Mediterranean. Then we said our goodbyes. Archie had a long, private goodbye with Capria that involved a lot of quiet talking, kisses on cheeks, hugs and tears. The tears were all Capria's.

I drove the limo back to Rome, wearing Paolo's hat. Paolo and Luc were zonked out in the back seat. Archie sat in front with me.

"I let her down easy," Archie whispered, leaning toward me. "She took it kind of hard at first but I think she's okay."

"That Capria is some special kind of woman," I whispered back.

CHAPTER 15

Swimming has become highly technical. Most sports have, and it's a good thing—mostly. People who understand the science have a leg up.

Science has influenced swimming technique profoundly. Coaches and physiologists study stroke mechanics and apply the laws of physics. They use swimmers as guinea pigs to try out their theories. At one time, freestyle was swum with the head out of the water and the dominant stroke was the "trudgeon," swum with a scissor kick. Innovative coaches proposed the flutter kick and putting one's face in the water. "Track" starts with staggered feet have replaced the old crouch and wind-up. Streamlining and dolphin kicking have been emphasized increasingly.

Pool and equipment technologies continue to advance. Some pools are faster than others. Why? Making a pool deep reduces turbulence reflecting from the bottom. Wash-through gutters absorb waves rather than bouncing them back. Lane markers are ever larger, lanes are wider, pools are well-lit and temperatures are tightly controlled.

Technical advances have meant that swimming times have gotten faster and faster. It's hard to compare swimmers from different eras. Mark Spitz won seven gold medals in 1972 and is venerated as one of the greatest swimmers of all time. He was far ahead of his competitors and revolutionized the sport. I was beating his times when I was a high school kid.

There are some downsides to the advance of science in swimming, as epitomized by the infamous "suit wars." Swimmers used to wear bulky trunks made of heavy wool. By the late 1990s, high tech fabrics and laser seam molding made suits "better than skin." Swimmers looked like cyborgs, covered with caps, goggles and metallic-looking fabric from head to toe. It got out of hand in 2009, as non-permeable, rubberized suits flooded the market. Some swimmers wore three or more suits to get extra compression and buoyancy. The suits got more publicity than the swimmers as technology produced a shower of records. FINA had to step in and in 2010 restricted male suits to non-buoyant, waist-to-knee jammers.

Scientific advances have also taken some of the mystery out of swimming. There are fewer surprises, like when someone comes out of nowhere to win a major event. There are fewer risks. The human element is smaller. But technology will never change the fact that good races require hard work, heart, guts and strategy.

"Archie, what happened in the 400 IM prelims?" Curtains didn't even greet us at the first practice after our return from Italy. Nor did he mention my win in the 400, or Archie's four gold medals.

Archie was tying his suit and had his goggle strap in his mouth, so I had a chance to come up with an answer myself. "It was my fault," I said. "I didn't set the alarm, and Archie missed the warm-up. The meet started two hours early the last day."

Curtains looked at Archie and he looked at me like he knew there was more to the story. "You got away with it this time," he said. "Next time you might not be so lucky." Curtains had no idea how lucky Archie was.

It was the end of March. The Olympic Trials were in early June, ten weeks away. We had seven weeks of hard work ahead. Seven weeks to put money in the bank. Forty-nine days until the start of the taper.

We did 20,000 meters the first day back, but Curtains told us to stay white. We were jet-lagged and out of sorts from the trip. Crack and Leor had swum in the NCAA championships while we were in Italy, Crack in his last, Leor in his first, and they were riding high in Lane 1. Every single person at the pool was now focused solely on the Olympic Trials. Everyone knew that the next seven weeks would be critical. No slacking would be tolerated. It was time to put up.

It took me three days to get back to pre-Worlds shape, but by the end of the first week I was back in the lead in Lane 1. In extreme distance sets I let Crack take the lead, and in the occasional sprint set Leor went first. Everyone looked to me to decide on the lead. I was the default leader. I stepped it up.

Curtains elevated his game as well. His game was to write up the workouts. He thought up some sets we had never tried before; sets that *no one* had tried before. One day he asked us to do fifty 100s on 1:10. This would ordinarily be a classic white set. The goal would be just to make the set. You'd get very little rest, five seconds or less at every 100. And that's the way we started. But as the set wore on, instead of getting fatigued we got juiced. I was getting close to a minute, then right at a minute, then under a minute on the last few. Curtains noticed. When the set was over, we congratulated each other. There was quite a bit of red in our faces, maybe even some blue. Curtains came over.

"How many could you guys do on 1:05?"

The smart answer would have been "zero." However, we were stoked from the set on 1:10. I asked the guys if we could do 20 on 1:05. They all nodded.

"Twenty-five," I said with apparent, but not actual, authority. Curtains seized on it.

"Twenty-five on 1:05," he said. "Tomorrow night. You guys are rocking." We congratulated each other again.

Leor said, "I thought we agreed on 20." Crack and Archie stared him down.

The next night we did 25 x 100 on 1:05. We had never done a significant number of 100s on 1:05 before. I led the lane, and after getting only three to four seconds rest on the first 10, I did the final 15 in 1:00 or better. Leor, Crack and Archie all nailed the set.

Nobody said anything, but we had a growing feeling of destiny in the animal lane. Our single little lane, inside a pool on a street corner in a modest-sized Midwestern town, was going to rock the world. We could feel it. There was a huge clock in the natatorium with big red numbers counting down the days, hours, minutes and seconds to the Opening Ceremony in Paris. Curtains had recently moved it from a remote corner to a prominent spot next to the main pace clock.

During the set of 100s on 1:05, Curtains had been pacing up and down the pool deck alongside Lane 1. "All right everybody!" he yelled, a minute after the set was over. "Stop what you are doing and listen up!" The other lanes were doing completely different sets, and some swimmers weren't done yet. It took a minute or two for everyone to get to the shallow end and stand at attention.

"We are going to do a Get Out swim," Curtains announced, when everyone was listening.

There was murmuring in every lane. Everybody loves Get Out swims. In a Get Out swim, one swimmer is chosen to represent the group. The coach sets a time that the swimmer must beat in order for the whole team to be excused from the rest of practice. If he fails to beat the challenge time, the team stays and finishes the workout. It's always a significant incentive, but when you've only done 5,000 meters, it's especially meaningful. A successful Get Out swim would save everybody an hour of swimming.

Curtains was pacing slowly behind the starting blocks. He looked like he was pondering something.

"All right, here is what we are going to do. Animals in Lane 1, you are all in. Caruso and Moses, you too. Six guys. I am hooking up the timing system—you will get about 15 minutes rest before we start. Distance is 200. Time is 1:50. I only need one of you to break it." He walked off to get the timing system going.

In Lane 1, we talked for a minute. "What do you guys think?" I asked.

I looked at Crack and he shook his head. "One-fitty? Unpossible."

"It's faster than my PB," Leor said. "But whatever."

I looked at Archie. "Can we do it?"

He spat into the gutter. "Not after the set we just did. It's just like that Russian fiend to do this after the toughest set of the year. He wants us to kill ourselves trying to beat the time, fail, and still have lots of hard work to do. He's a sadist." But I could see gears turning in his head. "What do *you* think, Doyle?"

I spat into the gutter. What I really thought was that Archie was the only one who had a chance to make it. I couldn't say that. I would have to come up with a way to motivate Archie. The two things that were likely to work were his hatred for Curtains and his competitive fire.

"I'm gonna do it," I said. "I'm gonna show Curtains who's boss. You guys have seen me—smoke on the water. You can cruise if you want. Leave it to me."

Crack and Leor were taken aback by my braggadocio. Archie looked at me out of the corner of his eye for a couple seconds, then spat into the gutter. I could see the gears turning again.

"You'll need someone to drag you," Archie said. "Come on, let's get up on deck and start resting up."

Archie likes to be the hero. He'd fallen into my trap.

We got out and sat in chairs behind the starting blocks. Within a minute, other swimmers came running up with towels and sweats for us to wear. They shouted encouraging words and gave us some impromptu amateur neck rubs that probably did more harm than good.

Curtains reappeared and announced he was ready. Just then, the pool's public address system erupted with sound—hip-hop music, Archie's favorite. It was deafening. Curtains had a scowl on his face and Archie was smiling. Then a voice came over the PA. Freddie Boxer, one of the sprinters, was attempting a French accent.

"Bon soir, Mesdames and Monsieurs. Welcome to ze Olympic finals of ze 200-meter freestyle!" Curtains bowed his head and massaged his temples. The swimmers all laughed and cheered.

"In Lane Deux, wearing ze gray trunks, from ze United States but having unknown exotic ancestry, Desmond Leor Walker!"

Loud applause followed, and then the chant "Lee-or…Lee-or…Lee-or." Leor waved to his fans on deck. He even turned and waved to the empty stands. Brook tossed him a cap, and he stretched it in every direction like a balloon before mounting it on his mane.

"In Lane Trois, also wearing ze gray trunks, he is ze great-great-great-great grandson of a United States President, it's John Buchanan, also known as Crack!"

There had been rumors about Crack's ancestry, but I happened to know that President James Buchanan had no children. Crack didn't acknowledge the crowd after his intro. There was a feeble attempt at a "Crack" chant, but it sounded like ducks quacking.

"In Lane Quatre, he is the man with four gold medals and one gold Jag, in ze gray trunks, Archie Hayes!"

Archie waved, and there was a huge cheer. The swimmers on deck knew that Archie was their best bet for an early shower.

"In Lane Cinque, ze recent world champion at 400 meters, Doyle Wilson." Polite golf clapping.

"In Lane Six, ze guy who sings in ze shower, ze Opera Man, Ca-rooooooooo-so Tucker!" Everybody loves Caruso. He got a big cheer.

"And in Lane Sept, ze outside smoker, ze man who can part ze sea, wearing ze gray trunks, Moses Weinberg!"

Freddie finished his routine: "Quiet for the start, plizz."

The introductions were funny, but it struck me that no one had ever given me a nickname. Why was that? And wasn't my suit just as gray as everyone else's? Gray is the final color in the chlorination spectrum. Every suit ultimately turns gray, and then it just rips apart. Was I too serious to be poked fun at? Too nerdly to be in on the fun? Those brief thoughts got my juices flowing. I had the Pavlovian nervousness. It felt like a real race. Curtains called us to the blocks.

"Take your marks…."

The electronic beep sounded and I dove hard. After three dolphin kicks I surfaced to find Archie half a body-length ahead of me. Caruso got a great start and was ahead of me as well. I felt a little stiff and sluggish after the tough set of 100s. I hung in there, though, and at the 100-meter turn, I was even with Caruso and still less than a body-length behind Archie. I moved over to the lane marker near Archie and felt his wake start to pull me. I made a move on the third 50 and was almost even with Archie as we turned for home. On the last length, I could see I was at his shoulders. I thought I might have a shot at beating him. I felt strong, so I turned up the kick. I tried to sprint the last 25. The last ten strokes were crazy hard but I could see Archie tying up. I inched ahead, and at the end I could tell I had him.

I looked up on deck and everyone was going crazy, jumping up and down, high-fiving each other. Then I remembered it was a Get Out Swim. I squinted at the clock and saw 1:49.22 next to Lane 5. Archie squeaked in under the challenge time at 1:49.95, and Leor was 1:49.99, his personal best. He was ecstatic— in a sad-looking, droopy-eyed sort of way. Even Curtains was ecstatic. He was running down the pool deck, writing furiously on his clipboard as he ran.

"All right, everyone. You are done for the day. Next time I will have to set a faster Get Out time."

There was no ecstasy in Lane 4. I leaned across the lane marker toward Archie. He saw me leaning and turned his back to me. Meanwhile, Caruso and Moses had come into my lane and mobbed me. The crowd on deck had come over to my lane as well, and people were shouting my name.

The whooping and hollering continued for five solid minutes, during which Archie quietly cleared the pool and headed to the locker room alone. I did a 200 cool down, then headed for the showers where I caught up with Archie.

"Momentous swim," I told him, as I cranked up the heat on my shower. He had, after all, beaten the Get Out time. He didn't congratulate me or even smile. He just nodded. Then he turned off his shower and headed for the lockers. I followed him.

"Hey Arch, before everyone leaves, why don't we make a plan for the six of us to have dinner together tonight, to celebrate. We can do it at my place, get some takeout, maybe watch *Knute Rockne, All American*." I wished it had been a different movie on CMC. Kind of on the hokey side but it was, after all, a sports movie.

"I got a better idea," Archie said. He always has a better idea. "Dinner at *my* crib, Chinese from Woo's, and Texas Hold 'Em."

"You're on. Since we have this extra hour, let's start early. Six o'clock?"

"Sure."

Crack and Leor entered the locker room together, so I told them the plan. They were in. I found Caruso and Moses in the showers, and they were in as well. Everybody was in. When I got back to the locker room, Archie was gone.

The back-slapping continued in the locker room until everyone realized that Archie had cleared out fast.

"Sup wit Arch?" Crack asked. There was something up. I knew what it was.

"He'll get over it," Caruso said. "He's sore that Doyle got all the credit." It's no surprise that Archie hates to lose, you just don't get to see it very often. But it was no big deal—he'd agreed to a celebration, he'd win at poker, and by the end of the night he'd be back to copacetic.

Archie's pad was not within walking distance of the pool, which was by choice—he liked to drive. He lived two miles south of campus on the outskirts of town. He owned a two-bedroom condo with no roommate. It had air conditioning, a big kitchen, a fireplace, a balcony and nice furniture. By comparison, my place was a dump and about 98 years older.

I arrived at Archie's pad at 6:00 sharp, with Leor in tow. Leor lived in the dorm, not far from my place, so I'd swung by and picked him up. He marveled at the raw power of my Taurus. Actually, he smirked a little when he saw it. Uppity little freshman, I thought. At least I *have* a car.

We were the first two to arrive at Archie's. He was on the phone with Woo. Woo, not surprisingly, was the owner of Woo's Chinese Garden. I don't know Woo's first name, we just called him Woo. He knew us all, and he treated Archie like royalty. Archie kept Woo in business, because believe me, Woo's Chinese Garden was no garden.

"I want three Triple Delight, two Muushu Woo, Human Chicken.... What?" Pause. "Okay, *Hunan* Chicken. Make it two of those. Kung Pao Chicken, two Sizzling Seafood, Tender Beef and Snow Peas. Got that?" Pause. "Okay, now double that. And rice for six, no eight. *Ten!* Rice for ten. A dozen egg rolls. Lots of that hot mustard." There was going to be a galaxy of food. "And no ducks' feet this time."

Woo always threw in an extra dish as a surprise. The ducks' feet hadn't gone over well the last time.

Leor and I looked around Archie's condo while we waited for the other guys. Archie was doing some straightening and getting out paper plates and poker supplies. The pad looked a lot better than the last time I was there. He used to have a Camille Cognac poster pinned to the wall, but it was gone. The only posters he had were framed travel posters from places he'd been. He had a cool poster from the 1896 Olympics in Athens. He had an old-time map of Paris. There were a few framed photographs, including a big one of Mt. Kilimanjaro. It looked professional. He also had a smaller photo taken from the top of Kili looking down. Archie had climbed Kilimanjaro. I had climbed Mt. Kenya. His mountain was higher; mine was harder.

Archie's bed was made and his clothes were picked up. In the spare bedroom, he had a nice desk and computer set up, with a huge flat-screen monitor. The desk was uncluttered. He had a bookshelf with a few books on it. *Ulysses* was not among them.

"Arch," I said, intending to compliment him, "your place looks like someone other than a slob lives here. What gives?"

"I got tired of imitating you," he said. "I'm blazing a new trail here."

Liar. I knew exactly why his pad looked so good. A network film crew had come to his place to take some footage for an Olympic promo piece. Archie hired a decorator and a housekeeper to make the place look spiffy.

The other guys arrived, and just a few minutes later, the food arrived. Woo brought it himself. We all greeted Woo like an old friend.

"Yo, Woo," Crack called out, "wuz the mystery dish?"

"Lion's Head," Woo answered. We all looked at each other like "here we go again." He saw us and rolled his eyes. "Come on. Lion's Head is just meatballs. You guys will like it." Woo had never been to China and his English was as close to having no accent as you can get. We invited him to stay and eat with us, but he declined.

If you ever have to watch swimmers eat, be prepared to shield your eyes. It's pretty savage. We need fuel, we need a lot of it, and we need it fast. The niceties of etiquette are unimportant to us. We're oblivious to the finer nuances of taste.

The six of us tore into the food like it was famine relief. Archie and Caruso used chopsticks deftly. I used them for fun, and if I put them in my good hand, I could get the food to my mouth. That's all that mattered to me. After about 15 minutes, the food was gone. Every scrap, every drop, every grain of rice. Woo had brought fortune cookies. Mine said: "Your lucky numbers are 3, 13, 21, 33, 36 and 45. You will gain the admiration of your pears." That fortune seemed so right on, I almost went out and bought a lottery ticket. My "pears" around the table kept telling me all evening long how much they "admired" me.

Archie had an "official" Texas Hold 'Em set including a tablecloth, playing cards and poker chips. I'm pretty good at cards because I'm a numbers guy. I count cards when I play Blackjack, not because I want to have an advantage, but because I can't help it. Coach Dewey noticed my instinct for numbers when I was a freshman. If I was watching a relay, I would call out the split the moment each swimmer finished. He complimented me on how fast I could do math in my head. I said "math?" I wasn't doing any math, I just knew the splits.

As a result of my affinity for numbers, I don't find it fascinating to bet on poker. I do find it fascinating to watch the guys play. I like the psychology, the bluffing, the banter. I offered to take the all-time dealer's role. The guys didn't let me. We decided to rotate the deal.

Archie was the first dealer, and he shuffled incessantly while the table banter played on. The guys continued to praise me for the Get Out swim. I said "three guys beat the time—Arch and Leor get some credit too." I looked at Archie, who was already staring at me.

"The point of the swim was to beat the time," he said, continuing to shuffle without taking his eyes off me. Everyone else looked at me.

"Right," I said. "Didn't matter who won." It mattered like crazy to me, but I was willing to be conciliatory.

"Wasn't a race," he said. "Otherwise…."

I could feel all the eyes on me. Archie was fronting an attitude, and it was boiling up some outrage inside me.

"So what're you saying? You didn't try to win?"

"I did exactly what I aimed to do," he said. "Five hundredths under the time." It held water, actually. Archie always knows precisely how fast he's swimming, and it would be typical of him to exert only the necessary effort and no more. On the other hand, he can't resist a race. Anyway, he should have let me bask. He didn't need to harsh me.

"Whatever," I muttered under my breath.

"What?" he said, his voice raised.

His trademark relentlessness was on display. I'd been ready to drop it, but now I was just about to blow. He had no idea how hard it was for me that he was gifted and lucky and carefree and standing in the way of my solitary goal, while raking in money and fame and babes and medals. He never thanked me for saving his bacon in Hawai`i and Italy and a million other places. And now he disses one of my rare triumphs? It was too hard to take.

But I knew it would be bad for everyone if I unloaded. So I kept it in. For the sake of the guys. "I said deal."

"Yeah, deal," Moses echoed. Archie started dealing the world's most thoroughly shuffled cards. When he came to me, he made a show of slowing down and snapping the card on the table in front of me.

After the cards were dealt for the first hand, Crack opened up a small case and put on his sunglasses. Crack thought of himself as a pro at poker. He watched it on TV. He played it at the back room of the Motor City Casino. The sunglasses, I suppose, kept his competitors from looking into his eyes to read his emotions.

"Nice shades," Caruso prodded him.

"Twelve layers of polarization," Crack answered, über-seriously.

"I'm not sure you're going to need all 12 layers indoors." Crack just made a scoffing sound.

The game bored me. I couldn't focus on it. I was annoyed by everything Archie did. When he won the first two hands he did a fist pump both times, as if the card game was putting him back on top. Like it mattered. I don't know why I decided to do it, but I couldn't help pushing Archie's buttons. I knew how to do it. I buddied up to Caruso, figuring it would make Archie jealous.

"Hey Caruso, you know Camille Cognac?"

"Never met her. But I'm a male and I'm breathing, so I know who she is."

"Would you be surprised if I told you that the last time I saw her, she was reading *Ulysses*?"

"You mean for a class?"

"I don't think so. It was this summer."

"Hmm. If she was reading it for enjoyment, I'd be fairly amazed, because it's a beast of a book. Hard to get through, not very pleasant, full of perversion. My guess is she was trying to impress you."

"To impress me?"

"Sure. She thinks you're smart, and you'll like her more if you think she's smart."

I looked at Archie, who pretended to be looking at his cards but I knew he'd been listening. I was asking Caruso for woman-advice, the kind Archie loved to give me, and it was killing him. And I wanted to make sure he heard Caruso call me "smart," because let's face it, I've got him there.

"Yak yak yak. We're playing cards here. Ante up." Archie was staring daggers from across the table.

I put my finger on a chip, slid it toward me to the edge of the table, picked it up between my thumb and forefinger, and arched a jump shot into the ante pile. It hit on an edge and bounced over in front of Archie. He grabbed it and whipped it at me. I ducked, and it sailed past. I sprang to my feet and so did he. We literally dove at each other, meeting in mid-air. We wrestled on the table, pushing each other's faces, drinks spilling and chips hitting the floor, for about five seconds before our corner-men pulled us apart. Caruso had me, and Crack grabbed Archie.

"I kicked your butt, man, and you can't handle it!" Nobody could believe I said that, including me.

Archie tried to wrestle free, but Crack had him immobilized. Before Archie could let loose a flow, a strong voice came from behind me.

"Shut up, Doyle." Caruso's command was as shocking as what I'd said. It stopped everyone from doing anything. I stopped trying to squirm out of his grip, and he loosened it. I was able to turn my head far enough to see his face peripherally. "Shut up," he said again, softly this time.

It seemed like I had a lot to say, but I forgot it all when Caruso issued his command. It brought me to my senses. He was right—I needed to shut up. Archie had said things that should have been left unsaid, and so had I. It was petty. And my pact with Curtains to watch out for Archie—how ironic would it be if I popped his shoulder in a stupid ego fight?

I pivoted and fell into the closest chair. With my hands finally free from Caruso's grip I straightened my glasses, which had been mashed into my face. Archie also stood down. The two of us stayed seated during the sentencing phase.

"You two are idiots in the first degree," Caruso began. The jurors nodded. "Archie, you and Leor deserve credit for beating the Get Out time, but you shouldn't begrudge Doyle his kudos. You couldn't have a better training partner than Doyle and you should be glad he pushes you as hard as he does. And you don't have to be superman every day. Okay?" Archie nodded.

"Doyle, I've never heard you brag like that or disrespect Archie. What's up with that? You guys are like flippin' *conjoined* or something. You can't hurt him without hurting yourself. You're the one on the high horse right now, so get off it." I nodded.

Everybody smiled when Caruso said "conjoined." He's an excellent exaggerator.

"Now," Caruso continued, "kiss and make up, and try not to slobber." Neither of us made a move. After an uncomfortable five seconds, I stretched my hand across the table, and Archie reached out simultaneously. He slid his palm across mine and it was done. I read remorse on his face. Mine felt more like shame, but it was a close enough match. We both got some backslaps from the guys.

Moses said "let there be cards!" and there were cards. The jibber-jabber resumed, the playing field was reconstructed, and cards were dealt.

Archie quickly expanded his lead. Leor became the first man on the brink. He was an aggressive bettor. In one of the early hands, he had completed an inside straight on the river card and won a decent pot, beating my three kings. That seemed to have buoyed him. He hardly ever folded, but he never won a hand after that.

Moses was the first to go "all in." He'd been getting poor cards all night and when an ace came up on the turn, he put it all in. But the ace had helped me, too. I had an ace and a seven in the hole, and with another seven showing, I had two pair. I called. Everyone else folded. We turned over our hole cards. Moses also had two pair, aces and twos. I had him unless he scored on the river. He did. A two came up, giving Moses a full house and a new lease on life.

Archie said "hey Doyle, I admire your guts for staying in." The other guys laughed and Archie looked proud of himself. He was mocking me with the fortune cookie. It was good-natured, unlike the previous needling. But my staying in wasn't attributable to guts; the percentages had been overwhelmingly in my favor.

Leor finally became the first loser, which was as it should be because his style was to take too many low-chance risks. He was young; he'd learn. The game continued with five players.

Leor was completely bored being a spectator. He shifted around in his seat, heaved a few sighs, and studied the walls and ceiling. Then he reached in his pocket, pulled something out and put it on the table. The rest of us froze. All words and movement stopped abruptly. A card that was being dealt stopped in mid-air. We stared at the thing on the table like it was a hand grenade. We knew exactly what we were looking at, it's just that no one knew what to do or say. It was a small baggie of marijuana.

Everybody looked at everybody. Crack finally broke the silence.

"What the *hell*, Dogg?" He was sitting next to Leor, and he contorted himself to face Leor and yet angle away from him. I wanted to see Crack's eyes, but the polarization was adequate.

Leor smiled and said "man, I'm just chillin'. Y'all need to chill. Who wants some?" He reached into his other pocket and pulled out papers.

I knew that as the elder statesman, the guys would be looking at me to make a ruling. Clearly, there would be no smoking. That wasn't the issue. The issue was how hard to come down on Leor. The kid was a rookie. If I blasted him in front of his teammates, he might get deflated. It was kind of like the situation with Archie and Capria. Demoralization was not an option.

"Put it away, Leor," I said firmly, but without raising my voice.

I looked right into his droopy eyes. His only choice was to comply or challenge me. He stared back at me, and his smile faded slowly. There was a tense moment while we all waited for his reaction. He didn't say anything, but he put the stuff away.

The faces around the table were aghast and nobody was saying anything. Caruso tried to cut the tension. "Take it easy on him, he's half Jamaican. It's probably in his blood."

"That's a stereotype," said Moses. "Not all Jamaicans are dope heads."

"I was just joking," Caruso volleyed. "And Leor's no dope head, either. Right, Leor?"

Leor didn't answer. He just leaned back in his chair, with his arms on the armrests, and stayed that way the rest of the night. His face, as always, was hard to read.

Cards were dealt, antes were made, and the banter resumed. My impression was that a potentially explosive situation had been defused. Leor's face was saved, no one had gotten mad, and no dope was being smoked.

The card game reached its climax as Archie and Crack became the final two players alive. Archie had five times as many chips as Crack, and he went for the kill early. Crack went all in with a pair of jacks, and Archie beat him with queens. Not a very impressive final hand, but it did the trick. While Archie didn't gloat, I could tell he was pleased to have won. It pleased me, too. All is right in the world when Archie's on top.

By the end of the card game it was getting late, and we had practice in the morning. We said our goodbyes and I was the last one out. I stopped at the door and told Archie I was sorry for provoking the fight. He took all the blame, which he didn't deserve.

"And by the way, man," he said, "that swim was *sonic*. I told you, you have something I don't have. I still haven't figured out what it is."

For the first time in my life, I felt like he really meant it. It occurred to me that all the pummeling of Archie I'd been doing in practice, my beating him in Rome and in the Get Out Swim and the fly set from hell, had gotten him worried. He'd never worried about anything. Now, maybe, just slightly, he was worried about me beating him. Good! It would be good for him to worry. And it would do me a whale of good to think he was worrying about me.

On the way home in the Taurus, I tried to say something to Leor that he didn't already know. He already knew that smoking marijuana was against

Team Jaguar rules and the laws of the State of Michigan. He knew that if he got caught, Curtains would kick him off the team and probably kill him.

One would think that the knowledge he already had would be sufficient to scare Leor away from dope. The kid was working so hard, every day, to achieve a goal that he risked destroying in a heartbeat. It was so obviously not worth the risk. Unfortunately, many 19-year-olds think they're invincible.

"Hey Leor, about the dope."

"No, my bad," he said. "I shouldn't… I thought you guys'd be cool with it."

"It's okay. And don't worry about trying to impress the guys. They're already impressed with you. Take my word for it, I've been here a long time. If they didn't like you, they wouldn't bother to razz you."

"Thanks," he said.

"So anyway, the dope—*very* big deal. Not just because it could ruin *your* chance for the Olympics. Archie's a celebrity. People want to know what he's doing 24-7. If a neighbor saw dope in his apartment, it would make news. If this car we're in right now got stopped by the cops for a broken taillight, and they discovered dope, *I'd* be in the soup. I have a lot invested in this season— more than you'll ever know."

I knew that monologue was heavy, and he'd need some time to let it soak in. The kid made a mistake. I just wanted him to learn from it. We drove in silence for a few blocks.

"How are your taillights?" Leor asked. Good, I made him nervous.

As I pulled up to Leor's dorm, he thanked me for the ride. I felt good about defusing the situation. My self-image about my role on the team as a helper of others, a protector, was growing. I'd done something good, correcting without demoralizing. I started whistling *"I'm a Lumberjack"* as Leor walked off.

After Leor took a few steps, I put down the passenger window.

"Hey Leor!" I called. He turned around, and I motioned him back to the car. I leaned toward the open window. "Give me the stuff and I'll get rid of it." He looked around to make sure no one was looking. He pulled the baggie out of his pocket and tossed it to me. I caught it and a shiver went through my body. The risk was all mine now.

It was only a few blocks from the dorm to my apartment, but I felt nervous carrying the pot. It was like holding a time bomb. How do you get rid of pot, anyway? I couldn't burn it—someone might smell it. If I threw it away, someone might dig through my trash and find it. If I flushed it down the toilet, the toilet might get clogged. I could see it in my mind. The pipes in the whole building are clogged and the building manager calls in a plumber. The plumber has this conspicuous butt crack and he says "I got your problem right here. It's a load of that mary-jay-wanna in the turlet pipe of 3A. Are you gonna call the police or am I?"

Okay, that's paranoia. Marijuana makes people paranoid. And hungry. After parking my car on the street, I walked over to Donut Dynasty for a nightcap. To my pleasant surprise, there were no other customers inside. When the guy behind the counter turned his back to get my donuts, I stealthily dumped the baggie into a trash can. I pushed my hand way down deep into the grime to make sure nobody would ever find it.

PART III

CHAPTER 16

The sport of swimming cannot be portrayed truthfully without talking about the boredom, the grinding and the relentlessness.

In swimming, you set a goal at the beginning of the season and then take a million small steps to achieve the goal. The goal will be achieved—or not achieved—at the end of the season, several months down the road. Every set, every swim in practice, is like putting money into the bank. When the big race comes, it's too late to make deposits. Day after day, you operate at your pain threshold for two hours in the morning, then you go back to the pool after school or work for another couple hours of pain. The next day is the same. Every day, week, and month is the same.

And then, out of this tunnel of relentless boredom comes a small light. You see it, it grows larger, then you're in it. It is swimming's three weeks of bliss. It's called The Taper.

In a taper, you cut back gradually on the yardage, increase the rest between swims, and focus on quality rather than quantity. The term has been traced to Frank "Doc" Cotton, a physiology professor in Sydney in the 1940s. His disciple, Forbes Carlile, became a great coach. He applied the technique successfully and described it in his 1963 book, Forbes Carlile on Swimming. Before the 1950s, there was no tapering because training itself was almost non-existent. Workouts were once a day, 2–3,000 meters per workout. There was no way to taper off that. Now, when training exceeds 100,000 meters per week, there's plenty of room to taper.

Athletes in other sports taper. It's an important part of the training regimen of runners, cyclists and triathletes. It has been studied extensively and people argue about why it works, but everyone agrees that it works.

I love tapering. It's like dessert. I see it coming about a month off and start counting down: 30 days, 20 days, a week until taper. Some people hate tapering. Distance swimmers who are addicted to training don't like to back off. Tapering carries a risk. If you taper too much, it can cut into your endurance capacity. There's a "hump" in the taper. After a few days, you feel sluggish and slow. You have to wait it out. You have to "trust the taper," as coaches are fond of saying. Some people can't stand the feeling and end up ruining the taper by doing extra work. Because of both the physiological and the psychological aspects of the taper, you tend to get edgy, anxious, occasionally surly.

Tapering takes faith. Like all faith, it must be placed in something trustworthy. Like all faith, there is an ambiguity, a subjectivity, a mystery about it. Experience has given me faith in the taper. When the coach does his part and the swimmer keeps the faith, it all comes together at the end.

I watched jealously from the pool deck as Archie paddled around with a bald 12-year-old girl and her two friends. The bald girl's mom was standing next to me, taking pictures, laughing and smiling. The girl was a cancer patient at SM Medical Center, and swimming with Archie was her "Make-a-Wish." She was riding Archie like a dolphin, and every time she came up from underwater, she was laughing hysterically. Archie was doing good again—the kind of good I'd dreamed of doing myself.

The Make-a-Wish swim was the last distraction Archie allowed himself before the Trials, and it happened eight weeks out. After the Get Out swim, Archie's focus seemed to sharpen and he stopped filming commercials. He bore down in practice. He hardly bagged anything, and threw in some amazing swims. I trained with a growing sense of urgency, knowing that my career had a short horizon. We fought every swim, every set, every day.

Swimming insiders say that there is more pressure in the air at the Olympic Trials than at any other swim meet. There's no second chance. In Australia, the great Ian Thorpe, who held several world records, got disqualified in the Australian trials in one of his best events. The Australian swimming federation made sure that he still got to swim the event in the Olympics. That would not happen in America. Many excellent swimmers have missed making the team. In the 1972 Olympic Trials, Kurt Krumpholz broke the world record in the prelims of the 400 free. He only got fifth place in the finals, and didn't make the team. His record held through the Olympics.

Most of us knew about Olympic Trials pressure, and I had personal experience. In the last Olympic Trials, I swam three events—the 200 free, the 200 fly and the 400 free. I got third in the 200 fly and fifth in the 400 free. Only the top two made the team in those events. In the 200 free, I only had to make the top six to make the team, because that is the qualifying event for the 800 free relay and they take extra swimmers as alternates to swim in the prelims. Alas, I barely missed qualifying for the finals, finishing ninth, .08 behind the guy in eighth place. That guy made the finals, made the team, and won a gold medal as a relay alternate.

So yeah, there's a lot of pressure at the Trials. You can feel the pressure building months ahead of time.

Twenty days to the start of taper became ten days, then one day. Finally the golden day came—Saturday, May 19, three weeks before the Trials.

Fanfare greeted the first day of the taper. Everyone was buzzing. Curtains gave us a speech about what was coming. He mapped out how the taper would go. He gave us some examples of great taper results in the past. He emphasized the importance of trusting the taper, watching our diet and weight, getting more sleep than usual. And he told us that everyone had a chance to make the Olympic Team. Every single person on the team had a chance to perform his or her very best on the world's biggest swimming stage.

Everyone was focused. Every swimmer in the pool had the Trials and nothing else in mind. School was out and the distant collegians like Kelton had returned. Team Jaguar was at full strength.

While the beginning of the taper is an exciting time, it's also utterly exhausting. In the first few workouts, you do almost as many meters as when you weren't tapering. You're trying to build speed, so you do more sets at the red-to-purple end of the rainbow. This makes you tired and sluggish. It is now a well-known phenomenon. At the cellular level your muscles are storing energy, and the initial phase of the process adds bulk to the muscles. You feel stiff. You also worry. I relived in my mind what it felt like to finish third in the Olympic Trials. The feeling in my arms and legs during the first week of taper was exactly the feeling I had experienced in Omaha. I blamed the ever-present bubble.

In the second week of the taper, we cut way back on the workout distance. We saw some amazing times in practice. The animal lane had done well going 100s on 1:05 a few weeks earlier. Now Curtains asked how many we could do on 1:00. I told Curtains we could do six, and we did. Curtains looked at that set, and did an analysis of our lactate sets through the year, and told us we were all on target to meet our goals. That got us jazzed.

The third week of the taper was mostly rest. We went down to one workout a day, and the distance was about 20% of our normal daily distance. The excitement built throughout that last week. That always happens. You have more time on your hands and your energy level is high. You're getting plenty of sleep, unlike during midseason training.

We drove down to Indianapolis for the Trials two days early. The Trials are frequently held in Indy. It's a great sports town and the pool is one of the best in the country. The natatorium is on the campus of Indiana University—Purdue University Indianapolis, or IUPUI. One thing I like about the IUPUI pool is that if you make the Olympic team, they write your name on the wall. There's a big wall with dozens of names on it behind the diving boards. I wanted my name on that wall.

The Olympic Trials followed an eight-day schedule, Saturday through Saturday, June 9-16. My lone event, the 400 freestyle, was on Saturday, June 16. We got to Indy on Thursday, June 7, which meant that I still had nine days before my race. It was more than a week of extra tapering. Curtains thought it would be a plus.

At precisely 11:00 a.m. on Saturday the 9th, the public address announcer asked everyone to rise and face the flag. The Star Spangled Banner began. I faced the flag, on the same wall as the names of past Olympians, and put my hand over my heart. Even though my race was still a week away, Pavlov was working a number on me.

Tension throbbed throughout the natatorium. In the very first heat of the first event, the 200 free, a guy named Jimmy Quinn false started and was disqualified. He didn't get to swim. I saw him sitting in a chair behind the starting blocks as his heat went off with his lane empty. The guy couldn't bear to watch. His head was in his hands and his body was convulsing. The first heat has the slowest swimmers, the ones who barely made the qualifying time. No one from the first heat has a realistic chance of making the team. I guess Jimmy Quinn didn't know that.

The 200 free was a big event for Team Jaguar. For one thing, we had several swimmers entered in the event with a legitimate shot. For another thing, it was the first event of the meet and everyone was dying to know how the taper worked. A couple good swims early in the meet can boost the confidence of the whole team.

Caruso swam a personal best in his heat of the 200. He had decided to concentrate on this event and he wasn't swimming anything else. He got third in the third-to-last heat, easily making the 16-person semifinal field.

Then it was Leor's turn. He was in the second-to-last heat, and showed up behind his lane with a knit hat on. He took off his sweats first and his hat last. He was standing there in his suit and hat, then removed the hat to reveal a shiny, bald, shaved head. A murmur rolled through the natatorium. Leor was the last person anyone expected to shave his head. He hadn't told anyone. He looked mental. He looked like a zombie, except most zombies don't have droopy eyebrows.

Leor was seeded fifth in the 200, and the top seed in his heat was Brick Lehman, a veteran 200 man—my roommate at the Worlds in Brisbane. Leor stayed right with Brick through the 150 point, then put on an amazing kick that blew Brick away. Leor won his heat by almost a full second and crushed his personal best. Leor's swim got the whole Team Jaguar bench pumped.

Archie was next. He was the top seed in the fastest heat of the 200. Curtains had given him strict instructions. There would be no bagging. There would be no "just make the semis" strategy. This was his first race, it was a fast field, and it made no sense to take any chances. Archie went out fast and broke the world record in the prelims. Team Jaguar had five of the 16 guys in the semifinals of the 200—Archie, Leor, Caruso, Pablo Zumaya and Freddie Boxer.

Vivian made a statement in the prelims of the women's 200. She didn't break any records, but she qualified first for the semis, ahead of Camille Cognac. Brook made it into the semis easily as well.

Team Jaguar was rolling.

The 200 free final on Sunday night was an epic race. Archie exploded off the start, then seemed to let Leor catch him, then he turned it on again. Leor didn't give up. He stayed right with Archie and they finished 1-2, to the delight of the Team Jaguar bench and fans. Archie lowered his world record. Leor got his name on the wall. I chuckled thinking about the names on the wall. They don't put nicknames up there.

There was also disappointment in the 200 final, however. Pablo Zumaya finished eighth. Caruso lowered his personal best again, but could only manage seventh place. The field was amazingly fast. Seventh in the 200 meant that Caruso did not make the team. He missed sixth place—the last spot for the 800 free relay—by one one-hundredth of a second. When I realized it, after the jubilation of Archie and Leor going 1-2, my heart shriveled.

I found Caruso a few minutes later in the showers. He wasn't singing; he had his head in the hot water. I knew the position. It was so steamy in the shower room, I'm not sure he recognized me at first.

"Caruso, man, *great* swim," I said, slapping him on the tricep. I got my sleeve wet. "I can't believe that time got seventh."

"You know what?" Caruso responded. "I'm okay with that. I left it all out there. I don't think I even had a hundredth of a second more to give. It just wasn't meant to be."

If it wasn't meant to be, it made no sense. Caruso represented everything that is good about our sport. He would have made an outstanding Olympian.

"So, are you done?" I asked him, knowing the answer. He could have taken a spot on a national "B" team and gotten a nice trip out of it. I knew Caruso was ready to move on.

"I'm so done," he said, and he was smiling. "No more workouts before dawn. No more 200 fly sets. I'm gonna enjoy the eternal off-season."

Caruso was not the type who would do a lot of sleeping in. Whatever was next for him, he'd be working hard at it.

"Well, I gotta run," I said. "I just wanted to say congratulations. Great swim, great career. It's been an honor being your teammate. I'm going to brag to my grandkids about having swum with Caruso Tucker."

"I'll be the one bragging about my famous teammates."

Caruso put his head back under the shower and closed his eyes. I went back and joined the team.

Archie had a big night. About an hour after setting a world record in the 200 free, he won the 400 IM by almost five seconds, setting another record. Crack got third, another close miss, just behind Jesse Vallejo. Moses was fifth.

Vivian was the first Jaguar female to make the team. She got second in the 200 free, just behind Camille. Brook got fourth, which earned her a spot on the women's 800 relay.

The next few days also went well, both for Team Jaguar and for Team USA. The stars of U.S. swimming all made the team. Camille and Vivian qualified in three events each, plus relays. Kelton won the 50 free and Crack won the 1500, so Team Jaguar had six Olympians. Archie won everything he swam.

On Friday the 15th, my parents arrived in Indy, along with Molly and a couple of my friends. I greeted them briefly at the pool, then apologized for being unable to socialize until after my race. They understood; they knew the routine. That night, I shaved down.

Let me give you a glimpse into the mysteries of shaving down. You think you know, but you don't. It's not like women who shave their legs all the time, a few swipes and they're done. This is different.

You start by growing your hair for several months. Curtains prohibited us from shaving our legs, armpits or faces for two months before the Trials. The female swimmers hated this rule. My leg hair had been growing for over a year and I'd been working on a scraggly beard.

The ritual began at 7 p.m. Caruso, my roommate at the hotel, turned on the TV, waiting for the time he'd be needed. I closed the drapes. You don't want anyone to see. I spread a towel on the floor and stripped to my boxers. I plugged in my barber clippers, a device used for removing the macro hair. When I turned the clippers on, they made an enormous buzzing sound, like a chainsaw. Caruso looked at me and I looked back at him. I turned the clippers off, then on again, and the sound was even louder. I shrugged, and Caruso turned up the TV volume a few notches.

I ran the clippers up and down my legs, and the hair fell off in clumps. Then I did my arms, my stomach and my chest. I paused before attacking my armpits. Swimmers didn't always shave their pits. It didn't seem worth it— when the hair grows back, it itches like *crazy*. Now, everybody does it, like it or not. I clipped my pits.

Body hair, like the hair on your head, gets discolored by chlorine. When I was done clipping, I had a nice pyramid of clipped, bleached body hair on my towel. There was also a significant amount of hair on the carpet and floating in the air.

I switched from boxers to a Speedo brief and moved the operation to the bathroom sector of the hotel room. I ran some warm water in the bathtub, and got out my supplies—two razors, six blade cartridges and two cans of shaving cream. As usual, I started with my left leg, covering the lower half with thick green gel that became creamy when I rubbed it in. I popped in a new blade cartridge and went to work on my toes, then my ankle, then my shin and calf, up to the knee.

"Ow! Son of a...."

I nicked my kneecap. I wiped the blood away and it immediately reappeared, so I moved on. Blood is inevitable in the shaving ritual, like pain in a race. The only question is *when* you'll see it.

Caruso poked his head in. "You okay? I heard you almost swear."

"Yeah," I said. "Just a nick."

I looked up and saw him grinning at me. You never get used to the sight of a guy shaving down. I was standing in the tub, squinting through my fogged-out spectacles, with one foot up on the tub ledge looking like God Bless America—white with foam—blood trickling down my shin. You just don't see that kind of thing every day.

"By the way," Caruso said, "nice legs." He chirped a kiss at me.

"Shut up! I have a fusion power razor and I know how to use it."

"Looks like you're still learning how to use it," he said, pointing at my bloody knee.

I cocked my razor and flicked a gob of shaving cream in Caruso's direction. He closed the door just in time. The cream went splat on the door, then trickled toward the floor, leaving a trail of tiny hairs. Hotel maids don't like swimmers.

If you ever shave your legs with a new razor, take my advice and go slowly around the toes, ankles, and knees. Those bony spots are especially vulnerable. Shaving down takes two hours. You have to get every single hair on every single surface. You have to press hard in order to remove the first layer of skin. You have to cover every section at least twice.

I shaved one leg, then the other. I shaved my left arm, then my right arm. I shaved my stomach, my neck, my face, my pits, my chest. Then I called for reinforcements.

"Ready, Caruso."

He reported to the bathroom. I transferred the razor and the shaving cream to him and he lathered up my back. I sat on the tub ledge with my feet inside. Caruso was a pro, and he had my back as smooth as silk in less than 15 minutes.

When it was all over, I surveyed the damage. I had used five of the six blade cartridges. There was some blood around both ankles and a knee, and Caruso nicked my shoulder blade, but nothing serious. I checked myself in the mirror, front and back. My legs looked longer without hair. My arm muscles were more visible.

There is a raging debate about shaving. Most people agree that it works, but there are competing theories on *why* it works. One school of thought says shaving changes the hydrodynamics, that hair produces microbubbles, that shaved skin is smoother and slicker. Another view is that wet hair adds weight. A third view is that shaving simply changes the way you feel in the water—you feel faster, and therefore you're more confident. This is why shaving the first layer of skin is so important—to produce the proper sensation in the water. A fourth view is that the mere act of shaving gets the swimmer mentally ready. Of course, there are unbelievers who say that shaving doesn't work at all, and may be counterproductive.

Studies have been done and data collected, but no one can say for sure why shaving works. Swimmers continue to shave for whatever reason. I wouldn't think of skipping it. In a meet where I swim multiple events on separate days, I re-shave every day. I'm obsessive about it. I carry a razor around with me. If I see a hair I missed, I whip out the razor and get rid of it.

Here are the reasons I hate shaving down: 1. The blood. 2. The itching. 3. The in-grown hairs. Here is the reason I love shaving down: 1. The slick feeling.

I finished shaving at 9:45 p.m. and hopped right into bed. The sheets felt like wax paper. I love that feeling. I relished it while watching TV for half an hour. We turned off the lights, but I was way too keyed. It took me forever to drift off, and I snoozed lightly.

When I woke up on Saturday morning, I felt good. I put myself on autopilot. I have a race day routine. I have learned, over the years, that I swim better later in the day. The prelims usually begin at 11 o'clock in the morning, so I get up early to fool my body into thinking the race is later in the day. I got to the IUPUI pool when it opened at 6:00 a.m. and did a long warm-up. When I got in the water, I could feel the effects of the shaving. I felt fast, light, confident.

I took care of business in the 400 free prelims. I swam a solid 3:43, and I didn't really push it on the last 100, so I knew I had a faster swim in me. Archie went 3:42 and so did Jesse Vallejo. I qualified third, just ahead of Leor. The finals were going to be loaded. Crack made it, as did Moses, so there were five Jaguars in the finals. Brick Lehman and Troy Conniff, who were already Olympians from the 200 free, rounded out the field.

During the afternoon, I stretched out on my bed, closed my eyes and tried to imagine myself winning the race. I couldn't sleep. Though I tried to push out all thoughts that would add to the pressure, there was no avoiding the fact that, once again, I was possibly facing the imminent end of my career.

That evening, there was a buzz in the crowd. The natatorium was packed; even the aisles were full. The 400 free final was a marquee race, featuring the best swimmer in the world in an event he might possibly lose. It was not a given that Archie would qualify for the team in this event. There were six Olympians in the race, plus Moses and me.

The men's 400 free final was the first event of the evening, so the competitors had to warm up and get out early. We were all in the ready room 20 minutes before the race. We twiddled our thumbs for 15 minutes, then Archie proceeded with our plan. He unhooked his earphones, stood up and took off his warm-up jacket. He did a few stretches, then motioned me up.

I stood up. We walked over to the corner of the ready room. We whispered back and forth to each other, occasionally gesturing and glancing at the other swimmers, all of whom pretended not to be watching us. We weren't actually planning anything, but it signaled that Archie and I were together, cooperating, that there was a mutual race strategy. It was a subtle move; a method. It messed with their heads.

As soon as Archie and I sat down, we heard the announcer say "all rise for the national anthem." It wasn't intended for us, but we all stood up. We couldn't see the flag, and we could barely hear the music, but every one of us put his hand over his heart. I mouthed the words while my hand bounced up and down on my chest.

After the Star Spangled Banner, Team Jaguar did some cheers that were answered by the Marlins team bench. We heard it all, faintly, distantly, beyond the walls of the ready room. The ready room is like water itself. When you're in it, everything else is muffled, dulled-down. When you emerge, sights and sounds seem heightened.

We marched out onto the pool deck and the cheers were deafening. When Moses was introduced as the swimmer in Lane 1, my pulse started racing. I took a swig of water to calm my nerves. I was in Lane 3; Archie was to my left in Lane 4. Vallejo was in 5 and Leor in 6. The starter called us up. I could feel the nervousness in my legs. They felt tingly, almost numb. I remembered the feeling from the previous Trials, and made sure to steady myself with my hands as I mounted the starting block.

"Take your marks..."—the pause was extra long—"...stand up!"

I heard a splash on the other side of the pool and came within a whisker of going in myself. When you're nervous and straining to get the best start of your life, you're ready to explode at the first sound. I caught myself. I crawled off the block, keeping a firm grip with my hands the whole time to avoid falling over. I thought my legs would crumple when my feet hit the deck.

When I was 15, on a trip to the Grand Canyon, I went right up to the rim and looked over. It was a thousand feet straight down, and I got this weird feeling in my stomach and legs. I crouched down to my knees, put my hands on the dirt and slowly backed away. That was the same feeling I got in Indy after the starter said "stand up."

I took a couple deep breaths and started to relax. Troy Conniff was the guy who'd gone in. He was disqualified. The rest of us shook it off, waited it out, and remounted. The second time up, I felt a little less nervous, a little more confident. I had survived a scare. I was okay.

The race started, and Archie already had a lead by the time we surfaced. But he relaxed on the first 100, so I quickly moved ahead of him. Two lanes over, Vallejo moved to the front. I hit my first two turns solidly. So far, so good.

On the second 100, a spread developed in the field. Vallejo was pushing the pace. Archie was a full body-length behind me, and I was at Vallejo's shoulders. The pace was a little faster than I would have wanted, but I decided to stay with Vallejo.

By the 250 mark, I was feeling the fatigue. Vallejo was still ahead of me, but just barely. Archie was so far back, I only saw him on turns. As far as I could tell, it was a two-man race between Vallejo and me. But I couldn't see Leor. Leor's insane, I remembered, and he could be way out ahead or way behind. The Marlins bench was going nuts, though, which meant that their guy—Vallejo—was probably in first.

When I surfaced after the turn at 300, I could hear the announcer say something. The crowd responded, and that meant Vallejo was ahead of record pace. I built up the speed. It was time to go after Vallejo. I had some pain, but I told myself Vallejo was hurting more than I was. I pulled even with him.

When I could see past Vallejo, I felt a need to know where Leor was. I took one breath on my left and I saw him. He was right with Vallejo. I also saw Archie on the move. I saw one other thing: the bubble on my thumb.

The turn came up on a half stroke, which is usually no problem. I typically just take a powerful, extra-long final stroke and glide into the wall. This time, however, I was distracted by Leor, Archie and the bubble, and my arms were too heavy to take an extra-long stroke. I could tell as soon as I was upside down that my feet weren't going to hit the wall at the normal time. I barely touched the wall, and my pushoff was nil. When I came out of the turn, Archie was ahead of me. He was doing dolphins.

I'm used to the feeling of Archie passing me on the last lap, but this was too much. The stupid bubble made me miss my turn. Archie was fresh and I was drained. And I wouldn't be able to see underwater past Archie, so Vallejo and Leor would be hidden from me for the rest of the race.

In swimming you cannot wallow. I felt like wallowing, but there was no time. Twenty-five seconds left, and all I had to draw on was guts. Like Dr. Nate with his bloody hands inside a dying man's chest, you can't quit. Do your best and let the chips fall.

I thought of my parents and all they had done for me. Curtains, Molly, my teammates—they were all there with me. I couldn't let them down. Come on. I reached down, and somewhere, inexplicably, I found a reserve of adrenaline. My legs were fresher than my arms, so I picked up the beat on my kick. The pain was making my arms rubbery, but Archie was no longer pulling away. In fact, he was over on my side of his lane and I felt his wake. I angled over to maximize the pull. There was hope. I put my head down and swam the last eight strokes without breathing.

After I touched, I looked up and there was Curtains kneeling above my lane. He was yelling at me. My ears were filled with water and I could only hear generalized noise. After a couple seconds, I could make out what he was yelling.

"3:39! Way to go Doyle! 3:39!"

I still didn't know where I finished. In the Olympic Trials, times are far less important than places. I glanced over at the Team Jaguar bench, and the team was ecstatic—high fives all around. They were doing the "1-2" chant. The Marlins were silent. Okay, but it could have been Archie and Leor. Archie had his fist in the air. I squinted at the scoreboard, but I couldn't focus right away.

As I was searching the scoreboard, Archie floated over to the lane marker that separated us. He came to hug me. Was it a congratulatory hug or a consoling hug? I was drowning in ambiguity.

"We did it, Doyle! Way to go!" I wrapped my arms around Archie and glanced at Curtains, who was now giving me the thumbs-up sign.

Yes! I yelled like crazy in my mind, but I had no voice. I tried to raise a fist, but my arm was too heavy. I was elated, relieved, but my body was empty.

I unclenched from Archie and sank down in the water. My strength was gone, and all I could do was float face down in the water. After a few seconds, my excitement took over. I came up, grabbed the lane marker and dipped underneath it. I floated over to shake hands with Vallejo and give Leor a hug.

I got out of the pool, put my glasses on and memorized the scoreboard. Archie won in 3:38.89, a world record time. I was second in 3:39.11. Vallejo was third in 3:39.20, and Leor went 3:39.33. Four guys under the old world record and less than half a second apart. Two of the guys were out of luck. Vallejo and Leor would not get to swim the 400 in the Olympics, even though either of them could win the event. They were young and would have another chance.

I had to give a urine sample for a drug test. I was so excited I couldn't pee. It took me half an hour to fill a cup. I felt sorry for the marshall who had to stay and watch me. With that out of the way, I rejoined the team and proudly wore my Team Jaguar sweats the rest of the night. My teammates were happy. Curtains was happy. Even *Leor* seemed happy for me.

Moses looked dejected. He finished fifth in a time that was his personal best by over two seconds. But his meet was over and he had not made the team. He had one more year of college, but he probably wouldn't hang on for a shot at the next Olympics.

For every triumph at the Olympic Trials, there are a dozen tragedies. For every goal that is fulfilled, a dozen hopes are dashed. Every emotion is present on the deck, from giddy elation to utter despair. The look on Moses's face made me feel lucky. A tenth of a second slower and my face would have looked like his. Later that night, back at the hotel, I gave Moses a speech similar to the one I'd given Caruso.

I don't wonder about the value of sports. They teach life lessons and instill disciplines in a way no other endeavor can. You can talk about hard work paying off and most people will assent intellectually, but swimming gets it from your head into your bone marrow. The thing I wonder about sports is whether we overplay the "dream" aspect. We push athletes to dream big, then watch as most of their dreams get crushed. Where does a guy like Moses, who has had one goal his whole life, go from here? He is talented, smart, funny and loaded with character. He just barely missed. Why should a guy like that go through life with "shattered dream" on his résumé?

I went upstairs and greeted my little entourage. Everybody hugged me. They were all excited and chatty, but I found it hard to chat. Everywhere I looked, there was a group with someone being consoled.

After everyone else left, I took my parents down onto the pool deck. I had watched on previous nights, and knew they put the names on the wall after the natatorium emptied out. We waited for a few minutes. A pair of double doors swung open and a cherry picker drove in. I stood between my mom and my dad as the bucket rose and a guy put my name on the wall. Mine was the only new name of the evening. Doyle. Wilson. My mom, my dad.

There were so many names on the wall, I knew mine would not be noticed by many people. The building was three decades old, and in a couple more decades, it would be bulldozed. I'd be long forgotten by then. Maybe it's not that big a deal to have your name on a wall, but it made my mom and dad kiss each other.

After the finals on the last day, the swimmers who made the team were herded into the ready room. All the chairs had been removed, and we stood there listening to Coach Ableman, the Olympic team head coach. He gave us instructions on what to do next—go home, swim every day, pack lightly and report to the U.S. Olympic Training Center in Colorado Springs in three days. He finished by barking out a warning to the greatest assemblage of swimming talent in the free world.

"I want to congratulate y'all on makin' the Olympic team. The team has a job to do in Paris, and what you've done so far has only given you the right to perform that job. The job is ahead of you, not behind you. As of right now, you represent the United States of America. Govern yerselves accordingly."

I think this was code for "don't get drunk." What it mainly communicated to me was that Coach Ableman was a tough-guy who wanted everyone to know he was the boss. I hoped that Archie wouldn't throw a flip-flop at him.

CHAPTER 17

It's possible that swimming is good for your soul. I bet it is, if there is such a thing as a soul.

I find it difficult to speak with certainty on this topic. The soul cannot be measured. It's not defined by a box on the wall spitting out numbers. There's some mystery about it, some ambiguity. I'm not good with stuff like that, but it intrigues me.

There's something akin to the soul in the math world: infinity. Infinity is real, though some people deny its existence. It operates in the background, exerting its influence on things like geometric progressions and hyperbolas in. You can make that little racetrack infinity sign: ∞, but that's about as close to describing infinity as $\heartsuit$ is to describing love. Like infinity, I imagine the soul is indescribable, untouchable. You can't box it

There are some very spiritual swimmers. Moses Weinberg studies the Torah. It seems to influence the way he lives. I talked to Moses about the spiritual side of swimming one time. He seemed pleased, almost relieved, to talk about it. He had put a lot of thought into it. He told me that his faith in God puts his swimming into perspective. It makes him humble. He thanks God for giving him his swimming talent, and prays that he can use his talent in a worthy manner. There's a passage in the Old Testament in which King David dances before the Lord with all his might. Moses believes God is pleased when he directs his swimming toward God and does it with all his might. I've heard similar things from other swimmers.

If there is a soul, I'm pretty sure swimming feeds it. When I was growing up, my dad used to say "suffering builds character." He overused the phrase and I got sick of it. Now that I'm an adult, I see the truth in it. Swimming is all about suffering, every day, and it builds us. Swimming introduces most people to defeat, and sometimes it's really hard to take, but we're forced to deal with it. Moses relates the suffering of swimming to the suffering of the Jewish people. Suffering is good for you, he believes. If suffering builds character, then swimmers should be loaded with character.

Swimming is also conducive to spirituality in that it is a contemplative sport. Self-assessment is constant. There's time for reflection and even prayer. I saw a survey once that said 75% of swimmers had prayed during swimming. I bet a lot of those prayers were "God, if you just let me win this race, I promise to go to church every Sunday." Many swimmers are not spiritual at all, some are highly spiritual, and most fall in the middle of the spectrum. I'm not sure where I fit. I think about it a lot.

My alarm started braying at an unconscionably early hour for a Sunday. When the buzzer sounded at 7:45 a.m., every muscle in my body reacted instinctively, like at the start of a race. I lunged and tried to judo-chop the snooze button. I missed, but took a swipe and knocked the infernal noise machine onto the floor. That shut it up.

I couldn't stay in bed. I had made a date with Molly and Samanda to go to their church. I regretted making the church plan. I'd arrived home from Indy after 1:00 a.m. and was too keyed up to fall asleep right away. I was in deep snore when the alarm went off.

There were two reasons I wanted to go to church with Molly and Sam. 1. I had a feeling of thankfulness, a sense that if there is a God, he might be somewhat responsible for my good fortune. 2. I wanted to see how Molly was doing in a spiritual setting, knowing it was such a big part of her, and that she'd wrestled with God.

Faith is like shaving down. Maybe it's just mental, or maybe there's more to it. I don't understand it, but it works—at least for some people. Faith works for Molly. When she's tight with God, it adds an evenness to her temperament, a solidity to her character. It gives weight to her reassurances. The fact that I don't understand it completely makes it even more intriguing.

Believe me, I don't know squat about God. I doubt that going to church is the equivalent of thanking God, or that God would be much impressed by someone simply setting foot into a building. But it seemed like a step in the right direction.

I was still rubbing the sleep out of my eyes when we arrived at the church. The first thing we did was to go to a room where Molly and Sam led a class. The students in their class looked about five years old. Several kids were in the classroom already, with their moms or dads, who left when we arrived. Within five minutes, the room was crawling with kids. Molly and Sam let them play and talk and even run. It was chaos.

One thing I noticed right away: the kids *adored* Molly and Sam. They didn't care much about me, which was fine. I was used to being in someone else's shadow. The kids included me in their games, but they didn't think I was anyone special. When it came time to introduce me, Molly didn't mention anything about me being a swimmer or an Olympian. She just said I was her friend. To the kids, *that* made me special.

Molly looked great. She was wearing a sun dress and flat sandals. Her hair was short, parted on the side, tucked behind her ear on that side. She had a bright, expectant, confident look in her eyes. When Molly spoke, the kids listened.

"Okay, boys and girls. Play time is over. Everyone come and find a seat."

There was such authority in Molly's command that it took me aback. The kids complied.

The chairs were arranged in two concentric semicircles with a larger chair facing them. Molly came over and sat in the larger chair with her hands folded in her lap. The kids got in their seats and settled down.

"Mr. Doyle," Molly called out to me, "there's a seat for you here." I'd been hanging in the back, leaning against the wall.

Every little neck craned to watch me. There was only one unoccupied chair, and it was a tenth of the size of a normal chair. I walked over and sat on it gingerly. My rear end was about a foot off the floor and my knees were two feet above that. To my relief, the chair held me. As soon as I got in it, the kids burst out in laughter. I deadpanned it. I raised my hand, and Molly nodded at me.

"Miss Molly," I said, proud of myself for picking up the lingo, "this chair doesn't seem to fit me. Can I use that one?" I pointed at a tiny little doll's chair. Every little neck craned to look where I pointed, and there was another burst of laughter.

"No, Mr. Doyle. You'll be fine in that one." She turned and looked at the kids. "How many people here know the story of Moses and the Red Sea?" Every little hand shot up except mine. Every little head turned and every little eye was on me. Slowly, sheepishly, I raised my hand. One kid nodded, like I was okay after all. He had enormous eyes that reminded me of the bug-eyed holographic goggles Archie wore on Halloween one time.

Molly proceeded to tell this great Bible story about Moses and Pharaoh, the Egyptian army and the chase. She knew how to tell the story—building tension, pausing at the right spots, lowering and raising her voice. The kids were mesmerized. I was impressed at how well she knew the details. She had a main point that she made clear to the kids: *God* did it, not Moses. Moses was a servant of God and a leader of the people, but he didn't part the Red Sea. God did. She asked if anyone had any questions, and two-thirds of the kids instantly raised their hands.

"What happened to the horses?" one girl wanted to know. Molly calmly explained that the Bible doesn't say what happened to the horses, other than that they were in the sea when God unparted it. Horses can swim, she said, so maybe some of them swam to shore. We don't know for sure; it's not the main point of the story.

"Who else has a question," Molly asked. The hands shot up again. One boy was straining to get his hand higher than the rest. Molly called on him and all the other hands went down.

"I saw a horse swimming one time," the boy said. Four more hands shot up.

"Dogs are good swimmers," said the girl who got selected next.

Samanda called out from the other side of the room. "Who wants a snack?" Every little neck swiveled and within a hundredth of a second, the kids were on their feet, headed for Sam, who was just finishing up laying out graham crackers on a table. I was the last kid to get up, and the chair was stuck to my rear end. But I hustled, because man, I wanted a graham cracker.

After snack time, Molly led the kids in some songs with motions. I didn't know the motions, but I tried, which earned me some laughs and a nod of approval from the kid with the giant eyeballs. After the third song, Molly looked at the clock on the wall and announced that it was time to clean up. She said it with the voice of authority, and the kids went at it without grumbling. Moms and dads started appearing at the door. Every kid got a hug from Molly or Sam on the way out. I shook a couple little hands to be helpful. A few kids got high-fives or fist bumps.

I told Molly and Sam how impressed I was at the way they ran the class. I said "those kids love you, you know?" Molly and Sam looked at each other and giggled.

"Yeah, we know," Sam said.

I didn't tell them, but I'd gotten what I came for. Molly was back in the saddle. After all she'd been through, including things I'd done to her, it was good to see. I made a check mark on my mental "to do" list.

Sam, Molly and I went out to a brunch buffet and stuffed ourselves. We made a date to watch *Mrs. Miniver* at 9:00 that night. I told them to invite as many people as they could. I lined up Caruso, Moses and Kelton, a real coup. Archie and Leor turned me down.

At 8:00, Sam and Molly showed up with Vivian and Brook in tow. Just as I was about to worry if I had enough food, Molly held up a big bowl of salad she'd tossed. Brook had popcorn and Sam had cookie dough. Guys never bring anything, or so I thought. Caruso surprised me once again by bringing an amazing pasta dish he'd made. I wondered if there was anything that guy couldn't do.

We watched *Mrs. Miniver*, and I had high hopes of converting a couple people, but it was too large a crowd to allow full concentration on the movie. I had to explain, at a critical point in the movie, about the Battle of Dunkirk in World War II where civilians in small boats helped rescue the trapped British army. Moses and Caruso were World War II buffs, and my explanation led to some tangential discussions. By the end of the movie, people were throwing popcorn kernels at each other. The movie wasn't properly showcased.

At the door on the way out, Caruso had a pep talk for the Olympians. He told us to "drown" the Aussies and "liberate" Paris. He told me to kiss the Eiffel Tower for him. I promised I would.

"And three French babes," Kelton piped in.

I spent the day Monday at my parents' farm after working out in the morning. When we finished lunch, my mom and I walked out to see the horses. We strolled past the gardens to the paddock. Two of the horses, Casper and Rhombus, were out. When they saw us coming, they whinnied and galloped around for a few seconds, then came over to the fence. We rubbed their noses and told them what good horses they were. I covered the basics of swimming with Rhombus in case he should ever find himself in deep water.

It was a nice, relaxing time at home with my mom. We made our plans for Paris. She was excited about the trip.

That evening, I saddled up the Taurus one more time for a trip to Three Rivers. I'd been making it a point to call Laura Dewey once a week, just to catch up, and she'd said she wanted to see me before I went to Paris. I arrived in time for dessert—Michigan cherry pie, my favorite. Laura and I sat on the back deck, chewing the fat and the pie, reminiscing about Coach D and anticipating the excitement of Paris. Laura had been to Paris with Coach D and loved the city.

In Michigan, the June sun stays out until almost 10:00. It was heading down as I sat there with Laura. Lightning bugs were dotting the landscape. There was no wind in the trees and it was quiet, serene. I wanted to ask Laura something, but my brain was fumbling it. I didn't know how to ask. It was too mushy to be described precisely in words.

"Laura, can I ask you something?"

"Of course, Dear. Anything." She smiled and put her hand on my shoulder.

"I don't really know how to ask this."

"Well, just say it, and we'll sort through it, whatever it is." She started gently rubbing my shoulder. It was the one that had been injured.

"Okay. I guess I just…I'm wondering about…I mean, how did you know you were in love with Coach D?" Asking that question was hard.

Laura's face took on some kind of glow. The sun had become a smoldering fire in the western sky. I think that was the reason for the glow.

"How did I know? I just knew, Doyle. I can't tell you how, but I knew."

"Like…*when* did you know?"

"When? A long time ago, that's for sure!" She got a distant, wistful look in her eyes and a trace of a smile graced her face. "Let me see. We were seniors in college. Bobby—that's what I called him then—invited me to go fishing with him at a place called Apple Valley Lake. Romantic, right? He planned everything for a big day; picked me up in his Chevy loaded with food, fishing poles, and supplies. We had a nice picnic on shore and then pushed off in our rented rowboat. When we were in the middle of the lake, he got out the poles and started looking for the bait. He turned everything in the boat upside down. When he finally realized he hadn't brought it, he looked at me, and I looked back at him, and then he laughed his big laugh. That was it, I think. That was the moment I knew he was the guy for me."

I didn't get it. I looked at her expectantly, hoping she'd explain.

"Bobby rigged out the fishing poles as if he'd *planned* to fish without bait," she continued. "We spent two hours casting and reeling, pulling in empty lines and admiring the imaginary fish on them. I never laughed so hard in my life."

I was still perplexed, but Laura looked completely satisfied, like it was clear as pool water.

"Just so I understand, are you saying there was a moment in time when you realized you and Coach were both insane?" It made her laugh.

"Yes, something like that. I wouldn't use the word 'insane.' 'Off center' is more like it—off center in the same direction."

She resumed the wistful look. I put my arm around her and we sat quietly for a few minutes. At first I'd thought the "off center" comment was weird, but as we sat there, it made more and more sense to me.

"Doyle...do you mind if I ask why you're interested in this?"

I didn't expect the question. The old Doyle would have shoveled some BS about Archie saying he was in love, like I was asking for him instead of me. But I'd come too far, learned too many lessons the hard way.

"I'm interested in someone," I said. Her face was glowing again. "And it seems like it would be good to have what you and Coach had."

Indeed, it occurred to me that Coach D had achieved a measure of greatness in his life with Laura. The satisfaction that he'd spoken about—that he'd enticed me with—could be attained in spheres other than swimming.

"That's sweet," she said, wiping her eyes. "And you're right—there's nothing better in the whole world."

"I believe that," I said. "It just seems...hard. Hard to understand. I think it'll be hard to recognize."

"No it won't," she said. She started rubbing my shoulder again. "You'll recognize it. You'll just know."

Love. I was out on Waterloo Lake one time with a couple teenage buddies. My friend Hughesy fumbled his cell phone and it went overboard. Instinctively I dove for it, and after leaving my feet I realized I had no idea how deep the water was. People paralyze themselves all the time diving into shallow water. I changed my dive in midair and belly-flopped, then swam around underwater looking for the celly. I dove down, and the further down I went, the darker and murkier the water got. I found the bottom with my hand and felt around to no avail. When I came up, Hughesy was holding his cell phone. It had a rubber sleeve on it and floated to the surface about the time I went under.

Listening to Laura, love sounded more imprecise, more dangerous than ever. If talking about it was this difficult, how hard would it be to find it? Or to dive into it? Or to keep it from paralyzing me?

After working out on Tuesday and before heading to the airport to catch my flight to Colorado, I walked over to Dr. Sandoval's office. No need to text ahead, I knew Molly would be there. She was helping a customer. While I waited for her to finish, I pretended to look at some frames.

"Is that Brad Pitt over there?" she called from across the room when the customer left. We walked toward each other.

"I wanted to say goodbye, and—and tell you I'm not going to kiss any French babes." She blushed.

"Goodbye," she said, and she came over to hug me. I stopped her before the hug.

"Actually, the reason I came by is to ask you to come to Paris with my parents to watch me swim."

"Doyle, I—"

"No pressure, no expectations. Just have fun, enjoy the Olympics, the city. It's six days. You'll be with my parents the whole time, you know, chaperoning them. My mom is the one who thought of it. We talked it over and they'd love to have you join them, help them see Paris. It's their treat. It's something they want. Besides, I need…."

"I know what you need," she said, matter-of-factly. She looked at me with her big brown eyes for ten solid seconds. It was more than the psych-student face reading. It was the ALS caregiver look, the search for codes, for what couldn't be said.

I dared not say it, but I was desperate for her to go. She was part of my crew, she could reassure me, but it was more than that. Something huge was going to happen and I wanted her to be there—to see it, yes, but also to help me through it, good or bad. But I couldn't make a big deal out of it for fear of scaring her off. The wait was almost unbearable.

"I'd love to go," she said, finally. She must have found what she was looking for in my eyes. "Let me ask the boss if I can get the time off." She walked away.

"August 3 through 9," I called after her.

She came back about two minutes later. "Dr. Sandoval wants to go too," she said. It took me a second to realize that that meant yes. I wanted to pump my fist, but I was still cautious, restrained.

"Okay," I concluded. "This will be great. Just great. I'll see you there, then." Now I got the hug—a good, solid, unrestrained hug. As I reached the door, she called my name and I turned around.

"I can't wait to see Paris," she said. "It's always been a dream of mine. I'm— I'm going to have a great time there." She didn't look giddy with excitement, she looked all serious, like she was about to cry or something. "Watching you."

Her words lifted me like air in the lungs. With Molly on board, it had all come together. I was ready to go.

Vivian, Brook, Crack, Leor, Archie, Kelton, Curtains and I were all on the same flight from Detroit to Denver. The captain made an announcement about the famous people on the flight and we got a cheer from the other passengers. There was a lot of well-wishing throughout the flight and as we disembarked at the end.

I sat in a window seat and eyed the mountains on the flight in. They reminded me about the conclusion to the Moses story in the Bible. When Moses was about to die, he was brought up to a mountain top to see the promised land. He wasn't allowed to go in because once, in the wilderness, he had hit a rock with a stick, making water come out. Forty years of hard, faithful service, and one slip-up got him DQ'd.

I was getting close enough to see the promised land. I wondered if I'd be allowed to go in.

CHAPTER 18

Swimming is not like the glamour sports, where the use of performance-enhancing drugs is taken for granted. We have our warts, our rogues and our history, but the polluting factors like money and fame have less influence in swimming. Swimmers are more internally driven.

Swimming is still mostly an amateur sport. Yes, a few people make money, but only one in a zillion swimmers makes any real money. There are college scholarships, but those are dwindling. More and more colleges are dropping their men's swimming teams. Only a miniscule percentage of swimmers get college scholarships. I once calculated that a scholarship was worth about ten dollars an hour of swimming. If you want to make real money, your chances are better playing the lottery.

Money is the primary motivation for steroid use. The absence of money in swimming should mean fewer drug problems. There have been, nonetheless, some notable steroid scandals in swimming.

In 1972, a 16-year-old Californian named Rick Demont won the Olympic 400 free by .01 over Australia's Brad Cooper. Two days later, as Demont was getting ready to swim the 1500 finals, he was disqualified from that race and retroactively disqualified from the 400. Demont had asthma and was taking a medicine that contained ephedrine, a banned substance. He had notified the USA team doctors that he was taking the medication, but somebody dropped the ball. The International Olympic Committee was initially going to leave the gold medal vacant, but after the Australians protested, the gold was awarded to Cooper, though he never accepted physical possession of it. Twenty-nine years later, the U.S. Olympic Committee cleared Demont's name and declared him, in its eyes, an "Olympic Champion." The IOC has not restored his gold medal. Demont was the first person to break the four minute barrier in the 400 free, and is one of my heroes. He's in the Swimming Hall of Fame.

Shortly after the Demont debacle, the East German team began dominating women's swimming. At the 1976 Olympics, they took eleven of the thirteen gold medals. The American coaches noticed how muscular the East German women were, and how deep their voices were. When they commented, they were written off as sore losers. "We are here to swim, not sing," said one East German coach.

The East German women were dominant again in 1980, and remained a power until the collapse of Communism. After the Berlin Wall fell and the secret files were opened, "State Plan 14.25"—detailing the systematic doping of athletes—was discovered. Female swimmers as young as 12 were given injections and pills described as "vitamins." Elaborate steps were taken to avoid positive drug tests. A couple of the swimmers have given back their medals. The official descriptions of East German swimmers from that era in the Hall of Fame carry disclaimers.

Swimming is an honorable struggle between competitors who respect each other. I'm positive that everyone on my team—and 99.9% of swimmers in general—feel the same way. I believe that today, steroid use among American swimmers is minimal. This is partly because of the honor code and partly because of widespread revulsion over what the East Germans did. We also have random and systematic drug testing. We're tested at every major competition and randomly tested throughout the year. The testers show up unannounced at the pool, at school, or at home. I was awakened after midnight one time and opened up the door of my apartment to find two guys demanding urine. I held up my hands and said "don't shoot." They didn't laugh.

The day we arrived in Colorado Springs, we learned the results of the Australian Olympic Trials. In the 400 free, Graham Dowling, the teenager, went 3:38 and beat Archie's world record. Ian Sinclair was right behind in 3:39 flat. The news got us hyped.

The plan for the U.S. Olympic swim team was to train hard in Colorado Springs for four weeks, then move to Manchester, England for ten days to get ourselves closer to the right time zone and altitude. We were set to arrive at the Olympic Village in Paris four days before the Opening Ceremony.

The first order of business at the Olympic Training Center was to get outfitted. We got every conceivable form of garment and doo-dad with "USA" emblazoned everywhere. USA t-shirts, caps, suits, sweats, towels, bags, key chains, pins, baseball caps, paddles, toys, flip-flops, jackets, playing cards, mugs, you name it. Underwear. Why do Olympic athletes need USA underwear? Most of the stuff couldn't be worn in Europe, where American self-promotion is unappreciated, so I packed it in a box and sent it home. I only kept the things I needed and a few items that would be good for trading.

We stayed in dorms at the OTC. The coaches wanted us to be as much like a real team as possible, so we had to mingle. We were required to room with people we didn't know, people who were swimming different events. I roomed with Jesse Vallejo. I shared a few Jaguar secrets with him and he shared a few Marlin secrets with me. We became friends. I learned that Jesse was devoted to Coach Ableman, who coached the Marlins in addition to the Olympic team. However, Jesse didn't like the way Ableman yelled all the time. It wore him down. He said he might not swim for the Marlins after graduating. I subtly recruited him to swim for Team Jaguar, and it turned out he had thought of it already.

The Aquatics Center at the USOTC has a ten-lane 50-meter indoor pool. It's a good pool, and we had some blazing workouts there. Colorado Springs is at altitude—over 6,000 feet. Altitude means less oxygen, and that affects your performance. Your times are slower and you get winded more quickly. The coaches and trainers were always shoving bottles of water at us, making us drink.

It was fun to swim with the new talent. Most of the guys were veterans I'd seen before, but I had never trained with them. Jesse Vallejo was definitely an animal in practice. Some of the younger women were inexhaustible in the water.

Coach Ableman, as the head coach, ran the practices. He was the dominant figure at the pool. Every morning, before assigning the first set, he'd yell out "wake up and smell the chlorine!" He never stood still, but pranced around the pool deck issuing orders and shouting aphorisms, like "the faster you go, the more rest you'll get." I was dying to give the guy a nickname but I learned he already had one—a name no one seemed to use: "Woody," a play on his real first name, "DeForrest." It was a clever name, and made me smile when I heard it, but I dared not become the one and only person to use it.

During one of the early workouts, I was having a bad thumb day. I noticed Coach Ableman watching me. I was in Lane 1, and he walked up and down the deck, right above me, for about ten minutes. At the end of the set, he motioned me out of the pool.

"Wilson," he said. He called all the swimmers by their last names. "Ya got a hitch in yer git along."

"Beg pardon?"

"There's somethin' *wrong* with your left hand." I wanted to git along with Ableman, so I stifled the urge to say "duh."

"Thanks, Coach," I replied. "Curtains and I have been working on it. I'd sure appreciate any suggestions you have." I knew, however, that the time for making any significant changes to my stroke had long since passed.

"Tell you what," he said, "I'll keep watchin'. We'll put you in the flume and see what it looks like."

The flume is a separate pool at the OTC. It's like a swimming treadmill with a current that can be adjusted from zero to three meters per second. It's built inside a hyperbaric chamber and the "altitude" can be adjusted from sea level to 8,000 feet.

The next day, I stayed after the morning practice and let Ableman order me around. Curtains and all the other assistant coaches participated as well. First they filmed me with cameras above and below the water. Then they put me in the flume. I was told to keep up with the water flow, which would be gradually increased, so that by the end I'd be sprinting. It was hard to do. During all of it, I could see the coaches talking together. I knew what they were talking about.

It reminded me of a bunch of doctors examining a patient who had some new kind of tumor. Have you seen this before? No. How are we going to eliminate it?

When it was all over, I went into an office and sat down with all the coaches.

"Wilson, ya got a big ol' bubble on yer thumb."

All the other coaches nodded. Coach Ableman shared one thing with Curtains: bluntness. No blowing smoke with this guy. I wondered if Curtains had filled him in on the fact that I was not only aware of the bubble but freaking obsessed with it.

"I know what you're talking about, Coach. I've seen it before. I've tried making changes to my stroke, but either the bubble on my thumb persists or new bubbles come along. I'll try anything you suggest, though."

"Let's try this," he said, holding up his left hand. "Tuck your thumb underneath the knuckle of your forefinger." He demonstrated. It looked like he'd lost half of his thumb in a thresher. I held up my left hand and tucked my thumb. "Exactly!" he said. "Just like that there."

"Okay, Coach. I'll try it. Thanks again for your help."

I didn't see how Ableman's suggestion could possibly work. Surface area on the hands works in your favor. You need more, not less. Tucking the thumb might get rid of the bubble, but it would remove half the thumb from doing positive work. I decided it wouldn't hurt to try. I talked to Curtains about it at lunch. He confirmed that the suggestion was unlikely to work.

"Ludicrous," Curtains said, shaking his head. "You should have told him to shove it. I almost told him that myself." It was rather demeaning for Ableman to think that Curtains had not fully analyzed the problem.

At the afternoon practice, I tried tucking my thumb, and sure enough, it got rid of the bubble. It felt really awkward, though, and it sure didn't make me swim faster.

"Looks good, Wilson," Ableman called out. Ableman, in fact, analyzed the problem far less thoroughly than Curtains had, and was willing to accept what looked good.

I talked to Curtains later that evening and asked him how long I had to humor Ableman.

"Couple days maximum," Curtains said. "Then he will forget about it."

Over the next couple days, I tucked the thumb only when Ableman was watching, and then I stopped altogether.

By the second week of training in Colorado Springs, we were really into it. On every swim in every set, guys were pushing each other. The intensity factor went up every day. So did the fatigue factor. We spent most of the time between practices, and at night, resting and nursing our sore, tired muscles.

On Wednesday of the second week, we had a brutal practice in the afternoon. Ableman was yelling like a madman, particularly at those of us in the animal lane. I was having a great workout, so the brunt of it fell on Archie. Ableman wasn't used to the fact that Archie almost never led the lane. You could count on Archie for a blazing swim or two every day, but it would be comical to have him lead the lane—we'd be swimming all over him.

Ableman didn't get it, and he sure didn't like it. His chewing on Archie became louder and more acerbic. "Hayes! Git your candy ass goin' on this one!" "Hayes! Don't be so yella—take the lead for once!" And my personal unfavorite: "Hayes! Here's a lady's suit for y'all to wear on the next set." He balled it up and fired it into our lane, right next to Archie. I tensed up, expecting another flip-flop moment. But Archie just ignored it, turned his back, and the suit sank slowly to the bottom. I was relieved that Archie had matured enough to stay calm during Ableman tirades.

Or had he? I didn't see Archie at dinner, and wondered if he'd skipped it. Jesse and I were dog tired and figured the most we could do that night was to get a card game together. Jesse went off to round up some Marlins for a game, and I went looking for Archie. I knocked on Archie's door, but he wasn't in his room. I walked down the hall, then into the next corridor, and finally took the elevator down. When I got to the bottom, Archie was there, waiting to get on.

"Hey, glad I found you," I said. "Want to play some cards? Jesse and I are getting a game together."

"Not tonight." His answer was short, like he was in a hurry.

"C'mon, it's cool. We can make fun of Ableman."

"I'm not up for any lame…just…not tonight." My antennae went up.

"What's up?"

"Nothin'. I'm just gonna hang out with the sprinters."

"Okay. Male or female?"

"Jack and Buddy." Jack DeVries and Buddy Clampett were sprint relay alternates who were rooming together. I didn't know them well. At least it wasn't the female sprinters, so it wouldn't be a repeat of Italy. Archie looked annoyed that I was delaying him.

"Well, if you're sure. You better get a good night's sleep."

"I wouldn't worry about it." Of course *he* wouldn't. I let go of the elevator door.

When I circled back with Jesse, we discovered that neither of us had been able to garner any playing partners. So we sat in a lounge, dealing hands of gin rummy. It was totally lame.

As Jesse was dealing the fifth hand, he asked what Archie was doing.

"I don't know. Hanging out with Jack and Buddy." I grabbed my cards and started sorting them.

"Jack and Buddy?"

"Yeah."

"Those guys are bad news."

"Meaning?"

"Buddy's a big time party boy. I heard he got kicked out of U of A and that's why he turned pro in the middle of the year."

We were right under an air conditioning vent and the cold air came blasting on. I rubbed my arms. Then I threw down my cards and ran for the elevator. There was no time to explain to Jesse. I knew where their room was. I knew Archie was in there. I knew what they were doing, or at least planning to do. My only hope was to get there in time.

I scolded myself as I ran. Why didn't I see it sooner? Archie can handle yelling, but what he can't stand is being ridiculed. Being dressed down flips a switch in him. It compels him to break rules. He can't help it. I should've seen it the moment Ableman threw the suit.

I got to Jack and Buddy's room and pounded on the door. After about 30 seconds, Buddy opened the door a crack. His eyes were eight inches from mine, and they were bloodshot. I said "I need to talk to Archie." I said it with as much authority as I could muster after having sprinted a quarter mile. The door closed.

Thirty seconds later, the door cracked open again and Buddy said "Archie's not here."

"Like hell," I said, and I blasted the door with my shoulder—my left shoulder, the one I'd injured—and put all my weight behind it. I bowled Buddy out of the way and stumbled into the room. Archie was in there. He stood up from his chair.

I quickly surveyed the room. It was just the three of them—Archie, Jack and Buddy. I didn't see anything or smell anything suspicious. But I noticed I was seriously outnumbered, not to mention outsized—Jack and Buddy were big jaspers. The door had closed itself. Buddy stood between me and the door. Okay, Mr. Hero, I said to myself, you busted through the door—now what?

"Arch, I need to talk to you."

"So talk."

"What's going on?"

"Nothin'."

"Then you won't be missing anything if we get out of here."

"I'm not goin' anywhere." And then he said it. "Mom."

It made my blood boil. I don't know exactly what came over me, but the calm, rational, clear-thinking Doyle we'd all come to know and love disappeared. In his place, a baser Doyle driven by animal instincts materialized. Unlike in *Dr. Jekyll and Mr. Hyde*, this transformation required no external potion. It was triggered by internal juices.

I punched Archie in the stomach. I sank my fist into that million-dollar gut.

It came out of nowhere and took everyone by surprise. Archie doubled over. I grabbed his arm, twisted it behind him, and pushed him toward the door. Jack and Buddy were too flabbergasted to do anything. I hip-checked Buddy out of the way, got the door open and pushed Archie into the hallway. The whole thing took less than ten seconds.

Once in the hallway, Archie started to protest. I pushed him three more times, sending him reeling each time, until we were several doors down from Jack and Buddy's room. There was enough of a commotion that a couple people came out into the hallway to see what was going on. An assistant coach came up to us. "You guys okay?"

"We're fine," I said. "Archie got Montezuma's from the tacos." Archie didn't say anything. He still had a hand on his stomach and was hunched slightly.

We got to an unpopulated lounge area and sat down. He still looked bewildered, and more than a little furious with me.

"Man," he said, "what the f—." I put a finger over my mouth to quiet him down. The rest of the conversation took place in whispers.

"Listen, I'm sorry about that. But I need to know something right now. Give it to me straight. Is there anything in your bloodstream?"

He shook his head. My blood pressure dropped 45 points.

"Okay. Good. Why don't we get some air?" We went downstairs and out into the Colorado summer night.

We walked quietly until we came to a statue called *Olympic Strength*. It had four sculpted athletes, bent halfway over and facing outwardly, away from each other. They were holding a giant globe—the world—on their backs. We walked around the statue twice. "I know how they feel," Archie said, breaking the silence.

I let him vent for a while. "Everyone thinks it's easy," he said. "They think I was just handed this talent, that I'm just lucky. Everyone expects perfection. Everyone wants to push. I don't need to be pushed. I've got it in here." He thumped his chest with his fist.

"I know. You've got a lot in there."

"You know what the hardest part is? The hardest part is that no one really gets it."

It hurt to hear that, but it was true. Even I didn't get what it was like to be Archie. I could come about as close as anyone because I knew him so well. I wanted to *be* him. Sadly, my failure to *be* him also prevented me from fully *understanding* him, which is exactly what he needed in a friend. It was a double whammy.

He didn't look angry any more, or defiant. He looked defeated. It wasn't a good look, believe me. I'm one of the few people who've seen that look on Archie. I felt sad to see it, and somewhat powerless. But it meant we were out of the danger zone.

We walked back quietly, and I wondered if Archie knew that I had his back. He'd never acknowledged it. He knew nothing of my pact with Curtains. Would it lift his spirits to know that he had someone like that—someone who might not understand him completely, but who was watching out for him? Of course it would. But it would be much more meaningful for him to figure it out himself than to have me tell him. I kept quiet.

I went to my room, where I found Jesse already asleep. I was keyed up but exhausted. The exhaustion won, and I fell asleep quickly. In the middle of the night, there was a loud knock on the door. It was pitch dark in our room, except for one digital clock with red numbers. I craned my neck to see 3:36 a.m.

I shuffled toward the door, hitching up my sagging boxers on the way. I opened the door and light from the hallway flooded in. I squinted and saw a bulky silhouette in the midst of the light. It was Coach Ableman.

"Turn on the light, Wilson," he said in a slightly muffled voice. "Get your roommate up and put on a shirt."

Ableman held the door open and watched while I complied. I poked Jesse, who woke up, startled. I told him what Ableman had said. He looked at the door, saw Ableman and shot right up. We put our shirts on and stumbled out into the hall.

Curtains was standing there in the hallway holding something. I walked over and looked at it. It was a box, containing cups of amber liquid. I looked at Curtains. I looked at the box. I looked at Curtains.

"That's not beer, is it?" I said to Curtains.

"Urine," he said. "I am holding a box of piss."

I chuckled and started to lean toward it. I didn't have to lean very far before the smell told me he wasn't joking. He sure wasn't smiling. For the first time ever, Curtains looked old. He had always looked younger than his age, thanks to his athleticism. He was usually clean shaven, but now he had a gray stubble on his face, accompanying some new worry lines. No one looks his best at 3:36 in the morning, that's for sure, but Curtains looked more than tired. He looked beaten down.

"This is why I got my PhD, so I could stand here holding a box of piss at 3:30 in the morning."

"3:36," I corrected him.

Ableman started pushing me down the hall. "You'll find out all about it later," he said. "Right now, yer comin' with me to the bathroom, and yer gonna pee in a cup."

Jesse and I went with Ableman to the john, and my bladder was very compliant. I had to wait in the bathroom for Jesse to finish. We walked back to our room behind Ableman, who was holding the samples, one in each hand, which he deposited in the box held by Curtains.

"Go back to sleep," Ableman ordered. "We'll have a team meeting at the pool at 0700. Set your alarm accordingly."

Jesse and I went back into our room and closed the door. We couldn't sleep, of course.

"Do you know what's going on?" Jesse asked me.

"I have an idea. It has something to do with drugs or alcohol. I don't think it's FINA or USADA. It's an internal thing." If it were an external thing, Curtains and Ableman wouldn't be handling the samples.

I thought about Curtains' face. Thank goodness I'd pulled Archie out of that room. And I talked him down, right? He wouldn't go back there, would he? A trace of worry stayed with me.

We heard a knock at the room next door, followed by groans, curses, and Ableman's muffled bark.

There was nothing more Jesse and I could talk about, so we turned off the lights. A few minutes later, I could hear Jesse's light snoring. I was as wide awake as a person could be. Couldn't be Archie, I kept telling myself. But then, why did Curtains' face look so ghastly? I finally fell asleep.

I was awakened by another knock on the door. I got up to answer it, throwing a quick glance at the clock. It was 6:30. The knock and the clock told me it wasn't going to be good.

It was Curtains. I invited him in and Jesse woke up.

Curtains addressed Jesse. "I am very sorry, Jesse. I need to talk to Doyle alone. Can you get dressed and find some place to go?"

"Sure, Coach," Jesse responded. "I'll go get something to eat before the meeting. Doyle, I'll see you over there." He got dressed and left. Curtains had the same expression on his face as he'd had in the hallway during the night.

"Is it Archie?" I asked quietly.

"No…Leor."

I had about two tenths of a second to enjoy the elation of the word "no," before utter deflation was brought by the name "Leor."

"Not Leor," I muttered in disbelief. He nodded. Not Leor. Not Leor. Leor. It wasn't hard to imagine, actually. Jack and Buddy had probably recruited him after I'd whisked Archie away. Leor was young and foolish. He had the proclivity.

"Coach Ableman received a tip that some guys were smoking marijuana in one of the dorm rooms. One person saw smoke and another one smelled it. They would not say who it was, so Ableman decided to test everybody. Three guys refused to give samples—Leor and two sprinters. Not Kelton. Ableman said he was going to have their rooms searched, and that is when they confessed. They are already on their way home."

"Leor confessed?" I mumbled, still reeling from the news. "He's...gone?"

"He is off the team. What will happen beyond that is open question. It was not a formal drug test. There may not be any sanction from FINA. But I have a tough decision to make as coach of Southern Michigan."

I felt sorry for Curtains. He was looking older by the minute.

"Well, thanks for telling me, I guess."

"Listen," he said. "Do not share details with anyone. Ableman is taking a tight-lipped approach. I wanted you to know because the guys look up to you. You may have to work some damage control."

Oh yeah, the guys look up to me. Leor looked up to me. I failed to prevent it. I blew it.

Curtains got up and started to open the door.

"Wait," I said. "I'm...sorry."

"Sorry? What for?"

"Leor. I could have done something."

"Leor has no one to blame but himself. Do not worry about him. Take care of yourself and rest of the guys." He opened the door. "I will see you over there."

I closed the door behind him and leaned against it. I banged my head on it softly three times.

Yes, I could have done something. Leor was in my charge. I had been too concerned with myself, too focused on Archie. I lost sight of Leor.

It was a lonely walk over to the pool. Everyone crammed into one of the offices and at precisely 0700, Coach Ableman stood up at the front. He was wearing a navy blue USA golf shirt, about a size too small, his ample biceps bulging below the short sleeves. He slowly surveyed the room from side to side, his hands on his hips, a glower featured prominently on his face. He growled out the news I already knew.

"Three swimmers have been suspended from the team for undisclosed violations of team rules," he began. "Y'all can tell by looking around you who they are." Everyone looked around. "We'll be issuing a press statement later today and there will be few details given. You are not to speculate about what happened or to supply any details to anyone outside the team. Any questions?"

Brook asked a question. "I understand the guys gave urine samples during the night. Why didn't the women give samples?" She was always noticing when males and females were treated differently.

"I am not going to confirm or deny that the men gave samples. The ladies were not asked for samples because the facts given to us indicated that the problem was isolated to the men's team."

Kelton the Bold asked the next question. "Are the samples going to be tested?" Ableman stared daggers at Kelton. I noticed that the Marlins knew better than to make waves.

"Maybe," said Ableman. "Maybe not. If anyone wants to 'fess up, I guarantee you it will be better for you than if we find out by other means." He slowly panned the room. "Okay, that's enough questions. Get some breakfast and be back here at 0900 for practice." People started turning to go.

"One more thing," Ableman bellowed. Everyone looked at him. "Let this be a warning. Violations of team rules will not be tolerated."

I walked over to the cafeteria by myself, deep in thought. Archie came up and fell into step beside me. He was smiling.

"Doyle," he said. "Ableman thought he was gonna bring me down, and I'm innocent." The statement was a glimpse of how Archie sees the world. There is always a winner and a loser, and Archie always comes out on top.

"Sweet. But do me a favor and stop smiling, wouldya? Leor got taken out."

We walked a few more steps before Archie stopped and grabbed my arm to stop me. The smile had disappeared. "Hey Doyle. Thanks." He gave me a bro handshake, and we walked the rest of the way without talking. It was the first time Archie had ever thanked me for anything other than a compliment. He'd gotten it.

And I wondered. My fist had found its target—just the right location with just the right force. If I'd hit him harder, I could've injured him seriously or thrown off his training. Softer, and he wouldn't have been stunned—he could've hit me back, or Buddy could've jumped me, and *I* might not have walked away intact. I wasn't even thinking clearly when the punch was thrown, so I can't claim the credit. What—or who—guided my fist to the sweet spot?

I thought about Leor all during breakfast and during both practices that day. I went through the various vectors of blame. I was furious at Leor for letting me down, letting Curtains down, letting his *country* down. I was miffed at myself for insufficiently watching out for Leor. I seethed at Coach Ableman for being such a dictator. I blamed the sprinters for luring Leor in like coyotes in a pack.

After a while, I blamed randomly in every direction. I'm not outwardly emotional. I usually keep it in. On this occasion, I let it out, or *took* it out is more like it. I pummeled the water. I burned it up in every set for two days. The other guys looked at me like "what's gotten into you?" I didn't care. I was itching to take on the Aussies right then and there. It was their fault, somehow. It was time to get a little revenge for Rick Demont.

Curtains came to my room again the second night after the Leor debacle. He asked Jesse to leave again. I was still fuming at the Australians.

"The coaches have been talking about relays," he said. "Leor was in the 200 free, no problem there. Jesse will move up and take his place in the 200. But Leor was also on the 800 free relay."

"Yeah, I know. We need to crush the Australians in that relay." They probably had something to do with the bombing of Pearl Harbor, too.

"Right. Well, we need to figure out who will swim in prelims and finals. Your name came up in the discussion." He paused to let that sink in. I was slow on the uptake.

"How did *my* name come up?"

"We discussed every single option. One was to bring the next guy from Trials onto the team."

"Caruso," I observed.

"Caruso has been out of the water almost two weeks. We would have to get him out here, get him processed, get him in shape, and get his head back in the game. The other option is to use someone who is already here. That is how your name came up."

"There are lots of guys here. Why me?"

"You have experience in international competition in the 800 relay. You just missed making the 800 relay four years ago. Most important thing is, you are killing it in practice. Coaches are very impressed. Ableman thinks if you put in a good split in prelims, you might even swim it in finals. Nobody else here is even being considered. By the way, even if you only swim it in prelims, you get the same medal as guys who swim it in finals."

"Gold," I said. Because the Australians are responsible for global warming and they've got to be stopped.

"So," Curtains continued, "the question is, if that is what the coaches want to do, are you willing to do it?"

"No."

"Maybe you need time to think about it."

"I don't. It's all clear to me. No."

"How about this, then. We bring Caruso here, get him in shape. Before we leave for Manchester, you and he have a swim-off. If he wins, the coaches have assurance we have a guy who is in shape and ready, the best man. If you win, then you deserve it, you will have swum your way onto the relay."

"No."

Curtains laser-beamed his eyes into my skull.

"Defend your position, Doyle. Because when I tell Coach Ableman, he will be next to knock on your door."

"There's nothing to defend," I said. "Caruso earned it. He swam the 200 in the Trials, I didn't. He got seventh, he's next in line. If he'd gone a hundredth of a second faster, he'd be here already. To make him do a swim-off is unfair. Besides, I thought this was settled in 1960 with Jeff Farrell. The Trials determine who swims."

"That is good reasoning, but according to the rules, the coaches have final discretion to put whoever they want on relays. We are following the rules. We want the best relays possible."

"It's not a question of rules," I said. "It's a question of tradition. It's a question of honor."

He thought about it for a few seconds and smiled. It was the same smile I'd seen in Hawai`i when I told him about my epiphany. It was a respectful sort of smile.

"I should have known this is how you would see it. I want to compliment you for saying no so forcefully. You are so compliant most of the time. Usually when I say swim, you say how far."

Caruso arrived in Colorado Springs the next evening. He had been getting in the water every day since the Trials. He couldn't shake the habit. Caruso was in fine shape.

"Caruso, you dog!" I said when I saw him. "You can kiss the Eiffel Tower yourself now!"

"And three French babes!" said Kelton.

Caruso wore his USA garments everywhere he went in Colorado, England and France. He even wore the USA underwear.

CHAPTER 19

There are several famous duos in swimming—rivals and teammates who are linked together in history.

Dawn Fraser and Lorraine Crapp of Australia will always be linked. They were born a year apart in Sydney. Lorraine broke 23 world records and Dawn broke 39. Lorraine won four Olympic medals and Dawn won eight, half of them gold in each case. In 1956, both women broke the 100 freestyle world record twice. In the Olympics that year in their home country, Dawn beat Lorraine in the 100 free and Lorraine beat Dawn in the 400 free. They teamed together on a victorious relay. At the 2000 Olympics in Sydney, Lorraine was a flag-bearer and Dawn was a torch-bearer. Dawn's middle name is Lorraine.

Gary Hall, Sr. and Mark Spitz were teammates at Indiana University during a stretch when the school won six straight NCAA titles. Hall set ten world records in his career, including one that he took from Spitz. At the 1970 Nationals in Los Angeles, Spitz set the world record in the 200 butterfly in the morning prelims, and Hall beat Spitz, setting a new record, in the finals later that day. In the 200 fly in the 1972 Olympics, Spitz won the gold and Hall got the silver medal. Spitz retired after those Olympics, having won nine gold medals in two Games. Hall kept swimming and qualified for his third Olympics in 1976, becoming the only swimmer ever to carry the flag for the U.S. Olympic Team.

Steve and Bruce Furniss weren't just teammates and rivals who swam the same events. They were brothers. Both were Olympians, NCAA champions and world record holders. Steve was in the race when his kid brother beat his 200 IM world record.

Rivals always push each other to greater heights. When your rival is your teammate, the pushing takes place on a daily basis. It can test the limits of teammate friendliness.

The television networks always stretch to create human interest stories as the Olympics approach. Somebody got the brilliant idea that Archie and I were a teammate-rival "duo." I'm sure it was Archie's idea.

The TV crews were in Colorado Springs to do stories on several athletes, not just swimmers. They spent quite a bit of time with Archie and Camille. When they were done with Archie, they said they wanted to include me in part of the Archie story. I wasn't insulted. I didn't suffer under the misimpression that I deserved a story of my own. Most swimmers didn't get their own stories or even the chance to be part of someone else's story. I participated gladly.

I tried to play up the fact that Archie and I were pals. I thought the TV guys would like it that way. We faked up some ways to pal around. The crew filmed us playing cards and ping-pong. I also told the interviewer, whose name was Bob, that I fully acknowledged Archie as my superior. I said he had greater talent. I said I wanted Archie to do his best in every event. I sensed Bob thought that was boring.

"I'm still going to beat him," I said, hoping that would meet with Bob's approval. I didn't want the story to be ruined just because I was boring. Bob still didn't seem interested; his face said "yeah, right."

"I have something Archie doesn't have," I blurted. That got Bob's attention.

"What is it?" Bob sounded skeptical.

"Archie knows," I said coyly, "ask him."

Bob and his crew went away. They came back and told me Archie had confirmed that I had something he didn't.

"What did he say it was?" I asked Bob. Bob repaid my coyness in kind.

"He told us, and we got it on camera, but he doesn't want us to tell you what he said. So, what do you say?" I had to think for a second. I wanted to be helpful but I hadn't yet figured out what it was that I had and Archie didn't, other than the bubble.

"I have a bubble on my thumb." I looked at Bob to see if any gears were turning. "Underwater, when I swim. Archie doesn't have one."

"He didn't say that. Is it good to have a bubble on your thumb?" Bob asked.

"No."

"Then how is it going to help you beat him?" Bob was getting impatient. He hadn't yet heard anything worth filming.

"I'm going to beat Archie because the bubble is something I've had to overcome, that makes me focus and makes me stronger mentally. It made me work harder."

Bob chewed on it for a few seconds. He was chewing on something, anyway.

"Okay, close enough," Bob said. "Let's get it on film and get out of here." Bob wanted to get out of there.

We filmed it. Before the crew left, Bob had to make a phone call and I chatted with the cameraman, a guy named Ramon. Ramon was a chill dude who wore a scraggle on his face and a knit hat that seemed unnecessary in July. We just joked around at first, then Ramon said "seriously, are you going to let him win?"

"*Let* him win? Why would I do that?"

"No, I'm just saying he's the legend, everybody in the U.S. wants him to sweep. If you beat him, you might not be so popular. Might be some money in it for you if he wins."

It was so far out that it took a while to hit me, and what hit me was nausea. Every drop of bile in my gut, every neuron in my brain, rebelled against the thought. I felt like telling Ramon to shove it, but he was good-natured. He had no stake; he was just verbalizing a thought that might be out there. He could never understand me. I tried to give him a measured response.

"Look, Ramon. I care about one thing on earth: winning the 400 free in Paris. It's within my grasp, too; I can taste it. I'm not going to give it up for money, or for popularity. I'd rather be dead."

Ramon looked at me like he was sorry he asked. "Okay, man. Good luck."

I should have said that on camera. I hadn't played it right in talking about Archie as my superior. I was beating him most of the time in practice. My confidence in my ability to beat him in Paris was growing. I should have sounded more aggressive, more confident. It might have made the story better. And I regretted mentioning the bubble. Now everyone was going to know. I hoped they'd edit it out.

The battles in practice raged on. The coaches, however, began taking Archie into other lanes to race the butterflyers, backstrokers and IM'ers. He had a lot of races and a lot of competitors to worry about besides me. A couple times, the coaches had me swim with the sprinters to build my speed. I enjoyed that, but I missed the day-in, day-out slugging with Archie. He was my only nemesis in the pool. Beating him in practice was my best chance to get an edge.

By the fourth week in Colorado Springs, everyone was getting restless. We had run out of things to do, the workouts were getting tedious, and we all wanted to move on. The coaches gave us a countdown at every workout— five days to go, three, two, one. Finally, the day came. We packed up and headed for the airport. We flew directly from Denver to Heathrow Airport in London, then got on the train for Manchester. By the time we got there, we were exhausted. It finally made sense to me why we had done this two weeks in advance of the Olympics. It took us two days to fully recover from the trip across the pond.

Manchester has a great swimming complex with two 50-meter pools and a diving well. It was built for the 2002 Commonwealth Games and has an Athletes' Village, which we moved into. The British team was also there. We were friendly enough with the Brits that we could share space with them. I was careful not to tell them any of our secrets, though, in case they were in cahoots with the Aussies.

The swimming in Manchester was more focused and more intense. It was the most critical period of our pre-Olympic preparations. We were tapering. It was an unusual taper because we had all tapered fully for the Trials. There was more uncertainty about how this one would go. Nervous energy filled the pool. Manchester was at a lower altitude than Colorado Springs, and that had a positive impact on our times in practice. Everybody was getting stoked.

We had three main goals in Manchester: 1. Acclimate to the time zone. 2. Get busy with tapering. 3. Start thinking about Paris.

We began to have team meetings every day. Coach Ableman put a giant map of Paris on the wall, and at every meeting, one of the assistant coaches gave us a miniature geography lesson. First she showed us all the Olympic sites—the Aquatics Center, the Stade de France, the Olympic Village and other venues. At later meetings she covered landmarks like the Eiffel Tower, the River Seine, the Louvre, Notre Dame. I felt like a bomber pilot being briefed for a raid. At one meeting she covered the Métro system of Paris—the subway. We would all have Métro passes and a very long list of restrictions, including chaperoning requirements, curfews and a dress code. I sensed trouble for Archie.

We were given French speaking lessons. This was unnecessary, because almost everyone in Paris speaks English. We had several team managers, and a couple of coaches and swimmers, who were fluent in French. I took some French in high school, but had forgotten most of it. Caruso would take care of me in a pinch, I thought. Coach Ableman wanted everyone to know a few phrases. To him, it was the polite thing to do. We learned to say "merci."

"Say it a lot," Ableman instructed. "Act thankful to everyone—workers, fans, and meet officials."

We also learned how to say "s'il vous plait" and "ou sont les toilettes?" We learned the alphabet and how to count. The only other phrase that made its way into the everyday vocabulary of our team was "eh bien, allons-y"—okay, let's go there. Whenever it was time to go somewhere, either Archie or I would utter the phrase. After a while, Archie bastardized it to "loan-zee." We all knew what that meant. The French people wouldn't, of course, which defeated the purpose.

We watched some movies that featured Paris. The offerings included *French Kiss* with Meg Ryan, the Woody Allen movie *Midnight in Paris*, and

Day of the Jackal with Edward Fox. Coach Ableman strongly encouraged all of us to turn out for *Casablanca*, which doesn't take place in Paris, but there is one Paris flashback and the line "we'll always have Paris." I guess Ableman wanted to implant the thought that what we did in Paris would stick with us the rest of our lives.

The main relief from boredom in Manchester was "Talent Night." Everyone was expected to participate, even the coaches. We all knew it was coming, and most people were excited about it. Some, like me, were dreading it.

"Here's the deal on Talent Night," Coach Ableman announced at one of the team meetings. "Y'all have four choices. You can do stand-up comedy, or you can get a team together and do a skit. You can do karaoke or something we call 'dancing like stars.' We have some experts here to give you some help. The show will be this Friday at 1930, so you have four days to work on it. I expect everyone to take this seriously—" he paused and scanned the room "—unless yer doin' comedy."

One person in the back laughed. Ableman got a big smile on his face, and that meant we were supposed to laugh. So we all laughed, uncomfortably. It was about as funny as Ableman could get.

I left the meeting with Archie and Crack, who were talking about doing a hip-hop routine. Someone behind me grabbed my arm. It was Camille.

"Doyle! We have to do 'dancing like stars.' We'll be great together." She was trying to work some charm on me with her eyes. I motioned Archie and Crack that I'd catch them later.

I was caught off guard and had to think for a moment. I was still unattached, technically, but I'd been making progress with Molly. At least I thought so. I wasn't sure what page Molly was on, but I had hopes. Fuzzy, unspecific hopes.

"Um, you know I'm not such a good dancer."

"It'll be fun," she said. "Come on, I *know* we'll be great together." She'd already said that.

I remembered Omaha—how good it felt to put my hands on Camille's hips, to hear her flattery, to kiss her. It was an ego boost to know she was still interested in me, that people would see us together. What could it hurt to do a little dancing with her? I agreed to do it.

At the next team meeting, we learned that there were six couples who had selected "dancing like stars," including two sets of coaches. At the end of the meeting, all the putative dancers went to a separate, larger room. A few extra coaches were there to chaperone.

Camille and I paired up. She was wearing a dress—something I'd never seen her in. It was a short, casual one, with spaghetti straps. She looked stunning.

Coach Ableman brought in the dance teacher. "Listen up," he yelled. "This is Francesca and she's goin' to teach you some dance moves. She knows what she's doin', so pay attention. I told her to be tough on you if necessary. Francesca, take it away."

"It is a pleasure to meet you, everyone." Francesca had a French accent. "We do not have much time. Today we are going to learn the waltz. It is a very basic dance. Tomorrow we will work on specific routines."

"First," she continued, "we are going to position the hands. The hands are very important in dancing. Ladies, hold your arms comme çi." Francesca was standing there like she was doing tai-chi, which the ladies imitated. "Gentlemen, you do what Coach Ableman is doing." Ableman was standing there in a slightly different tai-chi position.

"Now, come together," Francesca ordered. "Gentlemen, your left hand holds her right. Ladies, your left hand goes on top of his right shoulder. Gentlemen, your right hand goes on her left shoulder blade, in the back." It sounded complex, and many of the guys were having trouble.

I waddled toward Camille with tai chi arms and we came together. We locked hands. I put my other hand on her back, the bare part above the dress. Her left hand took its position on top of my right shoulder. We were like dancers.

I could see other couples squirming when they came together. Maybe they weren't doing it right, or maybe the invasion of personal space was discomforting. But Camille and I interlocked nicely. It was a good fit. I didn't mind her in my personal space. In fact, having my hand on her back renewed the feeling I'd had with my hands on her bare hips in Omaha. It was watered down, perhaps, but it was there. This time, I knew what it was: desire.

Francesca taught us how to do a series of waltz steps. One two three. One two three. We practiced it for a solid 15 minutes. Francesca went around the room observing people, barking out orders, moving people's hands. She came to Camille and me and watched us for about a minute.

"Très bon," Francesca said, then she moved on.

"She said we were good," Camille whispered. Her eyes were looking into mine from about six inches away. I looked into hers. I could see where she wanted to go. I gulped. It was getting complicated.

We practiced the rudimentary waltzing steps for fifteen minutes, then Francesca announced that we were done. "You all did a marvelous job and showed a great deal of promise. I will see you tomorrow night and we will build some routines. Anyone who wishes may stay for another half hour tonight. You can practice what you just learned."

Camille said she wanted to stay. I balked, thinking that walking away would be the easy way out. But she said "please," and I'm a sucker for that word. I said I would stay if we could talk a little while we danced, and she agreed. Only one other couple stayed. There were twice as many coaches and managers watching from the edges. There was soft waltzing music playing in the background.

"So, what do you want to talk about?" Camille asked.

"*Ulysses*," I said.

"Oh yeah, that. I...um, didn't really get it."

"I didn't like it either. Why were you reading it in the first place?" I asked.

She kept her eyes locked on mine for a few seconds before looking away and answering. "I don't know," she said. Her voice was barely above a whisper, and she looked around to make sure no one else could overhear. "I've got this…image. You know, the poster, the magazine. I have advisors who tell me what to do. I'm getting tired of it." She paused for a couple seconds, re-focusing on my eyes. "I want people to think of me as a person of substance…" another one of those dripping pauses "…like you."

It finally added up. She was an icon who wanted to become a real person. It was happening in front of me. I was part of her plan, and so was *Ulysses*.

"I think you're terrific without that stuff," I said quietly. "And just so you know, I don't mean that in some lustful way. Well, that too, but more than that." She blushed. It looked good on her.

I pulled her closer until her body was against mine. She put her head on my shoulder. We shuffled our feet. I could feel six pairs of chaperone eyes zeroing in on us.

"I think we'd make a good couple, Doyle," she whispered. "I feel like I could fall in love with you."

Love! That word again, in a context I didn't anticipate. Another curve ball coming toward my head. My first instinct was to duck.

"I'm totally flattered," I whispered back. "But I haven't really figured myself out yet. I don't know if I'd be good for you."

"What do you mean, you haven't figured yourself out yet?"

"I don't know where I fit in the grand scheme of things. I don't know what my life means. Swimming has been everything to me, but there's more. There's a lot more, and it's about to hit me big-time."

"It's hitting you right now, Doyle. I'm talking about more—more than swimming, more than fooling around. C'mon, let's give it a shot. We can figure it out together."

A glimpse from my future flashed before me. I saw a photo in a magazine: Camille, wearing her gold medals, me wearing mine, and two chlorine-haired kids with Camille's aquamarine eyes. It must have made me grin, because I noticed an assistant coach glaring at me disapprovingly.

I wanted it. I really did. Camille had become even more attractive to me with her talk about love. But something was stopping me. Maybe it was the spirit of Bogart telling me to nobly give up the gal. Maybe it was my soul. Maybe it was my fuzzy hope with Molly.

What do I know about love? I can't solve for the unknown variable. How do you know when it's love? Laura Dewey had said I'd recognize it—that I'd just know. She was right.

Are people really made for each other? Who makes them that way? What do you look for? What do you overlook? Camille seemed so right for me in so many ways, but even though I couldn't put my thumb on it exactly, I knew she wasn't the one.

"Camille, listen." We became unattached, except at the hands. "I'm not being straight with you." Her grip tightened. "The real thing is, you're like a dreamgirl to me and I feel something for you." I hesitated, knowing the import of the next words. "But it's not love."

I knew I was throwing away the possibility of something great. I knew the words would hurt her, and that worried me, made me sad. Based on my history of delivering disappointment to women, I expected tears.

Camille's eyes watered up, but she smiled. There was a hint of resignation in her smile. "I'm glad you said that, Doyle. I don't know if it's love either. That's what I want it to be. I thought we could try it and see if it headed that way." Even those words raised her in my estimation. They relieved me. They let me off the hook.

The music stopped and the chaperones closed in. There was no longer any excuse for touching each other. We walked outside with chaperones following, and were about to separate when she grabbed my hand.

"Doyle," she said, "thanks." I looked at her quizzically. "For being honest. For understanding me."

"You have no idea…." She put her finger to her lips, and looked sideways toward the chaperones.

"Are you sure, Doyle?" I nodded. "Then you have to promise me. We have to be something. More than friends."

"Teammates?" I almost choked on the word. It took her a couple seconds, but she got it. It fit us. She started laughing, and it made me laugh. We hugged, the chaperones closed in, and we parted ways. I kept smiling goofily all the way back to my dorm room.

Camille and I came back the next night and developed a routine. We got to be pretty good, I thought. Our routine included some twirls and back-bends, but we decided not to get too risky. I could take boos from a tough crowd, but an injury would be intolerable.

Talent Night came and, in general, proved that swimmers don't have much talent outside the pool. There were some notable exceptions. Caruso paired up with a 15-year-old distance swimmer who had braces on her teeth. They sang *Islands in the Stream*, and her sweet voice complemented his rich baritone. They sang the final chorus facing each other, and he kissed her on the cheek when it was over. The crowd of swimmers hooted and whistled.

Camille and I did a yeoman's job. We avoided major mistakes. I thought we were the best of the dancers until Coach Ableman came on with Francesca and blew us away. Talk about unfair.

The star of Talent Night, by a wide margin, was Archie. He dimmed the lights and turned up the amplifier. He came on stage with a giant gold necklace and a Detroit Tigers baseball cap turned 20 degrees to the side. He did a hip-hop number with Crack—sporting his 12 layers of polarization—playing the part of the guy who "answered" some of Archie's lyrics. There were two backup singers who mostly just said "uh-huh." Archie had all the moves, and he got the whole crowd clapping with the beat. When the song was over, he and his crew bowed to a thunderous cheer. It was seismic.

After Talent Night, Manchester became bloody boring for us. There was another countdown of days. On D-Day Minus One, we were told to pack up. We were leaving Manchester a day early. The plan was to take the train to

London, do a workout there, and then proceed to Paris. No one ever gave an official explanation, but I got the scoop from Curtains.

"Security alert," Curtains told me. "Our team is a target. We have to become unpredictable."

The thought of being a "target" was disturbing, but I analyzed it from all angles and decided to make the best of it. It cemented the image that we were soldiers going into battle. It all added up—the map of Paris with the bombing targets, mingling with our British allies, and now being a quarry for enemies. I was ready for battle. And I was definitely down with the idea of being unpredictable. I always wanted to be enigmatic.

When we got to London, we didn't even unpack. We headed over to the Crystal Palace for a workout, then it was straight back to the train station. We took the train underneath the English Channel, and when somebody announced that we had just crossed under the border into France, there was a cheer. It was real now. The invasion had begun. The liberators had arrived.

CHAPTER 20

Every sport has its legendary upsets. Swimming has had more than its share.

Most people in the swimming community agree that the greatest Olympic swimming upset occurred in the 1976 Olympics. Even at the time, the race was considered a fantastic upset, and hindsight has shown it to be more improbable than people knew in 1976. The East German women were considered shoo-ins to win the 4 x 100 freestyle relay. They won every other women's race except the 200 breaststroke. The 100 freestyle gold and silver medalists were on the East German relay. In head-to-head comparisons, the East German relay swimmers were better than the Americans by more than a second per person. The American team of Kim Peyton, Jill Sterkel, Wendy Boglioli and Shirley Babashoff shocked the world by winning the race and beating the East Germans' world record. The magnitude of the upset became clear years later when it was confirmed that East German swimmers had been involved in a systematic doping program.

David Berkoff revolutionized the backstroke by swimming half the race underwater, using just his legs. He set the world record in the 100 back at the 1988 Olympic Trials, then lowered it in the prelims at Seoul. In the finals, Daichi Suzuki of Japan surprised everybody by matching Berkoff underwater and touching him out at the end. He practiced Berkoff's technique in secret and then beat Berkoff at his own game.

Australians have pulled some big upsets. In 1984, Jon Sieben dropped from 2:01 to 1:57 in the 200 fly to beat Michael Gross, the world record holder. Gross was 11 inches taller than Sieben. In the 1988 200 free, Duncan Armstrong beat Matt Biondi, who won five golds in other events. Armstrong was ranked 46th going into the Games.

Upsets loom over every race. Every favorite wants to prevent an upset and swims with a target on his back. Spectators cheer for upsets. The possibility is on everyone's mind.

Caruso brought me a copy of *Le Monde* the day after we arrived in Paris. "Did you see this, Doyle?"

I had given it a glance, but it was in French. There was a special section on the Olympics and I had noted the ubiquitous photo of Archie.

"I saw it," I said, "but I didn't read it. Nice picture of Archie."

"The Australians are talking trash." That piqued my interest.

Caruso proceeded to translate one of the articles. It was underneath a photo of the Australian head swim coach, Teddy Balmer. Balmer was quoted as saying the Australians were going to win just as many medals as the Americans. He listed several events the Australians were sure to win, including the 400 free. Commenting on Archie, he said "Hayes is a good swimmer but this is not his race. It's time for him to move over. It's our race now." There was also a quote from Graham Dowling, the new world record holder. Asked to name his main competitor in the 400, he said "My teammate, Ian Sinclair."

Caruso kindly pointed out to me that my name was not mentioned by the Australians and did not appear anywhere in *Le Monde*. Neither was his, he admitted when I asked.

"We've got to show this to Archie," I said.

We trudged down to Archie's place. In the Olympic Village, each unit was a two-bedroom suite for four people, with a kitchen, two bathrooms, a living room and a balcony. We knocked on Archie's door and Brick Lehman opened up. We asked if Archie was around, and he motioned us to a couch where Archie was listening to rap music. There are two ways you can tell when Archie is listening to rap: 1. Whenever he has headphones on, it's rap. 2. His head moves up and down to rap music.

Archie motioned us over and pulled off his headphones. We sat down in plush chairs and spread out the newspaper on a coffee table. Caruso went through the same exercise he had gone through with me. I looked for a reaction on Archie's face. He had heard a lot of trash talk through the years. His face showed no reaction.

"I agree with Dowling," Archie said. Caruso seemed somewhat surprised, but I just waited for the punch line. "Sinclair *is* his main competitor—*for the bronze!*" We laughed.

"Hey, let's show this to Curtains," Archie suggested. Caruso and I nodded. "Loan-zee." We followed Archie out the door.

We trudged down to Curtains' room. The coaches roomed in suites that were similar to the athletes' and nearby. We descended a flight of stairs and walked down a few doors. Curtains answered our knock.

"This looks like trouble," Curtains said when he saw us.

"Hey Coach, did you see this?"

Archie thrust the newspaper in Curtains' direction. Curtains glanced at it and shook his head. Then he invited us in. Archie spread the paper out on the kitchen table, and Caruso went through the exercise for the third time.

"This is no big deal," Curtains said. "You know the Aussies are confident. So what? They will be tough. Do not take them lightly. But I cannot believe they are swimming as fast as you guys right now. You guys are burning up the pool."

Archie proposed that we call a press conference and trash talk them back. He was just about to suggest a few choice phrases for the Aussies when Curtains dismissed the whole plan.

"All that ever does is fire up your competitors. You guys should learn a lesson from this. I am surprised their coach let them say things like this to the media." He paused for a few seconds, thinking about something. "We should show this to Coach Ableman."

Ableman was in a different suite than Curtains, but on the same floor. We trudged down the hall—Curtains, Archie, Caruso and me—and Curtains knocked on the door. Ableman answered.

"Yeah? What are all these *Jaguars* doin' in the hallway?" He said the word "Jaguars" like an exterminator might say the word "cockroaches."

"Did you see this?" Curtains asked, holding up the newspaper. "Today's paper. Trash talk from Australians. Balmer is quoted."

Ableman looked at it like he'd never seen a newspaper before. He motioned us inside.

"Who's goin' to translate this for me?" Ableman asked.

We all looked at Caruso, who performed his task for the fourth time, with the newspaper spread out on a counter in the kitchen. Ableman didn't say anything while Caruso was translating, but you could see his neck getting redder and redder. Caruso finished and we all looked at Ableman. He pounded his fist on the counter.

"That just ain't right!" he thundered. "Just ain't right!" The rest of us wondered what it was that wasn't right. "Coaches don't trash the other team's swimmers. I'm goin' to have a talk with that Teddy Balmer." He said the name "Balmer" with even more contempt than when he'd said "Jaguars" at the doorway.

We left Coach Ableman's suite and headed back toward Archie's. Curtains peeled off from us. We walked out onto Archie's balcony. We could see the Aquatics Center and the Stade de France in the distance.

Caruso, Archie and I gazed toward the Aquatics Center as if it were a mountain we would soon be climbing. It had a stylized design. The roof sloped downward to one side and looked like a beret. Its nickname was, in fact, Le Grand Beret.

"What are we going to do to the Aussies?" I wondered out loud. Archie took the Olympics section of *Le Monde* and slowly ripped it down the middle. He gave the two pieces to Caruso and me, and we followed suit.

The article in *Le Monde* got me fired up, but it didn't change my view that Archie was the man to beat. I liked it that way. I knew Archie. I knew how he swam, how he worked out. The fact is, I was highly confident that I was going to beat Archie. Curtains was right when he said we were burning up the pool. *I* was burning up the pool. I could visualize myself winning. I saw—in my mind—a fist raised at the end of the pool and the fist was mine. I saw a gold medal around someone's neck and it was my neck.

Le Grand Beret had three 50-meter pools inside. One was primarily for swimming. It was called "La Piscine Boiteux," named after Frenchman Jean Boiteux, who won the gold medal in the 400 free in the 1952 Olympics. The other two pools were for diving, synchro, water polo, and warm-ups. La Piscine Boiteux felt amazingly fast to me. Maybe I should say *I* felt fast *in* the pool. We weren't doing much hard work in the days before the start of the Olympics, but we did a couple fast swims every day. My times on push sprints were faster than I'd been going before the Trials.

The first day of swimming competition finally arrived, and we were all ready for it after the distractions of Opening Ceremony, press conferences and assorted pageantry. Archie looked smooth in the prelims of the 400 IM and almost broke his world record. In the finals that night, he smashed it. Jesse Vallejo got the silver. Seppo Teervinen of Finland was a surprise third, beating the medalist favorites from Belgium and Australia. Archie was giddy after the race.

"Way to go, Arch," I told him as he got out of the pool after warming down. He hugged me, which I wasn't expecting. He got me all wet.

"Thanks, man! Those hard workouts paid off, I guess." He skipped over to the USA team bench and high-fived every single person except Coach Ableman, who gave him a firm, manly, traditional handshake.

At the medal ceremony, Archie was singing the Star Spangled Banner. I didn't know he had learned the words—there must be a rap version. After the song ended, he posed for photos with Jesse and Seppo. It was an inspiring scene. I pictured myself in it.

The second day was also exciting for the American swimmers. Kelton and Camille had both made the finals of the 50 free. In the finals of the men's race, Kelton had an excellent chance to win. The 50 is such a short race, one false move or hesitation can make a difference. The starter held the swimmers extra long, and when the beep sounded, Kelton's reaction was slow. At the halfway point, it looked like he was out of it. Then he surged. At the end he took one long stroke and won it by a fingernail over Sergei Palnikov. For the next hour, Kelton wore a bird-eating grin. At the medal ceremony, he kissed the woman who brought the flowers.

The women's 50 free had been billed as one of the greatest sprint showdowns of all time. Camille Cognac and Capria Diamanti were the favorites, and they breezed into the finals. Capria broke Camille's world record in the semis. I watched the finals with a smile on my face, thinking about dancing with Camille, remembering Capria at Santa Marinella. I was an insider, someone who had seen them both like no one else ever had, with tears in their eyes. I wanted them both to win.

They tied. Capria and Camille hugged each other like they were best friends. They held hands on the top step of the medal stand for the duration of two national anthems. Tears streamed out of all four of those mythical eyes, and they were not like the tears I had seen previously.

Everything was going unbelievably well those first two days. I felt good when I swam. My teammates were swimming well. The food I ate tasted delicious. Every person I met was friendly. Every joke I heard was hilarious. My parents and Molly were having a great time. I was totally sanguine.

Archie continued to dominate the meet over the next three days. He had a grueling schedule but he seemed to get stronger as the meet wore on. He won gold in all his races.

Camille won the women's 100 free and Capria took the silver. The American women won the 400 free relay. Camille had three golds, with a chance for two more. She became the darling of the French media, partly because of her name. The morning after her 100 free victory, the headline in *Le Monde*'s sports section was "Paris Aime Cognac"—Paris loves Cognac.

The 400 free began to loom large on the horizon. The day before the race, I went through my usual routine, including the shaving ritual. Caruso shaved my back. I kept telling him to press harder. Three years earlier, at the World Championships, I had roomed with a guy named Art Landry. I shaved his back, he shaved mine. Art's theory was that you were not shaving adequately unless you brought blood. Thus saith Art: "without the shedding of blood, there is no remission of time." Whenever he said it, I bowed and said "Art 3:16." Art ordered me to shave over his moles. I did, and those things bleed. I guess I was thinking of Art when I ordered Caruso to press harder. He showed me the bloody razor.

"Hard enough?" he asked.

I nodded, but my head was already elsewhere. I hadn't noticed whatever slice it was that had produced the blood. I was thinking about "lasts." I would never again shave down. I would never again room with Caruso. Everything I did that day, I was doing for the last time. There were no contingencies anymore; no decisions to make. This was it.

It was unsettling. Swimming was my whole life. All my goals had been related to swimming. I literally did not know what I was going to do the day after the 400 free. Or the day after that.

Caruso announced he was done shaving my back. I admired my legs in the mirror. Caruso whistled. Man, I was getting nervous.

I received about a dozen telegrams and text messages from friends and long-lost acquaintances, wishing me luck. I had never seen a telegram before, but I got four that day. Moses sent me a text: "3 FRENCH BABES." I showed it to Caruso and Kelton.

Molly and my parents came over to the Olympic Village for dinner that night. The Village had a food court with a vast matrix of tables and chairs in the middle. We chose a table in a corner of the matrix. I didn't eat very much. I kept tapping my fingers on the table.

"How do you feel, Doyle?" my dad asked, watching me tap away.

"I feel great," I said. Tap tap tap. "Ready to go." Tappity tap.

"You look good," my mom said. "Very handsome with your face shaved." I'd been wearing a game face beard.

They talked about their walking tours, the cafés, their visits to the great museums. I tried to listen, but I barely heard them. It was like I was in the pool. External sounds were muffled, and only my thoughts were loud.

My parents got up to stroll around the Olympic Village, leaving Molly and me "alone" in the crowded food court. I asked Molly how my parents were behaving.

"I love your parents," Molly said. "Your mom is sweet, and your dad, he really treats her well."

I scanned the food court, watching the bustle and the hum of activity. People were filing in and out, eating and chatting, mostly athletes and coaches. Every one of them had a story. I wondered if they were as nervous as I was.

"I'm glad you came, Moll. Tomorrow is a big day. I have a feeling something historic is going to happen, and it's good that you're here to see it."

"Historic or not," she said, "there's no place I'd rather be." Assurance meter on full. Check.

I slept very lightly that night. I found myself awake frequently. I looked at the clock, I heard sounds down in the Village, my roommates snoring. I visualized the race, the fist-pump, the medal ceremony. In a rare moment of sleep, I had a dream. I dreamed I was swimming ahead of a wave. The wave grew and pushed me faster and faster. I saw the shore approach and I was way up high, on top of the wave, higher than I'd ever been. The wave started to crest. The moment of truth approached. I was flying, the wave rush exhilarating me and scaring me at the same time. I woke up.

At 5:30 a.m., I got out of bed. The small amount of sleep didn't bother me. And what kept me awake was a good thing: adrenaline. I felt good—not one bit sleepy. Caruso got up with me and we went over to the pool for a warm-up. I felt light, like I had a bounce in my stroke. I always feel fast in the first swim after a shave, but on this, the most important day of my life, I felt especially fast.

I was in the last heat of the 400 free prelims, the fourth seed, swimming right next to Graham Dowling. Curtains and I had plotted out my strategy for the prelims. He told me my nerves would try to take me out too fast. I needed to relax at the beginning. Also, he thought I shouldn't kill myself in the prelims but hold back a little for the finals. He told me if I got first or second in my heat, I would easily make the finals. If I found myself fighting for third, I should fight hard.

Ian Sinclair and Archie won the two heats before mine. As Archie's heat ended, I shook hands with Graham and wished him luck. It occurred to me briefly that *this* might be my last swim ever. If I swam a poor race, or didn't have the money in the bank, I could miss the finals. I dismissed the thought.

The beep sounded and we were off. At the first turn, I was a half body-length ahead of Graham, and it felt easy. I was ahead of everybody. I maintained the lead through the 200 turn. Graham began making a move on the third 100. I let him move up on me, but I didn't let him pass. He wasn't going for the lead anyway. He was content to stay right with me, and we stayed even, stroke for stroke, down to the finish. We both backed off on the last 25. He touched a couple tenths ahead of me.

When all the results were in, the seedings for the finals looked like this:

Prelim Place	Name	Country	Prelim Time	Final Lane
1	Dowling	AUS	3:40.25	4
2	Wilson	USA	3:40.51	5
3	Sinclair	AUS	3:41.97	3
4	Hayes	USA	3:42.22	6
5	Ionescu	ROM	3:43.87	2
6	Carvalho	BRA	3:43.94	7
7	Morell	CAN	3:44.36	1
8	Manoglu	TUR	3:45.01	8

Curtains found me in the warm-up pool and read me my splits.

"I am satisfied," Curtains said. "You got into finals and did not kill yourself. You are in a good lane, right between Archie and the Dowling kid. Perfect."

Curtains went off to talk to Archie. Archie also had the 200 IM prelims coming up. I didn't wait to watch Archie's 200 IM prelim. I figured it would be best not to interact with Archie at all before the 400 final. I went back to the Village.

My nervousness kept growing as the day wore on. I tried to watch TV but I couldn't concentrate. I tried to read but the book was too boring. I couldn't eat. I needed to stay off my feet, so walking around the Village wasn't an option. I pulled up a chair on the balcony and stared out over the city. It was an overcast day, still warm. There was a tint of brown in the haze, a reminder that Paris, a city of light and majesty, has some dirt under her French nails. I stared out at the Aquatics Center. I made sure the sight would be embedded in my brain.

Curtains came to my suite late in the afternoon. My roommates were all gone. I let him in, and he took a seat on Caruso's bed. I sat on my bed, facing him. Curtains and I had done this dozens of times, going over the race strategy before a big race. This would be the last time.

I waited while Curtains studied a piece of paper, then he took off his reading glasses.

"Look," he said. "There is no doubt in my mind you can go 3:36. I remember when I first told you that and you thought I was crazy. It was a tough goal, but you have gotten yourself in position to accomplish it. Swim a smart race and it is within your grasp."

"How should I swim it? Take it easy at the beginning and build the third 100?" That was my usual strategy.

Curtains looked at me, and it was the MRI look I had seen many times in his office. He was looking past my eyes, into my cranium.

"I recommend you try something different this time. Your nervousness will want to take you out fast. Why not go with how you feel in first 200? If you feel good, take the lead. It may produce more pain at the end, but you can sleep all day tomorrow."

He was sizing me up, looking to see if I could handle what I'd just heard. Taking a race out fast takes guts. The pain comes earlier and stays longer. You have to be prepared mentally to fight through it. If you go out too fast and die, you will suffer physical agony and the ignominy of being passed. I knew exactly what it meant to take control of the race early, and though it was not my usual style, I was game for it if Curtains thought it best. I tried to telegraph to him that I wasn't afraid to take on the pain.

"Great idea."

"This strategy is not for the faint of heart, you know. There will be no one to chase. They will be chasing you. Do not watch for them. Do not look back. They will charge at the end, but if they try to stay with you, the early pace will diminish their ability to charge."

"I like it. I'm up for it."

It was bold. I smiled, and we looked at each other for a few seconds. Curtains got up to leave, then sat back down.

"You know, Doyle, this is not just another race." I nodded and waited for what was coming. "I am going to miss coaching you."

"I'm going to miss it too, Coach. All this stuff. I'm going to miss it like crazy."

Curtains is not sentimental. Even if he knew it would help me to get sentimental—that it would add one more drop of adrenaline to my reservoir— he could never fake it. So what was he doing? It wasn't in his self-interest for me to win. He must have been speaking from the heart. He could never say he wanted me to beat Archie. But I could read it between the lines.

The time finally came. I was wearing my shark skin racing suit—one size smaller than usual—under my sweats, sitting in the ready room. I was already more nervous than I had ever been in my life. My legs felt weak, my stomach queasy. I took deep breaths but tried not to hyperventilate.

Molly had given me a song by a group called the Newsboys, and it started coming into my earphones. The piano riff at the beginning drew me in. "*Stay strong, you are not lost. Come on, fix your eyes ahead.*"

I closed my eyes and concentrated on the words. "*Get up, there's further to go. Get up, there's more to be done. Get up, this race can be won. This race can be won!*"

I got up. Archie was in the chair next to me, and I looked down at him. He looked up and saw something in my eyes, so he put his earphones away and stood up. There was no plan for this, no method like we had thrown at the Trials. It was spontaneous.

"Arch, this is it, my last race. *Our* last race together."

"I know, man. It's gonna be historic. We're gonna shock the world."

I put my hands on his shoulders and looked straight into his eyes. "Yes we are, Arch. Yes we are."

Historic. Everyone knows that Archie will go down in history. He wanted a friend to go down there with him. I wanted to go. Ever since I was eight years old, I wanted to go.

As I stood there with my hands on his shoulders, remembering all the races we'd swum together, all the *practices*, I realized that even my friendship with Archie was about to change. It's easy to be pals with a guy you hang out with six hours a day. How easy would it be after my last swim?

I tried not to dwell on it.

They marched us out to the pool deck and I sat down on the chair behind Lane 5. Swimmers were being introduced to my right. A gaggle of Australian fans had come to Paris, so there was a big cheer when Ian Sinclair's name was announced. There was an even bigger cheer for Graham Dowling. The American fans were more numerous, and louder, than any other country's, so Archie and I got the biggest cheers of all. The poor guys in Lanes 7 and 8 had only their mothers cheering for them.

Once the introductions were over, I was in a tunnel. I didn't want to see what was happening beside me. I only cared about the starting block and the water in my lane. I tuned out every sound except the voice of the starter, who called us up to the blocks.

You should have been there. It was historic.

"Take your marks." Step forward, set the toes, lean down, grab the front of the starting block. BEEP.

I spring out, pike a little with hips up, stretch for the water, and hit it like a paint brush dipping into paint. Three dolphin kicks, then up to the surface. Hey, not too bad. Archie usually gets ahead of me on the dive but not this time. I'm even with Archie and Dowling, the guys on either side of me. It's a relief to be in the water.

The first length feels easy, and I'm forging a lead. This is what Curtains was talking about. Go with it. Relax out of the turn and then go. Keep it smooth, but don't hold back. Here comes the 100 wall. I'm in a clear lead.

The second 100 is smooth and I'm building my lead. My stroke feels great, my arms feel light. I'm on top of the water. All my senses feel heightened. I can see and hear better than usual; my brain is on high alert. All reports from body systems are positive.

At the 150 wall, I come in on my left arm stroke. No harm in taking a peek, I breathe on my left. No one near me—good. I also see no bubble on my thumb. Same thing at the 200 wall. No bubble. This must be my day! My Lezak day! The day I transcend my genes, my technique and my training! The day I swim beyond myself, the day the dream comes true! It's all working. I'm ahead, I feel great and there's no bubble. I can visualize it now—me, in the familiar pose, on top of the medal stand with a gold medal hanging around my neck.

Coming out of the 200 turn, I'm in the lead by at least a body length. That's more than a second. I hear a spike in noise from the crowd, which means I'm ahead of world record pace. That's cool, but it's not important to me. What's important to me is that the current and former world record holders are behind me, soon to be making their moves. These guys aren't going to just roll over.

At the 250 wall, I'm still a body-length ahead. I'm feeling smooth, but there they are, the first signs of pain in my arms and stomach. Hello, Mr. Pain. I've been expecting you. I know you'll be visiting my competitors, too. But you won't be having your way with me today. I trained too hard, and I want this race too much. Take a back seat.

Here's the 300 wall I'm still ahead, but the charge is on. Archie and Dowling are moving up on either side of me. They're trying to drag off me. Each one is on my side of his lane. I can't give Dowling an inch. I slide slightly to Archie's side.

The crowd noise increases again after the 300 turn, and this time it does not die down. I know all too well that Archie is kicking it into a higher gear for the last 100. So is Dowling. I wonder if I've got another gear. I start to stretch out my stroke and kick harder. They're still coming. I clench my jaw when I'm not turning to breathe. I can't let them pass me. Not today. Time to fight.

I fight, but they catch me. As Archie pulls even, I skip a breath to increase my rhythm. While my head is down, I can see my left hand. There it is. The bubble is back. I don't care. I'm used to seeing it. I won't let it affect me. I've trained beyond it.

At the last turn, Archie and Dowling are slightly ahead of me. Where's Sinclair? I can't see him. Archie is doing dolphin kicks. Mr. Pain is turning the screws. He's laughing at me. Time is running out on the race, on my career.

My arms feel incredibly heavy, but I know the other guys are feeling it too. I set a blistering early pace, and it took as much of a toll on them as it did on me. This is not the usual race. Archie is not just going to swim away from me. Not this time.

Come on, Doyle. Now is the time. The song: *"this race can be won!"* Forty meters to go. Molly's slogan: "YOU CAN DO IT!" Thirty meters. Keep churning. Keep your stroke together. Kick hard. Twenty meters. Catching up. Ten meters. Just about there. Put your head down. No more breathing. Force the arms through. Kick. Big kick. Lunge.

There was an explosion of sound when I hit the touchpad. The crowd was going berserk. The announcer was shrieking something in French I couldn't understand. I couldn't tell if I had beaten either Dowling or Archie. We had finished together. I looked over at the USA team bench. No ecstasy there. No ecstasy at the Australian bench, either. No one in the pool had his fist in the air. Archie was leaning into the gutter, coughing, spitting, maybe puking. I leaned across the lane marker toward Archie.

"You okay, Arch?" I could barely muster a whisper.

"Yeah," he said, faintly.

He sounded and looked utterly spent. I had never seen him like that. He came over to the lane marker and put both arms around my neck, like he needed to in order to stay afloat. After a few seconds he unclenched and said "great race, Doyle. *Great* race." He said it softly. I turned toward the scoreboard and squinted.

Archie won. I was fourth. Dowling was second and Sinclair third. My time was 3:36.36. Sinclair's was 3:36.35. Archie's was 3:36.29.

Four guys had thoroughly destroyed the world record. Three of them got medals.

CHAPTER 21

I once saw a demotivational poster that said: "Dreams are like rainbows. Only idiots chase them."

Most swimmers' dreams do not come true. Most swimmers don't win Olympic gold medals. Hardly any swimmers get full ride scholarships. Only a few make it into the Hall of Fame.

In swimming, you can win gold medals and still not fulfill your dreams. In the 1984 Olympics, there was a swimmer who won three golds but he had hoped to swim faster times. On the medal stand, he looked disappointed in himself. He had a great career, but his failure to meet his own high standards showed through.

What about the rare swimmer who achieves everything he hoped for? Is he fulfilled? Is his life full of joy? Is he in harmony with the cosmos?

Like most swimmers, I'm fascinated by the life of Mark Spitz. Spitz won seven gold medals and set seven world records in his seven events at the 1972 Olympics. He set the standard against which all other Olympians are measured. His name gets spoken at every Olympics. Matt Biondi aimed for the "Spitz Seven" in 1988, but ended up with five golds, a silver and a bronze. Not a bad haul, but not as good as Spitz. Michael Phelps went after Spitz in 2004, and also came up one gold short. In 2008, when Phelps won eight golds, it was Spitz's standard that provided the motivation. Should we push swimmers to dream the Mark Spitz dream?

Mark Spitz was 22 years old when he retired from swimming. After swimming, Spitz shelved his plan to go to dental school. He tried acting, but wasn't good at it. One of his dreams was to be the first "Olympic astronaut," but that dream sputtered. At age 41, Spitz dreamed of making a comeback and started training for the 1992 Olympics. He participated in two televised challenge matches with Matt Biondi and Tom Jager. Though Spitz swam well, the younger swimmers blew him away.

You get the sense that Spitz remained unsatisfied, that he was on a quest to do "more." The drive that got him the gold medals in the first place was something deep inside him that couldn't be shut off at age 22. Michael Phelps reached the Spitz pinnacle. He says he suffered depression—depression!—after winning eight gold medals in 2008.

Maybe we should tell young swimmers that their swimming dreams are unlikely to come true. Most aren't good enough to achieve anything dreamlike. Even if you're good enough, you can get robbed by circumstances, like in 1980. And even if your swimming dreams do come true, that doesn't mean life will be a bed of roses. It won't ensure inner peace. Maybe we shouldn't talk about dreams at all. Maybe we shouldn't teach kids to let their dreams run free, because dreams and disappointment go hand in hand.

Wait a minute, I've got it. Let them dream and let them get disappointed. Disappointment breeds humility, and there isn't enough humility in the world. Living beyond disappointment brings toughness, and there's too much softness in the world. Behind every success there are a dozen disappointments.

People who don't fulfill their dreams aren't failures. Swimming helps people develop traits that serve them well later in life. There are more Dr. Nates in the world than Mark Spitzes.

Swimming is a microcosm of life. It brings victory and defeat, triumph and disappointment. You have to learn to live with both. Swimming brings them on early in life. Let the young swimmers dream.

Getting fourth place is like getting kicked in the groin. There are pains in swimming that feel good, in a way. The soreness of your muscles the day after a tough set reminds you how hard you worked. That's a good pain. I broke my finger once by jamming it into the wall at the end of a race. The pain reminded me of my victory. But there are pains in swimming that are God-awful, like when you snap your rotator cuff. That's a bad pain. The pain of getting fourth has an insulting quality to it. It's the kind that makes you want to forget rather than remember.

I stayed in the water, facing the scoreboard, memorizing it. My elbows were behind me, hooked over the gutter, my back against the wall. The pain from the race and the emotional letdown of fourth place left me breathing hard and almost unable to move. Emotions came at me in waves, the relentless kind of waves that pound you. As soon as I surfaced after one wave threw me down, the next one came.

Not all the emotions were bad. It wasn't all bad that Archie had won. His string of gold medals was intact and he had beaten the Aussies. I was proud of my time—3:36, the number that had haunted my sleep for the last year. If there is a heaven, Coach Dewey would be looking down and saying "sweet."

It was not the kind of sweetness I had imagined. The good emotions were drowned by the bad ones: disappointment, anger, despair, self-pity, sadness. I felt unlucky, ripped off. I hated Archie. Why should he get *everything*? He has all the talent in the world. Why should he get all the luck on top of that? Luck—good or bad—is the only conceivable explanation for the order of finish in a race like that.

I had wanted to be great, just once. My greatness would be measured in gallons of grief.

I floated over to the lane marker next to Graham Dowling and shook his hand. There was no way I was going to swim over to Sinclair's lane, but I caught his gaze and said "nice race." Then I got out. I didn't want to see anybody, so I walked over to the warm-down pool. On the way, my legs started to buckle and I had to stop for a second, leaning on a chair. I got in the water and started to swim, even though there was no next race for me, no need to work the lactic acid out. I just needed my head to be in liquid.

After a couple laps, I saw Curtains at the end of my lane. I stopped. He leaned down and patted my shoulder.

"Do you want your splits, Doyle?" I shook my head.

It was obvious that Curtains didn't know what to say to me. I was in for a long night of talking to people who didn't know what to say. I didn't know what to say, either.

"Swim a few more laps, then," he said. "We will talk later." I pushed off and swam. I knew I would have to work through the emotions, just let them roll over me, toss me around, before I could start talking to people.

Before, no matter how bad a race I swam, no matter how bad I felt, I knew what to do next. Work harder. Bounce back. Keep going. There was always a tomorrow. But I'd run out of tomorrows and I didn't know what to do.

I got out of the pool and hustled to the showers, hoping no one would see me. The emotions kept coming, and I felt like wallowing in them. I had time to wallow, a lifetime in fact, and people would understand if I did. I set the shower handle on wallow, got a good flow of hot water on my head, and closed my eyes.

"Hey, Doyle."

It was the golden baritone. I opened my eyes and looked at Caruso through the steam without saying anything. The shoe was on the other foot now, the irony not lost on either of us.

"I'm awed by what you just did," he said. "Inspired."

I didn't react, except to spit some water between my teeth. I eyed him, he eyed me. There was no point in telling him the obvious, that I wasn't happy.

"Thanks," I said. "Go get 'em in the relay."

"I'm psyched for it. And when it's over, you and me—the Eiffel Tower...."

I nodded. Then I waved my hand and closed my eyes. I had no intention of visiting the Eiffel Tower. Kissing three French babes was just a cruel joke.

I don't know how long I stayed in the hot water, but my fingers looked like prunes when I turned the water off. I didn't stay in long enough to work out all the issues. I stayed in long enough to develop a game plan.

First, I decided to go meet everyone. I couldn't avoid people or wait for them to come to me. Swimming is all about making yourself do things that you know are hard. It was going to be hard to have all those awkward conversations. So what? I had to do it anyway.

Second, I decided not to sulk or pout or be negative in any way. There were people who still had races. I was a leader on the team. I had to cheer, psych people up, encourage my teammates. You can't do that when you're acting sorry for yourself.

Third, I decided to acknowledge the positives of what I had done. I wasn't going to pretend that fourth place didn't matter, that I wasn't disappointed, but I could still accept compliments.

Fourth, I decided to be thankful. Coach Ableman had told us to thank everyone. It was time to do that. I needed to thank the meet officials, the coaches, the trainers, my teammates, my supporters. My parents.

Once I had a plan in place, I got out of the shower and put on my USA sweats. I walked out onto the pool deck, ready to interact with whomever I might encounter. The first person I saw was Archie. He was stretching, listening to rap music, getting ready for the 200 IM semifinals. He saw me coming and took out his earpieces.

"Man I'm glad to see you," he said. "I'm having a tough time psyching up for this IM. I feel like crap from the 400. I don't even care about this race anymore."

My admiration for Archie sprouted a new bud. I had the luxury of dwelling on a race that ended half an hour before. I would probably dwell on it the rest of my life. Archie was moving on to the next one. It must be hard to be good at so many events. The mental toughness required to pull it off must be immense. And, intentionally or not, Archie was making me feel useful.

"I'm not sure how much psyching I can give you, Arch. I'm pretty drained myself. I couldn't even imagine swimming another race right now."

"Jeez, the 400 free…that race was epic." Archie was staring off. "That was the best race I ever swam. Three thirty-six is *insane*! I thought you had me there."

"You swam a great race, and I'm glad you did. You and I…you know…it's like I had a part in what you did."

Archie jumped all over that. "Absolutely!" he said.

"So I'll have a part in the next one too. Nail it, man. Do it for me." He grinned like a crocodile.

I knew Archie had mixed feelings about the 400. That's why he didn't pump his fist. He was glad to beat the Aussies, glad to get the record, glad to win, sad for me. He was part of my performances and I was part of his. We understood each other. We exchanged a manly hug and I moved on.

Did it soften the blow, the fact that the producer of my life's great anguish was my friend? Let me put it this way: no.

Just as mixing matter and antimatter results in annihilation, love and hate are dangerous when combined. I was feeling some of that annihilation. It would have been easier to handle if I'd lost to just the Aussies. I could make them pure evil in my mind; I could hate them forever.

And yet, the sport of swimming itself is a love-hate proposition. Things you hate—pain, boredom and relentless hard work—purchase things you love, like achievement, satisfaction, and character. Physical and mental breakdown ultimately build you. It seems paradoxical, complicated—like life, where love and hate are rarely found in unadulterated forms.

The medal ceremony for the 400 free was awkward but I made myself watch. I stood by myself in a corner on the pool deck. The emotions swirled again as the Star Spangled Banner played. The Aussies looked frustrated that they hadn't won. Archie looked exhausted, and perhaps disappointed that I wasn't there. He did the appropriate amount of smiling, waving and posing for photos, but I could tell he was anxious for it to be over. As the national anthem ended and Archie mouthed the word "brave," it was like the final note of my career symphony. I swallowed hard.

I met my parents and Molly in the hallway outside the spectator stands. My mom's eyes were red, and she came right up to me and just about hugged the wind out of me. She cried a little while I held her. She never said a word, but words were unnecessary. I knew. Moms feel your pain.

My dad hugged me next. We don't hug a lot, and he's shorter than I am, so it was clumsy. He mumbled something into my shoulder—words that sounded like "I understand."

Molly had a hug for me, too, but otherwise she stayed in the background. I knew she and I would have a chance to talk later.

I implemented step four of the plan I had devised in the shower.

"Mom, Dad, Molly," I began, looking at each one in turn, "thank you for coming to Paris. It means a lot to me that you're here right now. And thanks for supporting me in general. Mom, Dad, you know, over the years. I love you guys."

My mom started crying again. I put my arm around her shoulder. I was glad I'd gotten out the speech without blubbering myself. It needed to be said.

We stood there talking about the race for a few minutes. I told them I was extremely satisfied with the way I had prepared and raced, and happy with the time I had swum. I was, of course, deflated that I hadn't won. I told them I wasn't completely sure how bad I felt; I wanted to think about it and let it sink in. They told me not to be disappointed, that I had obviously fought my hardest and I was so close to winning. They were trying to reassure me, but they were swimming upstream.

The four of us decided to spend the whole next day together, starting with breakfast at their hotel. I would return to the pool to watch Caruso swim the prelims of the 800 free relay, then I'd be free the rest of the afternoon. We planned to watch the finals at night, then go out to dinner at a fancy four-star restaurant.

I said goodnight to my parents and Molly, then headed to the Athletes' Village. The rest of my teammates had already headed back. I was alone with my thoughts. During the shuttle ride, I replayed the last 100 of the race over and over in my mind. Is there any way I could have shaved a tenth of a second off my time? Should I have taken it out a little slower and saved more for the end? Did I miss a hair somewhere when I was shaving? Could I have worked just a little bit harder in practice? Seven one-hundredths of a second is a microscopic amount of time. Could I have found it somewhere? I'll never know.

And what about the bubble—did it cost me the race? Why had it disappeared, almost as if divinely removed, for a moment in time, only to reappear at crunch time? What was the aberration, the bubble or its absence? Was this to be my lot in life, living on the edge of perfection, crossing over only briefly, just enough to whet my appetite but not enough to deliver me into the promised land?

Or did the bubble, as Curtains said it might, bring me a benefit? I will wonder forever.

I knew a place in the Village where I could get something similar to a hot fudge sundae. It had everything but the hot fudge, but I asked them to heat up some chocolate, and it was close enough. After 15 minutes, I had assembled a complete meal—two burgers, a mound of french fries and a sundae. I was just about to dip a french fry into the whipped cream when Curtains appeared out of nowhere. He sat down across from me.

"Some of your teammates are at your suite with a tape of the 400 free. They do not want to watch it without you there."

"No problem," I said. "It'll take me five minutes to finish this off and then we'll go watch. You want one of these burgers?"

I knew his diet didn't include burgers, but I wanted to be polite. He eyed the burger like I was offering moldy bread. He took it. We munched for a while without talking. I remembered the plans I had made in the shower, particularly the part about thanking people.

"Thanks for coaching me to a 3:36," I said. "I know that's a time I'll remember the rest of my life, and it's a good time. I'm happy with it."

"You did it, not me," Curtains answered, examining the burger. "Four guys went 3:36 thanks to you."

He took another bite and examined the burger again. "How do the French know how to make such good burgers?" he said. I pushed the fries in his direction.

"So Coach, you've been around swimming a long time. What does it mean in the grand scheme of things to get fourth in the Olympics?"

"I am not sure I understand your question." He was licking his fingers.

"I mean, when I was a kid, I dreamed of winning all these gold medals in the Olympics, like Mark Spitz. Swimming was my whole life. I was going to make money off it, you know, endorsements, whatever. I was going to leave my mark on the sport. People were going to remember my name forever. Now, all I have is my name on the wall in Indy, along with five hundred other names. Was it worth it?"

Curtains wiped his fingers on a napkin and leaned toward me, with his elbows on the table.

"Listen to me, Doyle. The value of swimming is not getting a hunk of metal or your name on a wall. It is something inside your chest cavity and it is measureless."

He leaned back and started eating the fries. I let his words soak in.

Measureless? How could the value of a sport defined by measurement be measureless? And what was up with that "chest cavity" statement? It was typical Curtains, blunt and graphic. I wasn't sure I understood. There was value in swimming, even in coming in fourth. I got that. But I had invested so much—was it worth it?

"If I had quit swimming after college, I could have been three years into med school by now."

"So what? You can still go to medical school. Look what experiences you have had in the last three years. Look at the friends you have made. Look at the respect you have earned. Even getting fourth—is going to toughen you. It will help you get through med school."

"All things considered, I'd still take the gold," I said.

"So would I." Curtains took a bite out of a french fry and continued. "You know, what you did in that race took guts. That is one thing you showed me throughout your career. You have guts."

"And where did it get me?"

"You can parlay that on dry land."

Dry land. Vivian's words echoed in my ears: *You're a tiger in the pool, but a pussycat on dry land.* I detested those words. Maybe I could change. Maybe I could be a tiger on dry land *because* I was a tiger in the pool. Curtains watched the gears meshing inside my brain and seemed to enjoy it. He took another bite of french fry and said, "Now that you are done with swimming, you need to change your eating habits."

I smiled and started packing up the trash. Curtains took one more bite of fries, and as I stood up, he made a motion with his hand for me to stay seated.

"Wait," he said. "I forgot something. Your question about med school reminded me. Remember Dr. Nate who came and spoke to the team?"

"I sure do. He's kind of a hero of mine."

Curtains pulled a folded piece of paper out of his pocket. "He got you in. You have to start class soon as you get home."

"Wow," I said, reaching for the paper. He pulled it back.

"I have another option for you. I need an assistant coach at SM. You would be a good one."

It was déjà vu—another tough choice. Coaching alongside Curtains would be a great experience that would lead to a cherry career in the sport. But I'd learned something about myself since Coach Dewey had laid out a similar offer. I didn't need to stay in the sport to reap its benefits. Even Curtains had said as much. I was ready to move on.

"I'll take the letter."

"I thought you would." He handed it to me. "Good choice. You will make a good doctor."

I opened it and scanned it quickly. It was on SM Medical School letterhead and had Dr. Nathan Sensibaugh's signature at the bottom. It was official. My dad would be proud.

Sixteen months earlier, I'd agonized over a similar decision, going back and forth and taking forever to decide, being uncertain and regretful after the decision was made. But tiger-Doyle was a more decisive fellow, the kind with guts, the kind who could take charge of a race. I felt confident about the decision.

"One more thing," Curtains said as I put the letter in my USA sweat jacket pocket. "I remember the pact we made in Hawai`i."

"Oh yeah, that." I smiled. My smile became a wistful, wry, goofy grin. Curtains read a story in the grin.

"It looks like you kept your end of the deal," he said. "Archie is safe and sound, racking up gold medals, and I am certain you had a hand in it. I do not know what you did, but you have my thanks as well."

"I can't tell you all about it right now, Coach. Someday I will. There are a few interesting stories."

"I bet there are. By the way, I think you have a gift." A *gift*? No one had ever said that to me before. Archie had all the gifts. Curtains was messing with me. And yet, maybe he knew. He'd seen me through the underwater window.

"Okay, I'm game. What's my gift?"

"You make other people better. You can parlay that on dry land too."

He watched my brain process it for a while. This one was even harder. My confusion was amusing to him.

"You will see," he said. "Come on. There are people waiting for us."

When we got to my suite and opened the door, there were a million people inside. Almost all of my teammates were there. It was like a surprise birthday party. Several of them yelled my name as a greeting.

"Sorry about all this," I said to Caruso, who had a race the next day and probably wanted to get to bed.

"No worries," he replied.

Caruso explained that people had been coming down over the past hour, one by one, two by two. There was no set plan, people just wanted to come by and see me. When they learned there was a DVD, they wouldn't leave.

Someone popped in the DVD. The first thing that came on was The Archie Story. I'd almost forgotten about it. The network elected to play it right before the 400 free, which I thought was odd, because Archie had already swum six events. There were old home movie clips from Archie's childhood, some footage from the previous Olympics, and segments from the interviews of Archie, Curtains and me. The editors left in only one sentence from my interview—the one where I conceded that Archie was the superior swimmer.

Near the end, the interviewer, Bob, asked Archie specifically about the 400 free. Archie praised the Aussies, then he said "the guy I fear most is my friend, Doyle Wilson. He has something I don't have." Bob asked what it was. The camera slowly zoomed in on Archie's face as he thought about it. "Vision," he said.

Vision?! I squinted at the TV set through my glasses. What was he talking about?

Archie explained it to Bob. "Doyle sees everything, he analyzes everything, he thinks everything through. He sees ahead, he sees behind. He sees things I don't see. I just go." The story closed with video of Archie and me playing ping-pong in the background while Bob's voice-over made a feeble attempt to tie up what Archie had just said. Bob explained that Archie was swimming 17 times in eight days, but his toughest competition was expected to come in the 400 free, which would pit the guy who "sees everything" against the guy who "just goes."

The DVD went to the 400 free introductions, but I was still fixated on what Archie had said. Yes, the brain can win races for you. You can outsmart or outpsych an opponent, or win with mental intensity. But can too much brain activity also *lose* a race for you? Is it possible that this difference between Archie and me—which Archie saw as an advantage for me—actually cost me the race?

Could it be that my "vision" created a sort of mental bubble? I envied Archie more than ever at that moment. I envied his ability to "just go." There was a purity to it.

It hit me that I was over-analyzing my tendency to over-analyze. I had to smile at that.

The swimmers on TV were in the water and the crowd in my suite was cheering as if it were happening in real time, like we didn't know the end result. At the halfway point, someone said "Shhhh!" so that we could hear the announcer, Bart Evans, a former Olympic swimmer. A blue line appeared on the screen—the world record pace line, well behind my feet and through the middle of Archie, Graham and Ian. Bart kept screaming, "they're *all* ahead of world record pace!" Twice, Bart said "Doyle Wilson *can* win this race."

During the last 50 meters, Bart was yelling so frantically you couldn't understand what he was saying. The drama onscreen was palpable enough that even I felt it. All four of us took our final three strokes in tandem, like synchronized swimmers, and you couldn't tell by watching who won. It looked like a dead heat. Bart yelled "It's Hayes! It's Hayes with the gold, Dowling of Australia in second and Sinclair in third. What a race! Best race I've ever seen!"

It was painful to watch the end. They replayed it five times in slow motion from three different cameras above and below the water line. I had a feeling I'd be seeing the end of that race in my mind the rest of my life.

Curtains announced that it was bedtime, and everyone started filing out. People filed past and congratulated me like I'd won something. I saw Camille across the room and watched as she made her way toward me. When she got to me, she took me by the hands, looked me up and down, and said "what a stud!" before clenching me in a bear hug.

Archie was the last to leave. "I hope that didn't sound too dumb," he said to me, referring to the vision thing. "I meant it as a compliment."

"I know you did, Arch, and I appreciate it. It is a compliment. And, I might add, a rather astute observation by someone who just goes."

I slapped him on the back and told him no one could touch him in the 200 IM. It wasn't even worth mentioning that Archie would anchor the 800 free relay to an Aussie stomping.

I couldn't sleep. I was still adrenalized. I continued analyzing everything. I played the race over in my mind, from the bird's eye view of the DVD to the Doyle's-eye view of the actual race. I watched as the digital clock in my bedroom rolled over from 3:35 to 3:36. That number wouldn't bother me anymore, I said to myself. But I noticed it.

I tossed around in bed like a Spinner Dolphin, so much so that I got tangled in the covers. I felt a magnetic pull, maybe a lunar pull, so I got up and sat on the balcony. I stared at the Aquatics Center, its slanted roof like a floating beret in the light of the waning moon. I soon realized that it was Le Grand Beret that was pulling me. Like the house of a dead guy—I needed to go there.

CHAPTER 22

You can hardly see anything underwater with your bare eyes. Most people squint to protect their eyeballs. You can only see shadows, bulky shapes, blunted colors. You can't judge distances. Everything is murky, wavy, distorted.

With goggles, you can see everything clearly. Your vision seems enhanced, even your peripheral vision. There is about a thousand-percent difference between how well you can see underwater with and without goggles. Goggles are, hands down, the greatest invention the sport of swimming has ever seen.

Goggles came into common use in competitive swimming in the 1960s. Before that, swimmers wore no goggles in chlorinated pools. They'd come home from swim practices and try to coax tears from their eyes to wash the chlorine out.

The first goggles were bulky and heavy. They were modified dive masks. There was no way you'd ever wear them in a race. So before every meet, swimmers would practice their turns endlessly, trying vainly to spot the wall from ten feet out, with variations in visibility from pool to pool due to light shading, tile color and water murkiness.

Goggles evolved over the years. For a while, you could wear goggles in a race, but you risked losing them on the dive, or having them fill up with fog or water. Now, goggles are lightweight, streamlined, watertight, and anti-fog. You can get prescription lenses.

Goggles improve your underwater vision so dramatically that no one would think of swimming a race without them.

They say that all motion is relative. We live life at high speed on a terrestrial ball that's hurtling through space at 67,000 miles an hour. We're moving the same speed as the earth, so we feel like we're standing still. That's the way it seemed in my mind as I replayed the race. I knew I was swimming fast, but it felt like I was standing still. Everyone, everything, was moving at exactly the same speed and it felt like being stuck. Stuck on planet earth, stuck in water, unable to evolve.

I replayed the race in my quasi-sleep. I replayed it in my suite as I put on my clothes. I replayed it in the shuttle on the way to Le Grand Beret. I replayed it in the locker room as I opened my locker and instinctively put a suit on. Idiot—you don't need to put a suit on just to take a shower. I was stuck in swimming mode and couldn't break out.

I walked over to the shower room and soaked in hot water for 20 minutes. I got out, got dressed and started walking around the pool area. I went into the side rooms, the hallways, taking mental snapshots. I inhaled the sights, the sounds, the chlorine. I sat in the stands to get the view of the pool from there. I stared at Lane 5 and re-swam the race in my mind. It was the same every time: expending supreme effort and getting nowhere.

I went into the ready room. I sat in the fifth chair, looked at the clock, looked at the chairs on both sides and pictured the guys who had sat in them. It wasn't very fulfilling. An empty ready room has no power, no electricity. They're made for looking forward, not backward. That very thought dawned on me, and it changed my thinking. I stopped replaying the race. I stopped thinking about things I'd never do again, and started thinking about med school, about Molly, about the day ahead. I stood up and took one last 360° look around the ready room. I left Le Grand Beret and boarded the Métro, headed south.

It was quiet on the Métro at 6:00 in the morning. I got off at St. Placide, a few blocks from my parents' hotel. I walked a block before I realized it was way too early to knock on my parents' door. There was a café, l'Horizon, just around the corner from their place. A lone waiter wearing an apron was opening up. There were no customers.

I decided to get a cup of coffee and watch normal French people going about their business. The waiter looked like he was in his thirties. He had a goatee and a soul patch, no mustache. He did not look happy to see me.

"Je voudrais une café au lait, s'il vous plait." I'd been practicing my French.

"Do you speak English?" he asked. When I nodded, he said "good. Let's speak English, then." He said it snootily.

"Fine." I followed him to where he fixed the coffee, and we conversed while he fixed it.

"Are you an American swimmer?" he queried.

"Yes, I am. How did you know?"

"The shaved arms." I looked down at my arms, which were glistening with baldness.

"Very good," I said.

"And you have medals, no? From the Olympics. How many?"

"I didn't win a medal. I got fourth. Yesterday."

He had poured the coffee and was about to add hot milk. I motioned him to nix the milk.

"I saw that maybe on the television last night," he said. "It was a very close race, no?"

"I came this close to getting the gold medal." I held my forefinger and thumb a centimeter apart.

"Ah, so you are the unlucky one," he said. I smiled, he smiled, and neither smile was a happy smile. "What did you do to piss off God?"

The question threw me off. While I was used to bluntness, rank cynicism was beyond my ken. But what really threw me was that I hadn't yet thought of it myself. I had asked every other question. How had I missed such an obvious one?

"I don't know," I answered, my head bowed. "Good question."

I took a sip of coffee while I stood there pondering. It was too hot. I blew on it.

"Take your pick of the seats," he instructed me.

Thank you, I thought. How nice of you. I can have any seat I want and enjoy the view while I mull over what I did to piss off God. I took a seat out front, on the sidewalk.

I stirred sugar into my coffee, watching the sweetness whirlpooling downward. I paddled the question around in my head. Could I have done something to make God angry? Moses hit a rock with a stick and got penalized by God. Did I strike a rock? When? Maybe I wasn't humble enough, too self-absorbed. Or maybe I was being punished for Leor's downfall. It happened on my watch.

I made a mental note to ask Molly about the God thing.

The streets around l'Horizon came to life and customers filled the place. I took my time with the coffee, watching people come and go. It was a different atmosphere than at the Olympic Village. The patrons all eyed me curiously. Even though I made sure not to wear any USA clothing, I must have had an American look about me. It was a new experience to be treated as "the strange one." In America I'm about as vanilla as you can get, but in France I stood out.

I got my cup refilled twice and lollygagged until it was safe to go to the hotel. I tossed ten euros on the table and left with a wave to my new friend in the apron.

My parents and Molly were staying at a little hotel called the Saint Gregoire. The owner intercepted me in the lobby. He introduced himself and asked if I was Doyle Wilson the Olympic swimmer. I said yes, and he let loose a torrent of praise, not for me but for my parents. And Molly.

"Mademoiselle Molly, she is a *fantastic* lady."

He told me he talked to Molly and my parents every day as they came and went. He gave them suggestions on things to do, and they told him what they liked and disliked. Molly, he said, spoke French to him, and her French was "magnificent." That was something I didn't know about Molly.

The owner showed me the elevator and I went up to the third floor. My parents were ready when I knocked. Their room was tiny by American hotel standards, but it had a nice balcony that looked out onto a garden. My mom showed me around the room, which took about five seconds. I could tell she liked it. Molly was staying next door and must have heard me in my parents' room. She appeared and greeted us. The room couldn't hold four people, so we headed to the basement for breakfast.

Breakfast was served in an old wine cellar with an arched stone ceiling. The croissants and brioches were fresh, and I ate three of each. Uncharacteristically, my mom was the big talker at breakfast. She told me all about the hotel, the area, and what they had been doing when not at the pool. She raved about Paris and even thought the people were "nice."

I showed my dad the letter from Dr. Nate. It had been folded about 20 different ways and had greasy french fry fingerprints all over it. To say he was thrilled wouldn't do justice to his reaction. Dimple city. My mom, too, was thrilled. Molly's reaction seemed guarded.

After breakfast, we walked to the Jardin du Luxembourg. Molly and my parents had been there and wanted to show it to me. The park featured a beautiful palace, a bunch of statues and a big fountain where kids were floating their little sailboats. "Yar," I said to Molly, pointing to a particularly nice boat, and she repeated the word, laughing.

We strolled through the gardens and the scent of lavender caught my attention. The only other smell in all the world that ever caught my attention was the scent of chlorine. I can smell a pool from a mile away. Before this, I had a reason to smell pools and no reason to smell flowers. I was starting to feel relaxed, like I was free to discover new things.

As we walked on, I noticed that there were people engaged in almost every conceivable activity, from walking to tai-chi to sword-fighting to dancing. Molly wanted me to watch the joggers. We sat down on a bench.

"I have a question for you, Moll. I stopped at a café on the way over to the hotel this morning. I struck up a conversation with the waiter, who had watched the race on TV last night. When he discovered that I was the guy who got fourth, he asked me what I had done to p...to make God mad. What do you think of that?"

She thought for a minute. I saw a group of joggers run by, smoking cigarettes.

"Was that the waiter at l'Horizon?" she asked.

I nodded.

"I don't know everything about God," Molly said, "but I'm pretty sure your coming in fourth was not a punishment."

She was being modest. She knew a lot about God. That's why I asked her.

"Do you think God wanted me to get fourth?"

Another jogger went by, smoking.

"Maybe," she said. "If so, then it'll turn out well for you."

"How?"

"That's the thing—God's plans aren't always easy for us to figure out right away. Maybe swimming prepared you for something, maybe something really meaningful."

One thing I like about Molly is that she says "maybe" a lot, even when she talks about God. Lots of people, when they talk about God, sound so sure of themselves. Like the waiter at l'Horizon. That guy didn't know jack squat about God but he was sure I had made God angry. He didn't hold a candle to Molly when it came to God things.

A pair of joggers ran past, cigarettes dangling from their lips.

Molly continued. "Doyle, I *desperately* wanted you to win. I thought you were going to win and I was going to be so happy for you. When I looked at the scoreboard at the end, I cried." It brought back bad memories to think of Molly crying. "But getting fourth didn't change how I feel about you."

She felt something about me! I suspected it, hoped for it, but she'd put it on the table. That was huge.

I turned and watched four joggers run past, and three of them were smoking. Just a darn minute—when that group ran by before, the fourth one was smoking. He probably just ran out of smokes.

"Do all the joggers here smoke?" I wondered aloud.

I turned back to Molly, and she was looking sideways at me with a smile that was wry, very wry. Smoking joggers—are you kidding me? I laughed so hard my ribs hurt. Molly laughed herself to the anaerobic threshold and turned red. We laughed together for a full minute.

It was just like Laura Dewey had described it: *off center in the same direction.* Molly's face said it all—laughing at the smoking joggers, the crooked smile, the twinkle in her eyes. I knew. *Sure as Kilimanjaro rises like Olympus above the Serengeti.* I just knew.

A smoking jogger ran by, took the cigarette from his lips and threw it down on the grass.

I'd been given the goggles from heaven again. It was clear. I could see ahead and behind.

I looked behind and saw difficulty. I'd continually blown it with women. I'd blown it with *Molly.* I'd seen her only through the watery lens of swimming. I didn't want a serious girlfriend…*why?* Because it would hurt my swimming career. She was Molly The Reassurer to me. What was I to her? Doyle The… *what?* I had earned no title. But I could. She'd been emotionally frail, angry at God. Maybe I could help her, make her better. I had a gift, didn't I?

I looked ahead and saw more difficulty. I'd have to make a move, put myself out there, take a risk. What if *she* wasn't ready? What if she wasn't on the same page? I'd have to go see her father. He had her on a pedestal—could anyone measure up? Other guys had failed. And what about med school—I'd be busy, committed, distracted. Could I juggle two big commitments at once?

The most important thing of all was this: I could never leave her. It was all or nothing. I'd have to take a giant leap to get to her end of the spectrum. I hadn't been willing to do that before. It would be harder than any race or workout. I'd have to go where no pussycat would dare to go. Was I ready?

When I was seven years old, I swam in one of those neighborhood meets at the middle school. Sheldon Kurtz, a kid who lived on my block, came to the meet. His dad dropped him off and when he returned at the end, after all the events had been swum, Sheldon was sitting there with his towel wrapped around his shoulders, his curly hair perfectly dry. "Didn't you swim anything?" his dad asked. "They didn't have my event," Sheldon answered. To this day, no one knows what Sheldon's event was.

There's a little Sheldon Kurtz in me, and possibly in every man, when it comes to women. You have to choose an event. You have to be ready to go at the right *time*. You have to dive in when the beep sounds, even if you're not totally ready.

I wasn't expecting it to come this quickly. But it didn't matter. Timing is critical, I'd learned the hard way.

I started sweating. My throat felt dry. Come on, Doyle, I told myself, like I do in the ready room, like I do in races when the pain shows up. Do what swimming taught you to do: something hard. Enter the discomfort zone.

Sheldon Kurtz be damned. I took my mark.

I turned and looked straight into her eyes. "Hey Moll, what color eyes did your mother have?"

She'd been smiling, and the smile faded. "Ocean green. The disease didn't affect the color." She swallowed hard. "Her eyes were radiant."

"Because I can see a splash of green in your eyes—hidden within the brown. I never noticed it before. It's a nice gift from your mother."

It brought an instant shower of tears. I pulled her into me and she cried onto my shoulder. I held her while she let it out. And I kept holding her while we talked—about her mom, about med school, about doing us. It was going to be hard for her, too. But she was ready. She'd been in her own ready room.

With my bionic vision I noticed my parents making themselves conspicuous, like it was time to go. I didn't want to go, but I had to catch the Métro to go watch Caruso swim. Molly and I stood up and started walking behind my parents. My hand searched for hers and found it. It fit perfectly. She took hold and squeezed.

Eh bien, allons-y.

EPILOGUE

What do swimmers do after they retire from the sport?

Very few swimmers parlay swimming into careers. Johnny Weissmuller was one of the few who pulled it off. He became an actor, the star of the popular Tarzan movies. Many people say he wasn't a good actor, that he just looked good in a loincloth, but he became rich and famous directly because of swimming. Esther Williams took a similar route on the female side.

A handful of swimmers were launched by swimming into related fields. Adolph Kiefer, the 100 backstroke champion in the 1936 Olympics, founded a swim supply company that has been successful for decades. Donna de Varona, John Naber, Rowdy Gaines and Summer Sanders became sports announcers. A few elite swimmers have been successful with endorsements or motivational speaking. Those gigs aren't very plentiful.

Some swimmers achieve greatness in unrelated fields. NBA basketball player Tim Duncan was one of the fastest swimmers in the country as an age-grouper. He switched to basketball in the ninth grade and became an NBA All-Star. Academy Award winner Clint Eastwood was a swimming instructor in the army and dug swimming pools for a living before he launched his movie career. President Ronald Reagan was a life-long swimmer who was captain of his college swim team. He credited swimming with helping forge his character.

The vast majority of swimmers don't become famous. They become doctors, lawyers, scientists, teachers, businesspeople, salesmen, accountants, laborers, mothers and fathers. Most give back to the sport and their communities. Most are solid citizens. I would like to think that swimming strengthens the dorsal fin of society.

Most former swimmers reminisce about the glory days of their swimming careers. They think about what they accomplished, and they dream. Even the old ones dream. They dream about what might have been.

"Bianca's doing great," I told him as I pulled off my scrub cap and ran my fingers through my hair. My mask was down around my Adam's apple. "And JuJu—she's the sweetest little…." I couldn't say any more.

Archie hugged me and let out a heavy breath. "Thanks, man."

His baby, Juliana, had a congenital condition known as hypoplastic left heart. We knew it *in utero*. We were ready for it. It wasn't that long ago when babies like that just died. There was nothing you could do. In this case, we whisked her to the operating room right after she was born. Not every hospital can handle a Norwood procedure on a neonate. People come from all over the Midwest to have it done at the SM Medical Center. The vast majority of the patients survive it.

I was the one who cut open Juliana's chest and led the surgical team. Heart surgery involves a lot of cutting and patching and sewing and tying knots. That's what we did with JuJu. With newborns, the scale is miniaturized. I'd done it dozens of times assisting Dr. Nate. This time, Archie asked me specifically to take the lead. Nate didn't hesitate and told me I could do it. It wasn't easy, but it went according to plan.

The waiting lounge was almost empty, as it usually is at 11:30 at night. Archie's mom was there, asleep in a chair. It had been a long day for everyone. We sat down in a corner away from his mom so we wouldn't wake her up. We spoke in soft voices.

"It went well," I said. "Everybody's resting."

"Out of the woods?"

I looked at him hard, knowing what was on the road ahead. "Yes. For now."

With hypoplastic left heart, you have to do three major surgeries when the patient is a child. Juju would need medicine, a pacemaker, and perhaps, ultimately, a transplant. Her activities would be limited; she'd never be a premier athlete like her parents. She'd have to be watched closely. It would take constant vigilance and effort, but she could grow into a near-normal adult. I knew from watching other families that there would be a special bond between parents and child.

"You're going to love that little girl, Arch. She'll be the best thing that ever happened to you."

He nodded. "I don't know if I can do it."

"You can," I said, grabbing his upper arm. "You can do this. But you're right, it's going to be hard. Have you ever done anything else hard?"

"Hell yeah." We both chuckled and looked away for a few seconds. I was thinking about birthday swims and rainbow sets. The fly set from hell.

"And you're not in it alone, either. You have a team."

We'd had several talks about it already. He'd been on the verge of going AWOL.

Archie met Bianca at his last Olympics. She was a beach volleyball player from Brazil. He'd gone to live in Brazil for a while, but there wasn't much for him to do down there and he grew restless. Then he got a primo job offer to work in the Detroit Red Wings' front office. I'd never figured Archie to be the type to settle in Michigan. But he took the job, and he and Bianca became the hot couple in Detroit society.

I don't know whose idea it was to become pregnant, if it was anybody's idea at all. In my mind, it was Archie's idea. They weren't married when it happened. Archie had been hanging around at my place more and more, playing "Uncle Archie" to my kids, enjoying the family life that Molly and I were building. I think he envied me. I could see it in how he looked at Molly and the kids. True or not, it gave me a dollop of satisfaction to think of Archie envying me.

Anyway, they were pregnant, and Archie came to me for advice. I advised him to get married. He talked all night about what he'd be giving up. I talked all night about what he'd be getting. It was a stalemate. However, we did agree on one thing: it would be hard. What turned it my way was when I talked about the night I asked Molly to marry me. I'd sweated bullets for three days leading up to it. Molly was surprised. When I got down on my knee at Bates Motel in front of all her fellow counselors, she screamed. She couldn't stop laughing when she found out I was serious. That's how Molly is.

So Archie and Bianca got engaged, and before the wedding they found out about the heart defect. It started with a simple ultrasound, then a battery of tests and consultations with several of my colleagues. Archie appeared on my doorstep at two in the morning after he learned the diagnosis. It was snowing hard, and when he came through the door he had white hair. Inside my foyer, he shook like a dog and the flakes became a small puddle on my floor. We stayed up the rest of the night, not really saying a whole lot but mostly just looking at the fire in my fireplace and watching the snow, illuminated by my porch light, falling outside the living room window.

Bianca, he said, had "freaked out" and then thrown him out. The baby's heart defect was his fault, she'd screamed at him, which was ridiculous. The pregnancy itself was hard for her to get used to because it would cost her modeling jobs. They were working through that when the heart issue surfaced. Archie, who'd spent his entire life worrying about nothing, was suddenly distraught. He was distraught in my living room, in the wee hours of the morning, with Molly and the kids asleep upstairs.

"Look," I'd said to him, as the rising sun started to seep light into the sky. "You're just going to have to tighten down your goggle strap and swim this race. Bianca needs you. The baby's going to need you. They'll need your strength." I paused to let the word "strength" sink in. "You have it in here," I said, thumping my chest, "I know you do. I've seen it." That's when I explained the surgeries to him, the limitations, the effort that would be required. "You'll be a better man for it, Arch. You'll get a lot out of it, too—more than if it all just came easy to you."

I doubt if it was my talk that did it, but Archie manned up. He and Bianca steeled their resolve and came up with a game plan. The wedding was a small affair, without the hassle of paparazzi because Archie's star had faded as time swam on. Curtains was there, and Crack and Caruso. I was the best man, as Archie had been in my wedding. He needed another pep talk from me right before his pregnant bride walked down the aisle.

A nurse came into the waiting lounge where Archie and I were discussing JuJu's surgery. I had to run off to look at another patient in the ICU. When I got back, Archie's mom was awake. I briefly explained to her how the surgery had gone. I offered to take them both to the pediatric ICU to see JuJu, but I warned them about what they'd see: a bloody chest tube, wires and tubes poking out of every part of her, machines surrounding her bed, and bandages all over her little torso. They wouldn't be able to touch her. But they wanted to see, and I showed them. It's heartbreaking when you first see it. They cried. Even Archie, I think, though he was busy holding on to his mom while she heaved. After a few minutes, I walked them down to Bianca's room and said goodnight.

The long day had taken a toll on my body and my nerves. I needed my head to be in liquid. It's so good to live in a college town where you can do Norwood procedures in a world-class hospital, then walk across campus to some of the finest athletic facilities in the country. I didn't need to break in to get inside the Don Jackson Natatorium. I had a key. I'd been invited to swim anytime, and I'd been putting that invitation to good use.

The pool within the natatorium had been given a name: the Aleksandr Kurtenska Pool. Curtains had retired, though you could still see him on deck at half the workouts. I got in Lane 1, of course—the animal lane, though I could hardly be called an animal anymore. New animals occupied the lane in prime time, and even Curtains' retirement hadn't stopped the stars from shining on that lane. I dove in and glided as long as I could, until the air in my lungs brought me up. I took a slow, easy stroke, then another, and swam for an hour.

I swim for pleasure now. Mostly the pleasure is in my head. I retired cold turkey after Paris and didn't touch water again for six solid years. I'd still go and watch the occasional practice and meet, each time trying to pretend that I didn't want to be in the water myself. Molly is the one who got me back into it, ironically enough. She told me I needed to do it. "For your heart," she said, and I wasn't sure if she meant the blood-pumper or the seat of the emotions. Anyway, that prodding didn't work, so she started to call me fat, subtly and indirectly, needling me with little comments like "you need new shorts." I was on to her. I went to the pool to take away her ammunition.

I take long, smooth strokes through the water, feeling the glide on every pull. Times, distances, and heart rates don't matter anymore. I just go, because that frees my mind. I don't have to think about any of the things I used to have to think about. Except one: the meaning of life.

I think about the meaning of swimming. Curtains had told me in Paris that the value of swimming is not in getting a hunk of metal or your name on a wall, that the value is inside your chest cavity and it's measureless. I didn't get it at first. I thought he was talking about something invisible. But it wasn't invisible. Not to someone who can see ahead and behind.

Coming in fourth made me desperate to peer inside my chest cavity. And I did. I've been in there with a microscope. There's a mark inside, a high water mark, left by swimming. It's a permanent mark. Records get broken, names are forgotten, and medals get shoved into a drawer. The character forged by swimming never goes away.

I wouldn't have been as obsessive about the value of swimming if I'd won the gold. Swimming created a thirst in me and then failed to quench it. The thirst wouldn't go away. It would have to be quenched on dry land.

Archie has a water mark, too. Of all the hearts I've seen on this planet—and by now that's quite a few—Archie's is the most visible to me. His mark is different than mine. Not better or worse, but it's a strong one. Stronger than gold. That's how I know Archie will get through this thing with JuJu. He'll step up. He won't just get through it, he'll excel. He'll be heroic. For the first time, he'll be an *unsung* hero.

Swimming in the animal lane makes me nostalgic for the old days. The daily slogging, the banter at the wall, the oxygen debt, the chlorine cologne. Even the bubble on my thumb, ever present, makes me smile now. I used to ask myself if I'd do it all over again, knowing the outcome. It's black and white. A no-brainer. In a heartbeat.

There's one thing I'd do differently: Molly. I was slow off the blocks on that one.

The house was dark and quiet when I got home from the pool. Molly had turned on the nightlights to guide my path. I climbed the stairs, went into one bedroom and then the other, kissing my son and my daughter in turn. I stripped down to my boxers and flipped the switch on the alarm so it would go off at the usual time, 5:30 a.m. I rolled into bed beside Molly, who was on her side, breathing the gentle, rhythmic breaths of someone deep in sleep. I got close and put my hand on her stomach—her bare, pregnant belly, one of my hand's favorite spots. Her breathing never broke rhythm, but she put her hand on top of mine.

I drifted off to sleep. As I drifted, my mind returned to that day in Paris when I had pronounced myself the unluckiest man on the face of the earth. I hadn't yet seen it Lou Gehrig's way. It took the perspective of years to show me how narrow my focus had been. I see it now. I'd ended up with a prize of greater worth than a gold medal.

I'm still figuring a few things out, but one thing I know for sure. I will keep my hand on her—my good hand, holding tightly.

AUTHOR'S NOTE

The teammate-rival "duo" personifies the love-hate duality of swimming, so it should come as no surprise that the phenomenon occurs frequently. I experienced such a rivalry in my own swimming career and was in a position to witness others first-hand. While Doyle and Archie are fictional characters, I drew on real-life observations and experiences in formulating their relationship.

I grew up in Ann Arbor, Michigan and punched my ticket to the mecca of swimming, California, in the fall of 1975. While swimming for UCLA, I encountered a nemesis. Bruce Furniss arrived at USC that same fall already owning the world record in my best event, the 200-meter freestyle. He went on to win two Olympic gold medals in 1976. During our college years, USC and UCLA were two of the top five teams in the country and engaged in a bitter cross-town rivalry. Bruce and I swam against each other in dual meets, relay meets, conference meets, NCAA championships, U.S. Nationals, and the Olympic Trials. We swam many of the same events and usually anchored our teams' relays. For four years, it seemed like half the time I got up on a starting block, Bruce was standing on the next block over. Needless to say, I wasn't thrilled to see him there. My record against him was similar to Doyle's record against Archie.

Things changed in the summer of 1977. Bruce Furniss and I became training partners, friends, and teammates on the same club team in Long Beach. We swam on relays together and cheered for each other. We did the same thing in the summer of 1978. In the fall of each year, we returned to our respective schools and became enemies again—but not complete enemies. He was no longer evil incarnate, no longer a masked supervillain, and I had to reconcile my desire to beat him with the fact that I actually liked him. While Doyle and Archie are much different than Bruce and me, the Doyle-Archie relationship borrows, at least subliminally, from my experiences with Bruce Furniss.

I returned to Ann Arbor after college to go to law school and start a dry land career. After a few years I returned to the pool as a spare-time Masters swimmer, and the University of Michigan pool became my primary workout venue. Dozens of Olympians trained in that same pool over the years. One of the sport's greatest teammate-rivalries played out in front of my eyes and was one of the things that inspired this book.

Eric Namesnik swam for Michigan from 1989 to 1993. He just missed making the 1988 Olympic team, and in 1992 he won the silver medal in the 400 IM. He stayed at Michigan after graduating in order to train for the 1996 Olympics. Having just missed the gold in 1992, Namesnik passionately wanted to win the 400 IM in the 1996 Olympics.

Tom Dolan arrived at Michigan in 1993. He was 6'7" tall and excelled in several events, but his best was the 400 IM. For the next three years, the workout battles between Dolan and Namesnik were legendary. Just before the 1996 Olympics, a TV network reporter interviewed Dolan and Namesnik on camera, trying to paint them as pals, with Dolan the superior athlete and Namesnik the sidekick pushing him to greater heights. Namesnik, however, rankled in Dolan's shadow and didn't concede Dolan's superiority. While he was polite and said the right things, it was clear how much he wanted to beat his more celebrated rival.

The 400 IM race between Tom Dolan and Eric Namesnik in the 1996 Olympics remains one of the best races in swimming history. Namesnik qualified first for the finals and swam in Lane 4 with Dolan next to him. They were tied to the hundredth of a second at the half-way point. Namesnik took the lead on the breaststroke leg. Dolan pulled even on the freestyle, and the two battled stroke for stroke down the stretch. Dolan touched barely ahead of Namesnik. The two did not shake hands or exchange words after the race. Dolan was triumphant; Namesnik inconsolable.

Events outside the Olympics made the Namesnik-Dolan story more poignant. Namesnik retired after the 1996 Olympics having placed second in virtually all of his international swims—the Olympics, the World Championships and the Pan Am Games. He stayed in Ann Arbor and became an assistant coach for Jon Urbanchek. He was a candidate for the head coaching job when Urbanchek retired, but he placed second in that competition as well. Less than two years after that disappointment, Eric Namesnik was killed in a car crash. He was 35 years old and left behind a wife and two small children.

There was a memorial service for Namesnik at the pool. I knew Eric personally and went to the memorial. One of his former teammates gave a speech in which he pointed out that Eric had been a gold medal husband, father, friend, teacher, and coach. To think of him as "second best" would be to ascribe an incomplete legacy. The speech stirred up something that had been brewing in me for years. Very few people reach the pinnacle they dream of in this sport that requires sacrificial commitment. What's in it for the rest of us? Over the years, in the course of my own dry land experiences, I'd struggled with that question—a question that is not unique to swimming, or to sports. My struggle with it motivated me to write.

I missed making the 1976 Olympic team by a few tenths of a second and then, in 1980, I was training for a shot at the Olympics when the boycott was announced. People have told me I should be proud and happy that I came so close. It's true that the sport has given me great experiences. I've bitten my fingernails in many a ready room, swum in dungeon pools and animal lanes, and succeeded and failed in Get Out swims. I trained at the Olympic Training Center in Colorado Springs, where the real "box of piss" incident occurred in 1978. I've set a few Masters world records, two of which I still hold at this writing, although Masters swimming is divided into narrow age-group increments, so the "world" in which I hold records is a small one.

While I went far in swimming, there's a wide gap, in my estimation, between "almost" and making the Olympic team. I'm living in that gap. Being an Olympian was my dream as a kid, and it's been more than 30 years since I gave up on that dream. Several of my friends and teammates made it. I have the greatest admiration for what they accomplished and one of the aims of this novel is to show what it takes to become an Olympian and win a gold medal.

The bottom line is that I'm as good as most of the swimmers in this book only in my dreams. The bubble on Doyle's thumb, which symbolizes his place in the duo hierarchy, is taken from real life. Jon Urbanchek watched me swim one morning in Ann Arbor a few years ago and concluded, in his no-nonsense way, "not bad for an old man—you've got one good hand." In drilling down on that comment, I learned from Jon that one of his great swimmers, Peter Vanderkaay, had "no bubbles" on his hands. Bubbles?! I started watching my hands more closely underwater and, sure enough, I had a prominent bubble on my left thumb. I can't get rid of the darn thing. Its discovery was another nudge toward the beckoning keyboard.

Los Angeles, May 18, 2012

ACKNOWLEDGMENTS

This book was a five-year project. I'm sure I've forgotten some of the people who helped along the way, and that saddens me, because this was a team sport from beginning to end.

My wife Tracey was a true partner. She read every page of every draft of the manuscript. This project began just after our nest emptied at home, so the characters became our surrogate children. Tracey helped guide the story at every stage. Her highest value was in telling me what stunk. A lot of it ended up in the shredder. What remains has Tracey's seal of approval, which tells me it must be pretty good.

Brian Goodell gave me enthusiastic support at crucial times, as did Dave and Brenda Bartlett, John Naber, Janet Evans, Tony Anderson, Vincent Morales, Rowdy Gaines, Natalie and Kyle Van Dusen, Barb Riazzi, Martha Fletcher, and Stephanie Black.

Jeff Kleinman, Jita Fumich, and the folks at Folio Literary Management steered me in the right direction, not just when it was time to publish, but as the characters and story were being formed. I'm pleased to be working with true professionals at Untreed Reads, K.D. Sullivan and Jay Hartman.

Many people read the manuscript and provided helpful input: John Morales, Jim and Linda Fletcher, Erin and Kathryn Black, John Stephenson, Kristen Fuhs, Alene Franklin, Ken Buttke, Tony Bartle, Kent Tschannen, Tom Fletcher, Scott and Kristen Stephenson. Several people provided anecdotes or phrases that I used—I can't remember them all, but the following come to mind: Steve Swanson, Denny Hill, Joe Waller, Art Griffith, and "Sheldon Kurtz," who probably would not want his real name to be revealed.

Jon Urbanchek helped me in ways he doesn't even realize, one of which is recounted in the Author's Note. He taught me a lot about training, and gave me permission to use the stories associated with him that made it into the book (notably, "go flip-flop, go").

I was coached by amazing people who taught me most of what I know about swimming, and in that way heavily influenced this book: Denny Hill, George Haines, Ron Ballatore. Most of my former coaches are Hall of Famers—a coincidence? I don't think so.

In a similar way, my teammates, past and present, have molded me as a swimmer and a person, and provided some rich stories. My UCLA college teammates, in particular, have stuck together for 33 years after graduation, which is a testament to the sport and the people who participate in it. And, yes, I still fraternize with some of my past and current nemeses, and they shaped me too.

Last and most, Stephen King refers to the writer's subconscious thoughts as "the boys in the basement." My boy is upstairs. Thanks.

CPSIA information can be obtained at www.ICGtesting.com
Printed in the USA
LVOW131425281112

309198LV00001B/55/P